THE APPRENTICE

THE KILLOUGH COMPANY
BOOK 4

M.D. GREGORY

If you enjoyed The Apprentice, *please encourage your friends to download their own copy from their favorite authorized retailer.*

Credits *or* It Takes a Team to Raise a Book

Line Editing by Jennifer Griffin at Marked and Read.
Early Reading by Shelby De Jesus, Madelyn Collins, Natalie Knox, Lauren Van Netta, Lucky Barnes, Amy Voce, Heather Waskom, Suzanne Irving, Joanne McCorkell, and Robin Chrusniak.
First Round Editing, Copy Editing, Proofing, and Editing Coordination by Kiyle Brosius.
Final Proofing by Julie Hanson.
E-book Formatting by Meg Bawden.
Cover Design by The Book Brander.
A special thanks to Heather Waskom for helping us sort out the New Gothenburg World timeline in excruciating detail so we could continue writing our universe without stress! Also another huge thank you to Shelby De Jesus for helping Meg compare the scenes that overlap this book with the Irish Roulette series. You are amazing.

Fionn Killough is a Killough Company man in both blood and loyalty. Sloan—his uncle and mob boss—is the only father figure that Fionn has had, and he would do anything for him. But when Fionn is assigned to sniff out a rat in the Company, he hesitates for one reason—Daire.

Daire Reardon is the Company's second-in-command and the man Fionn loves. Fionn has spent eight long years yearning for a relationship with Daire, but Daire refuses to give him more than his body. Sloan doesn't know the entire truth about their history, and Fionn would never reveal his darkest secret. As much as Fionn tries, he can't hide his feelings for Daire, even if the other man won't acknowledge them.

Daire knows Fionn wants more. He's known since the very beginning of their physical relationship. As much as he wants to, Daire can't bring himself to admit his feelings for Fionn, not when he has a secret of his own. The more time he spends with Fionn, the more his own loyalty to Sloan and the Company are put to the test.

The Killough Company is going to war. They're being attacked on all sides. To succeed in their mission to find the rat, Daire and Fionn need to deal with their feelings before they destroy them for good.

AUTHOR'S NOTE ABOUT PRONUNCIATION OF NAMES AND OTHER IRISH WORDS

The C in *Cillian* is pronounced like the C in cake. This is a variation on the name Killian.

Oisín is pronounced Oh-sheen.

The surname *Killough* can be pronounced Kee-low or Kill-off.

The surname *Morrissey* is typically pronounced Maw-ree-see.

Daire is pronounced Dar-ruh. *But Daire responds to "Dare" and "Dar-ruh" as people usually call him Dare.*

Fionn is pronounced Fee-on.

Aodhan is pronounced Aidan.

AUTHOR'S NOTE

Welcome back to the Killough Company! How quickly time flies! This book has given me hell while I was writing it, but I'm so proud of how it has ended. Finishing this story wouldn't have been possible without the people in my life who cheered me on.

The Killough Company is part of the New Gothenburg world, and while you don't need to read other series to understand this book, time *has* passed in the universe. Because of this, it has now been eight years since Sloan and Conall first met. I will be writing a snapshots book to show some important scenes between *The Assassin* and now from their point of view.

1

FIONN KILLOUGH

Dad's funeral was held on a Thursday afternoon, sometime in February. I couldn't remember the exact date, but when I thought back on it, I recalled the slate gray clouds. Rain on the verge of becoming ice dripped from an array of black umbrellas held by the grieving crowd. My mom knelt near Dad's coffin, shoulders shaking. Droplets of water soaked into her black dress and the bun she'd pulled her brown hair into, but she didn't care. When someone came over to her, she shrieked at them to leave her alone while she cried.

The only other thing I remembered clearly was my uncle, Sloan, stepping up to my side and laying a hand on my shoulder. Uncle Sloan's grip was warm and firm, and I wasn't afraid of him, even though we'd never spent much time together. Dad worked for Uncle Sloan, but I was never allowed to visit his house. Dad insisted that being there was too dangerous, and I never understood why.

"There are two types of people in this world, Fionn," Uncle Sloan said.

I, at the age of four, tilted my head to stare up at him in

wonder. Uncle Sloan didn't look at me, though. His gaze was planted firmly on the coffin and Mom.

"There are those who take what belongs to them. I think of them as wolves, the predators who get what they're hungry for. Then, there are the people who let life kick them while they're already down, nothing more than sheep waiting to be eaten." It was at that moment Uncle Sloan's icy blue eyes slid toward me, and while I should've been scared, I wasn't. I had the opposite reaction—I felt safe beside him. "Which one are you?"

I didn't hesitate. "I'm the wolf, Uncle Sloan." The word wolf came out like *woof*.

Sloan smirked. "Yes, you are, because you're a Killough. An Irishman by blood. We were born to be wolves."

―――――

I gripped the tumbler of whiskey until my knuckles turned white. I exhaled, caught between the urge to slap this prick stupid or to put a bullet in his head and end it all. Sloan hadn't asked me to murder anyone, though.

He'd ordered me to reason with Cunningham.

"Two types of people live in this world, Christopher. The wolves, those who take what belongs to them, and the sheep, those who are more than happy to be the prey and beg for scraps."

I didn't miss Daire out of the corner of my eye, pursing his lips in amusement as he quickly took a sip of his drink from where he stood with his shoulder pressed against the wall. His dark hair was neat, with the longer strands on top pushed back, while his beard was short against his chin. He had a pair of his favorite sunglasses on and the blue lenses gave away nothing, but Daire knew the analogy well because Sloan loved to use it, especially when it came to business partners and those who worked for the Killough Company.

"Which one are you?" I finished, rocking my tumbler to hear the ice cubes *clink* together. The amber liquid sloshed against the side and the movement was entrancing, a well-rehearsed dance I'd become addicted to seeing.

I'd been drinking whiskey since I was fourteen. I'd gotten into Sloan's stash and drunk myself into a stupor. Sloan had been furious when he'd found me, intoxicated and incredibly sick. As punishment, when I was sober, he'd taken away my credit cards for a month, leaving me bored. It could've been a lot worse, considering Sloan's temper, so I'd considered myself lucky.

"Well." Cunningham smiled and leaned back in his armchair. He dipped his cowboy hat forward and grinned. His Texan accent made the word sound more like *whale*.

I resisted the urge to roll my eyes. Cunningham had a backward mindset and couldn't get more conservative if he tried. I hated him.

"I like to think of myself as more of a rattlesnake." His smile widened.

I agreed. Cunningham was a snake, a vicious one at that, and I didn't trust him as far as I could throw him. I peeked at Daire, watching the flicker of irritation that slipped across his handsome features. Like me, he wasn't fond of Cunningham, and he'd offered to have my back while I was meeting with the bastard.

"Dangerous as all git-out." Cunningham laughed and turned his attention to Daire, pointing a bony finger at him. "You're the right-hand man, yeah? The one with a weird name. Saw it on the message Killough sent me. Is it pronounced Dare?"

Daire smiled sardonically, and I stiffened, even though Daire wouldn't act against Sloan's orders. He was the perfect soldier and a loyal second-in-command who'd been at Sloan's side since the beginning. "Dar-ruh."

That wasn't entirely true. Most people knew him as *Dare*,

but from what he'd told me, only his parents called him by the correct pronunciation, which was *Dar-ruh*. He'd explained once that after so many issues during his childhood on how to say his name, he answered to either. I preferred *Daddy*, if I was being completely honest.

If I had a choice about what I was doing right now, Daire and I would be upstairs in my bedroom. In that delicious scenario, he'd be fucking me until I didn't know how to pronounce *my* name.

"What a weird one." Cunningham stroked his gray beard and stared at Daire like he was a bug beneath his shoe.

Daire's gaze turned deadly, and I sat up straighter, fingers twitching toward the gun I had hidden in the side of my chair cushion, not that I was sure I'd use it. While I'd practiced, I'd never had a reason to shoot someone. Not yet.

"It's Irish," Daire said.

"Ah, like the rest of you folks." Cunningham nodded as if it all made sense. I couldn't understand why Sloan wanted to go into business with him. I'd heard stories about Cunningham's exploits, how he slipped cash into Mexican federales' pockets to transport coke through small towns to get it to the American border, but Sloan already had ways to get drugs into the US. I couldn't grasp his reasoning, but I didn't dare ask, either. Sloan didn't need another excuse to question whether I was the right decision as heir to the Company.

I shook my head and leaned back in my chair, taking a sip of whiskey. I cocked my head and studied the man in front of me.

Cunningham wasn't very impressive and reminded me of an old Western movie star, with his big salt-and-pepper moustache and matching hair that hung loosely around his shoulders. The smug grin irritated me more than anything because the bastard thought he was better than me.

Well, fuck that.

"Mr. Killough has me here to make a deal with you,

Christopher. You know the terms." I pursed my lips and rested my whiskey tumbler on the arm of the chair, holding it there.

Cunningham laughed and dropped his booted feet onto the coffee table, dislodging dirt onto the pristine wood.

I gritted my teeth so tightly I thought I'd break them.

"Listen, boy, is Killough here? I want to talk to an adult, not a child."

As far as insults went, I'd heard worse. Sure, I was twenty-six, but I wasn't as useless as Cunningham thought. I had more experience than a lot of men my age in the mob.

Daire placed his tumbler on a console table and stepped forward to offer his protection, but I held up my hand, stopping him in his tracks. He lowered his sunglasses on his nose and gave me a pointed look, but I was already aware of his desire to break Cunningham's neck for disrespect. I needed to do this alone.

Sloan gave us a job to do, and I wasn't going to disappoint him. Not again. One day the Company would be mine, and if Sloan thought I wasn't capable, he would give it to someone else . . . like *fucking* Conall, Sloan's favorite little pet.

I would cut off my balls before I let that happen.

I leaned forward and took a deep breath to keep calm. "You will listen to me right now, *Chris*. You are in our house, so you will respect me. You know exactly who I am and what I can do."

Cunningham shook his head and snorted. "Just because you're Killough's nephew doesn't mean you get my respect. Earn it."

"Fine." I smirked and glanced at Daire.

We didn't have to like Cunningham to do business with him.

"You want me to earn it, then here's how I'll do it. Let's make a deal. We know about the drugs you're running across the border. You paid the cops in Mexico well, but you're having trouble getting the product past border patrol. Your last load was seized, am I right?"

His expression turned sour, bushy eyebrows furrowing. "Maybe."

A spike of delight shot through me. "Then, this is what we're going to do. You scratch our back, we'll scratch yours. You can use our trade route to get into the US."

He snorted. "Boy, New York's too far for me to be sending my coke. It'll be hit by the time I get it to Texas."

"Not that route." I leaned back in my chair and took another sip of my drink, letting the smooth liquid slide down my throat. "Florida is ours. It's easier to get your product through there than risk the border patrol near Mexico. The men in Florida are on our payroll."

"For now." Cunningham's grin returned. "You see, I've been hearing stuff about your Miami setup. Apparently, you're not the only one with connections there. The Reyes Cartel has already offered me a deal, *friend*, and I like what they're offering. What are you prepared to give me?"

I stiffened. Thiago Reyes and his band of pricks again. I had no idea why Sloan was letting them test his limits. If I was in charge, I would've destroyed their hopes and dreams in Miami already, but Sloan did everything for a reason, even if I didn't know why.

"We would take thirty percent of your product."

Cunningham's laughter echoed through Sloan's office. "Reyes only wants ten."

Reyes wouldn't stoop as low as ten percent.

Shooting to my feet, I glared at Cunningham. Anger sent a burst of heat through me, igniting my insides with a raging fire. My grip on my tumbler tightened until my fingers hurt. "I wouldn't push your luck if I were you. Reyes won't be in Miami for long, trust me."

Cunningham's smile grew smug again as he dropped his dirty boots to the floor and stood. He was taller than me, but not by much. "Now, don't go pitching a hissy fit, son. Y'all are here to talk business and that's what we're doin'."

"We're done," I growled out, raising my chin. "If you wheel and deal with Reyes, you will lose a lot of money." I stepped in closer, aware of Daire right at my back, lending me support. "Get out of our home and don't come back unless you're on your knees begging for a second chance."

"That won't happen. The Killough Company is losing its touch." Cunningham shook his head, baring his teeth at me in a crooked grin before tipping his hat. He stalked through the doorway, and his men were waiting for him on the other side.

I watched him go, anger still stirring in my gut until it became unbearable. I hurled my tumbler against the wall. The glass exploded in every direction, but I wasn't done. I spun around, picked up a vase of fresh flowers that sat on the coffee table, and threw it. The vase hit the wall to my left and shattered, sprinkling glass and water all over the hardwood floor.

"Motherfucking redneck." I curled my hands into fists and stared up at the ceiling while breathing through the rage that had me in flames.

Daire turned me around and laid his hand on my shoulder, mouth pursed and thoughtful. His sunglasses were back in place, hiding his eyes from me. "What has Sloan taught you?"

"Patience," I said between breaths. "But fuck Cunningham." I uncurled my hands. "Fuck him and the horse he rode in on, Daire. He disrespected us and had the balls to bring up Reyes. Fucking *Reyes*. Sloan needs to kill both those pricks."

"And he will. Everything Sloan does—"

"He does for a reason. I know. You don't need to give me this lecture." I shrugged off his hold and glared. "While Sloan waits, Reyes is making fucking fools of us. Look what he's fucking doing right now in Miami."

"Language." Sloan's strong voice filled the room.

I froze, fear striking me through the heart and making me wheeze in surprise as I glanced toward the door. My uncle stood there, arms crossed over his white dress shirt and deep red suspenders—which reminded me of Conall, who had a collar the same color that Sloan had put around his neck. Sloan was big on marking his slut as his property.

"Uncle, he—"

"I know what Cunningham is like. You don't need to tell me." Sloan slid into the office and closed the door behind himself.

I suspected Sloan already had men leading Cunningham out of the mansion and off our property, and I wished it was me so I could flip Cunningham the bird before he left. But Killoughs didn't do that. We kept our cool under pressure and never let fear or panic influence our decisions. More lessons Sloan had taught me.

"He's siding with Reyes." I dropped my shoulders forward, disappointment stirring in my gut. I'd lost out on the deal Sloan had wanted, one of the first my uncle had entrusted to me. Maybe I wasn't meant to be the boss one day. *Fuck.* I wanted the position, though. I *deserved* to lead. I was born for it.

And I was a Killough.

"I know." Sloan stepped toward me and rested a hand on my shoulder, squeezing. The pressure of his hold had me relaxing, and Sloan let out a sigh. "Cunningham was always going to side with Reyes. I knew they had a deal in progress."

I stared at Sloan in surprise. "Then, why did you ask me to make an agreement with him?"

"Because you need to learn a lesson, boyo." He slid his hand to my cheek and patted it. "Not all men can be persuaded to see reason. Cunningham has always been stubborn, an old man in a young man's game. He's stuck in his ways. Racist, homophobic old bastard. I'm surprised he'd deal with the Reyes Cartel in the first place, but he's always hated me more. Not because of anything to do with the Company, but because of who I share my bed with. Even though Reyes is gay, too, Cunningham's making a point. What I wanted was to watch your reaction."

"I let my anger get the best of me." I didn't need Sloan to confirm what I already knew—I'd messed up.

"Yes, you did." He dropped his hand and straightened. "If you were on your own, that would've been fine, but you weren't. Daire is still part of the Company, and you should never show those emotions in front of your men, no matter who they are."

I swallowed around the lump lodged in my throat, disappointment clenching my insides. Another lecture Sloan had repeated ever since I'd taken on the role of his apprentice, and I still hadn't followed it. "I'm sorry, Uncle. But don't you ever . . . feel that way? Angry at these stupid men?"

Sloan stared at me for a long moment, light blue eyes curious, before he turned to Daire and nodded.

Daire backed out of the office, closing the door, and I watched him go, not quite sure what to feel. I was confident that Sloan knew Daire and I were fucking, even though he'd never said anything. Staring at Daire had become an obsession. I couldn't stop since *the* night that began it all.

The memories of Daire taking my virginity made my skin warm and belly tight, and it was the beginning of our sexual relationship. Despite me wanting so much more, Daire had made it clear that it couldn't happen. *Wouldn't.* I'd accepted that sex was the only thing I'd get from him and continued to take what I was offered like a stupid schoolboy with a crush.

"Sit down," Sloan ordered, startling me out of my thoughts.

I followed him and took the chair Cunningham had abandoned. Sloan took mine, crossing a leg over his knee and linking his fingers together in front of himself.

No matter what he did, Sloan looked like *the* boss. I longed to be like him: not fazed in the slightest by anything that happened. The only time I'd seen his facade slip was whenever Conall was in danger or hurt. His reaction said everything about how much Conall meant to him, and I didn't think Sloan's pet realized. He didn't comprehend how lucky he was, because while I begged for scraps, he got all of Sloan's attention.

"You can be as angry as you want, Fionn. You can throw things around your office." Sloan glanced toward the littered pieces of glass, and I winced. "You can take a gun to a range and imagine Cunningham's face on the target. Hell, tape Cunningham's picture on it for all I care." He smirked when I laughed. "But not in front of your men. No matter who they are or how much you trust them. They must never see your weakness. Emotions are exactly that."

I quirked a grin. "And what about your pet?"

"What about him?" he asked, the lines around his eyes tightening.

I laughed again, this time less in amusement. "Come on. Conall's not just a pet anymore. You love him, and our enemies can see it. That's emotion. I saw you when the rogue Italians kidnapped Conall. How you felt because he was hurt."

I expected Sloan would deny it, wave off the comment and tell me I was wrong, but he didn't. Instead, he nodded. "I admit that my pet caught me off guard." His face turned soft, a rare sight on Sloan Killough. He lived to look fearless and in control, but now love had overtaken him. "You once implied, when we were in Miami that first year I found him, that Conall was made of stronger stuff. It was you who made me believe he could handle what I threw at him. But now I think *you* underestimate Conall."

"I must have been in a good mood," I grumbled.

Sloan raised his dark eyebrows.

I shut my mouth quickly.

"My pet *is* smart. If you gave him a chance, you could be friends. Instead—" He leaned forward, staring intensely at me. "—you choose to be a jealous child who's afraid I'll forget about you."

"That isn't—"

One corner of Sloan's mouth curled.

"I don't trust him." At this point, I was repeating the same rhetoric over and over again, but I wasn't sure if I believed myself anymore.

"Has Conall given you a reason to doubt his loyalty?" Sloan leaned back in his chair and laid his hands in his lap. "We're not here to talk about my pet. We're talking about you. Jealousy is another emotion you should never show. If I was to walk out of this office and ask any of the men how you feel about Conall, do you know what they would tell me?"

My stomach churned and I gritted my teeth. If I didn't start getting my act together, Sloan would take my apprenticeship away from me for good. He'd never let me step up as boss if he thought Conall's life was in danger. "That I was envious of him."

"Yes. That isn't how a Killough leads. Do you *want* to be the boss of this company when it's time?"

"I do." I sat up straighter. "It's all I ever dreamed about."

"Then act like a Killough," he said. "Your father knew what was expected of us, and you should by now, too."

Shame churned in my stomach, and I glanced away, unable to look at him any longer. Did Sloan know bringing up Dad would cause this reaction? Of course he knew. Why else would he do it? I hadn't known Dad for long, but I had vague memories of him. I could still smell his favorite cologne, a cinnamon scent that hung in the air long after he'd left a room.

I pressed my lips together and gathered the courage to look back at Sloan. "He was a good man."

Sloan's mouth upturned into a rare smile. "He was the best. I loved your father."

I nodded.

It wasn't the first time we'd talked about Dad, but usually it wasn't me who initiated the conversation. It hurt speaking about a man I never really knew. Being four when Dad died, I didn't have many memories of him. My younger siblings had none, but after Dad's death, Mom chose to take my brothers away from the life. Not me, though. I'd stayed to live out Dad's legacy. More than that, I was going to be the boss one day.

Sloan stood, and I blinked at him when he straightened his suit. "You're not Eoin and you never will be."

I cringed. *Ouch.*

"But I don't expect you to be. He was a great Company man, but he wasn't passionate like you are about this business." He laid a hand on my shoulder, his hold a comforting weight. "You're meant for great things, but you're young and you have a lot to learn. Your father worked for the Company because he was a family man who wanted the best for his wife and children, but you're more than that. You're a leader." He leaned down to press his forehead to mine. We didn't touch like this much anymore, but when I was a kid, Sloan would do this with me when I was upset about something. "Stop fighting your emotions. I'm not asking you to rip them out by the roots, but don't let them rule you. It'll get you or someone else you care about killed. It's what got your father killed."

I swallowed. Sloan had never told me the full story about how Dad died, only that he'd been shot in the chest by an enemy. He'd died in Sloan's arms, begging Sloan to take care of his family, and Sloan had done that. He'd provided money to my mom and brothers, and he'd protected me while teaching me how to be a boss one day.

I never regretted becoming his apprentice. Not once. Not even when Sloan chastised or punished me for my wrongdoings. That was what fathers did, right? And Sloan was a better parent than Mom had ever been.

"Yes." I bowed my head in respect. "Forgive me."

Sloan gave me one more pat on the shoulder before he turned and exited the room, leaving me to wallow in a mixture of emotions. I'd disappointed him—*again*—and that hurt the most. Everything I'd done since I'd seen Sloan at the funeral was to make him happy, yet nothing seemed to work.

I followed him out of the office and into the hallway, walking past expensive artwork I had a feeling was obtained illegally by Oisín Kelly, the Company's best thief. Not that Sloan ever asked Oisín where he got the paintings. Deniability and all that. Not to mention, no one would ever know they were the *real* artwork when Oisín was known for replacing them in art galleries with near perfect replicas.

Sloan stopped in the entranceway, in front of the stairs, and I figured out why when I came to a halt behind him.

Lor O'Guinn—a guest who'd been staying at the mansion for a while now, though I couldn't figure out why Sloan cared about him—and Conall walked out of the dining room, deep in conversation. They didn't see me and Sloan until they reached us.

Conall grinned when his attention landed on Sloan, his entire face lighting up. The red collar on his neck was bright against the black T-shirt clinging to his muscles and the faded jeans that molded to his ass. His sneakers were nearly the exact same shade of red as the leather around his throat.

Sloan opened his arms and dragged Conall into them, laying a hard kiss on his lips. Conall's back arched as he got in closer and he hummed into the connection of their mouths.

Lor smiled but shifted his feet awkwardly at the display of affection. I didn't know how old he was, but he had to be my age or younger, what with his baby face and those innocent brown eyes. Then again, he was also a strange man, with dyed-black hair bisected by a white stripe. I couldn't decide if he was trying to be punk or a skunk.

I hadn't spent much time around the new guy in the house and didn't want to. From what Sloan had told me, Lor was a friend of Dr. Vail Mifflin, who in turn was the lover of four Company men.

Four.

I couldn't even get the one man I was interested in to want more than sex. No, Daire preferred to see me as nothing more than a hole. A body. Daire's excuses were always the same.

You're Sloan's nephew.

You're the future boss of the Company.

I was tired of hearing it.

Bitterness coated my tongue and left a bad taste in my mouth. I'd tried so hard to pretend my feelings for Daire didn't exist. We spent too much time together already, and Sloan trusted us to get the job done, but when the world around us grew quiet, when I had time to think, all I could focus on was Daire. How handsome he was. How much I desired his compliments and touch. And then, I remembered the heartache of rejection.

My mouth twisted, anger beating in my chest. Sloan thought me and Daire were fucking, and while he was right, that was all it was.

Fucking.

Sex.

Physical, because I wasn't worth more than that. Daire didn't want anything from me.

When we fucked, I was his, but only until we came, and then I was nobody but his boss's nephew again. I wasn't good enough to be in a public relationship with him, and it was that knowledge that had me choking back tears in the dead of night.

How pathetic was I? So desperate for a man who didn't want me in return.

"Why are you still here?" I snapped before I could stop myself, glaring at Lor. Taking my anger out on other people was easier than facing my own sadness. "Don't you have a home to go to?"

Lor startled, turning wide brown eyes on me. "I . . . ."

"He was invited to stay at *my* home by me." Sloan filled in for

Lor's panic, his eyes narrowed on me from over Conall's shoulder. His lips pursed together in a decisively irritated way.

I flinched.

"He lives in the city, and it's a long drive to the Hamptons for the work he does with Vail, so I offered him a room."

"Stop being a jealous brat," Conall teased with a wink.

"Stop being a—" *Slut.* I cut myself off before I went too far. Sloan would kill me if I actually said it out loud, and by the darkening of Sloan's eyes, he knew what I'd planned on saying wasn't anywhere near friendly.

"I wouldn't finish that sentence if I were you," he warned.

I kept my mouth closed and bowed my head in respect, bitterness growing in its force to dominate my entire being. I'd been here longer than Conall and Lor combined, yet I couldn't do anything right in Sloan's eyes, and that was the worst part of the entire situation. They got more attention from Sloan. Maybe Sloan was right, and I was making my jealousy too obvious, but I couldn't stop. I wanted Sloan to look at me and smile with pride, then tell me I was doing a fantastic job. Was that too much to ask?

"Pet, take Lor out to the garage. I know I promised to take you both out for a late lunch. I need to talk to Fionn for a moment." It sounded like Sloan was kissing Conall again, but I didn't dare look in case I said something I'd regret. Tension seeped into my stomach, burning as I kept my eyes on the floor.

Echoing footsteps caused me to finally glance up at Sloan and lick my lips nervously. "Sorry, Uncle."

Sloan raised his dark eyebrows and stepped in closer, crossing his arms. "Stop with the apologies. I'm sick and tired of them."

I winced. "Yes, Uncle."

"Everything I say to you is being ignored." The disappointment in Sloan's voice had acid rising in my throat. "I tell you to control your jealousy, and a moment later you nearly insult my pet. Again."

"I'm trying." I hated how small I sounded, but it was hard to be anything else around Sloan. He loomed over me and made me feel like a child again, tiny and naive. I wasn't those things anymore, yet Sloan still scared me.

"No, you're not." Sloan heaved a sigh and fixed his suspenders, and my attention slid to his fingers and the way they worked the material. "Maybe I was wrong, and you'll never be ready to be the boss of this company."

My heart stuttered and I sucked in a deep breath. "Uncle, I'm s—" I swallowed around my apology, anxiety making me sweat. The thought of losing the Company had my chest squeezing until it felt like I couldn't breathe. "I won't fail you, I swear." My voice wobbled and I gritted my teeth, trying to stop the fear that made me shake. "I *won't*. This is my legacy. *Mine*."

Sloan got in close to my face, baring his teeth so angrily that I thought he was going to hurt me. I knew better, though. He'd always threatened and made the men think he'd punish me, but he never did. "Then, earn it. Right now, you're acting like a child. You might be an adult, Fionn, but if you want this, you don't have time to act blasé about the Company. The moment you let your guard down, someone will *kill* you, and I won't have your death on my conscience, too. Not like your father. Do you understand?"

He straightened and took a deep breath, the coolness returning to his strong face. Any anger he'd shown had disappeared and the tightness around his sea-blue eyes loosened.

Shock had me frozen. "Uncle—"

"Stop disappointing me," he said sharply, startling me. "Tomorrow, you and Daire will start looking for that rat again. Get me results or I swear you won't like the consequences. This has gone on for far too long. Daire has a new lead. Follow up on it."

Tears of frustration welled in my eyes and I blinked, trying to force them back. I wouldn't cry in front of Sloan, yet the unbearable shame wasn't easy to ignore. I couldn't remember a time when Sloan had gotten *this* angry at me.

"Don't cry. For fuck's sake, Fionn. Don't." Sloan didn't wait for me to say anything else. He slipped past me and walked toward the hallway.

When I heard the back door slam open and close—causing me to jump—I dropped my head and let the tears slip down my face. *Fuck.* I was a Company man. I couldn't cry. Yet all the years of hard work and emotional pain had finally caught up to me. What would I have to do to make Sloan happy?

More footsteps had me rubbing the tears away from my face. I turned, sighing when I caught sight of Daire standing at the top of the split staircase. The white steps gleamed under the chandeliers, giving him an angelic glow like he was my savior. That's all I needed. More reasons to be ashamed. Daire had never seen me cry, and now here I was, eyes red and cheeks stained by tears.

Daire took each step slowly, his hand skimming the black handrails until he hit the bottom. He stopped when he stood in front of me and reached out to rub his thumb over my cheek.

I stiffened, the warmth of Daire's skin creating a ripple of pleasure that cannonballed through me. I couldn't remember the last time Daire had touched me affectionally outside of the bedroom.

"You're okay, boy," he whispered, smiling. "He's been in a bad mood this week. It's not you. He's worried about everything happening with the Reyes Cartel."

I nodded, unsure what else to do, but I didn't have a chance to consider Daire's touch before his hand snapped back to his side.

"Meet me here at eight tomorrow morning. We have business."

"Wait." One word and it was barely whispered, the hint of hesitation in my voice making me flinch.

He stopped and glanced back at me.

"Tonight? I could really . . . use you." I ignored the shame that curled inside me, but my hunger for him and the need for comfort took control. I craved more, so much more with Daire, but I'd take what I could get. Even if it was only getting fucked by Daddy Daire.

My Daddy was a completely different person from the Daire that I worked with. He gave me exactly what I needed and took care of me, while also fucking me until there were no anxious thoughts in my head.

"I'll be back in four hours."

Then, he was gone, out the front door, probably to go home.

I laid my hand on my cheek where Daire had touched me and sighed. I couldn't remember the last person who'd made me feel this good. He brought all my emotions to the surface. When we were together, I could let go of my shame and anger.

I sighed and dropped my hand. Who was I kidding? He felt sorry for me, just like the rest of the crazy assholes in the Company. They all thought of me as weak.

Fuck them. I would prove them wrong.

2

FIONN

My heart thumped under the hand I'd placed on my chest, a sturdy beat that reminded me of a song Dad once sang to me as a kid. I didn't remember the lyrics anymore, but I knew the tune, and it seemed like the muscle in my chest did as well.

Thump. Thump. Thump.

Steady. Strong. Fast.

I was nervous. Why? Daire and I had fucked plenty of times, and once we were finished, he left without a word. There were no lingering kisses or promises of something more. He'd made it clear when we'd first begun this—it was purely sex.

He didn't want a *relationship*.

What was so wrong with me that he couldn't stand the idea of dating me? That was the question I pushed out of my head. In the end, it didn't matter because he'd made his choice, and I wasn't it. I was only good enough to fuck.

A knock made me straighten from where I stood near the wide square window in my bedroom. Taking a deep breath, I centered myself before I headed toward the door. I turned the knob and opened it to find Daire on the other side, his broad shoulders taking up the threshold. He was still dressed in his black suit, but his tie was missing and a few buttons were undone around his neck.

He didn't smile or say a word as he walked forward. I matched his steps by backing away, and he shut the door with a sharp *click* that echoed around the room. My heart resumed its strange beating, and my breath caught in my throat as he moved into my personal space. Once the back of my knees hit the edge of the bed, I had nowhere to go, but I didn't want to escape.

The thing about having sex with Daire was that he didn't speak a lot. Other than "yes, boy," dirty talk, compliments, and blunt directions, he hardly said anything. I'd been fine with that before because I could have *him*, but now the missing words were weighing on my soul. I needed *more*. I didn't want to be merely a body for him to come inside of; I dreamed of being his partner.

"Daire—"

He grabbed my face between his large hands and slammed his mouth against mine. I gasped into his rough kiss, and he shoved his tongue between my lips, tasting me in a way that I could only describe as starving. Only I could sate his desires.

I moaned into the hard press of his mouth and sucked on his tongue. My eyes slipped closed and I curled my arms around his broad shoulders, dragging him closer to me until we were chest to chest. The strong leather smell of his cologne tickled my nose, and I couldn't get enough. Everything about him was an addiction, and I was his faithful junkie.

"Strip, then get me naked, boy," he growled into my ear between the kisses he trailed over my cheek and down my jaw.

I groaned and got rid of my suit as quickly as I could. There wasn't any finesse to the way I ripped my clothes off, too impatient about getting my hands on him. As soon as I was bare, my fingers went to the top button of his dress shirt, tugging at it desperately. One button after another slipped through their holes, revealing inked skin to my ravenous gaze. My mouth watered as the tattoos he hid beneath his clothes came into view.

With a shirt on, Daire was stunning, a man who looked put together and responsible. Without a shirt, though, Daire was a force to be reckoned with.

Weaving ink stretched across his chest, down his arms, and over his back. Celtic markings he'd chosen purposely for one reason or another told stories in the form of black lines, joined together by body art. The tattoos were all expertly hidden beneath his clothes, and nearly everyone—except me—was completely unaware of them. This was one secret that Daire allowed me to know.

Fuck, he was always so fucking beautiful. I remembered the first time I'd seen them, back when I was about nineteen or so. Daire had taken a long vacation for five months, and while I'd never asked where he'd gone, Sloan had him on a secret assignment. When he'd come back, the moment we were alone, I'd practically mauled him.

―――――

Eight Years Ago

Getting Daire out of his suit had been my main priority. I was *greedy* for him, and my hole ached with emptiness. Five months was way too long, and I needed him to fuck me until I saw stars.

But the moment I got him out of his suit, I froze. The entirety of his chest was no longer a blank canvas for my teeth and tongue to map. No. Now his skin was inked from his stomach to his collarbones to his arms.

The tattoos were numerous and didn't have an ounce of bright color but were artfully done. Celtic knots intertwined their way across his skin like maps, and they were joined by shamrocks, guns, two dogs that looked a lot like Dobermans on either side of his ribs, and in the center of his chest was the claddagh symbol—a heart with a crown and two hands reaching for it. The claddagh represented love, loyalty, and friendship, and the design of the ink left me breathless.

"You have tattoos," I stated rather obviously. "When did you get tattoos? You didn't have them before you left."

Daire glanced down at his chest in surprise, as if realizing they were there for the first time, and I chuckled. When he looked up at me again, he smiled. "I got one about a week after I went on vacation."

Vacation? I snorted.

"It was a random thing." He twisted his body, muscles rippling with the movement, and he tapped a heart-shaped Celtic knot on his hip.

I ate up the sight of the inked flesh. The last time I'd gotten a shirtless view of Daire like this, he had fucked me into the bed before he left.

"I developed a taste for tattoos." He shrugged. "I ended up doing my entire chest, arms, and back. I made sure the suit could cover it because Sloan isn't a fan of them, as you know."

I reached out a hand carefully, as though I was about to touch a wild animal. His shoulders tensed, but he didn't move. My fingers gently trailed over his chest.

"Can I see your back? Please?" My voice was barely audible in the silence, but it was loud enough that I could hear it tremble.

"You're the future of the Company. You don't need to ask." He tilted his chin.

"I'm not going to order you, *Daddy*. You're not a regular soldier. You're our second-in-command. So, I'm asking you. Can I see it?"

I was close enough that I could feel his breath tickle my cheek. I should back away and let him fuck me like every other time.

Emotionless.

Hungry.

Desperate.

I couldn't make my limbs move. When Daire slowly turned, I devoured him with my eyes, taking in every line of ink that covered his upper body. The artwork was flawless, and the knots fit him perfectly, especially the claddagh symbol across his chest.

But the tattoos on his back were even more spectacular, making me suck in a surprised breath. Across the expanse of his shoulders and down his spine was a magnificent Celtic cross with the triquetra—the trinity knot—embedded into the weaving lines. Around the cross were more intricate images, including one that looked like a tear in his skin, showing off the back of his ribs and heart.

I wanted to ask him what each one meant, but I couldn't string two words together. My tongue felt heavy, and all I could do was reach out and trace the lines in Daire's cross, my heart thumping painfully in my throat. I caressed along the black knots, and he tensed, muscles going hard under my touch. The air in the room thickened, and I found it hard to breathe. I licked my dry lips and scratched my fingers over warm skin.

A shudder went through him, and I froze, terrified that I would scare him off, which was crazy because he was no wuss. Except, when it came to me, Daire seemed to shy away like he was allergic. Our interactions were push and pull, and it was beginning to make a nervous energy rise inside me.

Regardless of the tension, I didn't move away. I stroked across his shoulders, my fingers shaking. I took deep breaths, calming my racing heart. My stomach turned to knots similar to the complex ones in his tattoos. I bit down hard on my bottom lip to stop myself from doing something stupid—like laying my mouth on Daire's back in an intimate kiss instead.

I stroked lower, following the outline of the Celtic cross

until I got to the base of his spine, close to the upper curves of his ass, and that was when he finally stepped away and turned to look at me.

An awkwardness settled between us as my gaze dropped to the front of Daire's stomach where his belt kept his pants on his hips, and Daire pursed his mouth. His eyes darkened and his upper lip curled, and there was an animalistic urge dancing in his stare that made me want to shout, *"Fucking kiss me!"*

"Come here, boy," he growled.

———

I focused on the present.

Daire raised his eyebrows at me. "Are you going to do something or just stare at me, boy?" His voice deepened, an edge of lust and need scraping up from his throat, and I shivered with the sound. I was Pavlov's dog reacting to the *ting* of Daire's bell.

An embarrassing mewl slipped from my mouth, and I flushed, heat flooding my cheeks. Laughing awkwardly when Daire smirked, I focused on his chest once all the buttons were undone. I danced my fingers over his pecs and down his stomach, not quite tracing the ink, but reveling in the feel of his skin.

When I reached his belt, I went to work on unbuckling it, then yanking the leather out of the loops of his pants. I threw it behind me, unconcerned where it landed, and glanced up at him from beneath my lashes. He gave me a small nod of approval, and a sharp blast of electricity skittered through my body to land straight in my balls.

Unbuttoning his pants took a few tries, since I'd began to shake in excitement. It didn't matter how many times I slept with him, I always looked forward to the next, my insides an explosion of fervor from just being around him, let alone undressing his sculpted body until he was naked for my eyes to feast on. He was a Greek god, all rippling muscles, and it felt as though simply staring at him was similar to looking at the sun. Gazing at him wasn't good for me, but I couldn't tear my eyes away. I didn't want to stop, and if that meant endangering my health, I'd take that risk.

Daire was worth it.

I fell to my knees on the floor. First, I maneuvered his shoes and socks off, not interested in the pieces of clothing getting in my way, before I yanked down his pants. Next came his underwear. When I had him gloriously naked, I stared up at the planes of his body, from his thick thighs grazed with hair, to his cock that stood proudly out from gray-infused brown trimmed pubes, to the ridges of his inked stomach and chest, and finally, up to his strong chin and the dark eyes staring down at me.

He didn't say a word, but he didn't need to. I itched to please him, to do whatever I could to get praise from him. Like every other time we found ourselves in this position, I did what I wanted.

I touched him.

Brushing my thumbs over his hip bones, I leaned my cheek against his thigh and inhaled. The muskiness of his natural scent invaded my nostrils as hair tickled my skin.

"I love your body, Daddy," I murmured, falling into the roles we'd been playing since the *first* time we'd had sex. It came naturally to call Daire my Daddy. No one outside of this room knew the truth, how our relationship came to be, and I didn't think they ever would.

Daire carded his fingers through my hair, nails scraping over my scalp, and I moaned. I leaned my head back as my eyes slipped closed. The pleasurable sensations teased their way down my spine and through my stomach, landing straight in my balls. All it took was one small touch, and I was putty beneath

Daddy Daire. He could do anything to me, and I'd thank him for it without a second thought.

"What do you want me to do, Daddy?" I peeked up at him from beneath my eyelashes. All the responsibilities of the outside world were gone, nothing more than a forgotten memory buried deep in the recesses of my mind while I was in this room with Daire. He had control, and I yearned to hear him say how proud of me he was, like he always did when we were alone. Compliments were my drug, and he was my dealer.

He smoothed his hand down my cheek, and I closed my eyes, leaning into his soft touch. His fingers were rough but gentle at the same time, as if he was caught between the urge to dominate me or take care of me. Though, a Daddy did both. I'd read up a lot about the kink after our first time. I hadn't expected the words *Daddy Daire* to slip from between my lips unprovoked, but once they had, everything felt right.

I was his boy, and he was Daddy.

He brushed his thumb over my bottom lip, and I moaned, opening my mouth so he could press the flat pad against my tongue. I wrapped my lips around his finger and sucked, humming with pleasure as I imagined it was his dick instead.

"Fuck. You're so beautiful, boy. So good for me."

My stomach clenched and my dick throbbed. I groaned around his digit when he slipped in two more—his pointer and middle finger—and pushed them into the back of my mouth until my gag reflex kicked in, then withdrew them.

"What do you need from *me*, boy?" He yanked me to my feet and leaned down to kiss across my jaw, and I tilted my head back to give him access.

"Make me forget," I murmured, a quiver of excitement sliding down my spine and settling at the base. I hungered to reach out and touch him, but I wasn't in charge inside this room.

"Sit on the edge of the bed," he growled out in a low,

dangerous tone that had goose bumps erupting across my skin. "I want you to suck my cock."

I moaned at the words and shoved backward to sit my ass on the mattress as he'd instructed. My cock leaked, the precum building up at my slit, but I didn't dare touch it.

He watched me, eyes hungry as he skated his gaze down the length of my body, stopping to appreciate my dripping cock. Humming, he stepped in closer, and my breath caught in my throat. He curled his fingers around my cockhead, and I reacted on impulse, jerking up toward him with a low whimper.

"Daddy." I closed my eyes and trembled. A mere touch from him, and I was a shaking mess. How fucking embarrassing.

He tightened his hold and squeezed the sensitive tip, and I rolled my hips up toward him again. "Does that feel good?"

I moaned in answer and resisted the urge to close my eyes. Licking my lips as pleasure stoked the fire inside my belly, I stared at him and gave him a nod. "Yes, Daddy Daire."

"You're so *pretty*, boy. I've never met anyone as pretty as you." Daire dipped forward and swiped his tongue over my neck before nibbling beneath my jaw, releasing his hold on me.

I whimpered. "Thank you, Daddy."

He hummed and shifted away. With a hand wrapped around his cock, he waved his shaft at me. "Suck."

I grabbed his hips and dragged him closer. Tilting my head, I darted my tongue out to lick a stripe across his slit. He hissed, the sound igniting a fire in my belly. Beyond his compliments, I thirsted for the sounds that left him when I made him happy. His deep-throated growls and moans fueled my passion and need for him.

The head of his cock slid into my mouth, and I sucked on it gently, raising my gaze to watch the pleasure cross his face. I wrapped my hand around the base of his thick shaft and took more of him between my lips. The salty taste of his skin danced across my tongue, and I whimpered, the need to satisfy and get him inside me burning hot in my chest. He could ask anything of me, and I'd do it, if only for him to tell me what a good boy I'd been.

He slid his fingers into my hair and tugged at the strands with enough force to create a sharp sting on my scalp. A spike of lust blasted down my spine and I trembled. Fuck, this was perfect. I couldn't get enough of my Daddy, even if he wanted it to only be sex. I'd take anything and everything he'd give me, despite my craving for more. Right now, the only things that mattered were his cock in my mouth, his hand in my hair, and the sweet words of praise.

"Fuck, boy, you've got the warmest mouth. So fucking good."

I mewled around his hardness and started a slow bob up and down the length of his cock. I sucked with enthusiasm, pressing my lips as firmly as I could around him.

He groaned, grip tightening in my hair. "Fuck, boy, you're so good at this. Remember when I first taught you how to do it?" Daire's voice took on a dark edge, deep and hungry in a way that had my cock jerking and a stream of precum sliding down the tip. "You're a quick study."

I made a happy sound and twisted my wrist, creating friction with the base of his shaft. He thrust, burying his cock deeper into my mouth and triggering my gag reflex. My throat constricted, and I exhaled heavily through my nose, pushing as much air out as I could so I didn't choke. I wanted him to stay inside me, needed it more than anything else.

"Good boy." He stroked his fingers down my temple and across my cheek. "You're so beautiful like this, taking my cock down your throat."

I removed my hand and lowered my mouth farther onto his cock until my nose was pressed into his pubes. My throat worked around his thick shaft as I swallowed, and he groaned, tugging my hair harder.

"Fuck, boy, if you keep going, this won't last long."

I moaned, pleased I had him veering toward an orgasm, but it quickly turned into a sigh of disappointment when he moved away, taking his gloriously thick cock with him. Panting, I stared up at him as I licked my lips. "I wasn't done, Daddy."

"I know, boy." He thumbed my chin and the corner of his mouth curled. "But I want to get into that pretty hole of yours. Get onto the middle of the bed like the good boy you are."

I jumped to my feet so fast that I nearly lost my balance. I crawled to the center of the mattress and fell onto my stomach exactly how I knew Daire wanted me. He always loved it when his chest was to my back, and I did, too, because that position meant he drilled straight against my prostate.

Daire opened the bottom drawer of my nightstand and threw the bottle of lube and a condom onto the mattress beside me. He knew where all the essentials were because we'd fucked a lot in my room.

He slid onto the bed and sat on his knees behind me before he slapped me hard on the ass. The sharp sting reverberated through me and pleasure coiled in my balls.

I gasped and rocked my hips forward, rubbing my throbbing cock against the soft bedding.

He smoothed his hand across my asscheek and grasped my meaty flesh, squeezing with a firm grip.

"Daddy Daire," I moaned out, rocking back toward his touch. "Daddy."

"What do you want, boy? What can I do for you?" He swooped down to place a kiss on my left cheek, then the right, and I spread my legs farther, giving him as much access as he wanted to my hole.

"You. I need you to fuck me. *Please*. Daddy, I've been so good. I promise."

He hummed and spread me wider before his tongue was at my hole, licking delicately with a teasing curl that had my back arching. "So good, boy. I'm so proud of you."

I shuddered under his compliments and sobbed into the mattress. "Thank you, Daddy."

He pressed his face between my cheeks and stuck his tongue in my hole, working me open with precise, slow movements. Daire sucked at my ring, and I groaned, caught between pushing my ass back against his mouth and trying to wriggle away from his tongue because of the sensitivity.

"Please, Daddy." My words came out garbled, and I wasn't sure if he could make out what I'd said because the only response I received was a sharp slap to my asscheek. "Oh God."

"God's not here to save you, boy," Daire said between licks to my hole. "But Daddy will take care of you."

I believed him, too. I trusted Daire with my life.

The sound of a pumping bottle had me stiffening, then relaxing. He usually didn't finger me much because I didn't mind the sting of the stretch, so when one finger joined with his tongue, I relaxed under the intrusion. I spread my legs wider and pushed up onto my knees, hiking my ass higher to give him better access, and he used it to his advantage, delving his tongue in deeper.

"Daddy, please," I whined out.

Daire slapped my ass before his tongue and finger disappeared from my hole. The pumping of the lube and a condom packet ripping open met my ears before something wider pressed against my opening, and it was exactly what I wanted and needed. His cock. The head pushed in, stretching me open with a delicious bite of pain.

He laid his hand on the middle of my back, pushing my chest deeper into the bed as he slid inside me too slowly. I whimpered, bucking toward him so he glided balls deep in with one swift movement, causing us both to groan.

"You're so tight, boy." Daire blanketed me with his body, chest against my back, his arms wrapped around me in a tight hug that pressed his cock even deeper.

Home. That's what Daire felt like. Sloan was my uncle, but Daire was the only one who'd ever made me feel like I was worth something. He didn't baby me, but he told me when I was doing well, praised me when I deserved it.

He was a true Daddy.

Daire's lips met my shoulder and he sucked a bruise into my skin, deep and satisfying in a pleasurable pain that had me rocking back against him.

"Daddy." My fingers curled in the bedsheets, and I gripped them tightly, electric currents of lust shooting through me and making my limbs ache. I shivered, fighting the urge to roll my hips and begging him to move. I gave in and did exactly that.

"Shh, boy." He trailed kisses over my shoulders and licked across the back of my neck. "Patience."

I whimpered and tilted my ass up farther. "Please, Daddy. I need you. Please move."

He laughed hotly into my ear and sucked the top of it into his mouth. His cock was heavy in my hole, thick and warm, and his body was the same as it covered mine.

Every touch that came from him was magnetic, and I was drawn into his presence the same as a pyromaniac to fire. Would he burn me? If he did, I'd let it happen.

Finally, he sat back on his knees and began a gentle pace. His cock slid in and out of my hole with the rock of his hips, and his hands clasped my waist, holding me still. The stretch and pressure of his shaft created an addicting friction, and my world centered on the feeling of my Daddy inside me, opening me up for our pleasure.

I threw my head back, and as if shifting on instinct, his hand wrapped around my neck, squeezing. I moaned and pursed my lips, and he tilted his head to press his mouth to mine. We kissed hungrily as his thrusts intensified. The gentle rocking was replaced with a hard punch of his hips against mine, his balls slapping my skin and his cock driving home.

The moment he pegged my prostate, my world turned on its axis, and a carnality assaulted me. I shouted, and he removed his hand from my neck to slap it over my mouth. I nibbled the skin on his palm and moaned again when he continued to hammer at my most sensitive spot.

"So good for me, boy. Look at you, Fionn, so fucking beautiful with your back arched and your ass in the air." He slammed forward, the head of his cock beating my prostate again. "Do you feel that? My hard cock inside you. That's what you do to me. You're so fucking sexy, boy."

His words came with a soft sentiment, and it took all my effort not to fall prey to them. He didn't mean it. I was nothing more than a hole he used and abused before he left when the act was done. He played a role, and I'd started this all those years ago. I'd tempted him and given him a free meal —me.

The hand covering my mouth went to my hip, and his fingers dug into the crevice near my hip bone, nails biting my flesh and marking me as his.

"So pretty, boy. I wish you could see your hole swallowing my cock."

I shuddered at the praise mixed in with the dirty talk and opened my hand to spit on my palm. Unsteadily, I reached under my body to wrap my fist around my cock. I rocked back to meet his thrusts, the low thrumming pleasure building up in my balls. My orgasm tickled my sack, teasing how close I was to erupting.

"Daddy Daire, please come in me. *Please*. I'm being a good boy for you." I reached behind me with the hand not jerking my cock and grabbed one of my asscheeks, tugging it to open myself more for him. "Give it to me. I need it."

"You *have* been good, haven't you?" He kissed across my shoulders again and paused to bruise the back of my neck with a sharp bite, and I hissed. "Show me how much you want it.

Come for me first. Squeeze that tight little hole around Daddy's cock. Milk what you want from me."

"Yes, Daddy Daire. I'll do anything for you. Anything."

I was so close already. Tightening my grip on my cock, I rolled my ass back to meet his thrusts as I began to stroke myself faster. Intense heat exploded inside me as my orgasm hit hard. My balls tightened and I squeezed my hole as cum shot from my slit and splattered across the bed beneath me.

His grip on my hip tightened and he thrust roughly inside, his ball sack smacking against mine. We moaned simultaneously, and he stilled, a low growl vibrating from his throat as the condom filled up in me.

I wished I could feel the heat of his cum, but we never had sex with the rubber.

"Thank you, Daddy. Thank you." I gripped the sheets and sobbed into them as he smoothed a hand along my back and swooped down to place a kiss on my shoulder.

"You're a good boy, Fionn. You made me proud."

I shuddered, and while I wish I could blame it on him sliding out of me, I knew it was because of his words.

Proud.

I fucking loved that word, especially coming from Daire.

He fell onto the bed beside me, chest rising and falling in harsh pants. I sat back on my knees, and then my ass, staring at him carefully as he ripped off the condom and tied it up, before throwing it into the trash can beside my bed. A need rose inside me, but it wasn't a physical necessity like it had been a few moments ago. There was a deeper feeling, an emotional desire for connection with him. We'd been doing this for eight years now, since my eighteenth birthday party.

"Daddy Daire, do you think we could ever—"

"I need to go." Daire rose and slipped out of bed with the ease that only a confident man possessed, or one who was fleeing from a question he didn't want to answer. He always found the opportune moment to leave, to run for the hills before I could ask for more.

He dressed.

I watched him, not quite sure what I felt or if I could keep doing this. How much longer would I let him use me if this wasn't going to go any further?

Pain etched a chaotic imprint on my heart, along with all the others left by the people who lacked the will to love me the way I needed them to.

I crawled across the bed to get to my feet and grabbed my pants, tugging them on without underwear. Daire didn't say a word as I grabbed my shirt and shoved my arms through the sleeves. I wasn't going to do this, I *couldn't*. If he wanted me, he needed to have a discussion with me.

Opening my mouth to say the words out loud, I froze when Daire's phone rang. I stared at him as he answered.

"Daire speaking." He paused, then hummed. "I'm here now. Yeah. I'll be right down." He ended the call and glanced at me, eyes shining like he wanted to say something before he shook his head. "I need to go. Sloan called a meeting about Reyes."

"Why wasn't I invited?" I tried and failed to keep the irritation out of my tone.

Usually, Sloan came to find me first and told me he was calling a meeting.

Daire sighed. "It's about Reyes, Fionn. You know how your uncle gets about that. He only calls you in when he *needs* you to be there. He's keeping you mostly out of the Reyes business."

"Why?" The question came out like a demand, and I winced when he gave me a sharp look.

"Reyes is dangerous."

"And I'm Uncle Sloan's apprentice. I need to understand what's happening." I shrugged, keeping my composure. If Sloan didn't think I could contain my emotions, I would prove him wrong.

"This is different." He glanced toward the door, mouth twitching like it did whenever we talked about Reyes. I didn't know what Reyes had done specifically, but I'd always had a feeling it was deeper than a rivalry. Daire's gaze returned to me for a moment before he slipped past me and out the door.

I followed because I was a sucker for punishment. I didn't care that my shirt was still unbuttoned or that I was a mess. I raced down the stairs after him and stopped at the bottom when Donal McMahon came through the door. He was one of Sloan's lieutenants and had worked for the Company for a long time. He'd been my grandfather's best friend, too.

"Donal." I grinned despite my anger at Daire, who'd turned to walk down the hallway toward the meeting room. "You're here, too."

Donal was a short man with thick white hair, sharp gray eyes, and a permanent grin. He was somewhere in his early seventies and was probably one of the only men who didn't treat me like a child.

"Hey, boyo." His thick Irish brogue made me smile as the familiarity of childhood created a warm cocoon around me. He'd been in my life since the moment I was born.

"You've been invited to the meeting?" I closed the distance between us.

He nodded seriously and offered me a sympathetic smile, as if he already knew I wasn't allowed to go. "Serious business. The Reyes Cartel again."

I groaned and rubbed my eyes. "Sloan doesn't trust me with this."

Donal made a sound that I couldn't interpret. He gripped my shoulder firmly. "This isn't on you, Fionn. Reyes is different."

"How? Sloan lets me in on meetings when he needs all hands on deck."

"Yes, but he has his reasons." He eyed me carefully and the

smile turned more mischievous as he perused my messy appearance. "Have fun?"

My cheeks turned hot and I groaned. "I . . . . Yeah. I suppose."

"I'm not even going to ask." He laughed, loud and booming, and I couldn't help but grin back at him. That was the thing about Donal—he didn't belittle me in his amusement.

"I'd rather you didn't mention this to my uncle, either?" I chuckled and glanced down at myself and my open shirt.

Donal made a zipping gesture over his mouth. "My lips are sealed." He patted me on the shoulder and winked.

After a few quick seconds, I remembered the date. I blinked at Donal, a sadness overtaking me as I gave him a sympathetic smile. "It's been nine years since Carolina passed, hasn't it?"

He startled, his eyes widening. "You remember?"

I nodded very seriously. It was hard to forget. I hadn't known Donal's daughter well because we'd never been *friends*, per se, but she'd always been special to him. She'd died of a drug overdose, and it'd changed Donal in a lot of ways. Even now, around his constant joy, there was a haunted look in his eyes.

"I'm sorry."

The corners of his lips tipped upward, and he patted me on the cheek gently. "Thank you, Fionn. It means a lot. Now, I've got business to attend to. If I was you, I'd head upstairs before anyone else comes in."

I nodded. "It was nice to see you, Don."

His entire face softened. "You too, Fionn."

Then, he left, and I watched him go. He was right. If I didn't get upstairs soon, others would come in and gossip about me, and I didn't want that. I'd talk to Daire later.

3

DAIRE REARDON

I had a first-class ticket to hell, I was sure of it. I'd have front-row seats and be known as the sinner of all sinners. Well . . . maybe it wasn't that bad, but it didn't seem that great, either.

If I closed my eyes, I could still see Fionn crying yesterday.

Subtle tears broke the walls of his lashes to slide delicately down his pale cheeks, only to drop to their death from his sharp chin. His plump lips trembled as he stared up toward the ceiling, so close to the breaking point that only a thin tether of control kept him where he was. I'd never seen such an erotic sight. Fionn's beauty was breathtaking already, but his vulnerability made him damned near irresistible.

Groaning, I shook my head and stared at myself in the full-length mirror in my bedroom. I wore a black suit, custom designed to fit my body perfectly, with a red tie that I'd stuffed into a black vest. My shoes were freshly polished and my hair was styled. I appeared professional, like a Company man. Sloan expected us to always look our best, and as second-in-command—or third, if you counted Fionn as the apprentice—I needed to impress, to be the man who caught everyone's attention as I strolled down the sidewalk like I owned it, because in a way, I *did*.

The Killough Company controlled the East Coast, and a large portion of that power was given to me to wield. When Sloan wasn't around, it was my job to manage our many employees and business partners.

Last night's meeting hadn't been anything unusual. Sloan had updated us about Reyes's movements and what we could expect from the Cartel. They were one of our biggest rivals, along with the Russians. Sloan had always hated Thiago Reyes, and it was for good reason, too.

Bang.

I froze and went on high alert when something clattered downstairs in my condo. The hair on my arms rose as I stalked to my closet and grabbed the gun I kept on a shelf. After checking to make sure the chamber was loaded, I clutched the Glock firmly as I snuck out of my bedroom and down the black steel stairs, taking each step carefully and quietly. I paused to glance around the corner into the kitchen, exhaling through my nose as I readied to shoot if need be, but the moment my gaze fell on a familiar back, I grunted and dropped the gun to my side.

"What are you doing here?" I strode the rest of the way toward the kitchen and placed the Glock on the round glass dining table. "Do you have a death wish? Sloan banned you from New York."

Aodhan, my older brother, turned from where he stood in front of the counter and grinned. Wearing a white dress shirt, he had his tie draped around his neck. His suit jacket hung over the back of a chair near the table, and he looked cocky as usual. "Did he? I can't remember that. Oh, wait . . . . Yeah, I do remember, but I just don't care."

I rolled my eyes and rubbed my forehead in frustration. "You're going to get yourself killed."

Aodhan shrugged and moved his head from side to side, the ugly sound of his neck cracking making me wince. I fucking hated when he did that shit, and he knew it. "It would be fun to see him try."

I kicked out one of the chairs at the table and took a seat. Peering at my brother carefully, I studied the hard lines of his face. Aodhan and I looked alike in a lot of ways. There was no mistaking we were related. Unfortunately for me, Aodhan was taller and wider, with a more defined jaw and thinner mouth. His messy dark hair was only one of his many features that had women and men swooning, and as far as I was aware, Aodhan could have anyone he wanted.

And he did.

He had no quarrels with fucking anything that moved. I knew for a fact he'd fucked Ardan, at the very least, and probably a few more guys in the Company.

"Why are you here?" I asked again, leaning back against the chair and throwing a leg over my knee. "The only reason you're alive right now is because Sloan respects me."

Aodhan laughed abruptly. "And here I thought he respected *me*."

I sighed. "Aodhan . . . ."

He blatantly ignored me, continuing with what he was doing before I'd come downstairs, and I took a moment to consider him. He was messing with one of my favorite mugs, stirring whatever was inside it with a spoon. He hummed a tune quietly.

"At least tell me what you're doing."

Aodhan sent me a grin. "I'm making tea. I spent a few years in Scotland, you remember, and I took a shine to the UK's English breakfast tea. It's a shame you don't own a kettle. I liked that fancy little device, too."

"You can buy them here." I ran a hand over the back of my neck and sighed. "I'm serious, though. You need to tell me why you're here."

He turned toward me and leaned his ass against the counter. The smug smile curling his lips gave me a bad feeling, I knew my brother too well. Nothing stopped him from doing what he wanted, not even me begging him not to do something he would regret. "I was bored."

"You were bored?" I stared incredulously at him. "Are you fucking kidding me?"

He laughed. "You know the rules of your master. No swearing."

I glared. "Fuck off with your smart-ass comments."

He shrugged and grabbed his mug from the counter. Taking a sip, he moaned in appreciation. "There's nothing better than good tea." His gaze turned wicked. "Except good sex. Are you still fucking Killough's nephew?"

I shook my head, refusing to give him an answer. I'd made the mistake of telling Aodhan about what happened between Fionn and me all those years ago, and now I regretted opening my mouth. Aodhan made sure to bring it up every chance he got, and it constantly reminded me of how different we were, even though we looked so alike. My brother enjoyed the thrill of danger and fucked everyone in his path. He lived for the risk, while I had to be the perfect rule follower for our parents.

A whine came from my left, and I glanced toward the laundry room door. My two Dobermans walked out lazily, ears floppy and movements languid. Sinead—all black with a couple patches of brown—bowed the front half of her body in a stretch, yawning wide, while her sister, Oona—who had more brown than Sinead—tilted her head in confusion, looking between Aodhan and me.

"What kind of guard dogs are you?" I asked.

Aodhan snorted. "Don't be too hard on them. They came to check out who I was, but these girls love me, don't they?" He crouched, and the dogs rushed over to him for ear scratches and pets.

I rolled my eyes but kept my mouth shut. It made sense that the dogs liked him because everyone else did. Well, nearly everyone else. Sloan hated Aodhan's guts, and he had a perfectly good reason for it, too. But, Aodhan had always been a shit stirrer, and if he could get one over on Sloan, he would.

I rose to my feet and smoothed my hands down my suit jacket. "If he decides to kill you, I'm not saving your ass this time."

"Don't need you to," he said with a shrug as he rose to grab his cup of tea again.

"Do I want to know how you got past my security system?"

"There's no security in the world that can stop me. You know that." He winked.

I did, unfortunately. That was what made him a perfect hit man, and his skills had taken him across the globe. The Society, a secret organization of assassins and hit men, wanted him in their ranks, but he'd brushed off multiple offers. He might even give Ardan Murphy a run for his money if it came down to it.

"Lock the door when you leave," I said nonchalantly as I slid the Glock into the holster in my jacket. I grabbed my keys from the counter that separated the kitchen from the open-plan living room and gave him a single-finger wave before I left out the front door and went to the elevator. There were twenty-five floors in the condo building, and I had the penthouse, giving me the perfect bird's-eye view of New York City. Buying the place had been expensive but worth it. I was in Manhattan, and anything I needed was minutes away . . . except Fionn.

Growling at the thought, I smashed the button in the elevator that took me to the garage, and once the doors opened, I stalked out and headed toward my motorcycle. Sleek, sporty, and pure black like the rest of my aesthetic, my bike was a Ducati Diavel 1260, and it was one of my most beloved possessions. I bought it four years ago, and the bike was the one thing I'd done for myself that my parents wouldn't support. It was sadly amusing that I relied on their approval, while Aodhan went about his day doing all the things they hated without a hint of criticism.

I grabbed my helmet off the bike and shoved it onto my head before hitting the ignition. The bike rumbled to life, and the vibrations moved deep into my soul, giving me a moment's peace. The feel of the Ducati between my legs was a luxury that I relished. When I needed time to think, I got on my motorcycle and took a long ride until my head was clear.

Fionn was one of the reasons I often took a drive, and now I would spend another day with him, convincing myself that I felt nothing for the young boss to be, even though we shared our bodies with each other.

I shook my head and drove out of the underground parking garage.

The drive through the city was long and tedious, but having a Ducati meant I was able to weave around traffic in a way a car couldn't. I took to the highway until I reached Sloan's mansion in Southampton at 7:50 a.m.

By the time I'd taken off my helmet, laid it on the bike seat, and arrived at the steps, the front door opened. Mr. Hopper, Sloan's loyal butler, appeared. Wearing a black suit, he stood tall and imposing with a hard stare. He had gray hair swept back off his forehead and a permanent sneer twisted his thin mouth.

"Mr. Hopper." I greeted him with a sharp nod. "I'm here to pick up Fionn."

Mr. Hopper's gaze narrowed on me and he huffed, turning on his heel and leaving the door open. I followed him and stopped right inside the grand foyer, which sparkled under the wide chandelier that hung from the high ceiling.

Fionn walked down the left side of the double staircase, his black shoes dark against the white marble, although, they matched the handrails. Even though I'd only seen him last night, I couldn't help but inhale sharply at the sight of him in an impeccable suit, designed to fit his slim swimmer's build with perfection. He was tall, and from this angle, he reminded me a lot of Sloan. The natural brown hair he'd finally ceased to dye was the same color as Sloan's when he didn't bleach it. There'd been a period when Fionn had tried to be like his uncle.

"You're on time as usual," Fionn said, lips pursed. He narrowed his hazel eyes.

"I did say we were leaving at eight."

"Always punctual. A good soldier." The sarcastic tone in Fionn's words had me tensing. He was known for his insults, but he'd never aimed them at me—another reason people suspected we were fucking. I escaped his poisonous tongue.

He reached the bottom of the stairs and stopped, staring at me carefully. "Are you going to tell me where we're going? I deserve to know."

"To find a rat," I said.

"The same rat we've been trying to find for over *eight* years? We keep getting led on chases with dead ends. Diaz was good at covering her tracks. She knew we would figure out she had an informant, and she made sure we wouldn't learn who it was." He shifted closer to me. "What's different now?"

"A retirement," I said with a shrug.

"Stop speaking in riddles," he snapped. "I hate it when you do that."

I chuckled. "I'm not. A detective who worked with Diaz is retiring, and with *encouragement*, he decided to shed some light on the situation."

"Money, you mean." He crossed his arms.

"Yes, money."

Fionn frowned. "Why is he good with taking bribes now if he was clearly not okay with it before?"

"Because divorces are expensive, and when your ex-wife takes half of your retirement fund to spend it with her new, younger lover, situations change." I tilted my head, letting Fionn comprehend what I'd said. "So, we're going to take a drive to Mastic Beach and have a talk."

"Mastic Beach?" Fionn poked his tongue into his cheek. "Sounds like this detective's been taking money from someone already."

"He has. Folliero."

Fionn straightened as soon as I delivered the news, frown deepening. "They're bribing cops who could give us answers and didn't tell us? What happened to being associates?"

"Don't worry about that right now. We'll figure it out later. Sloan wants this rat situation settled first. It's been going on long enough."

Two maids walked behind Fionn and caught his attention for a short moment. He waited until they were gone before he turned his gaze back to me. "But whoever this rat is clearly hasn't said anything else to the cops, have they? None of our other businesses have been affected."

I hummed. He had a point. "Only because Diaz is dead, and they were probably worried about being found out. Your uncle knows there is a rat, and the *rat* knows he knows, so whoever this guy is, he'll be keeping his head down. It's why he's been so quiet."

"So, we chase our tails until we find answers." He snorted. "How *fun*."

I couldn't help the smile that teased my lips, even if I'd wanted to. Fionn's snarky replies had always amused me more than they should, and it brought out a side of myself I shouldn't explore, the one that demanded I take Fionn over my knee for his insolence and spank him raw. While we'd been playing for eight years now, I hadn't actually smacked his ass for being naughty yet. To me, spanking came with a type of intimacy I couldn't explore with Fionn. I was Daddy Daire in the bedroom, but I wasn't *his* Daddy, and despite what I called him, he wasn't my boy. Not really. I pushed the thought aside. "We'll take one of the Company cars and head out now. The traffic will be chaos."

"When isn't it? It's New York." He turned and waved his hand at Mr. Hopper. "Call a car to meet us at the front."

Mr. Hopper nodded, but not before his mouth curled in disgust. Or, that might be his usual expression. I typically didn't give him a second glance at the best of times. While he was good at his job and Sloan trusted him, he wasn't the most pleasant person.

Fionn swept past me and grabbed his long wool jacket from Mr. Hopper near the front door. He slipped it on while he walked down the few steps at the front and turned back to look at me with raised eyebrows.

"Are you coming or what?"

My gaze moved down the length of his back to his ass, but there wasn't anything to see while he had his jacket on.

Not the way I'd like to right now.

Keeping my mouth shut, I followed him outside. The frigid air had bite today, with flurries of early December snow falling from the sheet of gray clouds that hovered in the sky. Winter hadn't seriously begun yet, but I was dreading the bad weather to come. Once it began to snow, it was extremely unlikely that I'd be able to ride my bike, and I'd have to drive my SUV instead. As much as I loved my SUV, there was nothing quite like feeling the freedom that came with riding my Ducati.

I didn't bother to grab my helmet from my bike or move it. Everyone knew both belonged to me, and no one would dare touch them. While I was civil and rule abiding, for the most part, I was overly protective of the Ducati and that wasn't a secret. I didn't get angry often, but when I did, even the toughest men feared me. Except Sloan, who'd always been amused by my anger.

I glanced at the sleek black fuel tank that gleamed in the

early morning sun and couldn't help but smile. I'd worked hard for my baby, and I would raise hell if something happened to it.

"You love that thing," Fionn commented, surprising me.

I studied him, taking in the pursed lips and tight jaw. "Yeah."

"More than what's good for you." He flipped a sour look over his shoulder toward the bike.

I read the clear message twisted into the words. I'd been around his sharp tongue too long not to know what he was saying, and now that he'd turned his vitriol on me, it got to the root of the problem: my use of Fionn's body combined with my unwillingness to go further than a physical relationship.

It'd all started at his eighteenth birthday party, where I'd been enticed by a confidence that he had never exhibited. In a moment of weakness, I'd let my need to dominate Fionn take control.

Fuck!

We'd spent years not talking about taking it further, but I knew how badly he craved something else. He wanted to be public and *more*. I couldn't, though. Fionn was *Eoin's son*. That should've been reason enough for me to stay away completely.

Sloan, in what he deemed his infinite wisdom, continued to pair us up on assignments, and I didn't have the balls to tell Sloan the truth—that Fionn and I weren't anything but physical.

Sloan and I were best friends, but when was the last time we'd really spoken the truth to each other about our personal lives? Too long. I'd begun pulling away when I'd fucked Fionn the first time, but Sloan had distanced himself before that. All I was useful for was to give Sloan some good advice every now and then.

Fionn's jealousy over the Ducati was adorable, though.

Fionn snapped his fingers in front of my face, dragging me back to reality. I'd been so caught up in my thoughts that I hadn't realized one of Sloan's men had parked a beautiful black

BMW in front of us. The driver slid out of the front seat and opened the back door for us, but I shook my head.

"I'll be driving from here," I said simply, and the driver merely bowed slightly before closing the door and disappearing up the front steps and through the entrance.

Fionn stared. "Why are you driving?"

I winked. "Because we're finding a rat, and we don't want any gossip about where you and I have been getting back to that person through regular conversation, do we?"

He shrugged and went straight for the front passenger side while I took the driver's seat. When we had our seat belts on, I pressed down on the accelerator, taking us out of the round driveway. Once we hit the streets, I settled back into my seat and considered safe topics of conversation with Fionn. The more we worked together, the thicker the tension became until it felt hard to breathe. After each round of sex, his disdain grew, and I could see it happening. There was nothing reasonable I could do to make him understand without telling him the truth. I should confess everything, but I also couldn't bring myself to do it.

Because that would be the end. And I wasn't ready to lose him.

"Mastic Beach is no Southampton," I said.

"I know. You can get cheap pieces of shit there, but I was right about him being paid off, wasn't I?" He shrugged.

"Yeah, you were." I stayed silent for a moment. "How was Sloan this morning?"

Fionn snorted and stared out the window, his elbow pressed against the glass. "Irritated as usual. Nothing I do ever makes him happy." He paused and glanced at me from the corner of his eye. "But I shouldn't be telling you that. I need to act like the boss, right? No emotions."

I sighed. "Sloan has a lot on his plate right now. A few years ago, not many people would have challenged him or his territory, but it seems like there are a lot more players in the game now who want to prove they can take down the big dog."

"Right, but this will be my business eventually," he said, turning his attention back to the side window. "I should be next to him every step of the way, but instead he sticks me with you, a man who can't stand me except when he wants to fuck."

"Who said I can't stand you?" I gripped the steering wheel tightly, twisting my fists on the smooth leather. Frustration had me taking deep breaths to keep my temper in check. I'd learned ways over the years to keep my control.

He laughed abruptly. "Don't worry about it."

"No. Tell me who said I can't stand you," I snapped.

"I did." He shot an expression of pure toxicity at me and slapped a hand against his chest hard enough to make me cringe. "You hate being around me unless you want a hole. Let's be honest. You don't want to acknowledge us. You barely look at me unless you want to fuck me. Am I that ugly that I fucking disgust you that much?" This time when he laughed, it sounded painful, like a wounded animal caught in a trap. "Sloan—" His laughter went higher. "—thinks we're fucking. I can see it in his eyes, how he looks at us when we're together. He doesn't care. Why don't you want me for more?"

"Fuck, Fionn."

And just like that, the world crashed in on me.

We'd gone years without speaking about it, pretending we both wanted the same thing, and then *boom*. It had all changed. By the volume of the outburst, I imagined it'd been on Fionn's mind for too long. He'd finally broken and spouted the words that had lingered on the tip of his tongue, the same ones he'd pushed back time and time again.

I didn't know what to say or how to explain it to him without hurting his feelings.

I'd hoped to avoid this conversation forever, and that was my first mistake.

"Fuck, Fionn," I repeated.

"*What?*" The hurt echoed in his gaze and his jaw tightened. "You have nothing to say for yourself? Nothing at all?"

"You know we can't take this any further. I thought we agreed on that."

"You're kidding me, right?" He stared. And stared. And stared. The scalding look kept going until it became uncomfortable. He wanted me to say something, and while I was a master of words most times, this wasn't one of those moments. The situation was too delicate, and there were too many emotions.

Fionn's eighteenth birthday party felt like yesterday. The beginning of us.

———

Eight Years Ago

"Kiss me." The words were whispered so softly I could barely hear them. Fionn's warmth was all encompassing, drawing me in like a moth to a very hot flame, and I went, ready to deal with the consequences by stepping in closer to press him against the wall.

He tilted his head back and smiled.

Desire skittered through me, swirling inside my chest and across my skin like a thousand electric currents. When was the last time I'd felt like this? I couldn't remember. Sex was about getting off, and I'd been attracted to people, but Fionn wasn't *people*. He was something entirely different.

Beautiful.

Innocent.

Untouchable.

But here I was, *touching* Fionn's smooth cheek and caressing my thumb over the corner of his pouty lips.

"Kiss me," he murmured again, fluttering long dark lashes at me. He'd recently dyed his hair a sandy blond to match Sloan's. I'd noticed he'd tried to be more like his uncle lately, and I didn't like it. I preferred the version of Fionn which was true to himself, dark haired and sweet.

More like . . . Eoin.

Fuck. No. Bad choice of thoughts.

"I shouldn't." I exhaled sharply but didn't move away. Instead, I shifted in closer and hooked my fingers beneath his chin, tilting his head up and ghosting my lips over Fionn's. I wanted to devour and corrupt him. "You're too young."

"I'm eighteen," he said breathlessly, cupping my neck.

"I'm too old."

"You're Sloan's age. That isn't too old."

"You're Eoin's son."

"You have a father, too. Any more excuses? Or are you going to kiss me?"

I did as Fionn asked.

———

"There's nothing I can say that'll give you what you want," I said bluntly, taking a deep breath. "We shouldn't be doing this at all. You're Sloan's nephew and his apprentice, the future of the Killough Company. It's best to keep things professional."

"Is that what you want?" Fionn snapped. "To go back to not fucking?"

"No."

Fionn glanced away and stared out the window again, causing my heart to ache. I wished there was something more I could say to make it better, but nothing would. If I could go back in time, I wouldn't have slept with him in the first place, no matter how much I'd enjoyed every second.

"I respect you—"

"Don't!" He huffed. "I don't need you to say those things. I'm not a fucking virgin damsel who needs you to marry me. I would rather you not speak to me at all unless it's about work right now."

I held back the urge to slam my hand on the steering wheel. I'd fucked up, and I would live with my mistake, but I never meant to hurt him. Of course, he didn't want to know that. I'd gone and broken his heart. How could I have been so stupid?

Instead of trying to talk, to tell him how I really felt, I kept my eyes on the road and stayed silent, exactly like he'd asked.

4

FIONN

Anger like I'd never felt thrummed inside my chest, making it hard to breathe. My fingers itched to turn into a fist and smash against the car window, but I held back the rage. This wasn't Daire's vehicle, it was Sloan's, and causing unnecessary damage would only give my uncle another reason to lecture me about responsibility.

"We're here," Daire said, and I turned to look ahead, focusing on the small cabin surrounded by an unmaintained lawn. It wasn't what I'd expected. I'd never actually been to Mastic Beach, but I'd anticipated something like Southampton, with long stretches of sand—covered in snow—and crashing waves. It wasn't quite that. Actually, it wasn't anything special. Even though this detective lived near water, it looked more like a swamp than an actual beach, and even with the majestic vision of freshly fallen snow brushed across the ground, a trailer-park version of any decent town would be prettier.

Daire had said it was no Southampton, and he wasn't wrong.

"Okay, I take what I said back. This is a dump."

"Not all of it. You're seeing one area."

I crinkled my nose. "It's a shithole."

"You're just spoiled." He quirked an amused grin in my direction. "You grew up in Southampton. You had it too good. Not everyone was raised by someone like Sloan."

I turned to stare at him. "It's. A. Shithole."

He sighed and shook his head as he opened his door, stepping out of the car. I considered staying in the cab and letting Daire do all the communicating with this disaster of a cop, but it would only disappoint Sloan further, so I reluctantly left the car. I met Daire on his side, and we walked toward the cabin together.

Before we could knock, he nudged me with his shoulder. "You do the talking."

"Why?" I glared at him. "Men like this look down on me because I'm younger than Sloan."

He gave me a soft smile. "Sloan became boss even younger than you are now. Do you think people wanted to listen to him? He *made* them listen. You do the same."

"You have more faith in me than my uncle does." The words slipped out before I could stop them. I wanted so badly for Sloan to see my potential, and every time it looked like he would, I let my emotions win and get the best of me. But I'd made it my mission to prove to Sloan I could do this.

No more tears.

Daire didn't say anything, and I was glad. Ignoring him, I knocked on the door of the crappy little house, which creaked with a strong gust of wind. It sounded ready to collapse.

We didn't have to wait long before the door opened. The man who stood on the other side was exactly the kind of person I'd expected. Tall with square shoulders, the ex-detective had pure white hair in a combed-back style. He had a beer gut and wore a white tank top and brown shorts, obviously unbothered about getting dressed for the guests he was expecting. He stared straight past me at Daire.

"You Daire?" he asked in a gruff, no-nonsense tone, his

Brooklyn accent thick and nasally. He sounded like a man who'd smoked too many cigarettes in his life. The acrid smell lingering in the air made me scrunch my nose.

"I am. This is Fionn Killough, the boss's nephew." He gestured at me.

The ex-detective gave me a once-over and grunted, throwing the door wide open and turning his back, then walking through a small living room littered with empty beer cans and dirty dishes. The stench was tear inducing, and I held my breath as I followed him through the disgusting room toward a kitchen with a small round table, which didn't look much better. The sink was overflowing with plates and empty glasses, and boxes and trash were piled on the counters. It took all my effort not to dry heave at the sight and smell.

The detective waved at the table, which was clear, as if he'd cleaned it for the visit, and I made sure to keep my face expressionless as I took a seat, careful that I wasn't sitting on anything gross. This suit cost a fortune.

Daire took the chair beside me. "Sir, this is former Detective John Pellegrini."

"Italian?" I asked automatically.

Pellegrini grunted. "Born and bred in Brooklyn, but my parents came over from Prato."

I nodded, assuming that was a city in Italy. It made sense why he was on Folliero's payroll; although, the Company had a fair few Italians on ours, too. When it came to money, it didn't matter who offered it, as long as the spies got it. I wouldn't be surprised if there were Irishmen in Folliero's little black book, too.

"Daire tells me that you have information about a rat problem we're experiencing." I couldn't help sliding my gaze over to the counter, where a mouse was standing on its hind legs, chewing a piece of dried cheese that looked like it had been sitting there for weeks. I held back a cringe. Ironic, considering he was a rat right now.

"Depends. What you got?" Pellegrini smiled, showing stained yellow teeth.

Daire cleared his throat. "I told you, what we have depends on what you give us."

"You got any money here?" Pellegrini narrowed his eyes on him.

"Maybe." Daire kept his voice calm and crossed his knee, his posture giving off a casual *I'm not fucking around* vibe that I'd always found sexy. It was hard to tear my attention from him— my mouth was watering—and glance back toward Pellegrini.

"Tell us what you know," I demanded, taking over.

Pellegrini's gaze shifted to me. He hummed, then stood, walking over to his fridge. Throwing open the door, he glanced at us over the top. "You want a beer?"

"No," I answered bluntly. "What I want are answers. I'm a busy man, Mr. Pellegrini. Come and sit down and give me what I want."

From the corner of my eye, I noticed Daire smiling proudly, and it was all I could do not to straighten my back and puff out my chest.

Pellegrini grunted and kicked the fridge door closed once he had a can in his hand. He walked back and threw himself down on his chair, like a child who'd gotten into trouble. He opened his beer and took a long slurp, some of the alcohol sloshing down his chin and onto his white shirt.

I cringed. "Mr. Pellegrini—"

"Yeah, yeah." He let out a loud belch and wiped his mouth with the back of his hand. "Diaz. You want to know about the informant she had."

"Yes." I sat up straighter. "What information and how much you provide us with will determine how much cash we hand you in return. So, talk."

"Hm." He leaned back in his chair and rubbed his belly thoughtfully. "Diaz was a bitch."

I stared, unamused. From what I understood, a lot of male detectives had the same view of any woman in their field.

"She was a pain in the ass to criminals, to cops, to everyone. She was a know-it-all bitch." He grunted, and for a brief moment, I felt bad for Diaz. She'd had to work with lazy bastards like this. Pellegrini looked like the type of man who liked criminals—even the lowest forms—to grease his palms, all while preaching about protecting the force from women detectives. If I didn't hate Diaz so much or want to know who she had as an informant, I might've shot Pellegrini right here and now. I'd be doing the world a favor.

"I don't care what Diaz was like. If this is all you have, we will be leaving." I went to stand, but Pellegrini moved lightning fast for a drunk and grabbed my elbow.

Daire slapped the hand away from me and glared at the former detective. Unmasked fury swept over his face and he gritted his teeth. "Never touch him. Ever."

Pleasure at the surprise protectiveness from Daire simmered low in my stomach and my cheeks heated in desire. The anger on his face transformed him from a regal, untouchable man—who rarely showed emotions—to one who was protective and furious and handsome.

Fuck. My cock twitched, and it took all my effort not to get hard in seconds. I crossed my legs to prevent them from seeing what the sight of his anger did to me. Damn it, I was mad at him. I couldn't let his reaction affect me like this.

Pellegrini held up his palms. "Sorry, sorry!"

"He is never to be touched," Daire growled out, eyes flashing. "I will cut your hands clean off if you do it again."

I let out an excited breath, my chest shuddering under the exhale, and focused on Pellegrini again. Butterflies danced inside me, making me feel fluttery and light.

Pellegrini grunted out a laugh and sat back in his chair. He grabbed his beer and took another large slurp, then slammed it down on the table. The empty can crumpled under the force. "Do you wanna know about Diaz or not?"

"Yes, we do." I kept my tone neutral, even though I was fucking giddy on the inside. Sloan would be proud. "Tell me what you know."

He burped and thumped his chest before answering. "Listen, Diaz didn't trust us, all right? She liked to keep her informants close to her chest."

I wonder why. "So, you don't know who her rat is, then? Are you wasting our time?"

"No," Pellegrini snapped, glaring. His fingers twitched where his hand rested on the table. "Like I said, she kept her informants close to her chest, but she needed to write down their contact information, didn't she? And I know where to find it."

"You think we haven't been through her belongings?" I asked. "We searched her house from top to bottom, and everything she owned has now been passed on to living relatives."

"Relatives who didn't give a damn about her," Pellegrini growled out, slamming his hand on the table. "They were happy to give us anything they found with names in it."

"And have they found something?"

"Yes, but I didn't know you were looking for it." He glared at the table. "I passed everything I found to the Folliero Family. They wanted to check if they knew anyone on her list, and if they did, they'd deal with them. After they were done with it, they were going to give it back so I could do some blackmailing of my own, but they haven't been returning my calls." His jaw clenched.

"So, let me get this right." Any pleasure I felt about seeing Daire's protectiveness disappeared, leaving behind a buzzing anger that beat against my temples at Pellegrini's confession. If the Follieros had the list of informants, they should've passed it on to Sloan.

They hadn't.

This was a termination of their association agreement with the Killough Company, and Sloan wouldn't like hearing that Elio had been hiding Diaz's rats from him. "You passed any interesting belongings from Diaz to the Follieros, believing you'd get it back. And now that you haven't, you're trying to convince us to give you money for telling us that you gave it to Elio Folliero's men?"

"Well . . . yeah." He grinned in a smarmy way. "It was six months ago that her relatives gave me the book. If you were such good friends, you'd have it already, wouldn't you? What does that say about your alliance with Folliero?"

The bastard knew he had us by the balls, and I wasn't awed by it. I sniffed and glanced at Daire, who had his composure again. His back was straight and his eyes dark as they rested on me, waiting for my move.

"How much did you expect for a small amount of information like that?" I clenched my teeth together, reminding myself of Sloan's lessons. *Stay calm, and don't let them know they've pissed you off. Your face must always be blank. Let them guess what you feel.* "You didn't give us what we wanted."

"But I told you where to get it. I at least deserve a quarter."

"A quarter of a million?" I chuckled, resting my fingers against my lips. "You want a quarter? Don't make me laugh. You've given us *nothing.*"

Pellegrini's smile fell and he shoved to his feet, pointing a finger at me. "You wouldn't know where to find that book without me."

I leaned forward. "And you only told us because your favorite little Italians aren't talking to you. Are they not playing nice?"

Daire chuckled low in his throat. "And now he's telling on them because he didn't get his way."

I laughed harder and glanced into his eyes, which twinkled with pride.

Pellegrini hissed between his teeth, spit flying and nearly landing on my freshly polished shoes. "You think this is funny? I gave you information, and now I want my cut, or I'll take you to my cop friends and make sure you land your ass in prison."

I shot to my feet. I towered over him to convey my dominance to the former detective, and it earned me a pained wince from Pellegrini.

"Do not threaten a Killough," I said calmly. "You're nothing but used goods, Mr. Pellegrini, and we can make you disappear like you never existed."

Pellegrini swallowed, his Adam's apple jumping in his throat. "I want my money."

"We'll give you ten, that's all." I took a step away and offered him a smile. "Take it or leave it. Either way, Mr. Reardon and I will be leaving, and if I get even a hint that your officer friends are sniffing around us, we will end you for good. Am I clear?"

His chest heaved and nostrils flared. "Ten is fucked."

"We're not going any higher." I crossed my arms. "Ten or nothing."

"Folliero's men gave me a hundred."

"And you gave them the rats' names. Something we wanted that you didn't give to us." I shrugged. "A shame for you. We would've given you half a million for that book."

He came toward me, stumbling. "You fucking—"

Daire shot in front of me like a wall of security, his posture defensive. Even in a suit, his body looked amazing, the kind of armor I enjoyed having. Too bad it didn't come with him wanting more than sex.

He raised his hand toward Pellegrini. "I'd be very careful about what you say next."

Pellegrini's cheeks and forehead turned a bright red and his glare intensified. "Ten is fine."

Daire grunted like he didn't believe him but nodded, backing away and guiding me to move with him. We walked out the door, and Pellegrini followed, half stumbling in a way that confirmed he'd most likely been drinking all morning or was still drunk from last night. When we got to the car, Daire pointed at the opposite side, and I moved to stand there while Daire popped the trunk, pulling out a few stacks of hundred dollar bills from a black duffel bag and passing them to him.

Pellegrini watched, jaw tight enough to shatter, and his attention caught on the bag with the many other stacks of cash he'd never get. "What if I can give you more?"

"Like what?" I asked, though I wasn't expecting much.

"The Follieros. Obviously, they aren't telling you what they should, are they? Maybe I can keep an eye on them for you. Share what they're doing." He tried to smile, but it was fake, and I didn't trust him as far as I could throw him.

I pressed my lips together and walked next to Daire beside the trunk. I grabbed out another ten grand and passed it to Pellegrini, and the ex-detective's smile was real this time— *almost* excited, as though thinking about how much beer he could buy with it.

"Keep us informed."

Pellegrini nodded and staggered his way back into the house.

Daire and I watched him until the door closed.

"You don't honestly believe he'll tell us anything, do you?" Daire frowned at me.

I blinked up at him. "Of course not. Elio isn't stupid, and with Pellegrini cut off from them, he won't ever find out anything of importance from the Italian mob."

"Why give him the extra cash?"

"To make him go away without trouble." I shrugged. "It was

worth it to know Elio's got something we want and hasn't told us about."

He gave me an impressed grin. "Smart."

"I know." My chest swelled with smugness as I flounced to my side of the car.

He chuckled as he unlocked the vehicle, and we both got into our respective sides. As soon as he hit the ignition, Daire put his foot down, and the SUV took off back toward the main highway and home.

I stared out the window, taking in the large houses we passed and the snowy landscape of the Hamptons. Everything was slow paced here, unlike the city, where the streets were filled with cars and people. I preferred the quiet, and I loved Sloan's home—I had since he took me in as a kid and later as his apprentice, much to my mom's distaste, which she made sure to tell me the last time I'd talked to her. But I didn't regret a moment, even with the punishments that came with my failures. Sloan was the only father figure I had.

"Question time," Daire murmured. "Pellegrini. If you were the boss, what would you do with him now?"

"Hm?" I glanced at him and settled into the leather of the BMW. The seats were toasty and the inside of the cab was warm from the heater blasting. Outside, winter was in full swing, gray clouds clumped together with snow beginning to fall again. I loved the cold—it came with skiing and snowmobiling, some of my favorite hobbies, even though I hadn't done them in a while.

"If you were in Sloan's position, what would you do with Pellegrini now?"

I thought about my options carefully. This was the most substantive conversation Daire had shared with me in a long time, and if it meant we'd have to discuss work to get him to talk more, I would take it. Usually, when we went off to find out information about the rat, he would keep his words to the bare minimum. When we fucked, it involved a lot of grunting, groaning, and sobs, but he didn't have a lot to say except to order me around.

"He's basically useless. He gave the book to Folliero, and now the Italians don't want anything to do with him. He's a threat who could call in his cop buddies to come after us because we didn't pay him what he wanted." I took in Daire's strong jaw. I couldn't keep my eyes to myself, even if I wanted. "If I were Sloan, I'd send Ardan to deal with him. Or maybe ask Cillian, Aspen, and Rowen to take him for some fun and games."

Daire smirked and drummed the steering wheel with his fingers, a sign I'd made the right choice. "Choose, then make the call."

"What?" My mouth popped open in surprise. "That's Sloan's decision, not mine."

"Your uncle wants you to start making some choices on your own. He trusts you, despite what you think." His gaze slid over to me and the softness in his eyes had my stomach melting. "He wanted me to guide you to be a boss, Fionn."

"Sloan's going to be around for a long time," I said in a rush, panic seizing my chest. I couldn't imagine a life without my uncle. As far as I was concerned, Sloan was the only family I had. Mom and my brothers had all but forgotten about me once I'd gone to live with Sloan. Mom called randomly—mostly when she wanted money. The last time I'd talked to her was a few years back. They lived in Erie, Pennsylvania, near the lake. I sent them money every month to help my two younger brothers, Diarmuid and Bellamy, with college fees and other expenses. I hadn't actually talked to my brothers for over ten years, though. I never tried and neither did they.

"Yes, he is, but the mafia life is dangerous. You never know what's going to happen." Daire smiled sadly. "He wants you prepared, and you made a choice with Pellegrini, a good one. Call Ardan to take him out."

Swallowing became difficult. I'd never made the phone call

to Ardan about killing someone. I'd never needed to because Sloan always made them. The fact that Sloan trusted me enough to decide how to handle someone was both terrifying and exciting. After the outburst yesterday, I was sure I'd fucked up one too many times.

Taking a deep breath, I grabbed my phone from the inside pocket of my jacket and scrolled the names, finding Ardan's, and then tapped it. A few rings later, Ardan answered.

"How can I help, sir?" Ardan's sharp, blunt voice was sobering. On the other end of the line was an assassin, ready to kill at my orders. I would finally take another person's life through one of our men. A first of many, probably.

Sloan was in the process of having someone design an advanced phone app that we could send secure messages on. Our last one had been compromised, so we had to go old school until everything was confidential again. The DEA and government agencies were upping their techniques on us.

I glanced at Daire from the corner of my eye and got a nod in response. Taking a deep breath, I straightened in my seat. "How are you today?"

"Good." I heard Ardan's controlled excitement through his voice, even though he stayed professional.

"Do you remember a man named John?" I asked, recalling the things Sloan had recently implemented to avoid directly saying what he wanted done, in case we ever had anyone listening to our calls. He'd never cared before, but the heat on us was growing.

"No sir, I don't. What was his last name?"

"I don't remember. He was a guy who lived across the street from me when I was younger. I think my father knew him." I glanced at Daire, who sent me a wink. "He was a funny man. He loved a woman with the last name Pellegrini."

"Really?" Ardan snorted. "An Italian, I presume."

"Of course. With a name like Pellegrini, she must be, right?

Last time I heard, she was living in Mastic Beach." It was simple, to the point.

"Don't know her. If you'll excuse me, sir, I need to go to work."

My throat constricted and I cleared it. "Yes, go ahead."

The line went dead, and I stared at the screen of my phone, which slipped back to the home picture of me and Sloan at my eighteenth birthday party. The trust my uncle had put in me to make decisions like this had me floating high on adrenaline. The blood in my veins pumped so loudly it sounded like a jet engine in my ears. My head pounded from the thrill.

"I did that," I whispered, staring at my phone in wonder. "Was it okay? It wasn't too obvious, was it?"

"You did that." Daire reached over to pat me on the shoulder. "A little obvious, but that's all right. You'll get more chances to practice."

I turned my head toward him, and his hand rose to my cheek, fingers caressing my skin gently. The act was intimate and my breath caught. As though he realized his mistake, he yanked his hand away and gripped the wheel again, focusing on the road.

My insides lit up with a mixture of pleasure and need, the warmth of his fingers still lingering on my cheek. This was the second time in two days he'd touched me outside of sex. I didn't know what had changed, but I drank in every tiny bit of affection Daire gave me, even if it was foolish.

My heart ached and so did my soul, the deep need growing inside me, even though I wanted to tamp it down and move on, find someone who would love me in return. What was wrong with me? I'd told Daire not to talk to me unless it was about work, and within an hour, I'd faltered.

Maybe I *was* weak.

5

DAIRE

I exhaled, extended my arms, and then inhaled, dropping toward the floor as I finished another push-up, muscles straining and skin soaked with sweat. It was freezing outside, and I had my penthouse's heater set to seventy-five degrees, the steamy air fogging the floor-to-ceiling windows that usually looked out at Manhattan's skyline. I kept exercising until I hit four hundred push-ups, my arms shaking before I shoved to my feet. My chest rose and fell in fast, sharp breaths, and my heart raced, thumping loud and hard against my ribs.

"Are you done?" Aodhan asked in a bored tone.

I rolled my eyes and my gaze landed on my brother lounging on the couch in front of me, one leg crossed over his knee and arms lying across the back. Sinead and Oona sat on either side of him, both curled up and snoozing. I wasn't surprised that they'd been captured by Aodhan's charm, even though they hadn't seen him in years.

"What has you worked up? The little kitten? You know, Sloan's nephew?"

"Don't call him a kitten." I raised my chin and ran my hands over my arms, gathering the sweat that beaded there, then wiped it on my shorts. "He's the boss's apprentice and the future of the Company."

"And?" Aodhan grinned. He bent his fingers like claws and made a high-pitched hissing noise. "Kitten."

I decided it was time to change the topic.

"Do Cillian and Aspen know you're here?" I asked instead, referring to two of Sloan's best killers. They worked directly under Jamie Shannon, Lieutenant of Illegal Operations, and were some of the most brutal soldiers the Company had. Their work was top-notch, and if Sloan ever wanted answers from someone, he would send them.

Aodhan's smile slid off his face, and for the first time since he'd arrived back home, his expression turned furious. "Why would I tell those traitors I was back? They'll run to their boss and lick his ass like they always do."

I smirked and raised my arms up over my head, then rocked my body side to side to stretch before dropping my arms again. "Sounds like you're jealous of Sloan."

"Jealous?" He laughed abruptly. "That piece of shit—"

"Aodhan," I warned carefully. "He's still my best friend."

He made a noise of irritation and moved his leg so both his feet were on the floor before leaning forward with his elbows on his knees. He wore a simple pair of workout shorts and a plain black T-shirt with no shoes, but he still looked like he'd walked off a runway. I'd always been envious of my brother's charisma.

"Cillian and Aspen chose to betray me to Sloan. I was stupid enough to trust them, but it won't happen again."

"He's their boss. You'd gone off the rails and were doing things *on your own* without consulting him. Killing people without Sloan's permission, then expecting the Company to stand behind you if the shit hit the fan. The only thing that saved you was that you're my brother." I shook my head. "Cillian and Aspen didn't have that luxury. They did what they were supposed to do—be loyal to the Company. When *anyone* joins this business, Sloan comes first. Always."

"I'm aware. Even my own brother chose him over me." Bitterness filled his tone. I ignored it. "From what I heard, he has a new pet."

I groaned. "Don't."

"Don't what?" Aodhan's cockiness was back, and he winked. "What do you say I test this pet's loyalty, too?"

I pointed at him. "The last time you did that, I had to beg Sloan for your life, and you got yourself kicked out of this city. You're lucky he was in the mood to show mercy. You aren't even allowed on this coast."

"Worth it. Adrian had a nice, tight hole." He chuckled.

"You were never interested in that weasel." I threw my hands up. "You were only concerned about fucking over Sloan by having sex with his pet. Adrian is lucky the boss sent him to Mexico and didn't kill him."

"Eh. Sloan was done with him by that point anyway. He was bored and was going to send him away with or without my intervention." He shrugged. "And Sloan couldn't kill me, even if he wanted to, little bro. I'm fucking unstoppable, and he knows it."

"He hasn't sent Ardan after you yet. You know Ardan's good at killing."

Aodhan laughed. "Ardan Murphy is as much of a pussy as Fionn. These ghost stories about him are fucking stupid."

"Tell that to the hundreds of people he's killed," I muttered, taking a step forward. I scratched behind Sinead's ear, and she perked up, tongue lolling out. Crouching in front of her, I bopped a kiss on her forehead. "You're a good girl."

Oona sat up on Aodhan's other side, head cocked and waiting patiently, and I laughed, rising so I could do the same to her. When I was done giving love to my girls, I left Aodhan in the living room to head up the steel stairs to my bedroom. I went directly into the connecting bathroom and shucked off my shorts before stepping into the shower and switching on the lever.

Hot water shot from the silver showerhead, kneading my sore muscles and shoulders. I leaned forward, resting my forehead against the black tiles that lined the inside of the shower. While I relaxed under the water, I thought back on the morning I'd spent with Fionn. I'd been telling Sloan for a couple of years to give Fionn more control, and only in the last week had Sloan finally let me know Fionn could start making decisions. Sloan had confided in me that with the escalating war with the Reyes Cartel and other gangs and mobs, he needed Fionn to be ready in case anything ever happened to him. It was a sign of a good leader that he was preparing for the worst.

While I hated the idea of Sloan no longer being boss— mostly because that'd mean he was dead—I thought that given the chance, Fionn would shine. He'd learned a lot from Sloan over the many years of his apprenticeship, and I didn't think he would absorb any more unless it was through real-world experience. By the time Sloan was Fionn's age, he'd controlled the most powerful mafia in the country. Fionn needed the opportunity to make the same decisions that Sloan dealt with every day.

I grabbed the loofah that hung from a hook on the wall and soaped it up. Running the rough sponge over my aching body, I closed my eyes in ecstasy. There was nothing better than a shower after a hard workout.

Fionn had been perfect today, a boss anyone could respect, even someone as drunk and stupid as Pellegrini. While he'd not directly given us the book we needed, he had told us a crucial piece of information that would help us get it. I hadn't stayed around for Sloan's return because I trusted Fionn to give his uncle the rundown of what had happened, and if anyone deserved the praise, it was him. He'd done an amazing job showing his power while not letting the retired detective get anything over him. I believed Fionn was ready, and I'd never been prouder of him than I was today.

Seeing Fionn in his element had done something to me, more so than what his tears had. I didn't like to put a name to it, but desire swirled inside me the entire time Fionn spoke to Pellegrini. And knowing I was at Fionn's side, guiding him and instructing him, was another surprising element that turned me on in ways it shouldn't. I didn't know why.

What was sexy about controlling a future mob boss?

Everything.

Then, there was Fionn, beautiful and delicate, like a dainty piece of china, but below that porcelain fragility was a leader who demanded loyalty.

Over the years, Fionn had reminded me of Eoin in a lot of ways. From the way he stood, to how he smiled, and even the deep hazel of his gaze, which was why sleeping with Fionn on his eighteenth birthday was an unforgivable act.

Eoin had trusted me and Sloan to take care of his family if anything happened to him . . . and I had lusted after Fionn instead.

Sleeping with him since then was beyond inexcusable. I repeated the words of shame through my mind every time I let it happen, yet I couldn't stop. I didn't want to. Fionn was a dangerous obsession for both my physical and mental health. His body called to me, even when I'd convinced myself once again that I couldn't do this. Eoin would certainly never condone my relationship with Fionn.

I sighed and slapped my hand against the soapy tiles.

Eoin.

I turned my back to the wall and raised my chin, letting the water cascade over my face. I ran my fingers through my hair and grabbed a handful, tugging. Eoin was a man I'd once loved, not that Eoin had ever known. Sloan had no idea, either, and I wanted to keep it that way. Eoin's death had been a knife in my heart, shattering me in ways I'd never expected. As a result, I'd kept my distance from Fionn for a very long time.

The first time I ever *really* spoke to him, Fionn was around sixteen or seventeen, though I couldn't say what age for certain. From that moment, I was met with strong conversation and a bold personality. He was smart and articulate and reminded me a lot of Sloan, making it easy for us to get along. I was the only one Fionn was nice to, even back then.

"Fuck." I opened my eyes and tickled my fingertips across my abs, heading downward toward my twitching cock. The thought of Fionn, with his tight hole, was enough to send every ounce of blood rushing south.

I grabbed a bottle of conditioner and tipped some into my hand before replacing it on the shelf and wrapping my palm around my cock. I stroked and leaned back against the wall, thinking about the night that started our sexual relationship. Fionn had looked beautiful, an innocent bird in a room of predatory carnivores searching for who to devour next.

———

Fionn's 18th Birthday Party

Gentle music vibrated from the massive speakers in the corners of Sloan's formal dining room, which he'd cleared out to make space for a large group of guests. The songs playing were traditional Irish music with fiddles that had me scrunching my nose up in distaste. I'd always preferred a good old rock song, with deep, rough vocals and a thumping bass.

I stood beside Jamie Shannon—who was working his way up the Company ladder—near the right side of the room, a beer in each of our hands. We were watching Ardan Murphy, assassin extraordinaire, by the refreshments bar as he sipped Coke timidly. Once upon a time, not too far in the past, he would've been downing alcohol, but Sloan had stepped in after a mistake that nearly cost Ardan his life. Even though we were both staring at Ardan, Jamie had been jabbering about the Exotic Virtue and some guy he saw there.

"So, the Virtue's run by these two wee brothers, right? The youngest, can't remember his name if I'm being honest, has an arse like this." He waved his hands in the shape of an hourglass. "I told the boss about him. Said he was sexy. Boss said he might have to visit there one day and see for himself."

"Mm-hmm." I wasn't interested in some guy from the Virtue or what Jamie had to say about his ass. Jamie had a lot to say about everyone's ass, and it wasn't anything new.

"Shite. This is some birthday. Though can't say this is the kind of music I had at any of my parties." Jamie laughed, taking a sip of his beer. I had long forgotten about my own, not really interested in drinking, even though I'd told Jamie to get me one when he'd gone to the bar. "Do ya remember what ya did for your eighteenth?"

I snorted and grinned. "Fortunately, I got too drunk and forgot most of the night. But I did remember how I woke up."

Jamie waggled his eyebrows and nudged me with his elbow. "Tell me more."

I finally took a sip of my beer, humming when the warm liquid met my tongue, and placed the bottle on a table nearby. "Eoin and Sloan took me out to party. They got me a fake ID and used their own, and we got into clubs and caused trouble."

Most of the bouncers would've let us in without a fake ID anyway because everyone knew Sloan, son of the Irish mob boss of New York City, but Sloan wanted to be safe, in case we ran into any cops who sought to cause issues.

"Toward the end of the night, we went to the Genie. Sloan commissioned every whore in the brothel, and when I woke up the next morning, I was bare assed with a spent cock."

Jamie let out a loud laugh, slapping his chest as he spat some of his beer from his mouth while he choked on the rest. "No fucking way. Mr. Killough did that?"

I shrugged. "He wasn't always the boss, you know?"

Most people didn't know the real Sloan, and I was glad Aodhan and I had the chance to grow up with him and see his softer side. We'd all known there would come a day when we'd have to mature, so as teenagers, it had been our mission to have fun whenever we could. Sloan and Eoin always got me into more trouble than I would've without them.

I caught sight of Fionn in the corner of the room, hitting on one of the Company's soldiers. I didn't know the soldier's name, but he was a low rung on the Company ladder, nothing more than a hired gun and a loyal Irishman.

Fionn had his back against the wall, and even from where I stood, I could see the sly smile he gave the soldier. It was the kind of expression that said *everything* about what he wanted, and that was only confirmed when Fionn tugged at the soldier's tie, pulling him toward the door at the back of the room that led into a hallway near the kitchen.

I moved without thought, striding forward with determination. Fionn could do what he wanted—he was the future of the Company, and he deserved to live his life before responsibility slapped him in the face—but I *wouldn't* allow him to sleep with a soldier.

I followed them out through an archway that led into another hallway beside the massive stairs near the entrance. Fionn pressed his back against the wall and dragged the soldier in closer than what he should've in public. He smoothed his hand over the soldier's shoulder, laughing, and that's when I saw it—Fionn glancing toward me challengingly. He'd *wanted* me to follow him.

I let out a surprised breath. I hadn't expected that from Fionn, of all people, but I supposed it made sense. Fionn was a

Killough, after all. He was . . . Eoin's son, and that was a very good reason why I shouldn't go over there.

I needed to leave.

I didn't.

"Hey!" I called out, voice strong and commanding.

The soldier spun around to face me, and I took him in carefully, making sure to remember this man so that I could reprimand him later. The man Fionn had lured into the hallway couldn't have been much older than him, with short brown hair and wide blue eyes. He had a narrow nose and a pouty mouth and was only inches shorter than Fionn. The soldier was attractive, but he wasn't worthy of Fionn. No one was.

"What's your name?" I asked.

"Liam, sir." He shuffled away from Fionn and hooked his fingers together in front of himself, head bowed to me. At least he knew when to respect his superiors, unlike Fionn, who sighed and crossed his arms as if he was bored. I hadn't seen this side of him. Yet, defiance was as pretty on his face as lust.

"Liam, leave us."

"Liam, don't go anywhere," Fionn said immediately, making Liam freeze, uncertainty crossing his face. He glanced between me and Fionn, confused.

Fionn stood straighter and ran a hand through his bleached sandy blond hair, which I *didn't* like at all. I hated that he was trying so hard to be Sloan. "This is my party."

"And you can cry if you want to?" I smirked.

Liam chuckled, but Fionn's confused frown confirmed that he'd never heard the old song.

"Liam." I nodded toward the archway we'd come through, and Liam shot forward, leaving us alone in the hallway.

Fionn glared. "You can't do that."

"Do what?" I matched his posture, crossing my arms. If anyone would win this battle of wills, it would be me. "Ruin your fuck session?"

"I can fuck who I want," Fionn muttered, dropping his arms as though he realized how stupid he looked now that I was doing it.

"No, you can't." I sighed. "Fionn, your uncle put together a birthday party. The least you could do is *not* leave it."

Fionn grunted. "He doesn't care about me. He did it to show off. You saw the people he invited. The Italians. What do the Italians have to do with me? Nothing. And what the fuck was that music? I'm not turning a hundred."

My heart ached for him, and I understood both sides. I'd seen Fionn's desperation from the moment I'd met him. Fionn *wanted* Sloan to tell him he was proud, and he desired Sloan's approval. Sloan raised Fionn the only way he knew how—exactly how Sloan's father had raised him. Both Killoughs were stubborn, though, and they wouldn't listen.

"You can't fuck your soldiers." I took a step closer to Fionn and laid a hand on his shoulder. "That's a line you don't want to cross. You don't shit where you eat. Trust me."

Fionn's gaze slipped to my hand, then slid up to my face. He smiled, so sweet and soft, and my anger dissipated. It was difficult to stay mad at Fionn. "What about my uncle's second-in-command?"

My breath caught, but I kept my face neutral, even as my gut squirmed in excitement. No. *No!* Fionn Killough was out of bounds, but my cock didn't get the memo. Blood headed south. I stood too close to Fionn, and I could smell him—the gentle aroma of sandalwood.

Fionn moved away, resting his body against the wall. A teasing smile curved his supple lips. "Kiss me."

Leave, my mind screamed, but I didn't. Instead, I stepped in closer until our chests met.

Fionn raised his chin and that grin enticed me to stay.

Even though Fionn was seducing me, he still looked innocent and too sweet for this world. He was the epitome of virtue, and here I was, about to corrupt him because my cock couldn't listen to my brain. Pleasure simmered low in my stomach and heat filled me as I cupped Fionn's cheek and stroked my thumb over soft skin.

"Kiss me." Fionn's lashes fluttered.

"I shouldn't." A harsh breath left me. I slid my fingers beneath Fionn's chin and raised it, staring at the bow of his lips —beautiful and tempting. *Fuck.* I wanted to kiss him so bad, and my mental fortitude was losing to my physical needs. "You're too young."

The last attempt to reason with Fionn was useless.

"I'm eighteen." Fionn grabbed the back of my neck and dragged me in a little closer, our mouths inches apart.

"I'm too old." I was losing to my desires.

"You're Sloan's age. That isn't too old." Fionn's gaze flicked to my mouth and his teeth came out to gnaw on his bottom lip.

My cock twitched, half hard and trapped in my briefs. "You're Eoin's son." If anything should've brought us back to reality, it was that. Like everything else, though, it failed.

"You have a father, too." Fionn's nails dug into my neck, and a delicious bite of pain stoked the desire inside me. "Any more excuses or are you going to kiss me?"

I smiled, and any concerns I had temporarily disappeared, along with my resolve. I kissed him, *hard.* Our mouths collided in a war of need, and Fionn tasted just as I had imagined—both sweet and spicy.

Fionn hauled me closer, and he was stronger than I'd expected, but I grabbed his hips, grinding my trapped cock against his, causing both of us to moan. Laughter from the party made me freeze, though, and I ripped my mouth away from him.

He whimpered in disappointment.

My chest rose and fell, and I stared down at Fionn's excited flushed face. This was another chance to walk away. I could go back to the party and pretend this never happened.

Useless.

I would never be strong enough to leave Fionn, not when another man could take my place. *No,* if someone was going to fuck Fionn on his eighteenth birthday, it was going to be me. But nobody could see us like this, *especially* not Sloan. He would kill me for touching Fionn.

"We need to take this upstairs," I whispered.

Fionn's eyes lit up and he flashed me a toothy smile. "Come with me. We'll go to my room." He slid his hand into mine and dragged me down the short hallway to the wide split staircase. We ascended the marble steps as quickly as we could, not giving me an opportunity to reconsider going back to the party, but by this point I was committed. Only an act of God could ruin what was about to happen.

When we finally got to the door of Fionn's room, I grabbed him by the back of the neck before he could open the door and spun him around, slamming him against the wall. A gasp escaped Fionn as I closed in on him, our mouths ghosting against each other in a teasing dance that had us both breathing hard.

"Do you want this?" I whispered, raising my thumb to pull on his bottom lip. "Because once we go in that room, there's no turning back. I'm going to take you apart, boy."

Fionn grinned and grasped my wrist, holding my hand against his mouth so he could suck my thumb between his lips. He moaned around the digit and nipped at the tip, and my cock jerked. My heavy balls drew a little closer to my body, and I cursed him for having a talented mouth. Now that I knew what his lips looked like wrapped around my flesh, it was burned into my memory.

"Please, Daddy Daire."

I tensed in surprise. The words were uttered with the kind

of naivety that I had only seen Fionn pull off, and I fumbled with the name in my head.

Daddy.

As if I was the replacement father he'd craved, an older man who would tell him what to do and throw him over my knee and spank his ass red when he needed to be punished.

Fionn stared up at me, worrying his bottom lip between his teeth. "Are you mad?"

I broke out of my thoughts and stared down at him, unsure what to say. No, I wasn't mad. If anything, my cock grew harder than ever. I thought I might explode in my underwear. The warmth that swelled in my body went from mild to a lava that had me ready to burst. I *wanted* Fionn so bad it fucking hurt.

"No." I smiled and tucked a piece of Fionn's sandy hair behind his ear, which earned me a sweet pout. "You're beautiful."

Fionn's eyes widened. "I am?"

His words broke my heart. It was as though he'd been waiting his entire life for someone to pay him a compliment, and now that someone finally had, he didn't know how to believe it.

The expression on his face had my chest clenching. He wanted to be loved, but I couldn't be that person. It wasn't fair for him. He didn't know that I had once been in love with his father. I *refused* to use Fionn as a replacement.

"Maybe we shouldn't—"

"Don't say that," he whispered harshly, desperation overtaking him. "Please. It's *my* birthday and I want this. I want you."

How could I say no? Only an idiot could deny Fionn with that attractive face. I leaned my forehead against his and sighed. I wasn't that idiot.

Clearly taking my silence as a yes, Fionn tilted his chin and slanted his mouth over mine, pulling me into a desperate kiss that ignited my desire to devour him. I cupped his face and shoved him back against the wall again. He moaned, weaving his arms around my shoulders and dragging me closer.

I slid my hand down to his neck and grasped it, holding tighter than necessary, but by the sounds he was making, he didn't mind.

"Oh, fuck. Daddy. Choke me more."

The second time hearing Daddy wasn't as shocking, and my cock twitched even more fiercely than before. I didn't think I could grow any harder, but my cock was damned well trying.

I didn't want to hurt him. If Sloan saw any bruises on him and Fionn admitted where he'd gotten them, Sloan would come for my head, and my cock, too.

I couldn't help but nip at Fionn's jaw, though, before laying a kiss where my teeth left a mark. If I had my way, I would give him hickeys all over his body to claim ownership—a deep desire that I had always fantasized about—but I couldn't go that far with him. It was out of bounds.

"Daddy Daire?" He tilted his head and smiled. "Tell me I'm beautiful again."

With the hand not holding his throat, I caressed his face gently, running my thumb over the sharp cheekbone that pointed to Fionn's soft lips like an arrow directing me toward what to claim. My heart gave a hard tug at the words that left my sweet boy's mouth.

"You are the most beautiful man I've ever seen," I murmured, sliding my thumb over Fionn's bottom lip. If I thought about it long enough, it was true. He was even more striking than Eoin. "And you're going to make an amazing boss for this company. Sloan is proud of you. *I'm* proud of you, and I know your dad would be, too."

Fionn shuddered and his eyes grew watery, but no tears slipped down his cheeks despite beading at the corners. He smiled gently. "Thank you."

I didn't like the emotions clumping together in my gut. A mixture of guilt, desire, and sympathy was a horrible combination, but still, I couldn't make myself walk away, even though my mind screamed at me to get out of there. I wouldn't leave Fionn now. This was more than sex. I couldn't quite put a name to it, but I had something he *needed*.

I gave him a kind smile. "Come on, boy. Let's go into your room."

He exhaled and slid to the door, grabbing the handle and opening it before dragging me in by my blue tie. I went willingly and kicked the door closed, then flipped on the light. Seizing him by the neck again, I spun him and shoved him against the wall near the door. He let out a grunt at the rough treatment but grinned, eyes darkening.

In slow, purposeful movements, I yanked him forward to grab the lapels of his charcoal suit jacket and slip it off his shoulders, letting it fall to the floor. The deep purple tie went, too. His shirt was next, and I undid the first button, then leaned forward to lay a gentle, teasing kiss against the base of his neck.

Another button was undone.

Another kiss.

My mouth followed the unbuttoning, nibbling and kissing every inch of skin exposed for my hungry gaze.

When I finally had Fionn's shirt open, I slid it off his shoulders with his jacket and pushed him against the wall again. I stepped back to appreciate the sight of his bare chest, which was mostly smooth except for a trail of hair between his small defined pecs and below his belly button. His abs were tight, and he had the build of a swimmer—slim yet muscular. My mouth watered. I wanted to take the time to press kisses across the entirety of his flesh. I'd stop only to suck on his small nipples and add my teeth marks to them so he was reminded of who he belonged to every time his shirt rubbed up against them.

Fionn watched me closely, intrigue and desire clouding his

eyes. He stayed still and didn't reach for me like I thought he would, and that gave me a control I'd never had before. Sure, I was second-in-command of the largest mafia on this side of the country, but this was different. Fionn *trusted* me. Wanted *me*.

"Turn around," I ordered, my voice strong and dominant. "Put your hands on the wall and spread your legs."

Fionn's eyes went bright, and he spun around, slapping his palms against the wall like I had instructed. He slid his knees apart, rocking his hips backward to give me a perfect view of his cute bubble butt. I paused for a moment to appreciate the way his cheeks looked in the custom-fit suit pants.

Perfection.

I smoothed my hands over each of Fionn's cheeks and slapped them, watching them wobble underneath the expensive clothing, and then licked my lips. "Boy, take your pants and underwear off. Now."

He whimpered and slid his hands to his belt, unbuckling and yanking on it, while I took a step back and watched him, happy to enjoy the show he was about to put on. But he didn't get the message, merely shoving his pants and underwear down quickly and attempting to step out of them after his shoes went flying. He nearly tripped in the process.

I would've laughed if I hadn't been so turned on. My cock throbbed, straining against my briefs as he slapped his palms back against the wall and spread his legs, resuming his previous position.

Some have said that Fionn wasn't the kind of man who could run a mafia. He was too innocent, too much of an "order taker," and while I'd understood why people thought that, I knew better. He was Sloan's nephew. Given the time, he would learn to grow as fierce as his uncle. Sloan had the same doubts as Fionn when he was a teenager.

"Am I just going to stand here, Daddy?" Fionn whispered. "Is this . . . a punishment?"

I shifted closer and laid my hand on the middle of his pale back.

He tensed and shivered under my touch.

"No. You're doing good, boy. So good."

He gasped. "Thank you, Daddy. I want to please you."

"But you're the one who's going to be the boss eventually, aren't you?" I asked, dragging the nail of my index finger down his spine, heading south toward his round ass.

"Yes?" He sounded uncertain, and his breath caught when my finger reached the top of his cheeks, where I stopped.

"I should be serving you, boy." I smirked and went to my knees behind him, laying my hands on his ass, spreading it.

He froze, spine going stiff. "I . . . ."

"What, boy?" I kissed his right cheek, then his left. "You got something to say?"

He trembled harder. "No, Daddy Daire."

"Are you sure?" I squeezed that delectable bubble butt and dipped my thumb into Fionn's crease, rubbing the pad over his hole, not quite pressing in but teasing. "Because I'm going to eat you out, boy, and I'm going to make you ready for my cock with my tongue alone. Do you want that?"

He bent his fingers and scratched the wall. He glanced over his shoulder, eyes filled with tears, and nodded. "Yes. I do."

That was all I needed to hear.

I moved forward and brushed my tongue around the edge of his pucker before dipping into his hole. Nails digging into Fionn's cheeks, I took the time to open him good, all the while listening to the moans and whimpers that left his pretty lips. The noises were everything and more, and my cock throbbed.

There were too many reasons why having sex with Fionn was a bad idea, but now that I'd had a taste, I worried I would become addicted. The moans and the way he trembled under my hands and tongue were alluring, and I couldn't remember a time when I'd been overwhelmed with a fiery need like I was now. I wanted to sink into his tight heat and come, balls deep inside him.

I used my fingers alongside my tongue, because while I'd told Fionn I wouldn't, I had a feeling Fionn wasn't as experienced as he pretended to be. And I was okay with that. The thought of other men touching someone so beautiful, so *innocent*, and so *mine* made my hands itch to hurt them. Another warning sign of how dangerous this all was.

"Please. Daddy, please. Fuck. Your tongue feels so good. I need you. I want you." Fionn was mumbling, tremble after tremble sliding through his body, until I thought his knees would give out completely. I had no choice but to hold his hips in case he collapsed.

"Is that what you want, boy?" I rose to my feet and grabbed Fionn's shoulders, turning him around. Hooking a finger under Fionn's chin, I raised his head so that we stared at each other. "Do you want me to fuck you?"

Fionn shoved forward, latching on to my mouth with his in a rough kiss that had me hungry for more. Grabbing Fionn's hips, I hauled him closer as we ate at each other's lips, starving and desperate and needy.

When we finally broke away for air, Fionn licked the corner of my mouth. "Please fuck me? I'll do whatever you want."

This boy—*man*—needed my orders. Begged for them.

I would be stupid not to give Fionn what he desired. I turned us and slowly led us to Fionn's bed, which was wide and took up a lot of space in the huge room. Decorated in deep blues, Fionn's bedding was neat as a pin—but not for long.

When I managed to get Fionn to sit on the edge of the bed, I smirked and spread my arms. "Undress me."

Fionn's mouth popped open for a short moment, and then he grinned and did as he was told. He took his time, but I didn't mind. With every piece of my suit that Fionn got rid of, he stopped to appreciate the skin that appeared beneath it. He ran his fingers over my body like I was a god to be worshiped. He mapped my chest and abs, then my hips and thighs. He stared at my exposed cock, hard and long and thick, and swallowed visibly.

"You're so big, Daddy Daire."

I smirked. Compared to average, I was huge, and while most people assumed that was a good thing, finding guys who liked a thick piece of meat in their holes wasn't easy. Some men took one look at me and started stammering out excuses, not willing to attempt to take the chance. Not Fionn, though. Like with every other challenge he was presented with, he squared his shoulders and looked at me.

"I want you." He rested his hand on my chest, combing his fingers through the short dark hair spread across my pecs. "Please. I fucking need you so bad."

This was my last chance to back out of the room and stop myself from doing something stupid. The reminder that Fionn was my future boss wasn't doing a damned thing, and neither was the fact that he was Sloan's nephew. *Sloan*. My best friend since we were kids. What the fuck was I doing?

I glanced toward the door, my chest heaving in anticipation. I could write this off now before it went too far.

"Daddy?" Fionn laid a palm on my pec and squeezed. "Please?"

His voice was so gentle and sweet, contradictory to the person he was outside this room. Everyone knew Fionn was snarky and rude and a brat, and I liked each version of him. Fionn's wittiness had always secretly amused me, especially when he aimed his ire at someone I didn't like. Lorcan Lee, for example. Fionn made it known he didn't enjoy the general's company one bit.

Hesitation passed over Fionn's face, and he pushed me gently so he could stand. He went to step away, but I grasped him around the waist, dragging him closer. There was no way in hell I was going to back out of this. I *wanted* Fionn, and for a night, I could ignore who we were and why it was a bad idea.

I kissed him, hard. My mouth melded against Fionn's roughly, and I grasped his face between my hands, holding him still so I could devour whatever innocence he had left. By the end of the night, there'd be none.

I pushed Fionn toward the bed, and he fell onto it, eyes wide and excited as he shuffled back farther.

"Lube?" I asked.

"In my closet." Fionn waved his hand toward the right side of the room, and I strode over to the closet he'd pointed out, opening it. After a few directions from Fionn, I found the lube, along with condoms. I didn't want to think about Fionn using the rubbers because it didn't matter. While I'd fuck him, Fionn didn't belong to me.

I shoved the thought out of my head. We had tonight, and I was going to make the most of it. I was going to show Fionn what it was like to be taken care of and have the best sex he could imagine. Hell, I'd ruin him for every other man in the future.

When I got back to the bed, I dropped the lube and condoms on the mattress beside Fionn, and he stared at them.

"Do you need the rubber?" He nodded toward the condoms.

I stared down at him seriously. "Yes." I fell forward, knees and hands digging into the bed on either side of Fionn's slim body. Eyebrows drawn in concern, I pursed my lips. "You must promise me that you'll never have sex without one unless it's someone you trust with your life."

"Daire—"

"Daddy," I said sharply, making Fionn jump. "You will only call me Daddy or Daddy Daire tonight."

Fionn's gaze clouded with lust and need, and his kiss-bruised lips curled into a sensual smile. He tilted his chin and the light above him cut across his cheeks like glittering diamonds. "Yes, Daddy."

"Good. Now, promise me." I nuzzled Fionn's throat and nipped the skin there, intending to leave a small mark as a reminder of what we'd done. I wanted Fionn to remember it always. At least, that's what I wanted *now*. Tomorrow, I might come back to my senses and realize I'd prefer Fionn to forget all about it.

"What if I don't?" The challenge in his tone and the way he stared at me had the skin on my back prickling with a mixture of excitement and the desire to teach him a lesson.

I smirked and grabbed his neck in a firm grip. He gasped, head falling back to expose more flesh for me to press my fingers into, and his submission was a beautiful sight. His back arched and his cock jerked, precum already beading at his slit. He was so receptive to my touch, entire body shaking under the pressure of my control.

I licked a stripe along Fionn's jaw, then nibbled on his ear. "Promise me or I won't fuck you. I'll lock you in this room so you'll only be able to get off with your own hand."

He whimpered, the muscles in his throat working against my fingers. "Daddy, please."

"No." Pleasure knotted inside me, tangling ropes of lust, and my chest grew heavy with need, making it difficult to breathe. My cock throbbed, stiff as a nail and ready to hammer into him. "You know what I want to hear." I nibbled on his ear and tugged at it before kissing back down his jaw again. "Say it."

His whimpers grew louder and he arched back so far that his cock tapped against my abs, leaving behind precum. "I promise." He moaned when I squeezed his neck a little tighter but not enough to trap the air. "I promise, Daddy Daire. I won't let anyone have sex with me without a condom unless I trust them."

"How much do you have to trust them?" I nuzzled his chin.

"With my life." He gasped.

"Good boy." I released my hold on his neck, and Fionn sucked in deep breaths, falling back onto the bed.

He looked up at me, eyelids half open and stare filled with uninhibited desire. "Why does it matter?" he whispered, voice croaky. "You'll be the only one—"

I slammed my mouth over Fionn's, effectively shutting him up before he could say something that would make me walk out the door and not come back. What we had right now couldn't be permanent.

It was one night.

Only one.

Fionn groaned into the kiss, and when I broke the lip-lock so I could reach over to grab the lube and a condom, Fionn grinned and spread his legs. His eagerness twisted my insides, reminding me of just how innocent he was.

"I'm going to prep you," I whispered, dropping a kiss on Fionn's shoulder, then his chin. "We're going to take this slow." He opened his mouth, but I shook my head. "You will not argue with me, boy. You said it yourself. I'm big. I refuse to hurt you."

He hesitated and sighed, nodding. "Okay."

"Okay," I repeated.

Flicking open the lube, I smiled down at him comfortingly. I took the time to prep him, using one, then two, and finally, three fingers. I scissored and stretched him, and Fionn grunted in pain at first before he began to relax and the sounds morphed into needy moans.

When I was sure I'd be able to enter him without hurting him, I grabbed the condom and slid it on my rock-hard cock. I spread more lube over my erection and settled between his parted thighs.

Fionn tilted his head, eyes hooded and a blissful expression dancing across his sharp features. "Please, fuck me, Daddy?"

How could I say no to that? There was no other word for

him but pretty, even if it sounded feminine. I had never seen anyone as beautiful as him, but he was more so now that he was dazed with lust, naked with a sheen of sweat covering his compact muscles, and with a full cock.

I grabbed his legs, hooking them over my shoulders, and lined up to his hole. "One last chance, boy. You sure about this?"

Fionn whimpered. "Please, Daddy. Fuck. Please."

I shushed him gently and smoothed my palm over his forehead, pushing his hair away from his face. I thumbed his cheekbone, mapping the softness of his skin. "Good boy. You're okay. I've got you."

I slowly pushed in, careful as the head of my cock opened him. I watched Fionn's expression, noting the flickers of pain. His nose twitched and his mouth twisted, and I stopped when the head made it past his ring. I placed my palm against his cheek again, caressing it.

He winced. "Sorry, Daddy Daire."

"Shh." I leaned down to lay a kiss on the opposite cheek. "You're fine. It's fine. Tell me when you're ready."

It took him a few long seconds, but I stayed patient. I kept still, body tense as I waited for his go-ahead, and the moment he nodded, I began to push in again. I eyed him carefully, but he kept nodding when I gave him a questioning look, until finally I was balls deep inside.

Fionn's breaths came quick and shallow, and his legs shook against my shoulders. "It feels so strange, Daddy."

I smiled, then kissed him. I cupped his face, and we kept our mouths mashed together in what started out as a soft meeting, then began to get rougher. He moaned into the kiss, his legs trembling fiercer.

"Please, fuck me, Daddy Daire? Fuck, I need you so bad."

Positioning myself on my knees, I bent him forward in a way that would lessen the pain and began to thrust. I started slow and didn't pull all the way out. It was more of hip rocking to get him used to the feeling of my width and length inside him, but when he began to hump back against me, I knew what he needed.

I picked up speed, spearing my cock into his hole harder and faster. The moment I pegged Fionn's prostate, he threw his head back and yelled, entire body shuddering.

"Oh my fucking God. Daire. Fuck." He kicked my shoulder with his heel in a spasm of pleasure. "Please, harder."

The sight of him losing control was absolutely fucking stunning. This stoic *man*, usually so restrained and blunt to people, other than a select few, came unraveled like a bow on a Christmas gift, and the result was the kind of present I had always wanted from a man. Pure, utterly abandoned bliss. He was milking my cock like the best boy, and I couldn't get enough.

He was practically riding me, even though I was on top, rutting into him.

"Please, please, please." The mantra leaving Fionn's lips had my blood pumping hot as it rushed south. If he kept pleading so prettily, I would lose it too quickly. His hole constricted around me, putting the perfect amount of pressure on my sensitive cock.

I gripped his knees, nails digging into his skin, as I focused on thrusting faster, hammering into Fionn's prostate with every stroke forward.

His whimpers grew louder, music to my ears. He grabbed his cock and jerked it along with my tempo, and it didn't take long for his spine to stiffen, his moans turning into cries of pleasure as he arched up and came. Spunk jetted from his slit and covered his stomach and chest. He trembled through the throes of ecstasy, his hole tightening around me.

The orgasm-inducing sight was all it took for my release to hit me like a bullet straight to the heart. Desire wielding enough power to make me breathless weaved its magic, and I froze balls deep inside Fionn as I came. I groaned, leaning my forehead on his leg as every drop of my cum filled the condom until I had nothing left to give.

Exhausted, I pulled out gently and took off the rubber, then tied it and threw it into the trash next to Fionn's bed. I collapsed beside him.

Fionn had his eyes closed, the biggest smile that I'd ever seen on his face. "Wow."

I kissed his shoulder and whispered, "You're so fucking perfect."

He gasped and trembled, eyes snapping open so he could stare at me. "Thank you, Daddy."

My heart ached. *Fuck.*

————

I tugged harder at the memory, jerking my cock as fast as I could.

That night, I'd slunk from the room after Fionn fell asleep. I'd tried to pretend nothing had happened, but he hadn't let me. He was relentless, and I discovered that when he wanted something, he'd stop at nothing to get it. I was weak when it came to him, and after a night like that, I couldn't resist the temptation of his body. Like a rubber band, my ability to reject him snapped.

Even so, I refused to be anything more than fuck buddies. Fionn wanted more—I saw it in the way he looked at me, eyes begging—but I'd set down my rules. Fucking *only*. Fionn always treated me much better than everyone else—minus Sloan—but his attitude had become more hostile recently. His anger at me and my refusal for anything more than sex had exploded.

I clenched my eyes and threw back my head as my orgasm ripped through me, making my spine straighten and my muscles tense. I called Fionn's name under my breath, cursing the man for controlling my thoughts. Regular sex didn't dwindle my desire for him. He was the only man since that night that had captured my attention.

Cum shot from my slit, spraying to the floor and washing away with the hot water as it circled the drain. I shuddered through my pleasure, and when my balls were empty, I finally managed to pry my eyes open again and stare down at myself. My tattoo-covered abs continued to quiver, and my cockhead was red, still caught by my white-knuckled fist.

"Fuck."

Sex with Fionn was honestly the best I'd ever had.

Groaning, I dropped my head forward. I was doomed. Spending time with Fionn was killing me. I had no idea what I'd done to deserve this torture, but what *sweet, sweet* agony it was.

A sharp knock on the door interrupted my thoughts, and I grunted. "What?"

"Get out of there, little bro. We're hitting the clubs like old times."

I cursed. Going out was the last thing I wanted, but Aodhan would never let it go if I said no.

6

FIONN

I held myself tall in the chair I sat in, keeping my presence imposing like Sloan had taught me. *"Being the boss is a game of wits and dominance."* Sloan had taken a deep drink of his favorite whiskey for an effective pause. *"Even if you aren't in the mood, you always have to be prepared."*

So, I stayed ready.

Across from me, sitting behind his desk in his leather office chair, was Sloan. Conall lounged in a seat beside him.

"The Italians are hiding valuable information," Sloan murmured, stroking his chin. "I wish I was surprised, but I'm not. You should never trust Follieros."

Conall sighed. "Elio's been fine, but he's been touchy recently because of what happened to Matteo."

"I know." Sloan made a displeased sound and stared at me thoughtfully. "This is the danger of being in love with your right-hand man. It's his job to protect you, and when he does that, you need to stay immune to feelings."

I startled.

Was Sloan saying that specifically for a reason or did he purely mean Elio and Matteo? Sloan knew I was fucking Daire.

I could tell by the way he watched us with a knowing stare. Most of the generals in the Company had the same idea, giving us pointed looks when they thought we weren't paying attention, but they didn't outright say it, so I couldn't approach anyone about it. A small part of me liked the idea of them knowing there was something going on because I wanted it to be that way with Daire—and more.

"Elio is young, and his concern for Matteo is a weakness," Sloan said.

Conall stared at me carefully, but I made a point of ignoring him. I wouldn't lash out like I wanted to because I was trying to prove to Sloan I could do this.

"What do you want me to do about it?" I asked, squaring my shoulders. "I can go over to Elio's immediately and demand access to the book."

Sloan shook his head and raised his hand, smoothing it over Conall's hair. The attention he gave his pet was sweet—or as much as it could be for a mob boss. His thumb worked over Conall's temple, and Conall tilted his head toward Sloan, enjoying the devotion. "No. We want to handle him subtly. We don't want Elio to know we're aware of what he has."

"Why?" I asked seriously.

Sloan ignored me for a moment as he leaned forward to lay a gentle kiss on Conall's lips.

Conall moved toward Sloan, eyelashes fluttering closed as he let out a small moan of appreciation.

Sloan smirked and murmured something to him before he fell back in his chair and concentrated on me again. "Because relations between the Irish and the Italians have always been fragile. Remember what I told you about the war we had with them?"

I nodded. "Grandpa was the one who made peace. He nearly destroyed their empire, and when the Italians, or more specifically, Elio's father, waved the white flag, Grandpa offered them a deal, and we became allies."

"Exactly. If we go in there with guns blazing while demanding answers, it'll get you killed." He linked his fingers together and rested his elbows on his desk, lips pursed. "I won't have that."

My chest ached. It wasn't often Sloan showed emotion toward me, but when he did, I drank in every second of his concern. After my father's funeral, I'd felt lost. I'd swum in a sea of doubt and confusion and begun acting out at an early age. I had no father anymore. My mom couldn't handle me, so she reached out to Sloan. I didn't know what kind of agreement they'd come up with, but shortly after my father's death, Sloan took me in and became my legal guardian. That was the last time my mom tried to be my parent.

While Sloan was very much a father figure, it wasn't often that he showed me how proud he was or that he truly cared. He was a hard man. He showed more emotion to his pet than me.

"So, what do you want to do?" I asked.

Sloan sat back in his seat again and stared at me with a narrowed gaze. The scar across his left eye was more prominent today, and I thought it was because Sloan had been frowning a lot lately. The continued uprising of our enemies had plagued my uncle's mind. Everything seemed to be happening at once.

"We let this die down for a few weeks. If the Italians know we visited their cop, they'll be expecting us to show up immediately. When things have cooled down, you and Daire will go to Elio under the guise of a friendly visit."

I frowned. "Is a few weeks long enough?"

"Yes." Sloan tapped his finger on the desk in thought. "You'll offer to help them rebuild the businesses that the Giordanos destroyed."

"Elio is still pissed at us for making a deal with the Giordanos."

Conall laid his hand on top of Sloan's, caressing his thumb across Sloan's skin to gain his attention, as though he didn't always have it. The action was enough to make me want to roll my eyes. "Do you think he'll accept Fionn and Daire's visit with open arms?"

"He'll have no choice," Sloan grunted out. He raised Conall's hand to his mouth and laid a kiss on the palm, and I couldn't look away. As much as I sought to despise Conall, I craved *that* kind of intimacy. I wanted to be adored like Sloan did his pet, but only by . . . Daire. "The boy has a lot to learn, but he knows his place. The Killough Company controls the East Coast."

"That hasn't stopped him from asking questions about the Company around the city." Conall shifted in closer to Sloan, visibly shuddering when Sloan placed a kiss on the pulse point of his wrist. "You need to send a few guards with Fionn and Daire."

"No," I snapped before I could stop.

Sloan's and Conall's gazes shot to me, and I sat up straighter. I didn't apologize for talking to Conall that way, even though Sloan would want me to, but I softened my voice, even as a bitter taste lay heavy on my tongue at the thought of giving Conall respect. "We need to show Elio we trust him or this won't work. If we show up with soldiers, he'll be suspicious."

"He's right, pet," Sloan murmured, glancing at Conall from the corner of his eye. "We don't want to appear as though we're coming into his territory with an army."

Conall frowned. "You show up in places with more guards than the couple I suggested. I want him to be protected. Fionn *is* the heir to the Company."

"And Sloan's nephew." My jaw tightened. I had the urge to add that point, though, it clearly didn't mean anything to Conall. I was more than the future of the mob, I was also related to Sloan by blood. I *was* a Killough. "I can take care of myself."

"Enough." Sloan cut a hand through the air, and I swallowed down the anger that had lodged in my throat. "My pet is worried about you, nephew. He cares about your well-being, and you should be thankful."

Bullshit. He was undermining me, but Sloan was too blind to see it. Conall hated me, like everyone else in this company.

Sloan's attention moved back to Conall. "Pet, Fionn is right. There are certain situations where soldiers will do more harm than good. But we can compromise."

"How?" I asked, surprised.

"You'll take Mancini with you."

My nose scrunched. "The hit man that Ardan's fucking?"

I suspected it was more than sex with them by now. They hadn't outright come out as being in a relationship, but they didn't need to, either. It didn't take a genius to figure out they cared for each other.

Sloan's mouth twitched in amusement. "Yes. Mancini is Italian, and he's worked with mobs. He knows what to expect."

"Uncle—"

"No arguing, Fionn. It's decided. I will get in contact with Mancini and let him know. In the meantime, I want you to work with Daire and the generals." He smirked. "Check in with each of them to see how they are doing and if they need any help. I don't want any mistakes."

I stood, keeping my back straight as I bowed slightly. "Yes, Uncle."

Walking out of the office took every ounce of control my body possessed. I didn't want Mancini there with us, but it wasn't my place to argue. Sloan already had Daire babysitting me. Did he still have such little faith in me after all these years? What would I have to do to finally earn his trust? Daire always said everything Sloan did was for a reason, but I wished Sloan would let me in on the secret sometimes.

As I reached the end of the hallway beside the split staircase in the foyer, I paused and stared at the front doors. The quiet house wasn't unusual during the evening, but faint voices caught in what sounded like a heated discussion had me frowning. I followed the noise around to the other side of the stairs and down the opposite hallway, which led to the kitchen. Here, I was close enough to hear what the two men—guards who kept night watch—were saying.

"I'm fucking telling you, dude, if he ever becomes boss, he'll be killed in a week. He's piss weak." The first laughed.

"Eh. He'd last longer than that. A week and a half maybe." The second gurgled out his own laugh, but this one sounded like he had food shoved in his mouth.

My stomach dropped, rage and shame making my jaw twitch as I stepped in closer to hear what they were saying. Either they thought I would be asleep or they didn't care who was listening because they weren't keeping their voices down.

"I reckon it would be better if Reardon stepped up, then the boss's nephew could be his whore." The first asshole snorted. "With lips like those, he's gotta be good at sucking cock. There are times I almost understand what Reardon is up to."

Hell, I already *was* Daire's whore. I swallowed around the acid rising in my throat, stomach churning.

A door opened and closed inside the kitchen. "What the hell are you talking about?" echoed the very familiar voice of Conall's bodyguard, Ronan.

"Little Fionn Killough." The first one laughed again. "The Little Bitch. That's what we like to call him. He never does anything that the boss doesn't tell him. A perfect follower, not a leader. I bet the only guy he's been fucked by is Reardon."

My heart gave a jerk. It was true.

"Shut up," Ronan snapped, the irritation clear in his tone. "You have no right to talk about the boss's nephew like that. Get back to work."

"You're not in charge. Just because you got the job of watching the boss's pet's ass doesn't mean you can order us around, you dick." This came from the second guy.

Fuck. I wanted to know who they were.

"Right. Well, let's see what the boss's pet thinks about what you're doing and talking about. Tongues have been cut out for less than disrespecting Mr. Killough's nephew."

Footsteps reverberated, and I shuffled backward, prepared to have Ronan open the door in front of me, but there was movement in the kitchen.

"Get your hands off me," Ronan barked.

"You're a fucking snitch," the second grunted out. "Whatever. We're going back to work."

I waited until a door slammed inside the kitchen, signaling either a couple of them, or all, had left out to the backyard, where they were supposed to be in the first place. But when the door near me swung open and Ronan appeared, we both froze.

Ronan's blue eyes widened. "Sir."

I stared at him and he stared back. A weird silence hung in the air between us. I thought about saying something about what I'd heard, but I couldn't bring myself to do it. If it'd been Sloan who'd listened to that conversation, he would've stalked in there and demanded respect—probably killed someone—but I wasn't my uncle. Instead, what the guards said only confirmed my fears. They didn't think I could do the job.

I was useless. A fucking failure. No guard would ever speak like that about Sloan. He'd put the fear of death in them, but I was weak enough that they thought it was okay. They thought they were *safe*. My chest ached.

Ronan's gaze softened and he clasped his hands in front of himself, bowing slightly. "You caught that gossip."

"I did." I took a deep breath. "Is that what they all think about me?"

Concern played across Ronan's face, and he sighed, running a hand through his short blond hair. "No, but you have those who like to mouth off about their bosses. There are guys who do the same about Sloan and Conall."

"Why haven't you reported them?" I snapped, more worried that someone would plan to attack either my uncle or my uncle's pet than me. Their hatred for me was understandable, but no one had the right to question Sloan's leadership. I had my reasons for being irritated at Conall, but I would never let anyone else disrespect him.

Ronan hesitated.

"Tell me." I gritted my teeth and added more force to my words.

"Because I have."

I frowned. "If you have, then why are they still here?"

Ronan glanced around the narrow hallway we were in before he touched my upper arm, leading me closer to the wall. "Men like that enjoy feeling powerful," he said, voice lowered. "But when you get them in front of the boss or his pet, they are nothing but cowards. Mr. Killough and Conall are aware of the issue. I keep them updated. They allow these men to say what they want, to an extent, but it's my job to make sure they don't get out of hand."

"You're essentially a spy," I murmured, in awe of the simple strategy. Our men were never guaranteed to be one-hundred-percent loyal, even if they came from families that were, so having a mole among the soldiers who kept an eye on them made a lot of sense.

"Yes, sir."

"That's smart."

Ronan quirked a half smile. "It was Conall's idea for me to show my respect to our bosses, while also listening to what the men have to say or what they may plan."

I should've hated that it was Conall who came up with making Ronan a spy hidden within our own men, but I couldn't. Instead, I nodded. "Thank you for explaining."

Ronan startled but inclined his head.

I ignored his surprise at my gratitude. Being considered a

joke had lasting effects I didn't enjoy. They'd been right to assume I'd only been fucked by Daire, and that made the hole in my chest even wider. It made me seem like a fool. I didn't have the experience most guys did. By the time Sloan was my age, he was already the boss and making a name for himself in the organized crime world. Then, there was me.

The Little Bitch.

"You're welcome, sir." Ronan inclined his head. "Now, if you'll excuse me—"

"You have the rest of the night off, don't you?" I asked abruptly. I gave Ronan a slow once-over, taking in his wide shoulders and high cheekbones, with a sharp jaw and nice eyes. Ronan was beyond handsome, but appreciating someone who worked for us wasn't a good idea.

"I do, sir."

"Call me Fionn. At least . . . while we're alone." I didn't have many friends. Outside of Sloan and Daire and Conall, no one really called me by my first name. I was sir to everyone else. How pathetic was that? "Would you like to come out with me tonight?"

Ronan blinked at me and opened his mouth.

"I want to go to a club, and I know my uncle wouldn't want me to go unguarded. *I trust you . . . .*" A huge thing for me to admit, though I wasn't sure if Ronan knew that. "And you don't have to babysit me. You can do what you want, but at least I could say I took someone with me to appease him."

Ronan exhaled and a small smile stretched across his mouth. "I'd like that, Fionn."

Warmth spread through me.

"You've got clothes, right?" I asked, ashamed that I wasn't sure. I thought all the personal bodyguards had rooms of their own in the mansion.

Ronan laughed, and the genuine, deep sound made me grin. I couldn't remember making someone laugh like that before.

"Yes, sir. Fionn, I do. Should I meet you at the front with a car?"

"Yeah, sounds good. I don't drive." An embarrassed flush flooded my cheeks.

"I'm aware."

"In an hour?"

"In an hour," Ronan agreed.

I let out a breath. I was actually going clubbing. With someone. With a . . . friend? Was he a friend? *Oh, fuck.* I didn't know how to dance.

———

More than a few hours later, we arrived at Club Bellissimo. While someone in my position might have informed the manager of the club and taken the VIP way in, I decided to experience the nightlife like everyone else. Ronan didn't seem to mind, and as we waited in line, Ronan talked about his life in high school with Conall. It was strange to hear that Conall was an outcast who'd preferred to spend time by himself than with other people.

"It doesn't really make sense until you know about his home life, you know?" Ronan said as we got closer to the front of the long line. He was dressed in a nice pair of jeans and a crisp white T-shirt. The jacket he wore on top was brown leather. "I guess when you get treated like a punching bag by your father, you don't want any human contact."

I frowned. I'd suspected there'd been some abuse there, but I'd never asked Sloan about it, and I'd certainly never talked to my uncle's pet.

"His father beat him?" I didn't know why I cared. I fucking hated Conall, didn't I? He made Sloan happy, and that was something, I supposed. Maybe I didn't hate him completely.

Ronan winced. "I thought you knew."

I shrugged. "I had an idea."

"Terrance mostly took the hits when he could from Morrissey Senior, but sometimes Conall was the easier target." Ronan's eyebrows scrunched. "At a certain age, Conall just broke, you know? His entire personality changed almost overnight, and he became this smart-ass. Always mouthing off to people. It got him into a lot of trouble."

I snorted. "My uncle enjoys it. Gives him a reason to spank him."

The bouncer at the door ushered the two women in front of us inside. He took a long look at us, probably trying to decide if we were good-looking enough for the club, and his nose crinkled.

"You two look familiar." The bouncer had a faint scar across his jaw and a shiner blooming on his left cheek, like he'd already been in a fight tonight. He pointed a finger at us. "You going to cause problems?"

"No," Ronan said, offering his best smile. "We're just here to dance and drink."

Another bouncer, this one bigger and broader, stepped out of the door and slapped the first on the shoulder, leaning close to whisper into his ear. The bouncer with a shiner grunted and offered us a curt nod before opening the door and gesturing us inside.

"Mr. Killough, sorry for the wait."

Ronan snorted, clearly amused that they'd figured out who I was, and together we slipped into the club. Music hit us in a wall of sound, the beat so loud that I could feel it in my chest. My breath stuttered for a short moment as I remembered how to breathe. I'd never been in a club and didn't know why I'd thought this was a smart idea, but the desire to prove to the men that I wasn't *The Little Bitch* had rankled me in new and awful ways.

Mostly, I hated that they were right about Daire being my only fuck.

Club Bellissimo belonged to the Folliero Family, and it was the go-to place for the mobsters who were associates of the Family. Word would quickly get back to everyone that I had been here and I went home with a guy.

Hopefully.

Daire had made it clear from the beginning that it was only sex between us. He'd even gone so far as to say I could fuck anyone else I wanted. I'd never had the desire to, and I didn't dwell on the fact that he might've slept with someone else. It was better to pretend I was the only one he'd been fucking.

Multicolored lights shot across the dance floor, and the fast beat of the bass had everyone jumping in the air, punching their arms in time with the music. The bar was crowded, and around the dancers were tables strewn across the rest of the club, covered in mostly darkness to give partiers their privacy. I spotted the VIP section—which was past red rope and up a set of steel stairs—and the security there watched me, like they expected me to head toward them and enter. I merely shook my head and stalked toward the bar, keeping my stride strong, chin raised. I was going to get smashed tonight, and then I was going home with a guy to get railed because fuck Daire and his attitude toward me.

If he didn't want a relationship, I'd find someone else who did.

Ronan was right behind me. When we made it to the bar, he shoved people aside—taking his bodyguard role seriously even if he wasn't on the clock. I wasn't going to complain as he sidled up to the smooth wooden bar. A slim man with skin that sparkled with body glitter and glossy lips headed straight for me, leaning over the surface to pat my hand.

"What can I get ya, hun?" he yelled above the commotion of the club.

The bartender was cute, with short dark hair and arched eyebrows, but he was petite and didn't have the power I wanted in a man. I needed someone who could throw me around and fuck me—*hard*. The bartender winked, though, offering me the chance to flirt. If I was smart, I would show the soldiers that I could pick up cuties just like Sloan. But if I was going to be boss one day, my men would have to respect the idea of me having someone different than a dainty little pet. The opposite. Someone bigger and wider. A man who could rip a person to shreds with his bare hands. A guard dog who wouldn't stand for an ounce of disrespect tossed my way.

I hesitated as the bartender's question caught up with me. The stupid thing was that I didn't know what I wanted to drink. I'd only ever drunk whiskey because that was what Sloan preferred, and I'd never given myself a chance to experiment. I'd wanted so badly to be my uncle, I hadn't discovered who *I* was. *Fuck*. Pathetic.

"We'll have two Blue Moons," Ronan said, taking over, and I gave him a smile in thanks.

The bartender nodded and sauntered off.

I turned to stare out at the crowd. Men and women rocked their bodies in ways that seemed surreal, and it was hard to tear my gaze away from how amazing these people looked. There was the odd embarrassing dancer, but most had clearly been here more than once and swayed with the pounding beat.

When the drinks came, Ronan paid for them before I could, and he passed me a bottle.

"Thanks." I raised the beer to him and took a sip, wincing at the horrible taste but holding in the urge to dump it back onto the bar. We stayed where we were, watching, and I thought Ronan was waiting for instructions. It was a cruel reminder that he wasn't my friend, merely a man paid by Sloan to keep us all safe.

Someone sidled up on my left, and I didn't glance at them

until a smooth voice said, "You've got to be the best-looking person in this place."

Surprised, I glanced toward the man to make sure he was talking to me. He was.

He wasn't anyone I'd met, but there was a certain familiarity about him that had my back straightening. I felt like I should know him off the top of my head, but I didn't. I needed the files I had on all the powerful mob men that I kept at home. The fact that I didn't remember him meant that he either wasn't an important player or he hadn't done anything to merit remembering. Yet. That could easily change.

With short dark hair like the bartender, this stranger had the large shoulders, hard chest, and height I was searching for in someone to fuck. He was taller than me by at least a few inches and had the kind of muscles I wanted to feel.

The man stuck out his hand. "Michele Scotti."

The name struck a chord, and I stared, not bothering to take his offering. "Scotti? As in . . . ."

It could've been a coincidence, right? Who was I kidding. Of course it wasn't. Matteo Scotti, Elio's right-hand man, had a younger brother named Michele. I had all the information in my notes about Matteo. Michele had a file of his own, though it wasn't as extensive as his brother's.

"As in Matteo Scotti's younger brother, yes." Michele's sinful mouth curved deliciously. He dropped his hand before taking a step closer.

Ronan tensed at my side.

"And I know who you are. Fionn Killough." Michele licked his bottom lip as his gaze slid down my body, catching on spots that seemed to hold his interest. "I've known since the moment I saw you."

"How did you spot me in a crowd like this?" I asked, amused. I couldn't help myself. He knew how to charm.

"I didn't mean tonight," he practically purred, dancing one of his fingers from the top of my shoulder down my arm, gaze tracking the movement. "Though, I'd have to be blind not to notice you come into the club. You light up the entire room."

I laughed in embarrassment, heat blooming on my cheeks. "Does that pickup line work often?"

"I don't know, I haven't used it on anyone." He leaned against the bar with his elbow. "I can tell you the exact moment I first saw you, Fionn Killough. It was during a meeting between Sloan and Elio. You were standing at your uncle's side, dressed in a dark gray suit with a navy tie. You had blond hair back then, but I admit, I prefer you this way." The man had no sense of personal boundaries as he raised his hand to run his fingers through my hair, an act so intimate that it felt like we were already lovers.

My eyes slipped closed before I could stop them. His nails teased against my scalp, sensual and pleasure inducing. A shudder swept through me, and I gasped. A simple touch had my skin buzzing. I didn't know this man, yet my body craved this unfamiliar soft touch. Despite it coming from a man other than Daire, all I could think about was *Daire* doing it—his fingers, his nails, his everything.

"Has anyone told you that you're gorgeous?"

His deep voice, *not Daire*, reminded me this wasn't who I wanted it to be.

"Sir . . . ." Ronan's quiet voice had my eyes snapping open again, and I glanced at him. "Are you okay?"

I cleared my throat. "Fine, Ronan. Why don't you go for a walk, maybe find a table?"

Ronan seemed unsure, a frown creasing his forehead, but he nodded and left us alone.

I watched until he disappeared before I switched my attention back to Michele. "You're a straightforward guy."

He threw his head back and laughed, slapping a hand to his chest, a reaction that had my insides turning to goo. Excitement squirmed inside me, and I shifted, not quite sure how to handle this new feeling. While Ronan's laughter before had been genuine, this was different. Better. This was a man who was interested in me in the way I wanted Daire to be.

"I am honest." Michele waved a hand. "I like to think I'm a true Italian. I tell it how it is, and I romance men I find attractive." He leaned in again and put his mouth close to my ear. "However, you're the first I've wanted to truly seduce."

I exhaled sharply. So, this was flirting. I'd never had someone try to pursue me with such vigor—or at all, for that matter. Daire didn't need to pull out all the tricks to get me into his bed. I'd always done the chasing with Daire, but now someone finally wanted me. It was fucking awesome.

My stomach erupted in butterflies and my fingers tingled in excitement. Pleasure bloomed in my chest, and everything felt light, like I was walking on air. Was this how having someone purposely choose you felt?

Michele placed his thumb on my bottom lip, dragging it across my mouth.

I froze, waiting to see what would happen next. I'd only just arrived, but I already wanted to leave. With Michele.

My heart gave a tug. What about Daire?

Daire was the only one I'd had any sexual experience with, and it felt weird to want someone else. No one would compare to my feelings for him, but for once, I needed someone to want *me*.

Michele shifted closer in a way that suggested he was going to kiss me, and my eyelids slid shut, my grip on my beer bottle tightening until my fingers hurt. I waited, and when he got so close that I felt his breath tickle my mouth, I went to close the distance.

I met air instead.

My eyes shot open and I gawked, surprised to see Michele's

back to me. In front of Michele was Daire and another man I didn't recognize. Daire's face was filled with rage I had never seen on him. Daire had Michele's shirt in his fist, and he snarled at him.

"What the fuck are you doing?" Michele growled out, shoving at Daire. It didn't knock Daire's grip off him. Instead, Daire tightened his fist.

"I should be asking you that," Daire snapped, baring his teeth at him. "Who the fuck do you think you are? You have no fucking right to touch him."

The words hit me hard and my mouth popped open. I'd never heard Daire swear like that. Other than Sloan not liking it, Daire had always been as refined and gentlemanly as Sloan. This was new and shocking.

Michele chuckled, but unlike before, this sound was dangerous. "You seem confused. I can do whatever I want. Fionn was willing."

I shot forward and grabbed Daire's wrist. "Let him go. He's right. I wanted him to kiss me."

"Stay out of this, Fionn." Daire kept his deadly stare on Michele. "I should kill you for even thinking about laying your dirty hands on him."

"He's an adult. That's something for him to decide," Michele said, smirking. "Not you."

Behind Daire, the stranger laughed. He stepped forward, snatched the beer out of my hand, and chugged it. When he was done, he passed the empty to a random guy walking past, and the guy glared, muttering something. The stranger then clapped his hands together. "This is so much fun."

I narrowed my eyes on him. "Who the hell are you?"

The crowd in our vicinity had stopped to gawk, and when my cheeks heated this time, it was from shame. If Sloan found out about this, I would never live it down. Everyone knew Daire and I—we represented the Company at all times. Sloan would punish us severely for embarrassing the Company name tonight.

The stranger offered me a wide grin. He bowed dramatically. "You can call me Aodhan Reardon."

Michele frowned. "Aren't you banned from the city by Killough?"

"He is?" My attention danced between the three of them, complete confusion toying with my brain as I wrestled with what was happening. "Wait. Reardon?"

"He's my older brother," Daire grunted out, though he hadn't let go of Michele yet. "It doesn't matter."

Aodhan grabbed my hand, laying a kiss on the back. "Aren't you a cute kitty?"

"What?" My nose scrunched.

"Aodhan." Daire shot his brother a glare. "Stop it."

Aodhan merely shrugged and winked at me. "He's a grumpy teddy bear, isn't he? I blame our parents. They put *so* much pressure on him to make them proud in the Company."

Daire let go of Michele and spun toward his brother. "I said stop it." The way his voice went deeper than usual in anger had my stomach tumbling, a weird lust slamming into me and making me lose my breath.

Aodhan raised his hands, cackling. "See, kitten? Grumpy."

Daire went to take a step forward, but Aodhan pointed a finger at him, a simple gesture that had Daire tensing and coming to a stop. I didn't know what was happening between them, but the air around us thickened with tension.

All I could do was watch as the brothers battled each other in a staring contest.

Michele shifted closer to me. "How about we get out of here?"

Daire's glare shot to him. "He's not going anywhere, especially not with you."

Anger exploded inside me, and I shoved between them to

stand in front of Daire. All the years of wanting this man—who'd never wanted me in return—welled to the surface like a dormant volcano that had finally awakened. My head spun from my fury, and every ounce of me wanted to punch Daire, but I kept myself in check. It was one thing to give Daire the tongue lashing that was coming, but another thing to punch Sloan's second-in-command. It couldn't happen.

"You have no right to tell me where I can and can't go, Daire." I got in close to him, keeping my voice calm, even as rage blasted through my veins. Sloan would've been proud. "I am in charge of you, not the other way around. You've made it clear. I can fuck who I want."

Even though the club was loud and the music blaring, silence fell between us. Daire stared with a deadly glare I would expect from an enemy. The look was a reminder that, like Sloan, he had killed men. Back in his younger years, he was known for his murder methods. They'd called him the Company Butcher, though the men rarely mentioned it these days because Daire gave the orders on behalf of Sloan now.

"Be careful, boy," he murmured, but I still heard him because every atom inside me was tuned to him.

"Or what?" I snapped, feeling powerful. Not only had someone shown interest in me tonight, but I was out on my own, living it up in a way I never had. My confidence soared.

What I didn't expect, though, was for Daire to grab me and throw me over his shoulder as if I weighed nothing. I let out an embarrassing sound, but he didn't acknowledge it as he stalked toward the front door with his hand on my ass, holding me in place. I struggled, but I had no chance against him.

I looked up to see Michele moving to follow us, but Aodhan grabbed him and yanked him back. That was the last thing I saw before Daire carried me out of the club like a damsel in distress.

I was going to *kill* Daire Reardon.

7

DAIRE

Every fiber of my being told me to take Fionn home for Sloan to handle. I had no doubt Sloan was unaware of where Fionn had gone. If he had known, he wouldn't have allowed it unless Fionn had a ton of guards, even if they had to go undercover. The most I had seen was Ronan, who'd wisely stayed out of my way when I'd carried Fionn out of the club. So even though I should take Fionn back to Southampton, I headed toward my penthouse in Manhattan instead, tightening my grip on the steering wheel of my SUV.

Fionn sat in the passenger seat, arms crossed, anger radiating off him as he stared out the window at the glittering streets of the city. With no music on, the silence in the SUV made it easy for me to hear his harsh breaths.

"You have no reason to be mad at me," I grunted out, some of my anger bleeding away now that we'd distanced ourselves from the threat. While I hadn't had many conversations with Michele Scotti, I didn't trust him. Michele had thrown himself at Fionn the moment he'd walked in. I'd seen it from where I sat at a VIP table with Aodhan. As a result, I'd reacted without the chance to think about my actions. I couldn't help myself. No one was good enough for Fionn. *No one*, not even me, and especially not Michele *fucking* Scotti.

Fionn let out a mean laugh. "Are you kidding?" He whipped around to glare. "You humiliated me in that club. I am nothing but a joke for the men to laugh about and you made it worse."

I sighed. I *had* overreacted. Throwing him over my shoulder was dramatic, but wrapped up in my anger, I hadn't thought about anyone else except Fionn and getting him out of there, away from men who weren't as pure or innocent.

"You shouldn't have been there," I argued, though the anger in my voice softened. "It was dangerous."

"I had Ronan with me." He laid his hands on his knees and curled them into fists. He straightened his spine, staring at me with a tightened jaw and blazing eyes. "You don't trust me to take care of myself?"

"It's not about trusting you, damn it!" I slammed my hand on the wheel. "Sloan never goes places like that without guards. You're going to be the head of the Company one day, and our enemies would love a chance to take you out and make Sloan start from scratch."

"What about you?" he snapped. "You were there, and you're the second-in-command. You had no guards." His eyebrows dipped. "Why were you at the club anyway? You don't like dancing."

I shook my head and took a deep breath, focusing on the road in front of us. There was no easy way to tell Fionn about Aodhan and his habit of finding quick fucks. While Fionn had been in Sloan's care since he was four, Sloan had kept him away from the Company until he was old enough. He'd never met my brother and wouldn't understand what Aodhan was like. Truth be told, I had never wanted Fionn to meet Aodhan. *Ever.*

Fionn snorted. "Looking for an easy fuck with someone drunk enough to forget about you?"

The pure disdain in his words had me inhaling in surprise.

Fionn had always been snarky, but most of the time his bark was worse than his bite. This wasn't the case now. He wanted to hurt me, and the dig was sharper than any barbed words he'd flung at me in the past.

"Are you done throwing a temper tantrum?" I asked, making sure to push as much disappointment as I could into my words in a way that would get a reaction from Fionn. There was nothing he hated worse than someone he respected being upset with him. And it wasn't about hurting him, like he had done to me, but rather about teaching him a lesson. Words came with consequences. If I'd wanted to do serious damage, I could've said *"Sloan wouldn't expect this behavior from his apprentice."*

I couldn't be cruel, though.

I got the response I was expecting. Fionn's shoulders slumped and he fell back against the seat, the fury leaving him like a fire being extinguished. Guilt gnawed at me and I felt the need to make things right.

"I'm sorry for throwing you over my shoulder and carrying you out of the club."

"You wouldn't have done that to Sloan," he fired back.

I winced. "You're right. I wouldn't have." Sloan would've killed me with his bare hands if I'd even tried.

He gave me a long look, those eyes poignant and knowing. The stare reminded me a lot of the way Sloan sometimes watched people, like he knew the secrets of the universe, but he wasn't willing to share them. Fionn was different, though. Instead of knowing the mysteries that plagued the world around him, he wanted to learn them. Live them. He was a student in every way, and the things I wanted to teach him and do to him . . . .

The thought made me wince.

"Where are we going?" he asked, back to staring out the window.

"My place." My grip on the steering wheel tightened, then

loosened. I used the texture to stay present and in the moment, instead of fantasizing about a relationship that couldn't happen.

"Why?" His attention slid to me. "Are you scared of what Sloan will do to you when he finds out how you handled the situation?"

I peered at him carefully. "You should be more afraid of what he'll do to *you* when he discovers you went to a club with only Ronan as backup."

The reaction was almost immediate, with Fionn wincing away from me, fear bleeding into his gaze. He let out a helpless breath, small and fragile, and my heart broke for him. It wasn't that Sloan was a terrible guardian, because he tried, it was that as a mob boss, he needed to be tough. Sometimes, Sloan took it to the extreme to make sure Fionn was ready for the future. Fionn had no idea the violence Sloan and I had seen, and I hoped he never would. But I wasn't stupid. Fionn would find out, eventually. He *needed* to, as future boss of the Company.

"I'm tired of being what he wants me to be."

The words were so quiet I almost missed them over the sounds of the outside world. Cars honking. People partying. And then, here was Fionn, with his abject sadness, his voice so tiny I almost didn't believe it had come from him.

"What?" My anger about the club disappeared, and when I stopped for a red light, I turned my attention completely to him. "What do you mean?"

He laughed quietly, but it wasn't from humor, and he dropped his head forward. "I am trying *so* fucking hard. And I don't want to anymore because I'll never be what he expects. Conall. Lor. Vail. They come in, and Sloan bends over backward for them. He gives them more than he gives me." He glanced up at me and his eyes sparkled with unshed tears. "What do I have to do? When is it my turn? When will he be proud of *me*?"

I couldn't remember a time when Fionn had ever broken down like this, and the surprise punched me in the gut. I froze. I didn't see the light change to green until someone beeped their horn behind us and startled me into hitting the accelerator.

Fionn twisted until his back was facing me again and gazed out the window. The silence returned and it made my skin crawl. I hated the tension stealing the air between us, making it difficult to breathe. I'd faced a lot in my life but nothing quite like this.

It wasn't until we finally made it to my penthouse's garage, positioned beneath the tall building in Manhattan, and I'd parked that I found my words.

"Sloan has high expectations for you," I murmured. It didn't get a reply from Fionn, who kept his back to me. "Believe it or not, he's a tough nut to crack, that one, but I've known him for a long time, boy. Sloan's proud of you, he just doesn't say it."

"Could've fooled me." He sent me a glare before throwing open his door. He shot out of the vehicle, and I sighed, doing the same.

I met Fionn at the back of the SUV and managed to grasp his upper arm before he could put any more distance between us. He shoved me in an attempt to dislodge my grip, and I crowded him in return. He ended up against the back of the SUV, eyes widening, as I slapped my hands on the SUV at the sides of his head.

Our bodies pressed against one another tightly. My mind sent out warning signals to back off again, but I'd already disconnected from the rational part of my brain, focusing on the emotions that thrummed through me. I *needed* him to listen to reason, even if that meant being too close. Any words I thought about saying disappeared now that our chests were pushed together.

The smell of his cologne drifted around me, all encompassing, and my breath caught. *Fuck.* I was in trouble. Why did I think this was a good idea? The corner of his mouth curved a little and he leaned his chin forward, as though waiting for me to man up and close the distance between us. It wouldn't take much, either, and I could haul Fionn upstairs to the penthouse and fuck him like I'd been doing for years. I wasn't so sure it'd be as emotionless as I'd always tried to make it, though.

Reality punched me hard in the gut, and I stumbled backward, nearly tripping over my own feet. I groaned and ran a hand over the side of my face, and when I glanced at him, guilt gnawed at my insides at the look of disappointment that passed across his pretty face. It disappeared quickly, and anger twisted his features again.

Fionn straightened. "You're a coward."

I didn't deny it, even though it was more than that. There were too many reasons why Fionn and I couldn't be in a deeper relationship. I cleared my throat and tilted my head toward the elevator. "Let's go."

Fionn snorted and turned his back on me, heading in the direction I gestured. We walked to an elevator, and as soon as the notification bell dinged and the doors opened, he went inside without a word.

I followed him in and hit the button for the penthouse floor. We rode in silence as the elevator ascended the many levels until it reached the very top. What was usually a comfort for me became something else. I'd never allowed him to see this part of my life, and now I was nervous to know what he would think. *Fionn*—a young man who already owned too many of my nighttime dreams and jerk-off sessions.

He stared around the penthouse when we got inside, eyes wide as he took in the darkness, from the large living room to the wide kitchen filled with ebony appliances and the black marble island, with the tall chairs pushed in around the sides. The only splash of color came from the few white pieces of furniture, like the couch and the chairs at the glass dining table.

I hit a couple of buttons on the security system and it beeped to let me know it was set and the alarm wouldn't blare. From the corner of my eyes, I caught sight of the dogs peeking their heads out of the laundry room, but once they saw it was me, they retreated again.

"I know what your favorite color is." He glanced at me with a small quirk tugging his lips. "There are other colors in the world, you know."

I chuckled. "Black is elegant and makes the home look more luxurious."

"I'm sure this penthouse in Manhattan is expensive enough without needing to make it *look luxurious*," he drawled seriously, shaking his head. He stepped farther inside, and I followed him, gaze straying to the tightness of Fionn's pants around his ass. His cheeks bounced with every step, and it was difficult not to eat up the sight of them—of *him*—and not think about all the nights we'd spent together. He'd always been so beautiful, the perfect boy.

I shook my head. Fuck. I couldn't think about it. No matter how much I wanted Fionn for more than sex, it was out of the question. If, God forbid, anything ever happened to Sloan, it was my job to lead and guide Fionn.

Not marry him.

A relationship was a bad idea because it created a weakness a boss didn't need. Sloan had Conall, but Sloan was also experienced in the business. He was able to take that risk because he was battle hardened and ready to make the tough choices. Fionn wasn't, and I was scared he never would be.

"Do you want to take a shower? I've got clothes you can use. Come on." I focused on heading toward the stairs, ignoring the impossibly handsome man standing in the middle of my penthouse, even though every inch of me wanted to turn around and possess and claim him. I wasn't an animal, and I could control myself.

He followed me up the staircase to the next floor. The dark gray hallway walls were lined with black-and-white scenic photos of Manhattan's skyline and a couple of pale lamps. The complementary dark carpet gave the area a longer and slimmer appearance.

"Yeah, your favorite color is definitely black." He raised his eyebrows. "How did I not know this?"

I gave him a half shrug, not denying it. Between my vehicles and my home, I didn't have an argument against Fionn's statement. I'd purposely not brought him here because this was my private space, a part of me he shouldn't see, but he was here *now*. A possessive side of me didn't want him to leave.

"So, what's the plan?" Fionn crossed his arms, head tilted in defiance. "Keep me here until Sloan comes to get me?" Every word was harsh and rude.

I stared at him for a long moment, studying him. His attitude had put him on Sloan's shit list more than once, but I understood Fionn. Every quip, insult, and nasty comment were used to hide the vulnerable man beneath the prickly facade.

"Yes and no." I kept my distance because regardless of what I knew about him, Fionn was a temptation I couldn't indulge in tonight. I *had* told him he could fuck who he wanted outside of us, but now I was beginning to regret it. I didn't want to share him and that was a dangerous road to travel. "You whine about not knowing the business as well as you should, so let's change that."

The tightness in his shoulders relaxed and he dropped his arms. "How?"

"Tomorrow, you're coming with me to do our rounds. We go to our men around the city and check on how they're doing. You're good with numbers, so you can use that skill to help me work out which areas are profitable and which aren't. If we find some men aren't making the cut, we move them to another location, somewhere they can sell. Sometimes someone needs to be put in a different job. Occasionally, they're just *done*." I didn't elaborate on that last bit because it needed no explanation.

He hesitated. "You're talking about drugs, right?"

My mouth twitched into a grin. I couldn't help it. "Yes, boy, I'm talking about product."

"What do they sell around here? Coke?" Intrigue glittered in his eyes as he took a step closer. Sloan hadn't trusted Fionn to get near our runners, and he'd told me it was because he preferred Fionn to take care of the bigger stuff, but I saw the hesitation for what it was—he didn't want him to get hurt. I'd questioned Sloan about his motives, and all I'd received in return was a grunt. Sloan couldn't be afraid for Fionn's life while simultaneously teaching him to take over. It was a sign that both Killoughs had their weaknesses.

I leaned my shoulder against the wall beside a photo of Times Square. "Coke can get a hefty profit in some areas, but we're moving stronger products in the business district. The rich enjoy the harder substances to take off the edge. Fentanyl's the big fish around Manhattan. You can mix it with heroin and morphine."

His eyebrows dipped. "But why do people do that to themselves?"

"You're not thinking like a Company man," I drawled. "We don't care *why*. We don't force it down their throat. We're only here to provide a service and product. They make the choice." I straightened and stepped closer to him, laying a hand on his shoulder, then squeezing. "Rule number one when you're going around to the distributors, Fionn. Never humanize our customers. They are nothing to us but cash. Why they come to us to get a hit is none of our business. We're not shrinks."

He nodded and took a deep breath. "All right. No humanizing."

My thumb brushed across the skin on his neck, right above his collar, and the trace of warmth sent my attention straight to where I was touching. Realization of what I was doing hit me and I snapped my hand back.

A hurt expression flickered across his face before it hardened again. "Why didn't I know you had a brother? And why did Michele say he was banned from New York by Sloan? That's something I should've known."

I sighed. I expected the question would come up sooner rather than later, but I'd hoped he would completely forget about the incident. Fionn was smart and had a memory that never failed when it came to the important things. It was why he held a grudge for so long. Even though there was no reason for him to *dislike* Conall, he still did because he couldn't rid himself of the bitterness of Conall's arrival, even if it had been eight years ago. Or at least, that was what I assumed.

But I didn't know how to tell Fionn what he wanted to hear while also asking him not to report Aodhan's arrival back to Sloan. It wouldn't matter anyway. Now that Aodhan had insisted on going to a club, Sloan would find out soon.

"The Italians know because they used to hire him. Aodhan . . . is a sore subject. He's rebellious and doesn't like to follow authority. When he was a kid, they diagnosed him with Oppositional Defiant Disorder, but I don't think they were right." I rubbed the back of my neck. There weren't many people I talked to about my brother. Sloan didn't want to hear Aodhan's name, let alone discuss him, and my parents thought he was perfect the way he was, and it was no use trying to converse about him with them, either. "Aodhan enjoys mentally torturing other people. He knows it's wrong, but he loves every second. He's a sociopath, if you ask me."

"Is that why you never told me about him?" Fionn crinkled his nose. "Actually, I don't know *anything* about you, Daire. You come to our home nearly every day. You sit in our meetings, and you support Sloan as his second-in-command, and we fuck and it's nice, but I don't know shit about you." He threw his hands in the air. "I don't know what you like doing in your spare time or your favorite foods. Before tonight, I didn't even know where you fucking lived." His eyes narrowed and he closed the space between us until our chests were inches apart and his breath teased my chin. "Why are you hiding from me? Because I bet my balls that Sloan knows all those things."

"Yes," I said simply.

"Yes?" The helplessness in his voice made my chest hurt.

"Sloan knows all those things." *But I keep them from you because I need you at a distance.* I left the rest unsaid, but I didn't need to because his gaze told me he *knew* what I hadn't spoken.

His eyes sparkled with pain as he shifted backward. He swallowed deeply, Adam's apple bobbing. "Fine. If you want it to stay business, we'll keep it that way. Hell, we won't even fuck anymore. You can keep your dick away from me. If I'm not good enough for you to date, then my hole isn't good enough for you to use." His teeth clenched and he raised his chin in defiance. "Just remember, this is what you wanted, not me."

I didn't know what to say. I already regretted my resolve in not taking this further than we had, and nothing he could say would make it worse. But I'd grown up getting used to being the one who had to take one for the team, always putting my own needs second to everything else. What made this time any different? It hurt more, though. I'd never seen him as anything more than Sloan's nephew and apprentice until that night . . . when I'd made Fionn my boy.

My boy. He was mine, yet I had to let him go. I *needed* to end this.

I squeezed my eyes shut for a brief moment and caught my breath. No. I wasn't going to think about it right now. Instead, I tilted my head in the direction of the hallway and began to walk toward my bedroom, which was the second door to the left. I opened it and looked at Fionn.

"Aodhan's in the guest room, so you can take my bed tonight."

He frowned and glanced around me into the room. "Where will you sleep?"

Inside was designed with a similar dark aesthetic, with the king-size bed draped in an inky blanket and pillows. The floor featured the same carpet as in the hallway and the curtains that covered the floor-to-ceiling windows were also black, but a pattern of circles and swirly lines danced across the thick material. There were other items that separated the duskiness of the room, with brown shaded lamps and a couch. More grayscale photographs broke up the space on the walls.

"The bed looks big enough for both of us." He gave me a pointed look. "We've fucked, and it's not like we haven't seen each other naked. I can keep my hands to myself."

I smiled. "I know, but you're the boss's nephew. You don't share the bed with men beneath you."

"Seriously, Daddy?"

I shuddered at the name and sucked in a breath between my teeth. He knew exactly what that did to me.

He blinked up at me with those big hazel eyes and pouted a little, his mouth popping adorably. "You're different. As annoying as you are, you're important to us, Daire. So yes, I will be sharing a bed with you. Don't fucking complain."

"Don't swear, boy," I snapped lightly before I could stop myself. I cursed inwardly. This wasn't helping the situation.

"Yes, Daddy Daire," he teased quietly.

My cock jerked and pleasure simmered low in my stomach. He was doing this on purpose. Torturing me.

Fionn's lips twitched into a smirk that made him look even more like Sloan. "I'd like to take a shower. Where are these clothes you mentioned?"

I inhaled as stealthily as I could and headed into the bedroom toward my walk-in closet. I grabbed out the smallest pair of pajama pants I had and a loose black T-shirt, then passed the clothing to Fionn. With a strange sense of dread, I pointed at the door across the room, which led to the en suite. The one where I regularly jerked off to Fionn. "In there. The maid went through this evening, so there should be fresh towels on the rack."

He sucked his bottom lip between his teeth and gazed at me from under his long lashes, almost as though he was going to ask me to join him. He didn't say a word, though, and he headed toward the bathroom. He closed the door behind himself and the soft *click* finally gave me a chance to breathe.

I turned and rested my forehead against the frame of my closet. *Fuck.* I was in trouble. Over the years, we'd walked a thin line between pretending our indiscretions hadn't happened or wordlessly agreeing it meant nothing. At least, that was what I'd thought. But now Fionn was poking a sleeping dragon, hoping to get a reaction, and it might not be the one he was expecting. Jealousy was a nasty beast, and I despised the idea of Scotti's hands on him.

My interests in Daddy kink had only begun that first night with Fionn, and his desire for me to dominate him had inspired a new need for me. I'd discovered the world outside of vanilla sex through rough, throat squeezing, brutally sweet sex, but I'd never given myself leeway to try different kinks. He'd opened that experience for me, but I wasn't sure I would ever be ready to take him on as a boy full time. I craved it, of course, but the reasons not to were stacked against us.

Fionn had fallen so beautifully into the role of a bratty boy, and I'd found I wanted it as much as he had. Even the little nudges he gave me were about testing the waters, and I'd reacted the way he needed me to. I'd given him not only compliments, but punishments, too. He wanted to see how far *Daddy* would let him go, and I gave him boundaries. It was a fun game that tested my strength against the temptation of making Fionn mine and only mine.

I shook my head to shove away the thoughts. I needed to call Sloan, and having a hard-on while I spoke to him because I was thinking about Fionn and the kink we enjoyed wasn't the best idea. Grabbing my phone out of the pocket of my jeans, I steeled myself for the conversation.

I slipped out of the bedroom and closed the door before I found Sloan's number and tapped his name. It took three rings before Sloan answered.

"What?" he grumbled.

I cleared my throat. "Sir, we have a situation."

"What kind?" In the background, I heard Conall mumble something, but Sloan whispered, "It's fine, pet. Go back to sleep."

"I went to Bellissimo tonight and Fionn was there." The silence on the other end of the line was deafening, and I winced. "I extracted him, and he's here at my penthouse."

Finally, Sloan's angry breath noisily came through the phone. "What was he doing there without my permission and without guards?"

"I believe he wanted to get laid." I massaged my forehead.

"I thought you and he had a thing."

I winced at the harsh reality of what he may or may not know. Sloan was the boss, but he was also my best friend. Sometimes I felt it was better to be that friend rather than the second-in-command, and this was one of those times. "We don't. He's in his twenties. He's young. What did you do at his age? How many guys did you screw? He deserves to live his life and fuck who he wants."

"That was different," Sloan growled.

"How? He's the heir to the Killough Company and so were you. The risks you took were a lot worse than whatever Fionn's done." I stared at one of the photos of the Empire State Building on the wall and tapped the back of my phone lightly with my finger. "Let me teach him about the rounds we do with the dealers."

"No." His sharp tone made me wince. "He's not ready."

"He is and has been for a long time." I fell back against the wall and used it to stay upright. My entire body was suddenly tired. I needed sleep. Clubbing was a young man's game, and I was past the age of partying. Why I'd thought I could keep up with Aodhan, I didn't know. My brother never had an off switch. "I don't like questioning you, Sloan. You're my boss, but you're also my friend, so I'm going to tell you this. If you don't let him spread his wings, he won't ever be ready to take over the Company. He's not Eoin." My heart gave a twinge, prompting me to remember that myself. "What we do is dangerous. We can't ever promise he'll stay safe, but you chose him as your apprentice, and that means you need to trust him. And trust your men, including me, to protect him."

He grunted. "Fine. He can stay there and go with you tomorrow. *But,* if anything happens to him, Daire—"

"It won't." I believed it wholeheartedly, too. "I would die before I let him get hurt."

"Good. I'll send some men over tomorrow with a couple of fresh suits for him."

The call ended, and I pulled the phone away from my ear to look at the screen. I smiled. It was good to know Sloan still trusted my advice, but now what was I going to do with Fionn? We would be spending more time together outside of the bedroom.

"Shit." I slammed my head back against the wall. I was in deeper trouble than before.

8

FIONN

I closed my eyes and leaned into the hot water pounding over my face and neck, sighing in delight. I didn't need another shower tonight, but I'd used it as an opportunity to get away from Daire and *think* about what had happened. When Sloan found out about Daire carrying me out of Bellissimo over his shoulder—and he *would* find out—he would be pissed. Which meant I needed a way to spin tonight's mess in a positive light.

But that wasn't the focal point of my thoughts right now—Daire was. Yet again, my desire for more than fucking had been rejected, and I was made to feel like a child playing in an adult's game, which both frustrated and angered me. I was twenty-six. Before Conall had come along, I'd been well on my way to learning about running the Company. I helped Sloan control the ports and deal with the rogue Italians. My uncle had used me for accounting and trusted me, but all that came to a halt the moment Sloan got his new pet. I was forgotten, left to watch from the sidelines.

Daire? He acted as though I was a nuisance. If that were the case, then I was done with the flirting and fucking and waiting for Daire to come to his senses. I deserved better. I deserved someone like Michele, who looked at me as though I'd built the entire world in a day.

I frowned at the black shower tiles. I didn't *want* Michele. I didn't know him, for one, and he wasn't Daire. Dating never hurt, though, right? The only man I'd had inside me didn't want me for more than sex, and I was clueless when it came to other men. My obsession with my uncle's best friend was ridiculous, but I couldn't get Daire and our wild, passionate nights out of my head. If getting Daire out of my wet dreams involved letting Michele date and fuck me, then so be it.

With my mind made up, I finished my shower and turned off the shiny knobs. I opened the glass door and stepped out, grabbing a fluffy black towel off the rack, then wiped myself down until I was nearly dry. Wrapping the towel around my hips and tying it in a knot, I stepped over to the wide mirror above the vanity and wiped away the condensation from the heat of the shower. I stared at my reflection, taking in the narrow face and high cheekbones that looked back.

The more I worked out at the gym, the more my abs became defined, but I was still lean and sinewy. My hair was a dark brown again. Like my father's. A soft dusting of light brown hair covered my chest, but it was barely visible, and my nipples were tiny on my pecs. I laid a hand across my right nipple and sighed. Pointing out everything wrong with myself wasn't going to help. To hell with Daire. It was his loss.

Mentally holding on to my decision, I dressed in the pajama pants and T-shirt Daire had given me, then hung the towel on the rack before finally exiting the bathroom. He wasn't anywhere to be seen, so I took the liberty of sliding under the comforter on the right side of the bed and flopping on my back. I huffed, staring up at the dark gray ceiling. The only light left on in the bedroom was the lamp sitting on the nightstand beside me.

I didn't know how long I lay there, staring at that high

ceiling, before I heard two people outside the door. Aodhan's and Daire's voices filled the hallway, and even though Daire tried to shush his brother, Aodhan's words seemed to grow louder until I could finally hear what was being said.

"I'm telling *you*, go into that room and fuck that sexy ass. He's a feisty little kitten with claws that I *know* you want to scratch up your back. You know you like fucking him." Aodhan laughed.

My breath caught and I stayed as still as I could, listening to every word my ears could catch. Did Daire's brother know we'd been having sex for years now? Clearly he knew something.

What did that say about this entire situation? Why did Daire tell his brother? Fuck. This was all so confusing.

"Shh. Aodhan, keep your voice down. He'll hear you." Daire sounded irritated.

"Oooh, here, kitty kitty."

"Stop it."

There was a scuffle, and Aodhan howled in laughter. "If you don't keep riding that ass, someone else will. That Italian was certainly interested in sticking his cock in your precious boss's nephew."

Daire whispered something I couldn't hear, and before I could decide to get to my feet and walk closer to the door to listen, he spoke louder again. "Leave it. I mean it. Fionn's the future of the Company, and he deserves respect."

"So, respect him with your spunk filling that tight little hole of his, *Daddy*."

More scuffling. A hard *thump* like someone had been thrown against a wall.

I stiffened, hoping Daire didn't get hurt, because it didn't sound like a friendly fight.

"Keep his name and everything about him out of your dirty fucking mouth," Daire snapped loudly. "He's better than you and always will be."

"Touché." Aodhan laughed again. "Now get your hands off me before I break every one of your fingers. Brother or not, you know I'll do it."

"I don't care what you do, but if you say one more word about Fionn, I'll kick you out and tell Sloan you're here so he can send his trusty little assassin after you. Mom and Dad will be upset with me, but don't think for one second that I wouldn't."

"Well, well, well. You do care about him." Aodhan laughed. "Color me not surprised after all. You're too loyal to the Killoughs."

"Sloan's been more of a brother than you."

I sucked in a breath and held it, listening carefully. The silence that fell was tense, and I could feel the high emotions from where I lay. If they said anything else, I couldn't hear it. The door to the bedroom opened. I shut my eyes tightly, pretending to be asleep.

Daire muttered under his breath, and even though I couldn't see him, I could pick out his scent in a room of a thousand men. I peeked through my lashes and watched as he walked straight to the bathroom. A moment later, the shower turned on. I relaxed and pondered the conversation I'd overheard.

He'd been quick to defend me, but I didn't know if that was a good thing or not. Maybe he'd been pissed and embarrassed about Aodhan suggesting he fuck me, even though he already had—numerous times. Daire had a considerable amount of respect for Sloan, and if he'd shown me anything, it was that he *wasn't* interested in anything deeper. Instead, he pushed me away every time I attempted to make a connection. So, what was the sex? A quick way to get off? Of course it was. I was a willing hole. Nothing more, nothing less.

I groaned. I was such a child about this. Lovestruck, like a fourteen-year-old.

The sound of shuffling against the carpet made me frown,

and I sat up in bed. What I saw nearly had me flying to the ceiling. Two dogs the size of bears—okay that was dramatic, but they certainly seemed like it—stared at me with dark eyes. In the shadows, they looked like hellhounds.

"Hi?" My voice wobbled and I stared down at them when they stayed frozen. "Don't kill me please."

The bathroom door opened, and I jumped in surprise because I hadn't heard the shower turn off again. Daire stood in the doorway in only a towel wrapped around his waist, beads of water trickling down his rippled and tattooed chest and stomach.

The dogs were forgotten as my mouth watered at the sight of Daire.

I loved his tattoos but had never had the chance to explore them all. Our sex was quick and dirty, and he left as soon as he was done.

He snapped his fingers at the dogs, breaking me from my thoughts. "Heel."

I gaped in surprise. The ink of the Dobermans made sense now. Of course they were his dogs. I had no idea that he had these majestic beasts until now, another sign that I didn't know him as well as I wanted to.

The dogs turned their stare away from me and ran over to Daire, sitting on their butts in front of him. They were at attention, like soldiers ready and waiting for orders, and I couldn't help but stare. I slid out of bed and followed them, ready to heel for him exactly as he'd ordered the dogs to. Instead of following through with the embarrassing thought, I stopped behind the dogs.

My head spun. I didn't know where to *start* with all these new revelations. "You have dogs."

Daire finally looked at me, mouth curled in a soft smile. "I do. Sinead and Oona."

"Where were they when we came in?" I asked, noticing the

dogs didn't react to my voice. Their sole focus was Daire, their boss. One of them, the black dog with patches of brown, had her tail wagging, and I smiled at the adorable sight.

"They sleep in the laundry room. They usually know it's me when I arrive because of my smell." He scratched both of their heads and grinned. There was a softness in his gaze that made my heart give a hard tug.

"They're Dobermans, right? I thought Dobermans have pointed ears and a stumpy tail?"

He frowned at me. "Those dogs have had their tails and ears cut. In extreme cases, it's done to resolve medical issues, but otherwise it's for appearance value."

My mouth fell open. "Cut? What do you mean?"

"You don't know about ear cropping or tail docking?" He straightened again and waved his hand toward the left. "Bed. Go."

The dogs ran to the side of the room that Daire had gestured at, and it took me a moment to realize there were dog-size cushions in the corner that they immediately curled up on.

I shuffled backward and returned to my side of the mattress, sliding beneath the blankets and resting my shoulders against the headboard. "I didn't know." I scrunched up my nose. Even though I loved dogs and had begged Sloan for a puppy, I'd never had one.

He tugged at the knot of his towel uncomfortably and cleared his throat. "It's a cruel practice that has no health benefits for the animals. It's people who do cosmetic surgery on their dogs to make them look better." The last two words held enough venom to kill and he grunted. "I should cut off the tips of their ears and a leg and see how they like it."

Finally. This was something Daire was obviously passionate about. I was seeing a different side of him, one that wasn't controlled and managed like the good and loyal Company man he was. No, this was the real Daire, angry at the cruelty of humans.

"I didn't know that," I whispered honestly. "I thought they were bred that way."

He snorted, and the way he unintentionally tugged at the towel gave me a view of the start of his trimmed pubic hair, something I shouldn't be looking at because I'd *just* made a deal with myself to move on from this ridiculous crush. But it was hard not to stare at the tattoos that curved with the natural shape of his body. I had never realized how much Daire's skin was meant for ink until I'd seen it for the first time.

"Some breeds can be, specifically an Australian cattle dog, but not Dobermans." His gaze strayed to his girls and the smile returned.

I licked my lips as I studied the magnificent canvas of his chest and arms, the desire to stride back over to him and drop to my knees growing like weeds inside me. Nothing good came from invasive thoughts, but he'd always been my addiction.

I didn't have to worry, though. Instead, Daire simply nodded and walked back into the bathroom, closing the door with a firm *click*.

I sighed.

So close, yet so far.

I listened to the soft snores that came from the dogs with a small smile. Sliding down the bed, I snuggled deeply into the mattress. My heart thumped steadily, a beating reminder of how desperate for Daire I was. I could join him in the bathroom and beg him to fuck me, but I also needed to expel him from my system. If he couldn't love me the way I deserved, then I'd find someone who would.

A few minutes later, he opened the door again, dressed in a pair of gray shorts and a shirt. He headed to the opposite side of the bed and slunk into it, keeping as far away from me as possible.

"I don't bite," I whispered with a small smirk.

He grunted but didn't say anything.

With another big sigh, I reached over to switch off the lamp. The silence hung in the air again, with the dogs' snoring the only sound to break the tension. They were clearly comfortable in their living situation.

Tomorrow was another day. With the resolution of moving on from the stupid crush, I was ready to start anew. Not only would I learn the nitty-gritty of the Company, but I would keep my eyes open for potential new lovers.

If only it were that easy, right?

9

FIONN

I spent the morning trying to think of what to say to Daire and came up with nothing, so we got ready in a silence I didn't particularly enjoy. He sent me off to brush my teeth first, and by the time I left the en suite, he had one of my suits lying on the bed. I assumed Daire had a Company man drop it off, but I didn't gather the courage to ask about it.

Once I slipped the suit on—an olive dress shirt with a forest green vest and jacket and light brown pants—I left the bedroom and headed along the hallway, then down the black steel stairs.

Daire was in the open-plan kitchen, wearing a dark charcoal suit with a black shirt, staring down in front of himself. I couldn't see what he was looking at because of the large island blocking my view, but I didn't have to guess before a bark gave me the answer to my unasked question.

He nodded and grinned, then laughed as he grabbed a piece of meat off a plate on the counter and passed it to one of the dogs. "Good girl."

The sultriness of his praise sent a shiver down my spine. I inhaled, closing my eyes for a moment to remind myself that I'd firmly decided last night it was time to move on. Opening my eyes again, I forced a smile and strode over to the kitchen.

Daire glanced up at me and the smile fell off his lips. His expression turned stoic as he straightened. "Sir."

My stomach churned in disappointment. Did he dislike seeing me that much?

Pushing aside the thought, I squared my shoulders and straightened. "I'm ready whenever you are." I paused and stared around the quiet penthouse. "Where's your brother?"

He made a sound that wasn't quite a snort but wasn't anything pleasant, either. "He left early. Or maybe he didn't stay at all. Aodhan's got the energy of a teenager. He doesn't need much sleep."

"How much older than you is he?" I walked around the island to stand directly in front of him, then looked down at the Dobermans and their stiff sitting position. Their attention was firmly on Daire—their eyes never leaving him. It was clear they were waiting for orders.

Me too, girls. I internally sighed. I was the future boss of the Killough Company, and while I yearned for that position and power when it was time for Sloan to step down, there was one man I wanted to take commands from. Daire was a Daddy, and he demanded compliance simply by speaking with his rough, dominant voice.

I needed that.

"A year and a half older." He brushed his hand down the side of his face. "But he's never acted like it."

"He's different from you," I said carefully.

He did snort this time, and it was a strange sound that didn't fit him. "Well, we both couldn't be reckless idiots. One of us had to step up and take care of our family."

He spoke the words as a fact, but what he hadn't realized was the information he'd shared with me. I picked up on what was left unsaid.

"And that was you. The responsible brother." I knew exactly how that felt. Most men in the Company, including Sloan, forgot that I had two younger brothers. It'd always been my job to step up and be the mature one. When my mom needed money, she came to me. When my brothers needed something to do with college, she came to me. Sloan had no idea it was happening because I purposely kept it secret. My uncle didn't know as much as he thought he did. Sloan wasn't the only Killough who could keep a secret.

Daire stared down at his dogs in thought for a long moment before he shook his head. "It doesn't matter." He straightened and snapped his fingers, and the dogs' attention broke. They turned to walk away, giving me a careful look as they trotted past and ran toward the living room to jump on the leather couch.

I watched them get comfortable and smiled. "They're beautiful." I turned my gaze back to him and chuckled. "I didn't know you were a dog person." My gaze slid to the sleeves of his suit, and I thought about what hid beneath the clothing. The ink I loved. Daire was a mystery, but there was also a lot I could gather through the small amount of information he did share. I was good at connecting the dots. "I had no idea you were a tattoo person until you came home from that trip, either, so . . . ."

"There's a lot you don't know about me." He cleared his throat and reached down to button up his jacket. "Let's go. We've got a big day, and Sloan gave me permission to show you around the city."

"Which parts?" I stepped back as he stalked past, and I followed him as he headed toward the entrance of the penthouse. As soon as we stepped over the threshold, he closed the large door, and the security system beeped to signal it was activated. "Sloan started teaching me that kind of stuff, then Conall happened."

Daire stopped suddenly, and I bumped into his back. I shifted away as he spun around to stare down at me. His brow creased in a frown. "Did you ever think it wasn't because of Conall?"

I blinked. "What?"

He chuckled in an unamused way and shook his head. "Boy, you're so quick to blame the boss's pet because of your jealousy that you don't stop to think with that big brain of yours." As if to make a point, he tapped my temple. "Conall came at the same time as trouble started brewing. Sure, Sloan had you doing important work like running some shipments or talking to the port associates, but things changed the moment Toscani started stirring the pot. Sloan pulling back on your training had nothing to do with Conall."

"He was pissed at me for snooping through Conall's belongings," I argued, shame causing heat to flood my cheeks. I didn't know why I'd gone into Conall's room and looked through his drawers, but my protectiveness for my uncle and our business made me irrational, and I'd acted on an impulse.

He grunted and crossed his arms. "That's child's play. He already made an example of you about that."

Sloan hadn't, though.

While he'd made a show of sending me away with soldiers, they'd left me in the basement where Sloan usually tortured people. Sloan had then sent Daire down to *deal* with me. And by deal, Daire did nothing but sit in a chair and ignore me.

I had demanded his attention, but he hadn't done a damned thing. When a few hours went down and went, he finally spoke, telling me to get my act together if I wanted to be a mob boss. I realized then it was a show of dominance. Sloan *wanted* his men, including Conall, to think he had hurt me. They'd thought my injuries were under my clothes, leaving the perfect appearance for an apprentice. They were wrong.

So, I'd played the role like I'd expected Sloan wanted me to by snubbing everyone I could for a reasonable amount of time, and the small smirk Sloan had given me had said I'd done a good job of acting.

Like the bratty nephew.

The kid who'd needed to be disciplined. Despite being relieved Sloan wasn't actually going to hurt me, the shame of it hadn't been any better.

Daire sighed. "I'm not going to spell it out for you. Come on. We don't have time for this." He spun on his heel and stalked toward the elevator. I sped after him so I could get through the doors before he closed them. We stayed silent on the way down and as we walked through the lobby. A few people stopped to stare, and they seemed to recognize Daire because a sharply dressed man with short dark hair, round tortoiseshell glasses, and a light gray tweed jacket nodded at him as he strode past. This guy was the only one Daire acknowledged.

I didn't ask who he was, but if I threw the handsome man a glare, who could blame me? All I got in return was a quirky smile. Snorting, I followed Daire out through the glass doors of the building.

"Are we going to take your bike?" I asked hopefully. I'd wanted a ride on that thing for too long, but I'd been denied every time I'd asked. The excuse was that Sloan hated motorcycles, and it wasn't a lie. Sloan never understood why Daire rode one, but I thought it was sexy as hell.

Daire sent me a pointed look over his shoulder. "Company business means—"

"Company car. Yeah, I know." I smiled, and I didn't miss the small, amused grin that he gave me in return.

We paused on the busy sidewalk, and a few moments later a sleek black BMW parked in front of us. I hated that most of the cars looked the same, but it made sense that they were identical. Sloan didn't want them to stand out. We were nobodies, like everyone else in this big city, and we were especially *not* doing anything illegal.

The driver stepped out of the car and opened the back door for us, and Daire nodded in thanks before he slipped inside. I went around to the other side and got in, not bothering to wait for the driver because I didn't have the patience.

As soon as the driver returned to his seat, raised the partition, and set off, I gave my attention to Daire. "So, what are we doing today? Before Conall came along, I was handling the port and some of the drugs. I was doing important things."

He gave me serious side-eye. "Stop being a brat."

"I'm not," I argued, but it came out in a whine. I snapped my mouth closed and huffed. I refused to cross my arms like I really wanted to do. "I was ready for more. When Conall was taken, I had an automatic rifle in my hands." I raised my palms at him, as if it was there for him to see. "I was prepared to kill for Sloan." I hadn't, but I didn't mention that. There was so much gunfire in the warehouse after Conall had been kidnapped that all I could do was freeze and watch the scene unfold. "I've always been the perfect apprentice, and then suddenly, I was nothing. Invisible to Sloan."

Daire leaned back in his leather seat and closed his eyes. "The boss gave you the job of finding the rat. That's a big assignment, boy. Appreciate what you've been given."

I noticed how much more often Daire was calling me "boy" outside the bedroom. The pet name was becoming more regular and it was music to my ears. *Boy.* I wanted so badly to be his full-time boy.

I turned my head to hide a smile and stared out the window as we passed by the New York high-rises. The sky was cloudy and gray, the beginnings of snow drifting through the cool winter air. Somewhere outside was shouting. We passed a recent car accident. Two men threw their arms up and pointed at each other, clearly furious, and I snorted. Just another day in the city.

"Where exactly are we going first?" I asked. "Where do we find our dealers who sell the product?"

"Everywhere." The amusement in Daire's tone made me roll my eyes.

"You're *so* funny."

He chuckled, and I shot a surprised look at him. The sight of him being carefree and genuinely entertained made my stomach twist into knots. I smiled, ignoring the lightness in my chest at the notion that *I*, Fionn Eoin Killough, made Daire Reardon *laugh*.

"We're suits, so we don't get too involved with the nitty-gritty stuff. We handle the high-profile areas, but there's a chain of command for a reason. It's best to keep our hands as clean as possible." His lips quirked into a half smirk that I thought was unusual for him. "If we lose a couple of runners or higher-ups, it won't matter. They'll get compensated and protected in prison. When they're out, if they keep their mouth shut, they get rewarded for doing their time and staying loyal."

The logic made sense. "So, why are we visiting them? You said last night that you wanted to run numbers, right? See which areas are profitable and which aren't."

"Yes, but we can do that from one location. The Amatory." He rolled his shoulders, and I watched him carefully, reminded again of the ink on the skin hidden beneath his suit. I'd never thought of myself as someone who liked tattoos on a man, but they were perfect on him—like intricately designed icing on a very delicious cake.

"That's a brothel." I frowned. "The Amatory Lane, right?"

He hummed in agreement. "It's on the Upper East Side and is now run by Bohdan, that Ukrainian Sloan likes. Sloan transferred him from the Genie to the Amatory a few months back."

"Why are we going there?"

"Because it's the best location we have to run our operation." Daire tapped the window with the knuckle of his pointer finger. "Out there, Fionn, the DEA and FBI are always hunting for ways to bring down the Company. The Amatory is the best place we've got. You've never been there, have you?"

I shook my head. "The only brothel I've been to is the Virtue." My nose scrunched. "They're disgusting."

"Why?" He squinted at me with a serious stare. "Sex workers are no different than any other career. They work hard. Sure, they give their bodies, but don't a lot of jobs expect that? Construction workers use their bodies, so do football players and ballerinas and nurses who are always on their feet. What's the difference?"

I straightened. "I didn't know you were a supporter of our whores."

"Sex workers," Daire replied simply. "Sloan calls them whores, and I respect that he's the boss and he can do what he wants, but trust me. These men and women are as important as drug runners or money launderers. Sex sells, boy. If you respect them, they'll show you their loyalty."

I pressed my lips together. "Do you have a lover in one of our brothels, Daire?" A weird feeling clenched my stomach, and I rubbed the area where it hurt. *Fuck.*

Moving on! Did my body not know what that meant?

"No—" His expression turned serious again and he clamped his lips into a thin line. "—but if you're going to be boss one day, you need to understand that every part of your company makes it a whole. If one piece of the puzzle is missing, then it's not complete." He turned his head to stare out the window.

After a long moment, I sighed. "Tell me about the Amatory and why it's important."

He sent me a small, proud smile. "Because, boy, it's a hub. It's fronted by a real business, unlike the Exotic Virtue, which is only real on paper. The Amatory is a private hospital."

"Right. I remember Sloan telling me about that one. He said it brought us the most money."

The hospital took years to build, and Sloan had been excited about the new venture. It'd opened up seven months ago. He hadn't moved any of the criminal parts into it until recently, which made sense because he needed the legal portion to run smoothly before adding more variables. He kept me up to date with what was happening, but I'd never been there yet. Sloan always let me know when it was the right time to get involved.

"Yes, because of what it includes. This business is exclusively for the upper crust. You need to be a member to even walk through the front doors, and that membership costs you three hundred grand a year."

I whistled. "That's a pretty chunk of change."

"Exactly. Once they're in those doors, they have access to top tier doctors and surgeons. Our products range from general practitioners to plastic surgeons to any other specialty you can think of, including holistic and mental health, and the privacy is immaculate. *Then*, behind the legitimate front are our exclusive services—private hands-on care for *all* your physical needs. Only members we trust are allowed in there, and they pay for the privilege of top-notch services."

"How do we know they won't go to the cops?"

"Because, if they do, we have dirt on them. And you know how Sloan works."

"He'd kill them or their families if they opened their mouths."

"You got it, boy."

"Okay, so the brothel's hidden behind the hospital, but the drugs work because it's a medical clinic. The feds *could* search the business, but they'd need some good proof to do it."

"See, that big brain of yours does work."

It helped that Sloan gave me a small rundown of the idea already, but I liked that I was getting more knowledge about it. The Killough Company was huge when it came to our legal businesses, and Sloan hired trusted men to manage them. One boss couldn't keep an eye on all of them.

"Shut up." My cheeks burned and I chuckled in embarrassment.

Daire grinned widely. "All our books and data are in the Amatory. You could call it our own little research facility. For the rich, going into a private hospital for drugs makes things a lot easier. No one knows what someone's in there for and it's impolite to ask why they're seeing a doctor."

I whistled. "Wow. That *is* smart."

"Thank you."

"It was your idea," I guessed, laughing.

"Yes, it was." He pressed his tongue to the inside of his cheek, and this was the smuggest I'd ever seen Daire, who never took credit for anything. "And on top of that, we get our percentage of medical fees, and the doctors won't say a word because they're just happy to get paid a lot more than anywhere else."

"I'm impressed. Why wasn't I let in on this sooner?"

"Because it's our golden project. You needed to be ready for it." He stared at me for a long, silent moment. "And now you are."

"Really?"

"Really," Daire confirmed. "To make the clinic more untouchable, Sloan's got a bit of a bleeding heart. We do charity work through the clinic. We do a free chemo clinic four times a month. We give out twenty free transition surgeries per year, based on a raffle, and offer free psychological sessions for up to one hundred members of the LGBTQ community a year. Now, imagine if the feds tried to investigate us."

"The people would rally."

His eyes sparkled. "Exactly. We might cater to the rich,

which has its own benefits because who wants to take on people with money and power, but we also help those who need that extra bit of support."

The more Daire spoke about the Amatory, the more attractive he became. He was sexy, but his brain made him damned irresistible.

I tilted my head, unable to break my gaze from him, and he stared directly back at me. As if he was a magnet I was drawn to, I began to lean forward. My need to feel his lips on my own was an unstoppable force. He began to move toward me as well.

The force of the car stopping jerked us apart, and Daire didn't waste a second, throwing open his door and stepping out, acting as though we hadn't been about to kiss.

I mentally cursed myself and exited my side, ignoring the burn that assaulted my cheeks and made my stomach churn. I straightened my jacket and raised my chin, gathering the courage to put on the stern expression I was known for.

I paused to stare at the building and took a moment to appreciate the hard lines and boring architecture. To everyone passing by, the business looked like any other with four walls of windows, over ten stories high. There was a driveway that wound around into a semicircle near two automatic doors, and I assumed it was a drop-off zone for patients. Our driver hadn't stopped there, though, and instead parked in one of two designated VIP spots near the side.

The large name on the building caught my attention.

The Eoin Killough Memorial Hospital.

My breath stuttered and drawing air into my lungs became difficult. Dad. Sloan had named it after Dad. Tears prickled the corners of my eyes, and I wiped them away quickly. The image of Dad's face from the photo on his grave flashed through my mind, and I wondered how he would've felt about this. Would he have loved it or hated it? I didn't know and that tore me up inside. I rubbed my chest to soothe the agony ripping my heart apart.

Daire stared, giving me a moment.

I inhaled deeply. When I nodded, he gestured for me to follow him. I didn't argue, forcing my feet into action as we headed toward the sliding glass doors. As soon as we entered, we were approached by a guard who stopped when he got a good view of us. He nodded at Daire and moved backward again, and Daire gave him a short finger wave in thanks.

He leaned close to me. "When you first enter, a patient is expected to show their membership card," he said, voice lowered.

"Do we accept emergencies? What if we accept someone and they aren't a member?" I asked.

He made a sound in the back of his throat. "Then, they can expect a hefty bill. The kind that's a lot worse than what they'd get from any other hospital." He shrugged. "We have our own EMS transport, and those who aren't under our employment know not to bring patients here unless they're a member."

I hummed in acknowledgement as we walked past a reception desk operated by an alert young man with short blond hair, green eyes, and a suit that looked slightly too big for him. He nodded with a small smile as we passed, and I couldn't help but return it. We went through a set of doors that Daire had a key card for and down a long light blue hallway that led to another desk, this one manned by nurses.

Daire stopped in front of the circular desk and grinned at one of the ladies in blue scrubs. She appeared to be the oldest, with fine gray hair pulled into a small bun and a pair of green cat-eye glasses. As soon as she saw Daire, she tugged her spectacles down to the end of her nose and looked over the top of them.

"Well, well, well. Look who decided to show their ugly mug."

The teasing lilt in her Brooklyn accent had me smiling. "What happened, kid? You lose a bet?"

"Ha ha. You're hilarious, Meredith." He flashed his white teeth and patted the desk ledge in front of him. "I'm here on business."

"Look at him." She laughed and glanced at the other nurses as she straightened her back with her arms against her side as though mocking Daire. "*I'm here on business.*" Deepening her voice, she mimicked him.

He shook his head. "One day, you're going to tease the wrong person."

She laughed. "Honey, I'm not that stupid. You don't see me doing the same thing to Mr. Killough, do you?"

He sighed and waved his hand at me. "This is Fionn Killough."

She clapped her hands. Eyes bright, she grinned wide. "Ah, the prodigy taking over the big business!"

I nearly choked and glanced at Daire. "She knows?"

He laughed in answer. "She's a nurse."

Meredith *tsked* a lot like Sloan did when he was lecturing me and waved her hand impatiently while slapping the other on her hip. "We know everything. We also know more than the doctors, but don't tell them that. You don't want to hurt their inflated egos."

"They're not *that* bad," Daire argued.

She shot him a narrowed stare. "The one doctor we do like, we don't see very often because you always take him away."

He winced. "I don't know what you're talking about." It was clearly a lie, and the small ashamed smile said otherwise.

She grunted and turned around toward one of the other nurses. "Gloria, do *you* remember Rory?"

Gloria was a tall, rotund redhead with bright lipstick the same color as her hair. She put her hands on her hips and gave Daire a disgruntled look even as she spoke to Meredith. "Rory?

Oh, yeah, the cute natural redhead doctor with the adorable Irish accent. The only one who treats us with respect. The same one who actually acknowledges all the work we do, but also the one who Daire pulls out of the clinic all the time for personal emergencies. That Rory?"

Daire held up his palms to them, laughing, as he gave in to their playful scowls. "Okay, fine. The boss makes that decision. Rory is better equipped to be his personal doctor than anyone else."

Meredith shook her head and *tsked* again before she turned her attention to Daire. She stared at him over her glasses, a friendly smile curving her mouth. "So, why's the young Killough here? Not that I don't appreciate the broody big boss. He's very delightful to stare at when he's scowling at everyone. And that pet of his is cute as a button." She shook a finger at me. "But you are even more adorable."

"Thank you?" I didn't know what else to say. The snappy banter between the nurses and Daire had my head spinning. They were obviously good friends, and it was the kind of interaction that I hadn't thought Daire could have with someone.

He stepped closer to me. "Don't listen to a word she says, Fionn. She only compliments you when she wants something."

Her jaw dropped open and her hands were back on her hips again. "*That* was rude. Now I'm not going to tell you what your men have been gossiping about this morning." She pursed her lips smugly at him, and he sighed. "They're like a bunch of old ladies getting together for morning coffee to *spill the tea*."

"What did they say?" he asked, straightening.

She huffed. "What makes you think you deserve to know after that?"

"Really? You want an apology." It wasn't a question, rather a statement. He cocked his head, and when he realized he obviously wasn't going to get what he wanted, he gave me an incredulous look that made me chuckle. "Fine. I'm sorry, Meredith. You're always the sweetest, most informed person in the building. No one else could find the gossip like you. You are just . . . a diamond. You blind me every time I walk through those doors. I need to wear sunglasses to look upon your beauty."

She dropped her hands from her hips. "That's much better. Now *the tea* I heard is that you threw Mr. Prodigy here—" She gestured at me with a small giggle. "—over your shoulder like a man possessed and carried him right out of some nightclub." She grinned at him, amused. "They called it a lover's tiff. You were *very* jealous of your boy toy talking to another man apparently."

"Please tell me you're joking." His voice hardened.

My spine went stiff. Fuck. I wasn't surprised. Mobsters *were* gossipers, and even though the Italians and Irish weren't entirely friends, more like acquaintances, some of them met up on occasion.

"Am I the type?" she asked, and it was the first time I'd heard her tone serious since we'd arrived.

Daire rubbed a hand down his face. "No. No, you're not." He offered her a small tilt of his head. "Thank you, Meredith. If you'll excuse us, we need to go educate some Company men about respect."

She fluttered her hand at him. "Have fun. Don't spank their pretty bums too hard. We're nearly at capacity and can't afford any more beds for them."

Daire spun on his heel and stalked down the hallway, and I was quick to follow him. We went through another set of locked doors that he used a key card—it seemed like a master key—to get through. This hallway looked like any other, except there were no doors leading into patient rooms. At the very end of the narrow hall was one door to the right, and he slammed his way through it.

Inside were ten men, all dressed in different styles of suits. Six were sitting around a circular table, two standing beside a coffee maker, and two were seated on a couch against the wall to our left. As soon as we entered, they all jumped in surprise but settled back into their chairs when they saw Daire.

I recognized one of the guys as Irving. With short brown hair and hazel eyes that always seemed angry, he wasn't the friendliest man to be around, but Sloan believed he could be trusted. He'd always told me that just because a man wasn't liked, didn't mean he was wrong for the job.

Irving grunted and hooked his thumbs in his pants pockets, standing tall. "Sir."

I didn't know which one of us he was talking to, but there was a touch of disgust in those hazel irises as they settled on me.

Daire stared around the room. "Sit down. *All* of you."

The men around the table and couch sat immediately, but the soldiers near the coffee maker walked over to join the others on the couch. When they were all seated as ordered, Daire stepped farther into the room. He opened his mouth to speak, but I grabbed his arm, effectively stopping him.

I shook my head at him. "It's my turn."

His eyebrows rose, but he tilted his head in acknowledgement and shifted out of my way.

I clasped my hands behind my back and straightened, moving closer toward the men. I kept my chin raised, hoping to look powerful. Inside, I was a mess. My stomach churned and my heart thumped rapidly. I'd never spoken this way to my uncle's men. I'd let them say what they wanted behind my back, and I might have this time, too, if I hadn't been told by the nurse that they were gossiping. I couldn't be seen as weak any longer. It was time for me to step up and be the person I wanted to be when I was boss.

"You think you have the right to disrespect me." I stared

around the room, focusing on Irving, who seemed to be the ringleader. "You think I'm *weak*."

The silence was heavy in the room.

"You're wrong." I gritted my teeth. "I'm not my uncle, but you'd be a fool to think I'm frail." I crossed my arms. "How I enjoy my personal time is no one's business, but I'm going to tell you this so you can *pass it on* like the twelve-year-olds you are."

Daire made an amused sound close to a stifled laugh.

"I'm young, but I know what I want, and I know what I am. Yes, your friends did see Daire throw me over his shoulder and carry me out of that club last night, but what they didn't see was him taking me home and fucking me." A lie, but an easy one to tell. They didn't need to know the truth. I stopped pacing and did another take of each of their faces. I tamped down a grin at the sight of their shocked expressions.

One of the men swallowed deeply, his Adam's apple bobbing. His eyes widened.

"That's *my* thing. I like a cock in my ass, and I like being manhandled when I'm having sex with someone. But don't mistake that as weakness. Just because I like to be fucked doesn't mean someone can fuck *with me* or the Company, which I will inherit. If you come for me, I will put you six feet under next to anyone else who crosses me. Daire is my toy when I choose for him to be, and we can play however I want."

I didn't miss the twitch of Daire's mouth. Good. If I was a hole to him, then he was nothing but a dick to me. He could chew on that.

"But you and the rest of the Company men belong to me." I poked my chest. "Mine. Don't forget that. If I hear any of you cowards speaking about my business behind my back again, I'll send you somewhere you'll learn what being a *little bitch* is really like."

The creak of the door had me turning in time to see Sloan

walk in wearing a deep crimson suit that matched the color of Conall's collar. Behind him, his pet leaned against the threshold.

Sloan smirked. "That explains a lot."

My cheeks flushed with scorching heat, and I refused to glance toward Daire. I didn't want to know what he thought about my little speech. "Uncle, I didn't know you were here."

"Clearly." He looked over my shoulder at his men. "Well, you heard Fionn. Get back to work."

The men scampered like roaches, striding past Sloan and Conall as fast and efficiently as they could. My heart raced, rattling hard against my ribs, and I ran a hand over my chest, willing it to slow down.

"Good job. I would've done it with less . . . language, but well said." Sloan patted me on the shoulder and walked toward Daire.

Adrenaline pounded through my veins, making it hard to breathe. I moved forward, eager to get out of the room as it pressed down around me.

When I got to the door, Conall grabbed my arm to stop me. He winked. "You had those men shitting their pants. I'm pleased, Fionn. You did good. Sloan was proud of you."

I didn't know what to do, but I forced myself to give him a small, tight smile. "Thanks. I need air. Yeah. Air."

Conall let me go, and I stumbled out of the room and headed back the same way we'd come in. I passed the nurses, and Meredith said something to me, but I didn't have the mental bandwidth to hear what.

I left through the front doors and froze, sucking in the cold fresh air as deeply as I could. My hands shook as the adrenaline began to seep out of me. Excitement took over. I'd basically told Company men to fuck off. I had stood up for myself and I was walking on air because of it.

Closing my eyes, I leaned my head back and inhaled. *Perfect.*

When the time came, I was going to dominate. The Killough

Company belonged to me. I could do whatever the hell I wanted, and Daire? Well, I would leave him alone and move on to someone who desired me back.

My moment was ruined when my phone buzzed in my pocket. I yanked it out to stare at the name that flashed across the screen.

Mom.

My heart froze and familiar pain throbbed there as I answered the call and laid the phone against my ear. "Mom."

"I need money."

I squeezed my eyes shut. Of course she did. "Why?"

"Your brothers are in college now, Fionn. They have needs." She huffed on the other end of the line and something clattered. "I don't get paid for another week, and it's urgent. Can you give me the money or not? I can ask your uncle."

I stiffened and glanced around the busy Manhattan neighborhood. Everyone went about their day, unaware of my struggles, something I was used to in my own house. My heart hurt, and as much as I wanted to tell her *no*, I'd started something I needed to finish. If Sloan found out about my stupidity, it would be another *X* in the negative column for me. After my win today, I refused to let that happen. Sloan had given her money regularly since he'd taken me in, but this was different. He gave her a set amount and never a cent more. I was the idiot who couldn't say no to her.

"How much do you need?"

10

DAIRE

Fionn's words played in my mind, an echoing voice that teased me in ways I didn't want to admit. The confidence was new and exciting, and while there was still an underlying hesitation that I was sure only I'd heard, the men would be fools not to respect the threat Fionn represented. He'd sounded more like Sloan than I was sure he'd wanted, and it was admirable to see, even if he'd admitted we were sleeping together. After my little show at the club, it was only fair for Fionn to regain some of his dignity. I owed him that much, at least.

Ignoring Sloan's reaction to Fionn's announcement wasn't going to be possible, though.

Sloan crossed his arms. "Do you have something to say?"

I ran a hand through my hair and sighed. I couldn't deny what Fionn had said, even though it wasn't technically the entire truth. Sloan didn't know as much as he thought he did, because he had no idea about my past feelings for Eoin, and he didn't know about the situation between Fionn and me now. Falling for Fionn was a mistake. I didn't want to *use* him as a replacement for Eoin.

Fionn deserved more than that.

Yet, I still had sex with him, didn't I?

I'd had ex-boyfriends who reminded me of Eoin, and I'd been fine with that. They didn't know Eoin, and they weren't related to him, either. The longest relationship I'd been in had lasted two and a half years, and we'd broken up about seven months before Fionn's eighteenth birthday party. Fionn had never met Trace, since I'd kept him far away from my work life.

Fuck. I needed to stop thinking about it. Eoin was dead.

"Well?" Sloan's hard tone shocked me out of my thoughts. "You and Fionn *are* a thing?"

Conall sidled up beside his partner, and when Sloan raised his arm, Conall snuggled against his body. "It was obvious, though, wasn't it?" He nudged Sloan with a smirk. "You even told me you thought they were fucking."

"Pet." Sloan slapped him on the ass, earning a pleasured hiss in answer. "Language."

"Are you going to gag me for using the F-word?" Conall stroked a finger down Sloan's chest. "Because I can get behind that, or should I say, *you* can get behind *me?*"

I cleared my throat to distract them from each other. If I gave them the chance, they'd turn a simple conversation into fucking in a matter of minutes, and while I didn't mind watching them have sex, this wasn't the time.

"Fionn's an adult. What happens between us is private." I smiled. "Not all of us enjoy an audience."

Conall's tongue poked out from the corner of his mouth. "Really? What do you call the whole throwing Fionn over your shoulder at the club, then? Isn't that how he got into this predicament in the first place?"

"Which reminds me. You called last night to tell me he was at Bellissimo, that you handled it. If it was a sex game, why did you bother contacting me?" The suspicion in Sloan's gaze had me shifting uncomfortably. Damn it.

"It wasn't a lie." I shrugged. "I didn't know he was going to be there, which is how it became so public. We hadn't planned on meeting there."

"And what?" he drawled, glaring. "You decided to take matters into your own hands?"

"No, he took Fionn into his own hands." Conall snickered and it earned him *another* smack to the ass, this one harder. A pained sound left him and he huffed. "I thought it was funny."

Sloan's lips quirked. "We're having a serious conversation, pet."

"What does it matter?" Conall waved his hand at me. "He and Fionn are fucking. They have their kinks, and we have ours. Let them have fun."

"It matters because Fionn represents my company." Sloan released his hold on Conall and stepped back, staring down at him with the kind of intensity that would've scared anyone who wasn't his pet. But Conall raised his chin, meeting the look with an expression of defiance. "He must not show weakness."

Conall gaped. "Really, Boss? Because I'm yours, and you show me off like you're whipping out your dick and swinging it around in the wind." He tugged at the red collar around his neck with a forefinger. "You even signed your name with this thing."

Sloan frowned. "Pet . . . ."

"You can't have double standards, Sloan. It's not fair." Conall's eyebrows furrowed and he pressed his mouth together. "If showing off your partner is okay for you, it should be the same for him. Let him flaunt Daire and their kinks, if that's what they want, but *teach* him how to look strong doing it— how to not give a shit what people might think of it. How you would, how a boss would."

I felt like I was intruding in a private argument. While Sloan had softened a lot toward Conall since he'd first claimed ownership over him, Conall didn't push many boundaries with Sloan. He respected the boss and refused to use Sloan's weakness for him to get his way. Well, most of the time. At least, when it came to business decisions.

Sloan glanced at me and waved his hand. "Go find Fionn. My pet and I have things we need to discuss."

I had a feeling instead of discussions that it would involve Sloan's cock in Conall's ass as he fucked him hard into submission. Tilting my head in acknowledgement, I left the room and walked down the hall. I passed the nurses' station again, and before I could ask, Meredith pointed in the direction of the entrance.

"Outside." Her lips pursed knowingly.

I nodded my quiet gratitude and headed out the doors that led into the waiting room, then out the entrance.

"Stop. The question is simple. How much do you actually need?"

Fionn's quiet, sad voice caught my attention, and I turned to see him standing with his back to me, still on the sidewalk but closer to the hospital's wall. His shoulders were hunched, and even though he was no more than murmuring, I would hear him in a crowd of a hundred yelling people. As much as I tried to deny it, his energy called to me.

"I know, Mom. It's just . . . that's a lot of money."

I tensed.

Fionn was talking to Annabelle?

I hadn't heard from her since Eoin's funeral, and while Sloan had told me he was giving her and the other boys a fair amount of money to live off monthly, I had always believed it wouldn't be enough for her. When Eoin was working, she'd always wanted *more*. A bigger house. A nicer car. New jewelry. Vacations in Europe. Eoin joked that she'd bleed him dry when it came to money.

"Of course I care about Deer and Bellamy. They're my brothers. But why do they need that kind of stuff? A car for Bellamy? Isn't he living on campus?" He heaved a sigh. "I know.

It's just—" He paused and listened, and his shoulders tensed. "That isn't fair. I'm taking care of business, all right? Don't do this."

My stomach squirmed with a fiery anger I didn't know I was capable of. I'd walked this Earth as a numb man for a long time, and rage was an emotion I'd forgotten how to feel. Until Fionn. It was easier and safer to live in this world as nothing more than a robot, a loyal servant to Sloan. Yet, the fury that thrummed in my chest like a drum was a welcome sensation as I realized what was happening.

Annabelle was manipulating Fionn for money.

Annabelle was making Fionn feel guilty.

Annabelle was using her son for her own gain.

No, this wasn't going to happen on my watch.

I shot forward and ripped the phone out of his hand. He gasped but didn't have time to react before I turned my back and slotted the phone against my ear.

"Annabelle?" I asked gruffly.

The sound of surprise she made was enough confirmation.

"It's Daire." Though, I suspected she already knew my voice. "If you ever call Fionn for money again, I won't hesitate to tell Sloan, and we both know how that'll go. This manipulation will stop now, or so help me God, I will make you regret it. Am I clear?"

She exhaled loudly. "Yes."

I ended the call just as Fionn launched himself at me. I caught him around the waist and lifted him like he weighed nothing, shifting him back toward the wall of the hospital. He struggled and bashed a fist against my chest, which stung but wasn't pain that would make me drop him. I'd been shot in the past and tortured in all kinds of ways, and worst of all, I was treated like a backup to my brother by my parents. A punch didn't hold a drop of the agony I'd been through.

"What did you do?" Fionn raged when I finally set him back on the ground. "Fuck. That was my mom!"

No, she wasn't. She'd stopped being anything to him the moment she'd given him to Sloan, but I understood Fionn. He wanted to hold on to the idea of her. Hope was where men went to die in these situations.

"I know who it was." I raised my arm, keeping the phone out of his reach. "And I know what she wanted. Your mother hasn't changed since the first day I met her, and she got her claws into your father. She wanted money. She always wants money."

His cheeks flooded a deep red and he winced. "So? *She's my mom.*"

"And you're her *son*," I hissed, surprising him into taking a step back with wide eyes. "It's her job to protect you, to help you, not the other way around. How long have you been giving her cash?"

He shook his head and glanced away. "It doesn't matter."

I grasped his chin in a tight hold and wrenched his head around so he was forced to look at me. "How. Long?"

"It's not for her, it's for Deer and Bell."

"Bullshit, boy." The words came out so savagely that Fionn sucked in a deep breath and took a step back, his body flush to the wall of the hospital. The expression in his stare wasn't fear, but something more animalistic—a deep-rooted desire that made my cock stir. "Diarmuid and Bellamy can take care of themselves. They're not teenagers anymore."

"Bell's twenty-two and a half. He's still basically a teen." He shrugged and the bratty tone made my spine stiffen. The urge to grab him and bend him over my knee for a spanking made my fingers twitch.

No, Fionn wasn't mine to punish. Sex was sex, punishment was different. Spanking came with trust and intimacy that I wasn't allowed to give him in that way.

"He's an adult, boy." My teeth ground together. "Your brothers don't need you to take care of them anymore."

"I'm the man of the house."

I slammed my hand against the wall near his head, and he tilted his chin up, meeting my hard gaze with his own. We were so close our noses brushed, and Fionn's breath tickled my lips.

"You're not in their house. Your mother gave you to Sloan because you were grieving, and she couldn't handle it. She should've supported you and grieved with you, but instead she was too busy spending the money Eoin put away for *you* and your education. Sloan became your guardian." I lowered my voice when he shuddered. My stare dipped to his lips, wet from his tongue, and fire burned in my belly. I was *so close* to him—I could smell my spicy cologne he'd used this morning—yet I was so far because kissing him in public was off-limits. I didn't deserve that right after everything I'd put him through. Fionn was too precious. "Your brothers got to go to college. You didn't."

"I could've," he argued, eyes narrowing. He pressed a hand to my chest, but he didn't push me away, just kept it there as though wanting to feel my heartbeat. "Sloan gave me a choice. He might be a hard man, but he was never outright cruel. He let me choose what I wanted to do with my life, and I decided to be his apprentice. I don't regret my choice."

I dropped my head and let out a sigh. Fionn was missing the point, and it was a reminder of how young he was and how different from Sloan he was. Fionn's innocence was complex and confusing. He'd seen men die and he'd watched as Sloan tore men's organs from their bodies, yet he missed his mother's manipulation. He was too pure for this world, and all I wanted to do was wrap him in a blanket and hide him away from everyone, including Sloan.

I straightened and stepped back, not missing the disappointment that flashed in his gaze. I shoved the hand not holding his phone into my pants pocket because then I couldn't reach out and touch Fionn's soft cheek, or worse, grab his face and kiss him hard.

"You don't know your mom." I tested the words in my mind first, but everything I came up with sounded vicious toward Annabelle. *She's a bitch who uses men* or *she pressured your father to stay in the mob, when he wanted to walk away and be a family man.* I didn't know how Fionn would react to my assessment. I thought about something gentler to say.

"You never got to know her because Sloan raised you." I shrugged. "You never spent time with her or your brothers, so I'm telling you this because I care about you. Giving her money won't help. It's not for Diarmuid or Bellamy, it's for *her*."

Annabelle was manipulative, and even Eoin fell for her lies.

"I know, okay?" The harshness of his tone made me rear back in shock. He glared at me and huffed, grabbing a handful of his dark hair and tugging in frustration. "Fuck. You all think I'm some dumb kid. I'm not. Not anymore. I know what she's doing, but she's my *mom*." His steam dissipated and his shoulders slouched. His sad eyes dug a hole in my chest. "She's my mom." His voice came out so quiet that I barely heard what he said. "Deer and Bell are my brothers. I can't lose them, even if I only talk to Mom when she's looking for money. Even if she doesn't want me in their lives."

I didn't know what to say, and the longer I stared at Fionn, the more I noticed the fight in his eyes. This was a man who *wasn't* as innocent as I wanted to believe, but a grown-ass adult who'd struggled in ways that neither me or Sloan knew about. He was fighting battles that we were oblivious to, and that knowledge made me see him in a new light.

"Fionn . . . . Fuck." I rubbed my face. "I didn't know."

"Of course you didn't." He chuckled unhappily and pointed at himself with his thumb. "Because I can hide things, too. You and Sloan aren't the only ones who can keep things quiet."

"Keep—"

"Don't act like you don't know what I'm talking about. You won't tell me what happened to Dad, how he *really* died." He stared up at me and snorted when I stayed silent. "If you're allowed to be secretive, I can, too."

"We're not doing it to be cruel, boy." I stepped forward, closing the distance between us again. I cupped his cheek, uncaring of the consequences. Fionn's eyelashes fluttered shut and the heat of his skin against my palm was addicting. I should've backed away as fast as I could, but I stayed there so I could whisper. "Your father never wanted you in this life. He told Sloan that he wanted you and your brothers to be free of the Company, and Sloan accepted that, agreed to it. Eoin was going to leave soon, too, but then . . . ."

His eyes flashed open. "Then, what?" He grasped my wrist tightly, fingers brushing over my pulse point. We were too close, and yet I couldn't move away. Tension sizzled between us, and the rest of the world vanished. In this moment, there was only us and the way we got lost in each other's gazes. "What happened, Daire? Please tell me."

I couldn't. No son deserved to hear how his father was killed, especially not in the way Eoin was.

Bang!

I shot around, reaching into my suit jacket for my gun and my back against Fionn's chest. He grabbed my suit jacket, holding on tightly as I pressed him against the wall. My heart pounded, adrenaline pumping in my veins, but the urge to protect him wasn't needed.

The noise came from a car. A damned backfiring car that looked ancient enough to not be allowed on the road!

I cursed inwardly and spun around again, removing my hand from my jacket. Fionn watched me, those eyes sparkling with an emotion that I didn't want to analyze or think about. I distanced myself and offered him a small nod.

"You were going to—"

I ignored him, stalking back into the hospital. I stopped at the door and glanced toward him. "Come on. Bohdan will show you around and give you a rundown on how it works."

Some of the spark in his posture disappeared and his jaw tightened. The iciness returning to his handsome face was like a knife to my heart, but I didn't dare reach out to touch his shoulder like I wanted to as he strode past. He stopped beside me and ripped his phone from my hand.

"This is mine. If you take something that belongs to me again, I'll make you regret it." The coldness in his tone made me stiffen, but I merely inclined my chin in acknowledgment.

I wanted to make a boss out of Fionn, and this was a step in that direction, but whether it was on the right or wrong track, I didn't know.

11

FIONN

I was on a mission, and nothing was going to stop me. The soldiers around the house glanced warily at me as I strode past, and while they each inclined their head—*Like Daire had done the day before, fuck him!*—they didn't stop me as I stalked down the hallways like a predator after prey. The closer I got to Sloan and Conall's room, though, the more wary the soldiers became. One looked ready to stop me as he hesitantly took a step forward, but another yanked him back with a shake of his head.

"Move," I hissed.

The men scattered like frightened mice as I passed them and finally stopped in front of my destination. Taking a deep breath, I gathered my courage and knocked on the door. Twice. Once to alert Conall I was here, and another to assert my dominance. At least, that's what I told myself.

The door swung open, and Conall stood on the other side in a pair of long red pajama pants with little hearts printed across the *very* thin material and a plain white T-shirt. His collar was still around his neck, even though it was nearing ten at night, and he was obviously getting ready for bed. Sloan was still in his office—I had checked.

Conall stared in surprise. "Hi?" He tilted his head to the side. "Are you looking for your uncle? He's still working. Something about paperwork for Elio."

"Can we talk?" I didn't wait for him to respond. I pushed past him. The guards must've reacted because when I spun around, Conall had raised his hand at someone outside the room, then closed the door.

He frowned at me. "Okay. Are you here to look through my drawers again? Let me tell you, that might get weird because they're Sloan's drawers, too. Have you ever wondered what kind of underwear your uncle wears? You'll find out if you go snooping."

Ah, a joke eight years in the making.

I would've mentioned how long it'd been since then if I wasn't wincing with a shame I didn't expect to ever feel. I'd always thought I would hate Conall, and while the jealousy still lingered, it didn't revolve so much around Sloan's pet anymore. It was easier to like Conall and *hate* Vail and Lor. I cleared my throat. "I'm sorry."

He cupped a hand behind his ear and leaned forward. "What did you say? I didn't catch that."

I huffed and crossed my arms. "I'm not saying it again."

He smirked, his nose wrinkling a bit. "Oh, you will because you want something, and I'm not going to help you until you say what you just said louder."

Fuck. I dropped my chin in defeat. The bastard knew he had me by the balls. Biting down hard on my bottom lip, I took a few short moments to ponder my options before realizing I truly had none. I sighed and finally raised my gaze to Conall again. "Fine. I. Am. Sorry. I was an ass."

"You still are." He grinned and shifted forward, bare feet padding across the thick carpet. "Luckily, I like that about you."

"You do?" I stared at him. He was joking, right?

His mouth quirked into a small smile, and he gestured for

me to follow him over to a small sitting area near the window, right behind a feature wall with a stone fireplace. He sat on the wide windowsill, stretching his legs along the ledge, while I took a comfy gray leather armchair. He'd changed up the style since moving into Sloan's room many, *many* years ago. The area itself was elegant, and they had the biggest bedroom in the house. It had plenty of light, with floor-to-ceiling windows, except for the nook that Conall had added to go with his sitting area.

"Believe it or not, yeah, I do like you, Fionn. You're a good guy, and behind that obnoxious exterior is a man who's loyal to Sloan and worries about his safety. I can respect that because I do, too."

"Oh." I shifted uncomfortably.

"Anyway, forget it. What do you want?" He relaxed and bent his knees while curling his arms around his stomach.

"Uh." All the confidence I'd had coming in here evaporated, and now I felt stupid. My cheeks heated, and I scratched the back of my neck. "I was wondering if you know Michele Scotti? He's Matteo's brother."

Conall's eyebrows rose high on his forehead. "The same Michele who flirted with you at the club? I heard the men talking before you put a stop to it."

I sighed. "Yeah. Listen, what happened between Daire and I—"

"Is none of my business." He shrugged. "You're an adult. You can do what you want." He smiled smugly. "And if you want to change it up to get some sexy Italian cock, that's your choice, as long as it doesn't affect the Company."

"It won't." I sat up straighter. "I just want his number, and maybe to talk to him."

"Phone sex?" He winked.

I held in a groan and wrung my hands together. "Maybe? I don't know."

Conall laughed. "You don't need to be embarrassed. I mean, you see me and Sloan fuck all the time."

"How do you do that?" I asked seriously, eyebrows furrowed. "In front of everyone? Isn't that . . . weird?"

He pursed his lips in thought and hummed before finally shaking his head. "At first it was a lot to handle, but I think it's hot now. I like people knowing I belong to Sloan. I want them to watch us and know Sloan's mine and he'll only fuck me from now on, you know?"

I didn't know, but I nodded anyway. Conall and I had very different ideas of what was sexy. "So, uh . . . would you happen to have Michele's number?"

He snorted and tapped his foot on the sill. "No. Can you imagine me having an insignificant man's number like that? Sloan would lose his shit, and Michele wouldn't be alive."

"Oh." Disappointment twisted in my gut and my shoulders slumped. After another conversation with Daire that had left me hot and horny and ready to be fucked—yet also gutted and alone because he didn't want to kiss me in public—I'd decided nothing with him would change. I needed a man who wasn't afraid to want me and be with me. Michele had been that person.

Conall chuckled. "But, I know someone who might. Give me a sec." He jumped to his feet and flounced over to the bed. Grabbing his phone off the mattress, he waved it at me. "I was playing a game when you knocked. *Chapters*. Have you ever played it? That shit is addicting. It's an app where . . . ." He broke off and laughed as he headed back to the windowsill and took his former position. "Never mind. You don't want to start it, trust me."

I squinted at him, not quite sure what to say. I didn't think I had any games on my phone other than the kind that involved math equations, and I was positive *Chapters* wasn't one of those.

Conall unlocked his phone and played with it for a second

before he held it up to his ear. After a moment, he smiled. "Ardan, I called Mancini's phone." He pulled the phone away and hit a button, switching it to speakerphone. The grunting in the background gave me an idea of what was happening.

Everyone was having sex but me!

"You did, sir." Ardan's calm demeanor wasn't anything new, but it was strange to hear him so controlled when he and Mancini were clearly doing something sexual.

Conall threw me an amused grin. "Mm-hmm. Is he available?"

"He's currently busy." It wasn't much of an answer, but it was the best Conall was going to get from him.

"Aw. Is his mouth full?" Conall chuckled and shifted—I didn't miss the noticeable bulge growing in his thin pants. I grabbed the chair by the arms and turned it away a little. I didn't want Sloan coming in here to see me too close to his pet, who was on his way to rock hard.

I doubted my uncle would kill me, but I was smart enough not to test my luck.

I thought I heard Mancini mutter "fuck, baby" in the background, followed by a grunt.

"Something like that, sir."

I snorted.

Conall poked his tongue out a little. "Now I'm curious."

Ardan made a humming sound and there was another grunt that didn't belong to him. "Best to stay that way, sir. We don't want to upset the boss."

Conall pouted. "Eh, I suppose not. You and Mancini know Michele Scotti, don't you?"

"Yes." A simple answer, but I supposed we were lucky to get anything right now.

"I want his number. Can you text it to me?" Conall was back to business, and he straightened, laying a hand over his hardening erection, hiding it from my view, as though I hadn't already seen it.

"On it."

"Thank you, Ardan. I love our witty banter. You're a man of many words. We should do it again sometime."

"Good night, sir." Conall's entertained voice was met with nothing but an unamused tone. The line went dead.

Conall stared at the phone with an even bigger pout. His gaze slipped to me and he shrugged. "Ardan's really no fun at all."

I held in the urge to roll my eyes. I could've told him that; although, he was clearly being sarcastic because anyone who'd had at least one conversation with Ardan knew what he was like. He was a no-nonsense, straight to the point guy, and he took his job seriously. So seriously, in fact, that he'd answered the phone when he was having sex with his partner.

A moment later, Conall's phone buzzed, and he glanced down at it. He made a sound of triumph and shook it in my direction. "Got it. Let me just . . . ." He typed quickly on the screen, then my phone vibrated in my jeans pocket. I kept the ringtone of my Samsung turned down because I hated talking to anyone but Sloan and Daire . . . and I supposed Conall now, too. "There. You now have Michele Scotti's contact information."

I tugged the phone out and checked the message, a knot of anxiety twisting in my stomach as my gaze settled on the digits. I usually liked working with numbers, but these came with expectations that I didn't know how to handle. From the age of seventeen, I'd found myself enraptured by how smart Daire was, and we had in-depth conversations about topics no one else would care about. When I turned eighteen, my interest turned into *more* and I'd figured out a way to get his attention so he'd have sex with me. After that, I'd spent another eight years in a loop of fantasies that involved me and Daire being in a relationship. *Stupid.*

This was the first time I'd ever truly considered having sex with another man.

I felt Conall's stare penetrate my skin and he cleared his throat. "Do you want to tell me about what happened between you and Daire?"

There was a sense of knowing in his eyes, like he *saw* something no one else could. I never imagined I'd want to tell Conall anything, but I didn't have anyone else to talk to, either. If Sloan found out that Daire had led me on for so long . . . . Well, I didn't know what he'd do.

"A lot of things." I clutched the phone tightly.

"But not like what you said to the men. You and Daire haven't fucked, have you?"

"We have. We do." I straightened, my cheeks heated as embarrassment swelled in my throat, making it hard to speak for a moment. "It started when I was eighteen, a few months before Sloan found you." I needed Conall to know that Daire hadn't done anything bad, that he hadn't started anything I couldn't consent to. "We've had sex ever since. *Only* sex."

"Yeah?" Conall's surprise made me shift uncomfortably in my chair.

"He didn't even care about me until I threw myself at another man, and I only flirted with the soldier to get his attention. Pathetic, huh?"

Conall shrugged. "You'd be shocked at what I do to get your uncle's attention. It's fun, though." He grinned and a dreamy expression brushed over his handsome face. "I love making Sloan jealous. Not enough for him to kill someone, but *just* enough for him to throw me over whatever flat surface is close enough and fuck me in front of everyone."

I cringed. "No offense, but I don't want to hear about my uncle fucking you. I see it enough as it is."

He laughed and waved his hand. "Understood. So, you flirted to get his attention."

"Yeah. I *was* eighteen when we started it."

Conall made a disinterested sound. "Not judging, if that's what you think. As long as you were an adult, I don't care."

"Anyway." I sighed. "We had sex at my party and it was fucking awesome."

"Did you just swear?" Conall's mouth curled into a large grin and he raised his eyebrows. "The icy Mr. Fionn Killough swore."

I rolled my eyes. "Conall, concentrate."

"Right. Sorry." He slid off the windowsill and came to sit on the other chair near me. He leaned his elbow on the arm. "Continue. You have my full attention."

I pressed my tongue to the top of my mouth as I thought about what else to say without sounding like a lovesick fool, but nothing I could think of made me sound any more mature. "He left before I woke up, but we still had sex. It became a thing, and it's nice. But I want more. Why can't we have a relationship? Why doesn't he want me? He keeps holding back. It's not even him teasing me at this point, it's him leading me on and using me." The frustration poured out with my words, and my hands moved on their own, swinging around in front of my face as I spoke. "It's infuriating. And I'm stupid because I keep hanging on to his every word and waiting for us to *be* something, but he acts like he doesn't want it. He just . . . . Ugh. I'm a hole to him, and I'm tired of being a puppy who follows him around."

By the time I was done, my chest heaved, and I fell back against the seat with a groan. I covered my face with my hands.

"Wow." Conall whistled. "And at the club?"

I laughed at the ridiculousness of what happened now that Conall asked. "Michele flirted with me. Daire showed up and he didn't like it. He said that I shouldn't have been there without guards. He picked me up and threw me over his shoulder and walked out of there as if he owned me. It was ridiculous and stupid and annoying and really fucking hot." My chest rose and fell fast and my cheeks burned warmer.

Conall's mouth quirked. "Mm-hmm. So, what you're saying is that you really enjoyed him being possessive."

I nodded, not sure what else to do. I clutched my phone even tighter.

"And now you're sick of his shit, so you're going to get with Michele?" he asked.

Again, I nodded.

"Interesting." His grin transformed into a smirk that reminded me of my uncle. "Do it. Go out with Michele. Flirt with him. Fuck him if you want. If you aren't exclusive, you have that right. Make Daire realize what he missed out on."

"That isn't . . . childish?" I winced. "Because Sloan always says I act childish."

He snorted. "You're what? Twenty-five?"

I opened my mouth to answer, but Conall was on a roll.

"I mean, you can't be with the man you want, but you aren't required to settle for less than you deserve. If Daire, a man in his *forties*, can lead you on like that, then fuck it. You can do whatever the fuck makes you happy. Make the fucker jealous. Make him a raging green monster, and while you're at it, shake your ass at him and say *you could've had this permanently, big boy, but you didn't have the balls to make me your boyfriend*, and enjoy every second."

The entire thing sounded very dramatic, and while I wasn't usually the kind of guy who liked to make a scene—*really*, I didn't—the idea intrigued me. At the same time . . . .

"I don't want to be like Daire and lead Michele on. It's not fair to him. I'm not going to use him like that."

Conall narrowed his eyes. "What happened to Fionn Killough?"

I snorted out a laugh. "What, because I'm selfish?"

"No. Fuck no. I don't think you're selfish. You're the

opposite, actually. You're protective of the people you love." He sighed. "Listen, Michele's an adult. You don't have to hurt him. There's no promises of eternal love or weddings. It's just dating and sex."

"I haven't even talked to the guy yet."

"So go." He jumped to his feet and grabbed my wrist, dragging me to stand. He patted me on the shoulders like a father encouraging his son. "Go and message him. Flirt. Plan dates. Fuck him. Anything you need to do to get Daire out of your system. Make that bastard regret ever leading you on."

I didn't think Daire had any cruel intentions, but it was interesting to witness the fierceness in Conall's eyes, a protectiveness that I hadn't seen in anyone but Sloan.

"Don't . . . don't tell Uncle Sloan, okay? I don't want him to make a mountain out of a mole hill."

Conall's ferocity evaporated and his expression softened. He squeezed my shoulders. "Believe it or not, unless it has to do with the Company or Sloan's health, I do keep things to myself. This has nothing to do with him."

My throat tightened again, and I nodded, not sure what else to say. I didn't need to find words, though, because Conall gently pushed me toward the door with understanding written all over his face. I didn't have it in me to say thank you, either, but the wink he gave me said he knew.

Once I was outside the bedroom, I sucked up my vulnerability and glared at the soldiers as I stalked past them again. I had a reputation to uphold, and I wasn't going to give them an ounce of weakness.

When I got to my bedroom, which on the opposite side of the second floor, I locked the door and threw my phone on the bed. I stared at it for a long, daunting moment, considering my options. Daire wasn't going to act on something serious, that much was clear, and the sizzling chemistry between us wouldn't be anything more than an urge

I had to continue to ignore. I didn't know *why* Daire was fighting the need, but I was also tired of pushing and getting nowhere with it.

If Michele wanted to flirt with me, then I was going to do the same back.

Inhaling deeply, I walked over to the bed and grabbed my phone. I typed a message.

> FIONN
>
> Hey. This is Fionn Killough. Hope you don't mind that I got your number. How are things?

I groaned. The message was so immature. I deleted the text and started again.

> FIONN
>
> Hey. This is Fionn Killough. Want to fuck?

I laughed at the absurdity and deleted it again. This was ridiculous. I had no idea what to say to another man that didn't involve mob business. Finally, I typed out a new message and hit Send so I couldn't rethink it.

> FIONN
>
> Hey. This is Fionn Killough. Hope you don't mind that I got your number.

Groaning, I threw the phone on the bed again and went to the bathroom connected to my room and took a quick shower. All the possible scenarios played out in my head, but I ignored the embarrassment that had me cringing. What was done was done, and now I had to roll with it.

Once I got out of the shower and dried off, I went to the bedroom and dressed in a pair of pajama pants and a plain blue T-shirt, ignoring the temptation to grab my phone and look. When I was ready to lie down, I walked over to the bed and snatched up my phone again. I drew back the blankets and slid in, my heart racing a million miles per hour as I settled onto the comfy mattress.

Finally, I looked at the screen. The sight of a message from Michele stopped my heart completely. Panic roiled in my stomach as I opened the reply.

> MICHELE
>
> Fionn who? I don't know Fionn.

I sucked in a breath, shame making me wince, but then I saw there was a second message.

> MICHELE
>
> Hah. Just joking. Hello, Fionn Killough ;) What's a sexy guy like you doing texting me tonight?

I laughed and I typed back. The words came more naturally as some of my anxiety bled away.

> FIONN
>
> Wait. Maybe I'm texting the wrong guy. Are you Sergio? The blond from Vertigo?

> MICHELE
>
> 😂😂😂

> MICHELE
>
> Nope. I'm the sexy Italian you tease every time you walk into a room. You never noticed me, but why would you? You're beautiful. Everyone wants you.

I blushed and ran a palm over my face. Michele seemed the type to compliment a lot, and I wasn't sure how to take it. I wasn't used to someone being so . . . flattering. It was as though he enjoyed making me flush, even when he couldn't see me. Not like Daire, who praised me but in a more reserved way. He was careful in the way he spoke, as though he didn't want to give me the wrong idea, yet still got in close enough that we always seemed to be touching in public.

I gritted my teeth and settled into bed. Fuck Daire. If he wanted to ignore me, then fine. At least Michele wasn't ashamed of his desire, and I was going to enjoy every second of our flirtation.

———

December came and went, and then the new year arrived with a flurry of snow. In January, Sloan gave us permission to approach the Italians. He told us to use caution with Elio because he'd been touchy lately, and he didn't know the reaction we'd be greeted with.

Mancini met us at the Folliero home in the Upper East Side. The house was a tall brownstone with a small courtyard at the front. Soldiers guarded the door and the rest of the property. As soon as Daire and I stopped the car, we were on alert, watching carefully as we exited.

Mancini was already there, leaning against the brick fence with an amused smile curling his mouth and arms crossed. Handsome was an understatement when describing him. He was naturally attractive with short dark hair, deep brown eyes, and high cheekbones. Tall with broad shoulders, he looked more like a soldier than a hit man, which made sense because from what Sloan had told me, he'd been a CIA agent before making unsanctioned murder into a career. Today was a cold January morning, so he was dressed in a thick gray wool jacket that reached his knees and black gloves.

I'd slid on a thick coat as well, but it didn't stop the chilly wind from making me shiver, and neither did the layer of clothes I wore under my suit.

Mancini straightened but kept his arms crossed. His mouth curled up at one side. "Ready to go through hell's gates?"

"We're allies, not enemies." I kept my tone even and professional. If I was excited to see Michele, I was trying not to show it. We'd been texting nearly every night since the first, and while Daire hadn't disappeared from my thoughts, Michele was a hot distraction.

Daire hadn't tried to contact me for sex, and I hadn't offered myself up to him like I had in the past. We'd acted *professional*.

"If you say so." Mancini smirked and gave me a knowing look. I suspected Ardan had told him that Conall called asking for Michele's phone number, and knowing Ardan, he would have found out *all* the details later. Which meant Mancini probably knew I'd been contacting Michele, too.

Refusing to blush, I squared my shoulders and walked through the tall brick fence and the open wrought iron gate. The guards straightened, eyeing me carefully as I strode past them, but they didn't stop me. When I got to the front door, it opened before I could knock, and Michele greeted me on the other side with a wide grin.

Wearing a green sweater and simple black pants, his handsomeness knew no bounds. His dark hair was shorter than I remembered from the club, but the new cut fit him.

"I hope you didn't dress this well to charm me," I teased.

Michele threw his head back and laughed. "I did. Do you like it? The sweater's new. You teased me about the brown one I wore on our video call last week." He pinched the green wool between his fingers and tugged it, staring down.

"The color looks good on you." I felt Daire's eyes on me, and a brief glance told me that he was glaring. A knot of guilt twisted in my stomach for enjoying the expression so much and using Michele to achieve it. I returned my attention to Michele. "It matches your eyes."

Mancini snorted in amusement. "When you two are done flirting, I've got things to do. Seduce each other over the phone, and let's get this over with."

Michele narrowed his eyes over my shoulder. "Ah, the traitor's back."

Mancini rolled his eyes. "And here I was thinking you look good in that sweater, too. Rude."

I sighed. I'd warned Sloan that bringing Mancini wasn't a good idea. After he'd killed Elio Folliero's uncle—unbeknownst to the Italians it was to protect someone—he'd been marked as a traitor. The Italians didn't like him, and from what I'd discovered, the feeling was mutual. Mancini had only joined the Killough Company because of his relationship with Ardan.

Daire's suspicious silence had me glancing at him again, but his face stayed neutral. Behind his eyes, something ugly raged, though.

Michele waved us into the brownstone. "Come with me. We'll go to Elio's office. He's waiting."

As much as I wanted to reach out and touch Daire, I didn't. Instead, I followed Michele inside. We went down a hallway to the left and toward Elio's office, which was the third door on the right. There wasn't anything amazing about this space, with the usual furniture for this kind of space, including a dark wooden desk, office chair—which Elio currently occupied—and a couple violet seats in front. On the other side of the room was a sitting area, with several purple armchairs and a coffee table between them. The carpet was a light plum, while behind Elio's desk was a wall of filled bookshelves.

The Italian don had a favorite color.

I took one of the seats in front of the desk, while Daire took the other. Mancini stood behind us, quiet as a shadow. Michele left the room, closing the door, but not before he sent me a wink. Beside Elio was Matteo, Michele's older brother and Elio's right-hand man, and he appeared as stoic as Daire. There wasn't an ounce of emotion on his face. If anything, he winced every so often in pain, which made sense considering he'd been shot a few months ago.

"Young Fionn Killough." Elio threaded his fingers together, resting his elbows on the desk. He wasn't much older than me, and if I had to guess, he was around Conall's age. Taking over as boss for his father so young, he'd achieved feats I only dreamed of. I would never want anything to happen to Sloan, but my goal was to lead like Elio. While it'd been a rocky start for him, his men respected him.

"Elio." I offered him a reserved smile. "It's been a while."

"It has." His blue-eyed gaze narrowed on me. "To what do I owe the pleasure? Sloan informed me that his apprentice would be paying me a visit, but he never mentioned why."

Regardless of his position and power, he appeared no older than he had the last time I'd seen him. He had the same youthful handsome face and short dark hair, styled precisely as he'd always done it—short and slicked back off his forehead. Wearing a blue pinstriped suit that fit him perfectly, he sat tall in his chair. He *almost* dared me to mess with his mafia.

Sloan had given us instructions to tread carefully. We'd been told to ask about Elio's businesses and poke him to see if he'd let any information slip, but my judgment said that he wasn't that stupid and Sloan knew it, too. This was a test. I wasn't going to fail.

"I'm going to be blunt with you." I laid my arms beside myself on the chair and settled into the comfortable cushions. "Because as allies, you deserve that."

Elio tilted his head, a small smile curling one corner of his lips. "I appreciate it."

"We've learned that you've been given a book. It came from Detective Diaz, and it contains knowledge about her informants, including the rat who whispered in her ear about the Killough Company. We want it."

He frowned at me and shook his head. "I'm not quite sure what book you're referring to. Would you care to elaborate?"

I hesitated. His confusion seemed genuine, and I had the

inclination to give him the benefit of the doubt. Sloan would call what I was doing weakness, but I had no reason to distrust Elio. "We came across an Italian detective, now *retired*, who told us he gave the book to your men for money. Like I said, we want it, and to be completely honest with you, the fact that you haven't shared it with us is quite disheartening from the perspective of our business relationship."

He made a disgruntled sound and threaded his fingers together, resting his elbows on his desk. "I could say the same for you. This Reyes situation is putting a strain on our business in New York. Also, this feud between Sloan and Thiago, not us, is less than great. As your allies, we're suffering the consequences."

"I understand. I'll pass on your frustration to my uncle—I promise. I can assure you that the Reyes issue will be dealt with ASAP." I raised my chin. "Now, the book?"

Elio squinted at me and sighed. "I'm not sure what you're referring to, but we don't have this book that you claim passed into our hands." He raised a finger when I opened my mouth to speak. "However, if this detective says he gave it to one of my men, I will investigate, because if he did, that means someone is hiding very valuable information from me, and I don't treat that kind of betrayal lightly."

I tilted my head in respect. "We appreciate it, Elio, and we value your friendship."

He snorted. "I like you more than Sloan."

"Don't tell him that." I smiled politely. "But I've learned a lot from Sloan. You and I are both new to this game, and we had good teachers. Your father and my uncle have been through hell and back to give us not only a future but a business to run. If it wasn't for them, we wouldn't be here."

Something akin to respect slid across his face and he nodded. "I agree. It hasn't been an easy journey." He stood and held out his hand. "Now, if that's all, I have work to do."

I rose and took the proposed peace offering from Elio by shaking his palm. We gave each other a final smile before Matteo strode over to the door, opening it for myself, Daire, and Mancini.

Daire led the charge to get out of the house, but as soon as we reached the front door and were ready to exit, Michele called my name.

I grinned as Daire spun around and glared over his shoulder. "We don't have time for this. We're busy men."

"Speak for yourself." Mancini smirked and leaned against the threshold, arms crossed and foot kicked up. "This is about to get good."

Daire shot him a glare as I turned to meet Michele.

"I had to catch you before you went." Michele lit up the room with a wide smile, but as handsome as he was, I was more interested in watching Daire from the corner of my eye. Guilt gnawed on my insides because I couldn't stop myself. Michele deserved my attention more than Daire.

"Really?" I licked my lips and tried to focus on Michele because while I wasn't as interested as I *should* be, he was still a pretty nice guy. Hot, too. It wasn't a mental strain to stare at him.

"Yeah." He stopped right in front of me and leaned down slightly, and the room seemed to fill with tension.

Daire moved closer and so did Mancini and a few of Elio's men, as though they expected Daire to hit Michele. They might not have jumped to the wrong conclusion, either.

I held my breath.

"Go out with me tonight. Have you heard of Vincenzo's Italian Esperienza Culinaria?"

"Do you mean Vincenzo's down near the Hudson?"

He winced, and I thought I might have said something insulting. "Eh, yes. That's what the locals call it, though, I personally prefer the full name. It gives the restaurant the true reputation it deserves."

"What *does* it mean?" I asked.

He chuckled. "Vincenzo's Italian Culinary Experience."

"It sounds delicious." I smiled.

"You're a busy man," Daire snapped, earning a surprised glance from me.

I frowned. "I'm not needed tonight. Sloan's got paperwork to do, and he already gave me the night off." I flicked my gaze back to Michele. "I'm available. I can meet you there."

"I could pick you up." He winked. "I've got quite the collection of cars. I'll even give you a choice on which one we'll drive into the city."

I chuckled and shook my head. "That's an unnecessary drive, and I doubt my uncle would want you on his grounds without his permission."

"Well, how am I supposed to seduce you, then?" Michele's grin was salacious, and my cheeks went hot.

"You can do that at the restaurant." I didn't look at Daire, afraid of his reaction to everything that was happening.

Mancini, on the other hand, seemed thoroughly entertained by the situation. He chuckled and let out a low wolf whistle, but I ignored him. I hated that my uncle made us bring him along. We didn't need him at all.

"Tonight at six?" Michele's eyes sparkled with wickedness that I should've been interested in seeing, but I couldn't help but peek at Daire from the corner of my eye.

Daire had his arms crossed and his jaw clenched, but he didn't look at me. His unhappiness made my stomach squirm with guilt.

Raising my chin, I focused on Michele with a smile. "I'll be there."

Daire didn't look at me for the entire drive home.

I felt like I'd done something horrible, like cheat on him. But

Daire had made it clear—we couldn't be in a relationship. You can't cheat on someone who won't date you. Yet, the remorse gnawed at my insides, a beast wanting to escape a cage, which only made me angry because *he* chose this. Not me. Now he had to live with the consequences.

When we got back to the Killough mansion, I slipped out of the sleek black car and stalked up the steps to the front door, where Mr. Hopper was waiting with it open.

Mr. Hopper gave me a short bow, but I ignored him as I stormed into the foyer and up the stairs. I heard someone behind me, but I didn't bother to look back until I was spun around by the arm.

I raised my fist, ready to strike, but dropped it immediately when I came face-to-face with Conall. If I'd hit my uncle's partner, I would be dead on the spot, nephew or not.

He grinned. "What happened? Daire's furious, and you look like someone pissed in your cornflakes. I want to know *everything.*"

I shook my head and held up my palms. I stepped back and moved toward my room. Conall's footsteps signaled he was right behind me, but I ignored him until I walked through the door into my bedroom. If we were going to have this conversation, it wasn't going to be in the hallway where every guard could hear us.

I shut the door behind him and crossed my arms. "Michele asked me on a date tonight, finally, and I accepted."

"Is that why Daire's stomping around like a kid who lost his favorite toy?" Conall looked too damned smug for his own good. He bounced on the tips of his toes.

I groaned. "He wasn't happy, but I'm tired of waiting around for him."

"Good. You should be." He walked over to the desk near the window and fell into the comfortable black office chair. I hated the furniture in my room because I always believed bedrooms were for sleeping only, but Sloan had insisted it would be useful in the future. I could never say no to my uncle. Conall spun on the chair to face me. "Do you want to know one thing I learned working in a whore house?"

"How to deep throat?" The corner of my mouth twitched. This new relationship with Conall was strange, and even though we'd become more like friends over the last month, I was waiting for the entire thing to explode in my face. If Sloan noticed the difference between us, he hadn't said a word, but there was more smiling in my direction.

"I'm naturally talented in that department." He chuckled. "Men are stupid. And yeah, that does include us." He shrugged. "We're built to enjoy sex and made to believe by society we can't love like women can. Fuck that shit. We can have as much fun as we want with fucking, but also be in love with that person, too. You wanna know how I keep Sloan's attention?"

I didn't think he'd have to try hard. He might've been right about men being stupid because I suspected Conall couldn't see how much Sloan loved him. I decided to humor him anyway. "How?"

"I make him fight for it. I don't just give in to him. Men like Sloan and Daire, they want a challenge. That's why Sloan chose me that day at the Virtue. I wasn't on offer, and he wanted someone to fight him. He was bored, and I was a game." He smirked. "I'm not saying Daire's the exact same, but that man has pushed you around for too long. You've chased him and waited for him. He's never seen you with another person. You've never threatened him with another potential lover because you were a puppy dog, panting for his attention."

"I wasn't his puppy," I snapped, although, I'd had the same thoughts.

He raised his eyebrows.

"I was his boy."

He blinked. "What?"

"His boy. He was . . . is Daddy Daire. Well, when we fuck anyway." The words sounded pathetic to my ears. I gritted my teeth. "But you're right. I'm done."

"Remember what you said to those men at the Amatory, Fionn?" Conall shot to his feet and strode toward him. *"You're* the future of this company. You're not a nobody, you're Fionn fucking Killough. Change things up. Now it's Daire's turn to grovel and chase *you*. You're in charge of your life."

A renewed vigor had me straightening, and I squared my shoulders. I smiled. "Conall, will you help me choose the clothes for my date?"

He snickered. "Fuck yeah, I will."

12

DAIRE

I couldn't stop pacing the foyer hours after I'd given Sloan a rundown of the meeting. My fingers itched, and it felt like ants were crawling under my skin. I burned to go back to the Folliero brownstone, strangle Michele Scotti, and bury his body with all the others I'd killed for Sloan. But, this wouldn't be for the boss. No, this murder would be for me.

"Problem?" Conall's smug tone caused me to freeze and glance over my shoulder. He stood on the stairs that led up to the second floor, leaning his elbow on the polished black railing.

I cleared my throat. "No, sir."

"Really?" The tone stiffened my spine. There was an underlining danger in Conall's voice I hadn't really heard from him. After a few moments, his mouth curved into a smirk. "Your mood doesn't have anything to do with Fionn going on a date with a certain Italian, does it?"

I swallowed and gripped my hands behind my back to stop him from seeing them clench into fists. "I worry that Scotti isn't good enough for him."

"Who is then? You?" He pushed off from the railing and

moved down the last few steps to the foyer before he strode toward me. He stopped mere inches away. "From what I heard, you've been leading him on for years. Maybe he deserves a man who'll give him what he needs."

"You don't know the full story." The words tumbled out of my mouth before I could stop them.

"Does Fionn?" He smirked when I didn't answer immediately. "Does Sloan?"

I stiffened. "No. Sloan's my friend and boss, but there's things he doesn't need to worry about. If you tell him—"

"I promised Fionn I wouldn't. That's the *only* reason I haven't." He narrowed his eyes at me. "But I *promise you* I will do everything in my power to get Fionn the perfect man. From what I heard, you're not it."

I stared at him for a long moment, and the last remaining threads of control I held on to slipped away from me. "I am. Fionn belongs to me."

Conall's smirk widened and he poked my chest. "Then stop being a little bitch. Do something about it. You're going to need to grovel, Daire, because he's done with your mind games. He wants a *relationship*, not a fuck buddy."

"He was never a game to me," I snapped in a way I shouldn't to the boss's pet.

He snorted and leaned in closer. "You better do something now or you'll lose him forever. Don't be a coward. Grow some balls."

I gritted my teeth but didn't leave. It was the wrong move to go anywhere near Fionn, but my heart demanded something different because it wanted what it couldn't have. If I said it out loud, I might consider my reasoning to be stupid, but I'd done everything I was supposed to my entire life. I'd kept my family afloat when Aodhan had gone off to do something reckless. Following my brain over my heart kept me alive.

"What's going on?" Sloan came walking down the hallway to

the left of the grand staircase, his suit jacket missing, leaving him in his white dress shirt with the sleeves rolled to his elbows and black pants. He looked good, but there was never a time when Sloan didn't. I had grown up listening to men and women swoon over my best friend.

Sloan walked over to Conall, who tilted his head back to receive the kiss Sloan dropped on his lips.

Conall smirked. "Daire and I were just talking about taking what we want."

"Really?" Sloan's ocean blue eyes slid from me back to him. "And what do you want, pet?"

Conall made a show of slowly licking his upper lip as he raised a hand to play with his collar. "I think you know what, Boss."

Sloan slid a thumb over his mouth, chasing after his tongue, and Conall grinned, playfully nipping at Sloan's finger. "Hm. You're a tease. What am I going to do with you?"

Conall's gaze went back to me. "Take what *you* want. We all know what it is. Otherwise, someone else might get it instead."

Even though he was clearly talking to Sloan, I was also aware his infuriating advice was directed at me, too. If Sloan noticed Conall pointing the words at me, he didn't say anything as he grabbed Conall and lifted him up against his chest. Conall laughed and wrapped his legs around Sloan's waist, arms around Sloan's neck.

"No one gets you but me, pet." Sloan's voice came out as a growl, and then he slammed his mouth against Conall's. Their kiss was intense, and Sloan used his grip on Conall's ass to keep his pet pressed against him.

My desire for Fionn swirled deep in my stomach.

Something snapped inside me as I watched Sloan walk off with Conall in his arms. Throwing aside every rational thought I'd had in my head, I stalked up the stairs. The few guards I passed gave me suspicious stares before averting their eyes.

There were certain people they couldn't question—I was one of them.

I only got halfway down the hall toward Fionn's room when he slipped out the door, dressed in a way that had my mouth watering. The jeans melded with his long legs and ass, showing off every curve he had, while his shirt was the tightest I'd ever seen on him. The black material clung to his sinewy torso, and as he turned toward me, I lost my breath and came to an abrupt halt.

He squared his shoulders and stormed toward me until he was in my face. "Move."

"No." I gritted my teeth and crossed my arms. "You're being ridiculous, boy."

"Me? Ridiculous?" He laughed and mirrored me by folding his arms. His eyes flashed with a rage unlike anything I'd seen from him. "Move, Daire, or I'll make you."

I didn't. I stood firm, and even though I was acting like a selfish prick after denying us both for so long, I couldn't bring myself to shift out of his way.

Fionn was *not* going on a date with Michele fucking Scotti, the Italian bastard who could flirt the boxers off a saint.

Fionn stepped forward, and for a moment, I thought he was going to try and shove me, which wouldn't have gone well, but he rocked back again at the last minute. "You don't get a choice anymore, Daire," he hissed low enough that none of the guards would be able to hear him. His mouth curled and there was a smirk that reminded me more of Conall than my sweet Fionn. "I let you lead me on like a naive idiot. You fucked me, and I enjoyed our time together, but I want more. I'm done waiting. I'm going out on a date, and somewhere around dessert I'll beg Michele to fuck me. Then later, we can go public, like you and I should've years ago." He poked me on the chest. "You. Are. A. Coward."

Fionn stepped backward and went to stalk around me, but I

seized his arm and spun him, slamming him against the wall. He huffed out a gasp, and two of the guards near the staircase straightened and began to walk toward us, but Fionn held up a palm at them, effectively stopping them.

I didn't care if they came for him. I would lay them flat on the floor, and they would learn *why* I was second-in-command. Most of the younger Company men had no idea what I could do or what I'd *done* to get where I was now, including Fionn. They saw a businessman, not a killer.

I grabbed his face between my fingers, squishing his lips until he looked like an adorable goldfish. "Scotti doesn't get to touch you."

"And you do?" he spat out, even though I still had a firm grip on his face. "You had the chance. For over *eight* years, I sniffed behind you like a puppy—pathetic, begging for scraps, *longing* for more from you. I wanted to be your partner in *everything*. You don't deserve me."

"You're right, I don't." I steeled my jaw. "But you're mine, Fionn, you've always been mine."

"I *was* yours," he snarled. "Not anymore. Michele can put his cock wherever he wants because at least he treats me like I'm a fucking human being."

I growled between my teeth. Every ounce of guilt inside me ate at my gut because he was right, and I hated myself for what I'd done. "I tried to push you away more than once."

"And then, you dragged me back in. I'm nothing but a gullible fish you caught on the line you threw out as bait." He finally slapped my hand away, but I gripped his throat instead, and he left my fingers pressed there. "Don't worry, that wasn't all your fault. I was the idiot who thought you actually wanted me." He choked on a laugh, the toxic sadness and anger seeping through it, poisoning me until I couldn't breathe. "You listened and taught me lessons, and I latched on to you because you were acting like you were invested in my future. I considered you *my* . . . Daddy. Daddy Daire." He gnashed his teeth and the fire in his eyes was directed at me. I deserved this, didn't I? "But now I'm going to find a new Daddy. What do you think about Daddy Michele? Has a nice ring to it, doesn't it?"

"Boy, stop pushing," I growled out. Fury swept through me in a blazing inferno, an overwhelming and unbearable heat that I couldn't control.

"What are you going to do about it?" He tilted his chin. "Come on, Daddy Daire. Show me how *little* I mean to you."

My grip on his throat tightened, and Fionn gasped. "I care about you, boy."

He needed to know. He *had* to know how much he meant to me. Desperation clawed at me. I couldn't lose him. Not now.

"Do you?" He pressed his lips together. "Prove it. Get on your knees, right here, right now, and suck my dick. Show me that I have your loyalty. Show *me* what I mean to you."

"Stop this." I glanced at the men from the corner of my eye. The two standing closest to the stairs were Healy and Walsh, and they were two of the most trusted guards, but that didn't mean a damned thing. I didn't want to share Fionn like Sloan did with Conall. Fionn deserved to be worshiped by only one man—*me*.

"Come on, Daddy Daire." His grin was mean, and my heart hurt. This wasn't my boy, and the realization of how much pain he was in only made the agony of my breaking heart worse. I'd fucking done this because I'd convinced myself I was doing the right thing. *Fuck.* "Get on your knees and show me you think I'm worth it." He tilted his chin. "Or are you a coward?"

I stared at him for a long moment before I finally dropped to my knees. It was a strange sensation to be in front of Fionn like this, and he obviously hadn't expected me to actually do it because his eyes widened and he let out a shaky breath, back pressed tightly against the wall.

"If this is what you want, boy, then I'll happily do it because I am loyal to you. I always have been."

He stayed silent as I reached for his jeans, unbuttoning them and grasping the zipper between my fingers, then tugging it down slowly. From the corner of my eye, I noticed the guards watching, and while I wasn't one for public displays, I didn't care, either, because maybe they'd spread the word that Fionn was *mine*.

The apple in Fionn's throat bobbed and he opened his legs with uncertainty. If this was what he wanted, then I would do it, if only to prove to him that he belonged with me.

Hooking my fingers into his waistband, I yanked down his jeans and underwear until they were around his thighs. His cock bounced free—already half hard and flushed red at the tip. Over eight years of having him didn't dull his beauty. Everything about him was exquisite.

"Well?" Fionn had regained some of his confident composure, lips pursed as he wrapped his fingers around his cock, tapping the head against my mouth. "Get to work, Daddy Daire."

If I wasn't on my knees in front of some of our men, I'd be proud of Fionn for standing tall and exuding the energy of a mob boss. Hell, I was always proud of him. Mouth curling into a half smile, I batted his hand away and took hold of his cock around the base, holding it out so I could suck him between my lips. I licked across his slit, watching the shudder that worked its way through him. The taste of precum lingered on my tongue and I swallowed.

I trailed kisses down the length of his cock, tongue darting out to taste and trace the lines across his silky skin. Cupping his balls, I squeezed, and a sinful moan spilled from his lips. He threw his head back and clonked it against the wall.

"Fuck." He trembled.

I wished I could stand and pull him into my arms, but I stayed where I was, where I *belonged*, at Fionn's feet.

I took his cock into my mouth again, stroking my tongue on the underside of the head, before sucking him in deeper until he was touching the back of my throat. He grasped my hair, then moaned and his grip tightened.

Pain exploded from my scalp as he tugged on my strands, but it added to a buildup of need inside me that had been growing since I'd seen him walk out of the room dressed good enough to eat.

I pulled away to lick the tip before tilting my chin back to stare up at him.

"Is this what you want, boy?" I murmured, swiping a line up his cock and across his slit.

Fionn whimpered and bit down on his bottom lip. "Yeah. It's where you deserve to be after the bullshit way you treated me."

"You're right," I murmured, nuzzling the side of his length. I laid a couple of kisses along his hardness and watched him shiver. "I'm sorry, boy. Let Daddy Daire make it up to you. Let *me*."

He snorted, clearly in disbelief. It hurt that he didn't trust me, but I didn't blame him. I'd royally fucked up. "You'll be more than making it up to me. You'll be begging for forgiveness until I say it's enough."

I laid my hands on Fionn's thighs and ran my palms along them, getting a good feel of hard yet wiry muscle beneath. I couldn't get enough, wanted to touch his skin all day, every day. I slid my right hand under him until I was where I wanted to be and pressed my finger to his hole.

He bit his lip hard enough that it began turning white and spread his knees farther, giving me more access to work with. He quivered and his chest heaved in deep, fast breaths. "Do it. Lube in the pocket of my pants."

My heart gave a painful tug. He was going to use that tonight

—with Michele. I'd nearly lost him. The reality was a baseball bat to the chest. I held back a gasp that threatened to slip out.

I licked my lips and pulled my hand back so I could grab the lube packet out of his pocket. Once I had the foil open and lube on my fingers, I returned my hand to its former position. I nuzzled his cock again, tongue dragging along the hard flesh, before I pushed my finger inside his tight hole.

A moan slipped out of him. I couldn't decide what I wanted to do more—watch every reaction I dragged from my boy or suck him off until he exploded in my mouth.

He'd given me an order, though, and I wasn't going to ignore it. No, I wasn't going to *ignore him* anymore. I'd done enough of that for a lifetime, and he deserved more. I'd be a better Daddy for him.

I took Fionn's cock back into my mouth, sucking the head before I took the entire length in. He shuddered and jerked forward, his cock shoving deep into the back of my throat. I choked, but he pushed in deeper until he was halfway down my windpipe and my nose was pressed into his groin. He stayed there, his hand at the back of my head holding me in place, and I gagged, but stayed perfectly still. I was at his service. I shoved my finger into his hole even deeper, searching for that magic bundle of nerves that would make my boy lose his mind.

He deserved my submission in this way. I'd give him the world, if only to say sorry for all the past mistakes and the pain I'd caused him. I'd *hurt* him and that destroyed me. Fucking idiot.

The moment my finger hit his prostate, he trembled and moaned. His cock exploded, filling my mouth with delicious creamy cum that I swallowed down effortlessly. Usually, I took pleasure in receiving a blowjob, and while I gave when I could, over the years he'd preferred to do the worshiping.

Now Fionn didn't ask, he didn't give, he'd *demanded*.

He release me, and I retreated.

I licked up the final drops of cum and sat back on my knees. I pulled my finger out of him and stared up at him. "How was that, boy?"

Fionn shivered where he leaned against the wall and rolled his head, as though still escaping the last throes of his release. Exhaling, he reached down to pull up his jeans, but I slapped his hands out of the way and did it for him, going as far as zipping and buttoning him up.

"I'll think about it." He straightened and swiped his tongue over his bottom lip. His knees shook, but he kept his position above me. "You will hear from me."

He went to leave, but I jumped to my feet and grasped his arm again, spinning him around. "You're not still going on a date with Scotti," I growled.

Fionn's eyes turned to flint. "Yes, I am. If you think I'm going to forgive you after one blowjob, then you're insane." He leaned in. "You fucked me for years and used me when you should've treated me like a goddamned prince, *Daddy* Daire," he said, voice lowered. "You don't get to be let off the hook so easily. So yes, I'm still going on a date with Michele. Now, if you'll excuse me."

He went to turn again, but I kept my hold on his arm.

No! Fuck no. I wasn't going to lose him to Michele's foolish romantic gestures. I couldn't. Panic held my lungs hostage and breathing felt like walking through fire. It burned. It hurt. I was going to lose Fionn if I didn't act.

I needed to tell him the truth. "I was in love with your father."

He froze. "What?"

"Fuck." I ran my hands down my face and sighed in defeat. Maybe I'd lose him by telling the truth. "That's why I didn't want a relationship with you. I was in love with your father, and I didn't want to use you as a replacement, boy. I was afraid that by being with you, I'd make you one."

He blinked slowly. "Are you . . . fucking kidding me?" He spun around and shoved me back a few steps. The anger in his gaze was a fire so hot that it could've burned me into ash. I'd deserve it. "You let me pant after you like a fucking dog because you loved my father and thought you were sparing my feelings because you didn't want to *use* me?" He laughed abruptly, and the guards nearby stared at him as though he'd gone insane. I didn't blame them. The sound was unsettling, and the terror I felt hearing it worked its way deep into my bones. This wasn't my Fionn.

Maybe he had finally lost all sense of reality.

He was mad and had every right to be.

"That is the most ridiculous excuse I've heard in my life."

"Boy—" I started to advance, but he held up his hand.

The smile fell off his handsome face and his eyes went wild with rage. They flashed dangerously and he became perfectly still. "I don't give a flying fuck that you loved my father. Hell, you could've fucked him for all I care." The pure agony in his voice ripped me into shreds.

He stalked forward and pointed an accusing finger at me. His usually beautiful, flawless face had turned a blotchy red, and moisture was caught in his eyes. "But you broke my heart. All because you were feeling guilty that you had sex with me? Thought you were using me as a replacement for a father I never knew well? You're selfish. You could've come to me and told me, but instead you chose to be a coward and hide. It's been over eight years, Daire. *Eight years* of me pining for you— desperate for more. You *took* my virginity."

He didn't cry, but I realized it was furious tears that flooded his eyes.

I froze, his words echoing in my head. *Virginity?*

"What?"

His laugh was manic. "You were my first. I gave my everything to you."

I wanted to reach for him, to fall back on my knees and apologize and beg for forgiveness. I'd deserve it if he walked away, but I couldn't let him. Desperation wouldn't let me. He was mine and I wasn't going to let another man have him.

Yet . . . I fucked up. He was a virgin? How didn't I know? I should've been gentler with him, took it slow. I didn't deserve his forgiveness. I swallowed around the emotions that lodged in my throat, making it hard to breathe or speak.

"You were the only one I ever slept with. I never wanted anyone else." His voice broke and his glare intensified.

"I had no idea. Fionn, you should've told me. I thought—shit." My head was a mess.

He stared at me for a long moment. "You are weak." He stepped back again.

The sharp, angry words hit their target—my vulnerable heart. I flinched. Ouch.

"You could've had me, but never again. I'm not your boy anymore. You don't get to tell me what to do. You've had enough chances. *This*—" He gestured between us. "—is done."

Fuck, what could I do? How could I show him that I'd changed, that I wouldn't hurt him again? I would kill any man who touched him. Despair tore at me from the inside, shredding me until I felt wretched in a thousand different ways. This wasn't how it was going to happen. The only way we'd be apart was in death.

When he went to walk away, I grabbed his arm again and slammed him back against the wall. He aimed a fist at me, but I caught his wrists and pinned them against the wall above his head.

He writhed when I pressed my full weight against him. We panted as we struggled, his chest heaving. A rush of adrenaline swept through me as need had my cock throbbing. The hard-on that nudged me said he wasn't really interested in pushing me away.

"You. Are. My. Boy." I nipped his earlobe, and he sucked in a breath. "You're right. I *was* a coward, and more than that, I was an idiot who made the biggest mistake of my life. I fucked up bad. I hurt you, but not anymore. I'm going to make it up to you, sweet boy. I won't let you go to Scotti because you're mine. I own your body—your ass, your mouth, and that spicy attitude of yours." I brushed a kiss across his lips, *needing* him to see my hunger but also my love for him. "I can't wait to spank that feistiness out of you. I'm your Daddy, and you're *my* boy."

"All those pretty little words and empty promises. You think I should believe them? What are you going to do if I don't?" he snapped. "Do you even have the balls to do it?"

The challenge stoked a fire in the pit of my belly, and I growled before I threw him over my shoulder.

Fionn kicked and nearly got me in the balls, but I managed to keep a hold of him as I walked toward his room.

"I'll show you what I'm going to do, boy." I slapped his ass— *hard*—and he moaned. It was the prettiest sound I'd ever heard, and my cock thrummed with need. My entire body was alight with lust, goose bumps prickling over my arms. "And by the end of the night, you'll only be calling me Daddy Daire again."

"Never."

I smirked. We would see about that.

13

FIONN

I gasped when Daire dropped me back on my feet and shoved me against the inside of the bedroom door. His mouth was on mine, sucking the life out of me with a kiss so poisonous it left my knees weak. I was desperate for his touch. I could never get enough.

I wanted more.

So much fucking more.

I grabbed a handful of his shirt and tugged him closer until our bodies were nearly melded together. I tilted my chin back to gain better access to his sinful mouth, and we ate each other's lips like we were starving men. Having Daire against me felt like taking a drug after years of being clean, and I needed him *inside me*. I wanted to crack open my chest and bury him deep in the cavity because he was already my beating heart.

"Fuck me," I growled into the kiss. "That's an order."

He chuckled and nipped my bottom lip. "Whatever you want, boy."

I shoved him, and he fell back a few steps, confusion passing over his face, but I didn't wait for him to say anything before pushing him again.

Daire's expression hardened. "What are you doing, boy?"

I stepped forward to do the same exact thing again, but he caught my wrists this time. His strength sent a shiver down my spine.

I smirked.

"Are you pushing me on purpose?" he growled, low in his throat.

"You're a Daddy. Figure it out yourself." I struggled, but Daire's grip was firm, and he wouldn't let me go anytime soon. I would have bruises by tomorrow morning. The thought sent a shiver of excitement through me. "Everyone tiptoes around me and thinks I'm weak. They treat me like a child throwing a tantrum, and they don't listen. You are the only one who handles me like an adult. Don't get scared now, *Daddy Daire*."

I wasn't weak and I'd show him. He could toss me around, and I'd fucking thank him for it. Right now, I needed him to be my Daddy, the only man who was allowed to control me.

He stared for too long, and my heart battered against my ribs as I waited. Just when my hope that he would give me what I wanted was about to crumble, his mouth curled up in the right corner. "No."

I frowned. "No?"

"I take the lead in the bedroom. You are my boy, and I will treat you how I see fit. You've been a brat, and you've pushed and prodded for a reaction from anyone. I *saw* you, my sweet Fi."

I startled at the nickname and swallowed, my lips dry. The name was juvenile, but I didn't mind it coming from his mouth. Anyone else wouldn't get away with it so lightly.

"This temper tantrum stops now." He yanked me close, breath tickling my cheek. "I'll make sure of it." He laid a kiss on my jaw. "I'm going to step up and be the Daddy you need."

I laughed at the absurdity and tried to tug my wrists out of his hold, but it was useless. He should've done that from the beginning, when I first gave myself to him. I wanted to hate him for everything he hadn't done, but *I loved him.* "If you think—"

"I don't think, boy. I know. Come here." Daire dragged me toward the bed, and as much as I pretended to struggle, I wasn't trying to escape. A burst of pleasure streaked through me, and my tired dick twitched, ready to rally for another round of mind-melting orgasms.

He shoved me toward the bed, and I went flying face-first onto the mattress. I started to turn, but he was right behind me, a hand placed in the middle of my shoulders holding me flat against the Italian woven blanket.

"Stay right there, boy." He licked a stripe up my neck below my ear.

I grunted and tried to bat his arm away but froze when a hand came down on my ass. I gasped, the breath *whooshing* from my lungs. "Did you just spank me?"

"I'm going to do more than that, boy." He held me down and playfully patted my ass. "Lift this cute peach."

I was tempted to tell him no, to remind him that he didn't deserve a single thing, but I wanted Daire inside me. I would do anything to get it. This wasn't about him, but rather about me and everything I'd *earned.* I lifted my hips.

He reached underneath me to pop the button and pull at the zipper on my pants before he yanked them past my hips. He tugged the clothing all the way down my legs. When the material bunched around my ankles, he got rid of my shoes, then finished the job of extracting the pants. My underwear followed the same path until I was bare assed on the bed, my dick pressing insistently against the soft blanket.

Daire stood and got rid of his jacket before taking the time to roll up his sleeves to his elbows. I couldn't help but twist to look at him and appreciate the view of his forearms, straining with protruding veins under black ink that had my mouth watering.

Fuck.

I wanted him.

He had a glint in his eyes as he returned to the bed. His hand was back on my asscheek, but this time he was rubbing his palm in a slow, teasing circle, the heat of his skin sending sizzles of need from my ass through my entire nervous system. My brain was ready to short-circuit, and we hadn't even begun.

Fuck.

I should've gone out and made him jealous earlier. If Daire kept going like this, I would come again embarrassingly fast.

I wriggled, and he slapped me across the ass. The sting made me freeze again, and my mind went blank. My dick surged, blood traveling south and straight to my rock-hard cock. "Fuck."

"Language."

I moaned. After another crack, his hand licked heat across my ass. I trembled, tingles spreading over my skin.

"Fuck off. You've never cared," I grunted out, half tempting him to make another move. Just because I let him touch me again didn't mean I was letting him off the hook. He had a long journey full of groveling in his future.

"Fine, boy. You asked for this." When his palm came down on my bare ass again, the sound echoed around the room. My asscheeks jiggled under the force. The mixed feeling of pleasure and pain burst inside me. My dick jerked where it was trapped, and I rocked forward, a needy whimper spilling from my lips before I could stop it. I cursed myself and sent a glare over my shoulder at him.

I wasn't going to give Daire what he wanted.

Not until he'd earned it.

"Is that what you call spanking?" I raised my chin and laughed. "I'm sure Michele could do better than that. Maybe I should go find out."

"Boy." He shook his head and chuckled.

I frowned because it wasn't the reaction I was expecting. I went to move, but Daire held me down and slapped me across the ass again, this time hard enough that it had to have left a handprint. I hissed and my insides throbbed.

"You're going to regret saying that."

I hoped he was right.

Daire used his hand as a weapon, striking my tender flesh with his palm until I was writhing with excruciating need. Heat exploded from my asscheeks, and my balls drew tighter to my body, threatening a release I didn't want before he got inside me.

"Fuck me," I moaned out desperately, shuddering under another firm smack across the ass.

"You don't get to tell me what you want right now." He brought down his palm again, striking a spot on my cheeks that was already hot and deliciously painful. "Not after the insults you threw at me."

I wriggled and glared over my shoulder. My dick pulsed, and I clenched my ass, trying to hold back the orgasm threatening to rip through me—from a spanking, no less. "Please." I swallowed and huffed. "Please, Daddy Daire. *Please.* You *owe* me."

He paused, hand caressing my right cheek, and glanced at me with a frown. "Boy. Fionn. Listen to me." He tickled his fingers up my spine, and I shivered. "I am sorry and will make up for the hurt I caused you. I will be the man you need, and I will support you the same as I do with Sloan, but what you need to understand is in this bedroom, you are my boy. I am your Daddy. *I* am the one who calls the shots. I choose what you need and deserve. So, while we're playing or having sex, you can tell me what you want, but don't try to guilt me for my mistakes. You can do that all you want outside of this room, and I'll be sure to make up for it, but when you're my boy, I'm in charge."

Guilt clocked me in the stomach, and I flinched. As much as he *had* been in the wrong and I wanted him to make up for it, I hadn't meant what I'd said to sound that way. Not really. I never wanted to manipulate Daire into anything he didn't want to do, no matter how furious I was with him. While I *should* be good at that type of game, because Sloan used all sorts of tricks to his advantage, I never wanted to do that with Daire. Ever.

Yet his words brought tears to my eyes. He was my Daddy. This man who I'd loved for eight years was finally *with me* in every way. He was promising me a future. Forever.

"I'm sorry."

"Don't be." He brushed his lips across the burning skin of my asscheek and continued to rub up my back. "I understand your anger. I'm mad at myself, too. We'll talk about it later. For now, let me be the Daddy you need."

I licked my dry lips. "I . . . . I don't know what that involves. When we've had sex, it was amazing, and I enjoyed calling you Daddy Daire, but I don't know what it really means."

"I don't know everything, but I do know it means that as your Daddy, it's my job to take care of you. The rest we can figure out. Together." He leaned down to lay a kiss at the base of my spine, then licked up the length of my back. "You've been pushing since Conall came into the house, begging for this, and I was stupid and let it slide."

"Then, why didn't you give it to me? Why now?" I hated how my voice wobbled, but despite the heartache, he always made me feel safe. I could be vulnerable because he never judged me when we were together. I buried my face against the pillow rather than look at Daire, but I raised my mouth enough that he could hear me. "Why weren't you the Daddy I needed you to be?"

"I thought I was doing the right thing." He sighed. "Keeping distance. I'd let you call me Daddy, and we didn't need to get deeper into the lifestyle. I was always a step through that door, wanting you and needing you and living the Daddy life with you, but also trying to stay away from you so I didn't hurt you. I ended up doing that anyway."

I twisted to look at him. "So, as your boy, it's *my* job to tell you that you were in the wrong this time."

His mouth twitched and he nodded seriously. "You're right. Thank you." He smoothed his hand up my back again, fingers tickling my sensitive skin, then went higher to card his fingers through my hair.

I wouldn't get over all the years of pain quickly, but I trusted him to make it right. I'd ached for this relationship for too long to let it slip through my fingers. He'd have the rest of our lives to be better.

I shivered under his touch, then pouted. "Can you fuck me now, Daddy Daire? It's been too long."

"Yes, my sweet boy. For you, I can." Daire grabbed me by the hips and flipped me. My world spun and my stomach knotted with anxiety now that I was on my back. My breath caught in my throat, and I tried hard to swallow around the nerves that had begun to multiply. Any confidence I had earlier disappeared now that I was below him, staring up at my Daddy.

Daire smoothed his palm up my thigh and smiled—that was all it took for my heart to skip a beat. How could I be so in love with the one man who'd hurt me so much? When I was younger, Sloan had told me love was a weakness and nothing but pain—I now understood what he meant. Yet, Sloan still succumbed to the temptation of loving, and I did, too. Hell, I'd been in love since the first time Daire kissed me.

He stared at me with devotion that shouldn't have been possible, eyes full of promises that had me squirming in delight. He leaned down to kiss the inside of my knee, then my thigh. "Lube still where it always is, boy?"

I let out a harsh breath. "Yeah. In the drawer." I pointed shakily at the nightstand on the left side of the bed. It had been over a month since we'd fucked. Did he think I'd brought another man in here?

He hummed and kissed my thigh again before sliding off the bed. I sat up to watch him. My heated ass rubbed against the soft blanket and a shiver slid down my spine.

With a smirk, he opened the top drawer. My cheeks burned as I thought about what was inside—two dildos, lube, and condoms—and clenched my eyes shut. The dildos were new, since I'd missed Daire's cock in me over the time we'd been apart.

Daire raised his eyebrows in surprise. He threw the lube on the bed beside me.

"We'll be using those toys at a later date," he growled out, his tone going deep and guttural. "Get rid of that shirt, boy."

I shuddered, ripping off my top and throwing it to the floor.

He unbuttoned his shirt slowly, revealing tattoos, along with the rest of his body. My gaze traveled over his chest, unable to stop on one design because there was so much to see. Every time I looked, I found something new. Now that we were taking things more seriously, I craved a quiet moment to lick and trace every line that worked its way over his sculpted muscles.

"Good." His eyes darkened as he got to the bottom button. He unrolled each shirt sleeve before sliding it off his shoulders, and I couldn't look away even if I *wanted* to because the sight was too delicious.

He went for his pants next, and he took too long as my patience unraveled. His movements were slow and teasing. His fingers brushed the buckle of his belt as his mouth curled deeper into a smirk.

I bit down on my lip and stayed still, being the *good boy* that Daire insisted I was, because if I rushed it, then he would only go slower. I wanted to see him naked again.

Finally, he unbuckled his belt and unbuttoned his pants. My

breath caught in my throat. Daire was the most beautiful man I'd ever set eyes on, and I never wanted to look away.

When he was finally naked, I licked my lips. His hard dick stretched out from his body and curved a little to the right. The head was flushed red and precum built at the slit.

My mouth watered.

"Fuck. Let me have a taste?" My words were breathy, and I winced at how desperate I sounded.

"No." He stalked forward, dick bouncing as he shifted closer, and carded his fingers through my hair.

I moaned as my eyes slipped shut. His nails scratched lightly over my scalp, and the simmering pleasure burned hotter in my stomach. I didn't know how long I'd last. I'd prepared for this moment with *Michele* tonight, not Daire. Being with my Daddy made every touch so much sexier.

"I want to fuck you, boy."

"You can have me any time you want me now that you've wised up." The words slipped out before I could stop them and my eyes shot open again.

His mouth twitched. "Hm. I really do need to spank you into being a good boy, don't I?"

I tilted my head and smiled. "Just making sure I chose the right Daddy."

His hand shot out and captured my throat, *just* tight enough to steal my breath and make me gasp. My dick jerked and I trembled under his hold.

"I'm the *only* one for you, boy." He slammed his mouth over mine—the hard press of his lips was violent and needy.

I whimpered and returned his kiss just as ferociously. Spreading my legs, I made room for him.

Daire took the welcoming gesture and slid in between them. He lay on top of me, our dicks sliding against each other as we rutted. I wanted *this* so badly that I thought I'd die if I didn't get it soon. I'd waited too long, and I deserved Daire.

"I'm going to fuck you now, boy," he growled against my mouth.

I moaned. "Please."

He trailed kisses over my jaw and down my neck.

My entire body went weak. I was too far gone to worry about the embarrassing sounds escaping me because everything felt so fucking amazing. I couldn't get enough. I *needed* more.

He grabbed the lube and flicked open the lid before sitting back on his knees. He pumped a couple of drops of the liquid onto his fingers. "You ready?"

I nodded fast. "Yeah. Do it."

He raised his eyebrows and almost immediately, I knew what I'd done.

"Please, Daddy Daire."

"Good boy," he murmured.

The words went right to my core and twisted. They repeated over and over in my head, and I couldn't get enough of him. I was his good boy.

I tilted my hips as he guided two fingers to my ass. The breach of his digits in my hole created an explosive reaction inside me. An array of heat and pleasure assaulted my stomach, and every inch of skin was too sensitive to touch. My dick jerked and slapped against my abs, and I groaned before spreading my legs wider.

He was taking too long, but I didn't dare complain in case he decided to stop. His fingers were second-knuckle deep and stretching me just right. I wriggled as waves of heat weaved their way through me and straight to my balls.

Fuck. How much longer would I last?

"Shh. Good boy." Daire kissed the inside of my knee before he pulled his fingers out. He reached for the lube again, and he *finally* slicked his dick up. It was about time. I was going to combust.

I couldn't look away. I didn't *want* to do anything other than stare because Daire's dick was the sexiest thing I'd ever seen in my life. Okay, everything about Daire was fucking sexy. I'd watched my fair share of porn, but none of the dicks I'd seen had anything on Daire's. "Let me get a condom—"

"No," I said sharply, shaking my head. "Please, Daddy Daire. I haven't been with anyone else, you know that. You're the only one. I want this, I want *you*. Please. Give me what I need."

He stared at me for a long moment, then nodded. "If you're sure. But remember—"

"Daire, don't lecture me right now." I hated how pleading I sounded. "Just fuck me like I mean something to you."

He smiled and dipped to slant his mouth over mine. We kissed aggressively, and I hadn't even realized he had lined his dick up to my hole until he was pushing inside. I broke the kiss, gasping, and threw my head back as pain and bliss punched me in the stomach.

I whimpered, delighting in every second of the stretch as Daire filled me. I wrapped my arms around Daire and held tight, my fingers clawing at his back. Our lips melded together again in another deep, fierce kiss that had my toes curling and my mind turning to jelly. I wrapped my legs around his waist, holding on in case he decided to back away. I couldn't let him go, not after getting a taste of this rapture.

Daire didn't retreat, though. He pushed deeper until his balls were snug against my ass. His mouth claimed ownership over mine, nipping my bottom lip and swiping his tongue over the top before shoving in. Outside the bedroom, he would be mine, but behind closed doors and away from our men, he was my Daddy Daire and I was his boy.

His width spread me and gave me exactly what I needed and wanted. He kissed the corner of my mouth. "You're so perfect, boy. Tight, just for Daddy. *Only* for Daddy. Am I clear? No one else gets this hole. It's mine. You're mine."

I shuddered and raised my chin, then grinned. "Prove it, Daddy. Make it worth my time."

Daire laughed deeply. He started slow, each thrust nothing more than a warm-up while I got accustomed to his size before his pace grew faster. His dick drilled into me, the head nudging against that perfect spot inside. Stars exploded in my sight, a million bright lights dancing in front of me as bliss flooded all my senses and my length jerked. Precum leaked from my slit.

Daire knew exactly what he was doing, and he was driving me crazy.

The sounds of my moans, his grunts, and his balls slapping against me all mixed together, creating a soundtrack that I wanted to relive over and over again.

I squeezed him tighter between my thighs and clawed his shoulders. His muscles bunched under my touch, solid and hard. We kissed again, just as brutally as before, lips possessing me body and soul. Every part of me was floaty, drifting into the throes of lust, and I was going to implode. I would've shattered into a thousand pieces if Daire hadn't been holding me so tightly.

"You're so sexy, boy," he whispered, nipping my bottom lip. "I want you to come for me. Show your Daddy how much you want him."

I moaned and reached between our bodies. I grabbed my dick. Using the copious precum from my slit as lube, I began to jerk off to the same rhythm as Daire's thrusts. The pressure built at my spine, and I wouldn't last long. How could I when I'd waited years for this? I'd fantasized about him taking me seriously and now it was finally happening.

Two more strokes was all it took before my muscles locked and my balls tightened. My dick shuddered in my palm, and my orgasm ripped through me like a bolt of electricity. My vision wobbled as I came so hard light burst behind my eyes. Everything went black for a short moment.

"Daire!" My dick jerked and cum shot from my tip, splashing across our abs.

He drilled faster into me and froze after a few more thrusts. I couldn't look away from him, caught by his eyebrows dipping low as his mouth opened in a silent moan. He cursed under his breath before warmth filled my hole, marking me—*claiming me*.

"Mine, boy. You're mine."

He panted as his orgasm rocked him, and he kissed me desperately, whispering my name like a prayer until he was done, then collapsed on top of me.

My lips split into a smile even though I was completely *wrecked*. "Wow. Fuck."

Daire laughed, his breath brushing across my warm face, and pressed a lazy kiss on my jaw. "Right."

"That was . . . ." I frowned. "I still haven't forgiven you."

His laughter grew louder. "I know, boy. I've got a lot to make up for." His kisses trailed from my cheek to my lips again. He cupped my face and stroked my jaw, gazing into my eyes. "I promise."

I grinned, a bubble of happiness in my chest—a shield around my healing heart. "Good. Now let's fuck again."

"Boy, I'm a lot older than you and I just came. Give me time to recover."

I chuckled. "When you get some energy back, old man, pass me my phone. I have a text I need to send."

I received a slap on the side for that comment.

———

"Faster, boy. Come on Daddy's cock."

Anchoring my hands to his chest, I raised my hips before crashing back down onto his dick. This was my first time riding on top, and the angle pegged my prostate just right. I was nervous at first, but with my Daddy's encouragement, I couldn't say no. I'd do anything to be his good boy.

"Fuck, yes. Daddy Daire." I whimpered as my dick shuddered from another direct hit to my prostate.

A soft ringing filled the room. My phone. Tucked beside Daire's thigh. One quick glance at it, and I winced. Michele's name flashed across the screen and the happy tune continued to play.

Daire gave it a dirty look, and after a moment, he grinned. He grabbed my thighs as he began to pound up into my already tender hole.

A moan tore from my throat and it hurt in the most pleasant way. I'd be feeling a lot tomorrow.

"Answer it," he growled.

"What?" I rasped out as he pegged my prostate again. Over and over. He knew exactly where to hit. I was so close it was painful. Even though I had barely any cum left in my balls, my orgasm strained and teased at my teetering control.

"You heard me, boy. Answer the phone." His voice turned gruff and his thrusts grew more aggressive. His grip on my legs tightened—a punishing hold that reminded me who was in charge. His nails dug into my skin, leaving crescent shapes in my flesh. "Do it."

I shivered at the intensity in his tone as I picked up the phone and accepted the call.

"Hello?" My voice was wrecked, a guttural mess that made me sound like I'd chain-smoked for decades.

Daire paused, much to my relief.

"Fionn, you're not here." Michele sounded confused. Fuck, I was an asshole. I'd never meant to stand him up, but Daire happened, like he always did.

"Didn't you get my text? I'm sorry, I have to cancel." *A little late for that.* I groaned. I'd fucked this entire thing up. I shouldn't have started what I couldn't finish.

Daire's hands rubbed against my thighs. He smirked at me, and my heart caught as he began to move again. The thrusts were fast and hard. I bounced on him like a rag doll, his dick slamming straight into my sweet spot. There was nothing on this Earth that could stop the needy, desperate sounds that slipped from my lips.

Michele said something, but I couldn't hear him over the pulse throbbing in my ears or the sounds of our skin slapping.

"What?" I asked, then whined when Daire shoved so deep inside me I swore I could feel him in my stomach. I placed a hand on my abs to check if there was a belly bulge, but that'd be impossible. Right?

Silence reigned on the other end of the line for a moment before Michele sighed. "You're with him."

A shaky breath fell from my lips. "I . . . . *Fuck.*"

"Say my name," Daire growled. "Tell him who you belong to, boy. Tell him who has their dick in your sweet hole."

I stuttered, trying to say something, *anything*, but it was all too much. I choked on my words.

"Tell him."

Michele cleared his throat. He couldn't have heard Daire, right? Who was I kidding, of course he could. "I thought there was something going on, but I'd assumed . . . . Well, it was stupid to assume anything. You are too beautiful not to have someone else in love with you."

"I'm so—"

Daire slammed up into me so roughly that I nearly bounced completely off him. I grappled at his chest to keep myself upright.

"Daddy Daire," I whimpered.

"Good night, Fionn." The call ended.

No matter how much I wanted to feel guilty for what I'd done, I couldn't because I was riding a high—addicted to every ounce of Daddy Daire I could milk out.

With one hand, he pinched my nipple and twisted, and that was all it took.

I threw my head back and yelled out my release, my hard-on jerking as cum splattered across his stomach.

"Fuck, boy. You're so tight." A few more thrusts, and he came, too, filling my battered asshole once more.

Before I could collapse on top of him, Daire carefully helped me off his dick to lie at his side. He rose, leaving me in a messy heap on the bed as he went into the bathroom. When he came back, he had a washcloth and took the time to clean me before he did the same to himself. After disposing of the cloth, he returned to lie beside me.

He laid a gentle kiss on my lips. "How are you feeling?"

I groaned, exhaustion catching up to me. "Fucked."

He chuckled as he tickled his fingers over my chest. "I hope so."

I hummed happily. "Sleep now?"

He pressed another kiss on my already bruised mouth. "Sleep."

This was the first time we would doze in the same bed after sex. Together. Next to each other. The thought made me grin widely despite the fatigue. I'd wanted this from the beginning, and now it was happening. All my dreams were coming true. I'd finally landed my prize. My Daddy.

I laid my hand on his chest, across his heart, and left it there for a moment to feel the fast beat beneath my palm. Then, I traced the lines of one of his tattoos, and he turned his head to smile. He grasped my wrist and brought it to his lips, laying a kiss over my pulse.

"Boy, sleep. I mean it."

"Yes, Daddy."

14

DAIRE

I woke first but couldn't manage to make it out of bed. I was captivated by the rise and fall of Fionn's chest. He was even more beautiful asleep, his lashes long and dark against his creamy cheeks, mouth curved in a hint of a smile that had my heart thundering. He appeared content, lost in a world where nothing bothered him. This was the Fionn not many people had the privilege to see.

I trailed my fingers down his neck and over his collarbone, delighting in the shiver that swept through him. I'd always left after sex, but not this time. How could I have given this up for so long? I was stupid and proud and . . . me. My role in life was clear—I was the son who always did *right*.

The good son.

The caretaker.

The one who fixed all the mistakes my older brother made.

The thought of Aodhan made me groan. I had to tell Sloan about my brother soon. Aodhan was still in town, and every time I questioned him about how long he would be here, he brushed me off with a wink. Getting a real answer out of him was like getting through a month at the Killough Company without bloodshed.

Impossible.

My parents still thought Aodhan was the light of their lives, though, because he was their perfect oldest son. If I left telling Sloan any longer, all hell would break loose, and I might not get out alive this time.

Fionn groaned and shifted, his eyes slowly prying open to peek up at me with a half-lidded stare. He smiled and his long lashes fluttered. "You're still here."

I flinched, his words a violent punch to the stomach. I'd done that to him, hadn't I? I broke his heart and made him think he didn't deserve this. But I'd make it up to him for the rest of our lives.

"Where else would I be?" I kissed the corner of his mouth and smoothed a finger down his cheek. "I'm your Daddy now, boy."

He hummed, the dimples in his cheeks so sweet I was tempted to steal a taste. "I like that. Daddy Daire." As Fionn's eyebrows dipped, my gut dropped. One night wasn't going to change everything I'd done to him. I had to find a way to reassure my boy that I was here for him. Prove to him that I was in this to the day the last breath left my lungs.

"I'm not going anywhere. I'm past the point of trying to keep it casual with you." I brushed my nose against his. "I'm sorry, boy."

"Don't worry, you'll be making up for it for years to come." His mouth twisted into a devious smirk that reminded me of Sloan. Killoughs had their own special expression that promised retribution, and as soft as Fionn seemed, he would only grow more vicious.

Sloan's violent tendencies started young, but he had also been exposed to it a lot earlier than Fionn, and Sloan had to step up to take over the Company after his father died. Hopefully, becoming the boss wasn't something Fionn had to concern himself about anytime soon.

"I'm looking forward to it." I winked and tugged him against my chest.

He snuggled in closer and laid his cheek over my heart. His delicate fingers traced the lines of my ink, mapping my chest as though he wanted to memorize every inch. Against the morning light that filtered through the bedroom window, my tattoos were a stark contrast to my skin. "What does all of this mean for us?"

"Well, what do you want it to mean?"

"What do you think?" He stopped sketching one of the tattoos and stared at it. For a moment, I wondered if he saw *it*, a message hidden in plain sight in my ink work. He started to move his finger again.

"I'm right here, boy. You're mine."

He snorted. "I've always been yours. That hasn't changed. But do you belong to me?"

My chest went light at his admission, and a fluttery sensation started in my stomach. I really was a fucking idiot.

I'd spent too much time fighting the chemistry that ignited between us. I was ready for the flames and the injuries that came with our forever. If I ever hurt Fionn again, I'd take care of myself because I wouldn't deserve to live. Then, there was Sloan. If he ever found out about all the years of misery I'd put Fionn through, then I might not live to see another day anyway —*if* he didn't kill me for the Aodhan thing first.

"Yes." I captured Fionn's hand and brought it to my lips, laying a kiss over his knuckles. "I'm yours."

"Good." He sighed happily, and my body was wired to his responses. Every little sound he made created a chain reaction, and his pleasure was mine. My skin tingled at how carefree he looked. "You still owe me for all the years of hell."

"What do you want?" I asked carefully.

Fionn's eyes sharpened and there was a seriousness that had me on edge. A spike of concern swelled inside my chest. I wanted to hand him whatever he desired on a golden platter, but there were certain things that weren't easy to give.

"Dad," he finally whispered. "Tell me how he really died."

"You know how," I said. Part of me hoped he'd let this go, but I knew him too well. He'd always craved the knowledge of his father's death. He wouldn't give up until he had the truth.

"And you know there's more to the story," he snapped in return. He sat up, shoving at my chest. "All I know was that he was shot by a cartel member. I want to know who and why and what happened to the bastard."

"What you're asking me to do will go against Sloan's orders. It was his choice not to tell you." I sat up in the bed with my back against the headboard. I needed him to understand how serious this was. The repercussions could get him killed, and I'd only just gotten my shit together. I couldn't lose him.

"Why, though?" He threw his hands up in obvious frustration, a terse line creasing his forehead. "There's no reason, unless he's hiding something." He pointed at me. "This is the only thing I'm asking from you, Daddy Daire. The *only* thing. Please."

I sighed, fingers gripping the short strands of my hair in frustration. I banged my back against the headboard again and stared up at the ceiling, praying for strength to deal with the sad puppy eyes he was currently giving me. I *did* owe him something, but this was . . . . *Shit.*

"It was violent," I murmured. "What happened was cruel and vicious and your uncle blames himself."

"Why?" Fionn swallowed, Adam's apple bobbing as he wriggled closer. He pressed his back beside me and leaned against me.

I wrapped an arm around his shoulders and closed my eyes. The image of Eoin's dead body was seared into my brain as a memory that would never fade. "Because Eoin was done with the Company. He had permission from your grandfather to walk away to be a father and husband." I opened my eyes again and glanced at Fionn. "He wanted to be around for you, and he could because Sloan was your grandfather's apprentice. He would be the one to take the reins when your grandfather died."

Fionn nodded slowly, encouraging me to keep talking.

I shouldn't, but now that I'd started, I couldn't stop. I owed him this. "Sloan wasn't happy that Eoin chose his family over the Company. He's never had kids, so he didn't know what it was like to be a father. Eoin . . . never wanted Sloan to be upset with him. They were brothers. They had always been close." I glided my fingers over Fionn's shoulder, nails scraping across his warm bare skin.

"So what happened?" He leaned into the touch, gaze never leaving mine.

"Eoin asked Sloan to forgive him for leaving. Sloan never did. At least, not that Eoin ever knew." I pressed my lips together for a short moment to gather my emotions. The images that came with Eoin's death were more than enough to haunt me for the rest of my life. I couldn't give that trauma to Fionn. "After Eoin left, Sloan threw himself into his work. He hadn't talked to your dad for months. Sloan was gunning for the Cartel. He pushed their buttons, killed their men, and took their product. He wanted to show your grandfather he was born to be the boss. He pushed too hard." I sighed.

Fionn's jaw tightened.

"Sloan was warned that the Cartel was out for blood, but he never expected them to go for Eoin. We don't know if they did it on purpose or if they confused him for Sloan. But they took him. We told you that your dad was shot, and he was, but he was tortured beforehand. He was . . . ." I exhaled loudly, and my breath came out shaky. The truth was that I'd never forgiven myself, either. I should've done more, advised Sloan to pull back. I didn't. Bile rose at the back of my throat, and I had to swallow it down at the memories of finding Eion's broken body. The things they did to him . . . . No child should know that happened to their parent. "Fuck, I don't think I can tell you what they did to him, boy. Your dad wasn't recognizable by the time they shot him. His death was a message for Sloan, and Sloan never got the chance to see him alive again despite what Sloan always told you."

He let out a shuddery breath. "Oh." He touched a palm to my chest, above my heart, searching for the beat beneath my skin. "Did Sloan back off?"

"Have you met your uncle?" I shook my head. "No, he pushed the Cartel back to the West Coast where they belonged. It was the Reyes Cartel."

Fionn sucked in air sharply, rage twisting his features. "What?"

"Thiago Reyes's uncle—Jesús Montero. You've never met him because Sloan killed him. Thiago's father pushed to try to take the East Coast and that's why Jesús was over here. They thought they could take New York, but they failed. Montero failed. That's when the rivalry broke out."

"I didn't realize it'd been going on for that long," Fionn murmured, his fingers falling back into tracing over my tattoos.

"Enemy relationships wax and wane." I drew him closer to my chest and shivered when his nails scraped over a particularly sensitive spot above my rib cage. "Some years they are more dangerous than others. It always depends on how stupid they want to be."

He frowned. "I don't know why Sloan didn't tell me. That wasn't his fault. It was the Reyes Cartel's."

"Sloan antagonized them." I laid my palm on his arm and trailed it over his skin, petting him in slow, long strokes. "And what they did to Eoin . . . . I don't think I'll ever forget the state of your dad's body."

Fionn brushed the dip of my brow, a sadness passing over his face. "I understand. Is that why Sloan took me in? He felt guilty?"

"Your mother couldn't handle you because you were acting out. So, she gave you to Sloan." I smiled because if that hadn't happened, I would never have met Fionn. I trusted Sloan with him more than his mother. "And then, you became his. His son. His apprentice. I don't think he wanted to give you back."

"Well, it was a good thing my mom didn't want me back then, huh?" Bitterness dripped from his voice.

I hugged him tightly. "Your mother never fully recovered after your dad died. She blamed the Company and Sloan."

"If she blamed him, why did she leave me with him?"

"I don't know," I answered honestly. "Maybe she didn't know what else to do with you. The truth is, you have more drive for the business than your dad had. Eoin was good at what he did, but he never loved being in the mob. He never wanted to learn how to be boss one day, which is why Sloan became your grandfather's apprentice."

"There's also the fact that I've never been her favorite." He laid his cheek against my shoulder. "That title goes to Bell."

"She's ruined them both," I said with a shake of my head. I hadn't seen Fionn's younger brothers since she left with them, but with everything she'd been asking Sloan for, it was obvious they were both spoiled. "They can't fend for themselves and never will." I didn't know much about Fionn's brothers. They could walk past me in the street and I wouldn't recognize them. The last time I'd seen them was at Eoin's funeral, but I imagined after growing up under the influence of their mother, they were exactly like her. "You won't be giving them any more money, boy."

"But—"

"No buts, Fionn." I slapped him on the thigh, hard, and he hissed. "Your mother doesn't need your money. She's a full-grown adult who must learn to take care of herself. She doesn't need you to look after her, and your brothers are old enough, too."

"You don't understand," Fionn argued, but I gave him another smack, this time even harder than the first.

"I do—better than you. I've known your mom since before you were born. So this is me being your Daddy, boy. You will *not* give her money. None. If you do, I will rat you out to Sloan, and we both know you, or she, won't like how he deals with it."

He frowned. "That's mean."

"That's life. She can't continue to rely on you." I hooked a finger under Fionn's chin and tipped his head up before laying a gentle kiss on his mouth. "Trust me, boy, I'm looking out for you. No more money."

He hesitated but finally nodded. "Okay."

I smiled, pleased. I smoothed my hand over his ass, fingers delving between his cheeks and teasing his hole with gentle pets around his ring. "I'm going to fuck you again, boy."

He moaned.

———

After we finally got out of bed, Fionn said he was going to take a shower, and I made my way to Sloan's office. Men and staff milled around the house, going about their day and job efficiently. I passed Ronan as he headed down the hallway, and we exchanged short nods in greeting.

When I reached the door to Sloan's office, I knocked lightly and waited.

"Come in," Sloan said, voice raspy and laced with pleasure.

I chuckled while opening the door before stepping over the threshold. I wasn't surprised to see Conall between Sloan's knees, lips wrapped around Sloan's cock. Sloan's hips rocked up, his hard-on driving deep into Conall's willing mouth as he tipped his head backward against his leather desk chair.

Walking in on scenes like this wasn't uncommon, especially when it came to Sloan and Conall. Sloan'd had pets in the past, but they'd never been *right* for him, at least, not until Conall came along. I'd been Sloan's friend for a long time, and I'd never seen him happier than when he was with Conall. Not that I'd ever tell him that. It was easier to let him work on his own timeline. The man wore armor as thick as steel around himself and for good reason. Being a mob boss came with duties and danger.

I ignored what Conall was doing and took a seat in the chair on the opposite side of Sloan's desk. I settled in, throwing a leg over my knee while I waited for Sloan and Conall to finish. Judging by Sloan's quiet hums, he wouldn't be much longer.

A few moments later, Sloan tensed and groaned low in his throat. His hips jutted forward. Sounds of Conall choking on Sloan's cock filled the room, followed by a breathy inhale as Conall pulled off the boss.

"Such a pretty mouth, pet." Sloan stroked his thumb over Conall's bottom lip and smirked. "Now, go upstairs and wash up. We have some work to do today, and I want you with me."

Conall hummed and shoved to his feet. He leaned down to kiss Sloan gently before he sent me a wink and left the office.

Once the door closed, Sloan turned his full attention to me.

I cleared my throat. "There's something I need to tell you."

He raised an eyebrow and linked his fingers together. "Talk."

I cursed Aodhan for making me do this. I should've told Sloan from the beginning, but I'd thought Aodhan would get bored of New York City and disappear again.

"My brother's in town." As soon as my words hit air, I lowered my eyes and head in respect.

"Aodhan?" His tone dropped dangerously, and even though

it sounded like a question, it wasn't. I only had one brother. "Why?"

"I don't know," I said with sigh. "He won't tell me. He turned up at my penthouse and hasn't left."

"Hasn't left?" The creak of Sloan's chair told me he rose and was probably making his way toward me, but I didn't need to see him to feel the space of the room disappear and become hard to breathe in. His presence on a good day was menacing; on a bad day, like now, it was downright terrifying. Fear coiled in my chest. "*When* did he get here, Daire?"

"Before Christmas, sir." I held back the urge to flinch. I dropped my leg and sat with both feet flat against the wooden floorboards, hands clasped in my lap like the soldier I was. In the end, being boss came first to Sloan. In a situation like this, I wasn't his best friend or second-in-command. I was his employee, one who'd fucked up by not telling him about Aodhan as soon as I'd become aware that he was in Sloan's territory.

"And you're only coming to me now?" His voice grew closer, and then he was right beside me, nudging my shoulder.

This time I winced. "I was trying to convince him to leave before it became an issue, sir."

He laughed, and it wasn't pleasant—the coldness of the sound seeping through to my bones. "You should've come to me immediately. *That's* your job."

I finally raised my gaze to meet his. "Sloan, he's my brother."

"And I'm your boss," he snarled, baring his teeth with anger that had a spike of fear shooting through me. Only one person could draw that reaction from me, and he was towering over me. "You made a commitment to me—to my company. Stand up. Now."

I swallowed and stood as ordered. I turned toward Sloan, keeping my shoulders squared. Now that I was facing the boss, I kept my eyes on him. "My loyalty is to you, but Aodhan is blood. I gave him a chance to leave."

"Jesus fuck, Daire!"

I flinched. Sloan didn't swear . . . ever. This had taken a deadly turn, and I had to tread carefully if I wanted to leave this room alive.

"You're the one I *need* to trust. You're my right-hand man. And you do this?" He surged forward, his fist connecting with my jaw.

I tumbled backward into the chair and over the top of it, landing on the hard floor on the other side. Agony exploded through my jaw, ricocheting through my head, and my shoulder ached where I landed on it. I groaned, touching my fingers to the spot he'd connected with, then rose slowly. I didn't attempt to retaliate. He was my boss, and I deserved it. I'd fucked up. But I didn't regret it. Aodhan was my *brother*, and as much as he drove me crazy, I also had a commitment to him.

"Don't you have anything to say for yourself?" Sloan's eyes sparked with fury, the ocean blue darkening to resemble a storm rather than the calm sea. His chest heaved and his jaw tightened, the muscles bunching. "You should've told me the moment you saw him."

"I'm aware, sir, but he's my brother. If you knew immediately, you would've killed him."

"What makes you think I won't now?" Sloan sneered, stalking close so our faces nearly touched. I was taller and wider than him but not by much. "What makes you think I won't torture him until he's inches from death as a consequence for your lies?"

"Because I'm your friend and I've been nothing but loyal to you."

"Until now?" His anger radiated off him in waves, deadly and toxic, and it made it hard for me to breathe. I knew what he was capable of, and if I didn't talk him down off a ledge, I might not be around for much longer. Sloan wasn't the kind of person to easily show anger, but Aodhan was a sore subject. He was the only person who could get a rise like this out of Sloan. I could usually handle Sloan's outbursts, but a new fear stirred to life in my chest. I'd just gotten Fionn back in my arms. I couldn't leave him yet—especially not this way.

"Sloan—"

He reached into his jacket and pulled out his gun before aiming it at my forehead.

I tensed, heart racing and chest aching, and let out a shaky breath. I stilled and swallowed around the anguish in my throat. I'd been ready for death for a long time, but I didn't expect it to come from my boss. I thought about Fionn and how angry he would be at Sloan. I hated the idea of the disconnection it would cause between uncle and nephew. He'd never forgive Sloan.

While I'd been ready for death, I didn't want it to happen, either. I was ready to treat Fionn the way he deserved. To take him out on dates and show him off to the world like he'd begged me to. Now, it was over before it had begun.

"Uncle, no!"

Before I knew what was going on, Fionn was there, shoving his way between me and the gun.

Fear struck me violently in the chest, and the overwhelming need to protect Fionn rose and lodged itself as a lump in my throat. Would Sloan hurt Fionn? Part of me wanted to believe he wouldn't, but I had no fucking idea. The terror of what Sloan would do to him had me rooted on the spot.

Sloan glared. "Move, Fionn."

"No." Fionn stood tall, but his height wasn't enough to hide my bulk. "What the hell is going on?"

Sloan's jaw tightened. "Move. Now."

"What is this about?" he snapped.

"Aodhan." I sighed. Laying my hands on Fionn's shoulders, I

tried to shift him out of the way, but he planted his feet and refused to move.

"If you want to shoot Daire for that, then you need to shoot me, too." Fionn raised his chin. Disobedient boy. I would have to teach him a lesson about that later—if I got the chance. Regardless, my heart throbbed at the thought of Fionn protecting me. He loved me enough to risk his own life. I was the luckiest fucking man who ever existed. His loyalty never wavered. "I knew about Aodhan being here, too."

Sloan stared, gun hand lowering. The anger stayed in his gaze, but some of the danger slipped away. "You don't know him."

"I do." Fionn stepped forward and the tension in his shoulders bled away. "Sloan, Daire's always been your most faithful soldier. Fuck, he's your best friend, but Aodhan is Daire's brother. Imagine if it was Dad. You'd defend him, too."

"Don't tell me what I would or wouldn't do," Sloan growled out.

"It's true, though." Fionn crossed his arms. "Has Aodhan crossed you or the Company, Uncle? Are your feelings getting in the way of business? He could be useful."

Sloan snorted. "You don't know Aodhan or what he's done. He's a wild card who can't be controlled."

"Maybe." Fionn exhaled loudly. "Please, don't hurt Daire. You know if there was any risk to our business, he would've told you."

Except I didn't know why Aodhan was here, which was a huge fucking problem.

Sloan had a stare off with Fionn and time passed as slow as molasses—my breath caught in my throat as I waited—before Sloan slipped the gun back into his holster under his suit jacket. He grunted and glanced at me over Fionn's shoulder. "You are a lucky bastard to have my nephew on your side."

I bowed my head in respect because it was true. I'd never expected Fionn to defend me—especially against Sloan.

"Fine." Sloan's gaze continued to burn. "You will tell Aodhan he has two choices. If he wants to stay, he needs to pay me a visit tomorrow, and only tomorrow. Otherwise, he has until the weekend to leave alive. Am I clear?"

"Sloan—"

"Am. I. Clear?" He stepped in closer again, and Fionn shifted so he made sure he was between us. "There are no more chances. I'm done with traitors and men who think they can beat me at my own game."

I inclined my head. "Yes, sir."

"Get out of my office."

I didn't need to be told twice. I grabbed Fionn by the elbow and led him outside.

Once we were farther away from Sloan, I spun on him. "What the hell were you thinking, getting between me and that gun, boy?"

He shrugged, a small grin tugging on his lips. "I just got you, Daddy Daire. I'm not letting you go anytime soon."

I pinched the bridge of my nose. Concern ate at me, kneading my gut and making it churn. I couldn't stand the thought of losing Fionn. He was playing a dangerous game. "Never do that again. I mean it. What happens between me and Sloan is just that. Between us. I don't want Sloan to think you're choosing me over him."

He flicked his gaze to the side, then back to me, like he was considering what to say. Finally, his smile grew bigger. "If I don't listen, will you spank me?"

I smirked. "Test me and find out, boy."

"I might take you up on that."

15

FIONN

I traced my finger down the middle of Daire's chest, nail scraping through the tuft of hair between his pecs. As I dragged my digit over the ridges of his abs, I studied every microexpression that passed over his face. Although Daire was still asleep, it was clear he felt everything and enjoyed my touch.

It was hard to believe I was here again, in his bed, and finally, in his heart. His resolve had shattered, and the only thing that mattered was us.

And Sloan.

The thought made me wince. What I walked in on this morning was my worst nightmare. I'd expected Sloan to pull the trigger because when my uncle threatened something, he followed through with it. I'd never seen him point a gun in Daire's direction, and the sight had nearly made me vomit. I'd reacted on an impulse, getting between the gun and Daire before offering Sloan an ultimatum. If he was going to shoot Daire for keeping Aodhan's visit a secret, then he should do the same to me. Sloan would relent. It wasn't that I thought Sloan wouldn't shoot his own blood, because he would if he had a damned good reason, but not over this.

At least, that's what I had told myself.

Now, I truly wondered what Aodhan had done to Sloan to make him so furious. Sloan was calm and collected. He didn't get angry, yet Aodhan had brought out a reaction in him that I wasn't sure I'd ever seen in the past.

I frowned.

"I can hear you thinking, boy," Daire murmured softly without opening his eyes. His mouth curled into a smile, and after a few moments, his inky lashes fluttered and he turned his head to stare at me.

We'd spent the day fucking before having a small afternoon nap. Aodhan hadn't come home to the penthouse yet, and Daire had tried to call him, only to get sent to voicemail every time. I saw the irritation rise with every call Daire made. I tried to soothe him the best way I could—by giving him one amazing orgasm after another. Well, at least as many as his dick could take.

Now I lay with my head on Daire's shoulder, cuddled close to his side.

"Why does Sloan hate Aodhan so much?" I asked.

He exhaled loudly and closed his eyes again, tilting his chin back as though he'd fallen into a memory. I waited, fingers dancing across the many lines of his tattoos, the Celtic symbolism distinct and proudly inked into his skin. "He slept with one of Sloan's pets."

I blinked, stilled, then blinked rapidly again. "*How* is he still alive?"

Daire laughed. "It's only because by that point, Sloan didn't care for Adrian."

"Adrian?" I scrunched up my nose in distaste. I'd never really met Adrian prior to Sloan shipping him off to Mexico. Adrian had only been around for a couple of months, but the few interactions I *did* have with him had ended with Adrian looking down on me as though I was nothing more than a fly to swat. It might have been around that time that I started to hate the idea of Sloan having a pet. "He was an asshole."

Daire hummed in agreement. "Can't argue with that. Part of me thinks Aodhan knew that Sloan was done with Adrian and he wanted to make a point."

"What point is that? How to get his brains blown out?" I drawled with a snort. There were no words for how lucky Aodhan was. I honestly didn't expect Sloan to let anyone get away with something like that.

"He enjoys playing with fire, choosing the riskiest plans and seeing where it gets him." He nuzzled my hair and inhaled deeply, dragging me in closer. His grip on my shoulder tightened. "He's always been like that, and it's what makes him a good hit man, but it also put him in a lot of danger. Can't tell you how many times he's had someone try to kill him for something stupid he's done."

I kissed Daire's shoulder, the warmth of his skin a sensation I never wanted to forget. "It's not like Sloan to let Aodhan go for something like that."

"Aodhan got lucky." He closed his eyes and sighed. "It helped that he was your dad's friend. Eoin and Aodhan grew up commiserating over being the oldest sons." The corner of his mouth quirked into half a smile. "It used to be Sloan and me against them in a lot of the games we played growing up." His eyes slipped open again and his expression hardened, mouth pressed into a thin line. "When Eoin died, Aodhan never went to his funeral. Never checked in on you or your family. It was almost as though he didn't know Eoin."

I frowned. "Yeah, well, I'd never met him until last month."

"Your mom knows him." Daire reached up to rub his eyes. "I guess Sloan always had an attachment to Aodhan. When he fucked Adrian and Sloan found out, I begged your uncle not to kill him. Other than me and Sloan being friends since we were young, he owed me for all the things I've done for him. That was the only time in our relationship I asked for anything, and I only did it for my parents."

"Your parents?" I shifted until I could rest my chin on his chest and wrap an arm around his waist.

Daire's teeth clenched, a tic working through the muscles in his jaw. He focused on the ceiling. I'd hit a sore point. "They have so many dreams for Aodhan. They think he'll make them proud, even though they *know* he's trouble."

I studied his face carefully, taking in the tension lines and the way his eyes hardened. "And what about you?" I whispered, finger stroking down the middle of his chest again. "Are they proud of *you*, Daddy?"

"Don't be silly, boy," he drawled, the tic in his jaw pulsing. "I'm the one who's supposed to fix all their golden boy's mistakes."

I didn't know exactly how that felt, but I understood Daire's need to please his parents. I'd been doing the same thing with Sloan, hadn't I? I was so desperate for his approval that I would do anything for him.

"*I'm* proud of you," I whispered, placing featherlight kisses over his pecs. "I'm proud to have you as my Daddy."

The blinding smile he gave me made my words all worth it.

"Will I ever meet them?" I asked timidly. I held my breath and waited for his answer. We'd played this game of ignoring the feelings between us for so long that I wondered if he thought I was worth introducing to his family.

"If you want." He smoothed his thumb over my chin and smiled. "Despite their flaws when it comes to Aodhan, they are good people. They'd love you."

"Really?" I couldn't stop the wide grin from spreading across my face.

He laughed. "How would you like to go somewhere tonight, boy?"

"Where?" I stared, mouth parted. His offer took me off

guard. Like a date? No, that wasn't possible. Right? "To see your parents?"

He made a wounded sound. "No, let's not do that yet. I'd rather have you to myself for a little longer before Mom decides to take you from me. No, I was thinking we could go for a drive, do something together."

"On your bike?" I fluttered my lashes at him hopefully, and his laughter was back.

"No." He played with my lower lip when I pouted at him. "It's too dangerous on the bike right now. The roads are too icy, and I don't want you to get hurt."

"I trust your driving skills," I whispered, settling tighter against him. "You're good on the bike."

"I know." It wasn't arrogance in his voice, but confidence, and that was so fucking hot. "But I'd never risk your life like that. I promise when it gets warmer, I'll take you out on it."

"Really?" My excitement bubbled up and I had to hold back from wriggling. I'd asked Daire to take me on his motorcycle for as long as I'd known he had one, and each time he'd refused. He'd never once showed an inkling that he'd consider it, but now he was agreeing. *Finally.*

"Only if you hold on to me very tightly." He cupped my cheek and slanted his mouth over mine in a soft kiss that had my toes curling. "We have to trust each other. You need to hug my back and move with me. Give me complete control. Only my special person is allowed on my bike."

I stared at him with wide eyes. Was he admitting that I was that person? Damn it, he was. Excitement churned in my stomach and I kissed him hard. He rolled us over so he was on top of me, and I melted into his strong body.

"I love you, Daddy Daire," I whispered against his lips.

He froze, and my stomach dropped. Panic welled behind my eyes. Had I gotten this all wrong? Did I fuck this up before it even began? Before I could spiral out of control, he stunned me with another brilliant smile. Somehow, he looked younger like this, even as his eyes crinkled in the corners. "I love you, too. For longer than I knew."

The words blasted happiness through me until I thought my heart would burst from my chest. He loved me. *He fucking loved me, too.* I'd waited for this moment for too long and it was finally happening.

"So, you don't have any guilt about the whole loving my dad thing anymore?" I didn't care that he had feelings for a man I never really knew, as long as what he felt for me was real.

"You know . . . ." He stroked the length of my face as he stared down at me. "I think I stopped feeling that way a long time ago. I held on to Eoin's memory because he was the first person I loved."

"But not the last," I murmured with a grin.

"No, you get that honor."

I bit my lip to hold in a gasp of joy. My body was floating and I had tingles all the way to my toes.

"Till the day I die, you have me, Fionn. My loyalty, my love, my everything. I am yours." He cleared his throat and sat up on the bed. I followed him, head cocked curiously as he touched one of the many weaving tattoos with Celtic knots. He touched a spot and smiled at me. "Look closely."

Frowning, I shuffled forward and leaned in to stare at where he was pointing. At first, I didn't see what he was getting at, then I saw it. He grasped my hand and guided me to the tattoo before tracing my finger over the letters. The word blended in with the lines of the tattoo, and if one wasn't familiar with where to look, they wouldn't see it, but it was there. Cursive black ink was interwoven with the knots.

Fionn.

My name.

Mine.

"What . . . ?" My gaze shot up to him. "That's me!"

He chuckled. "You are special. You always have been, even all those years ago when I got these tattoos. You're Fionn, the future of the Company. My boy. My . . . Fifi."

"Fifi?" I laughed, but it came out wet. Something like joy prickled behind my eyes. I tried to swipe at the moisture threatening to spill down my cheeks, but Daire caught my wrists to stop me. His lips chased away every tear and something settled in my chest.

"You're beautiful, boy. You're mine as much as I'm yours. When you need to be strong for the Company, I will have your back. When it feels like too much, lean on me. Let it out in front of me—I can take it. Let me be your strength. I will catch every tear, push you past any outburst, and I'll remind you of the incredible, strong, good boy you are." He cradled my face between his large hands and kissed me roughly, and I returned it with fervor.

"Why did you fight this for so long?" Desperation bled into my words as I whispered against his lips.

"I was an idiot, Fifi. A complete fucking idiot."

I couldn't agree more, but he was here now.

As much as I wanted to spend the rest of the day in bed, Daire dragged me out to shower. We got ready as quickly as we could.

He had a few of my suits here from when the boys dropped them off after the club incident, so I chose a dark maroon one. Daire went with a dark navy gray with a subtle plaid, and he looked as delicious as always. I couldn't help but drag him in for a kiss.

"If you start this, boy, we won't be leaving this bedroom," he growled out against my lips.

"Is that a bad thing, Deedee?"

"Deedee?" He pulled back to stare incredulously at me.

"What? You called me Fifi," I said with a laugh. "Deedee stands for Daddy Daire."

"No, I'm Daddy Daire and nothing else." He nipped my bottom lip, and I moaned. "Say it."

"What's wrong with Deedee? I'll let you keep calling me Fifi."

He chuckled. "Deedee and Fifi sound like a couple of poodles."

"I won't tell if you won't," I whispered.

He laughed harder and pinched my ass before I could twist away from him.

"You can call me Fifo, then," I offered with a grin.

He gave me *the look*—the one I'd come to know as his Daddy stare. Unimpressed, yet amused, but I'd hear about it later. "Now that definitely sounds like a dog's name."

I curled my hands in front of my chest like paws. "Woof. Woof."

He rolled his eyes and dragged me closer, dropping a quick peck on my forehead this time. "You are my boy, not my puppy. I'm not into pet play."

"A shame," I teased, and it earned me an ass smack.

The sound of the door opening downstairs interrupted us, and almost immediately the playfulness on Daire's face disappeared, leaving behind a clenched jaw and hard eyes. He swept past me, and I followed him as closely as I could. He took the steel black stairs two at a time with his long legs to race to the bottom.

Aodhan was sitting at the kitchen island, playing on his phone, when we reached him.

"You." Daire slapped his hand down on the marble counter next to Aodhan. His brother glanced up lazily, as though he wasn't surprised that me and Daire put in an appearance.

The dogs came out from the laundry room, eyeing us carefully, but all it took was one flick of Daire's hand and they retreated.

"Can I help you, little brother?" Aodhan drawled, first glancing at Daire, then me. He raised his eyebrows and grinned.

"Well, hello there, little kitty. Looks like you finally got Daire where you want him, huh? Did he declaw you?"

I glared. "You are a piece of work."

He laid a hand on his chest and pouted. "That's the nicest thing anyone's ever said to me. Are you sure you don't have a thing for *me?*"

"Aodhan," Daire snapped. "Sloan knows you're here."

Aodhan shrugged. "How is that my problem?"

"He wants you to come see him tomorrow."

Aodhan barked out a laugh.

Daire crossed his arms and glowered at his brother.

"And you think I'm going to listen to him? Funny." He shook his head. "Sloan's not my boss, and I'm not doing jack shit. Why should I?"

I swallowed and opened my mouth, ready to argue, but Daire beat me to it.

"Because I asked you to." Daire didn't need to raise his voice to get his point across. He was always firm yet calm—a quiet strength. He clenched his jaw. "Because I'm your brother, and I've done *everything* I can to protect you. I have put my life on the line for you more times than I can count. I'm asking you to do *one* thing for me, Aodhan. One thing."

Aodhan stared at him with a frown for a long moment before something shifted in his eyes. The teasing was gone and a steeliness overtook his expression. He nodded. "What time?"

Daire straightened, clearly surprised, before clearing his throat. "We'll go together. We'll leave here at eight."

Aodhan stood. "Will do. Eight sharp." He pointed between us. "Going on a date?"

"We are, actually," I said, raising my chin to dare him to say anything rude.

He laughed. "About fucking time. Have fun, kids." He winked as he sashayed his way past us and up the steps.

I watched him go until he'd disappeared, then sighed. "At least he agreed to see Sloan, right?"

Daire's eyebrows furrowed and he pursed his lips. "Yeah, he did, but that's not like him to agree so fast. I thought I'd have to knock his ass out and drag him there."

"You think he's up to no good?" I asked, unease slithering through me.

"I don't know." He pinched the bridge of his nose. "Maybe he decided to do something for me for once. God knows, I've risked a lot for him in the past."

"So, it was about time he gave back to you." I shifted closer to him and curled my arms around his neck.

He smiled and leaned in for a soft, sweet kiss. "Come on, boy, let me take you out for the night."

He guided me out of the penthouse and to the elevator. I couldn't keep my hands off him but had to when an older couple walked in. They gave me a pointed stare after they caught me with my lips on Daire's.

I nearly raced out of the doors when we reached the garage, and Daire laughed, letting me drag him out and toward his SUV.

"Oooh, Daddy. This car's as manly as you are," I teased, earning a laugh from Daire.

He paused beside me and stroked a line down my back thoughtfully. "It's time you get your license, Fifi."

"Me?" I scrunched my nose. "I have people to drive me around."

He tapped me on the nose, and my mouth dropped open. "You can't rely on others all the time, Fionn. You should've gone for your license when you were eighteen, at least, so this is me putting my foot down. You're going to get it."

I hesitated. "I . . . don't know how to, Daddy Daire." Heat spread across my cheeks and I groaned. "I never asked Uncle to teach me. He's always so busy."

"Then, I will." He caressed my cheek. "Because there may come a time when you need to know, boy, and I won't have that be the reason something happens to you." He kissed my forehead. "You'll be a good boy and do what I say. Now in you go."

Warmth spread over my cheeks and I did as he'd instructed, eager to please him by following orders. We both got into his spotless SUV.

"So, where are we going?" I asked.

Daire leaned over and grabbed my hand, linking our fingers together. I enjoyed the feel of his strong, rough hold. "You'll see." He sent me a wink.

I settled in as he began to drive. The afternoon sun was close to being swallowed by the darkness of the night.

Every so often Daire peeked over at me with a smile so sweet I could only offer one of my own in return. His home was in a busy part of the city and there were cars everywhere, so I wasn't sure how long we were going to travel, but I didn't mind the drive. I relished the chance to finally be out on a date with Daire. It was a situation I'd never expected to experience, but here we were. *Fuck.* We were together. It was surreal.

We drove for thirty minutes before he pulled into a parking lot. The moment I realized where we were, I quirked a brow back toward Daire.

High Tech Laser Tag.

"Laser tag?" I chuckled. "I don't think I've ever played."

He raised our hands so he could kiss the back of mine. "Then, your first time will be with me."

"It already was," I teased, earning a laugh from him. "Why are we dressed in suits for laser tag?"

"Well, to be honest, I was going to take you somewhere nice for dinner, but I thought this would be a good idea." He released my hand to stroke my cheek, and I leaned into his touch. "You've been trained to be Sloan's apprentice all your life, boy, but you never had the chance to be young and have fun. We can kick ass and look good doing it."

"By shooting a bunch of teenagers?"

He laughed again. "Don't underestimate them. They're good."

"Ah, you've been here?" I shifted in the seat so my body was facing him. "The truth comes out, Daddy Daire."

He shrugged—unashamed. "It's good to let off steam and have fun. Remember that, Fifi."

I stared at him for a second before I burst into laughter. "Every time you call me that, I can't take you seriously. You're a grown-assed man in your forties calling me Fifi."

"Hey!" He pinched my arm playfully, and I twisted away from him, too amused to do anything but curl up and laugh until it hurt. His smile said he wasn't upset with me, but I forced myself to stop and wipe the tears from my eyes.

"Sorry. I like you calling me Fifi, I do. It's just funny."

"I know," he murmured, running his fingers through my hair. "But it's worth it just to hear you laugh. Do you know how long it's been since I've seen you this happy, Fionn?"

I paused, ruminating on his words. How long *had* it been since I'd laughed like that? Too long. The pressure and stress of being Sloan's apprentice had taken its toll on me. Daire was right, I never really had fun growing up. It wasn't Sloan's fault, but rather my own desire to make my uncle proud. Sloan had offered to send me to college, but I'd turned him down, eager to start learning everything. Fun hadn't been in my vocabulary.

"Come on." Daire tugged my hand gently before letting it go and stepping from the SUV. I followed him out, and he met me as soon as I closed the door. Once he locked the vehicle, we walked into the boxy brown brick building with flashing LED lights illuminating the business name.

Inside was dark and foggy, smoke machines giving it an eerie atmosphere. The lights blinked red, blue, yellow, and green, while loud music pounded from big wall speakers. The large room was crowded with people of all ages, and to the right was a bar and tall tables and stools. I'd never been to a place like this. I felt like you needed friends to play laser tag, and I never had anyone. All my life, I grew up around men older than me or just as interested in the mob as me. We never had time for games.

"Food first or laser tag?" Daire asked.

I glanced at him with a wide grin. "Tag."

He pressed a kiss to my forehead. "Prepare to lose, boy."

I rolled my eyes with a chuckle. "Whatever, old man."

His eyes widened. "Did you just . . . . Never mind. We'll handle this inside."

He drew me in for a hard kiss, and I relaxed into his embrace before he broke away and strode toward the cashier. I watched, a little starstruck over my boyfriend, because that's what he was, wasn't he? Boyfriend. Partner. Either way, he was mine, and I didn't know how I'd become so lucky. As much as I'd wanted this to happen, I hadn't actually expected that it ever would. But here I was, on a date with Daire.

He came back with some tickets and linked his fingers with mine again before dragging me toward a door to the right. A man stood out front and he took the tickets from Daire, gesturing for us to go inside.

"The next game is about to start. Gear up with the rest, and we'll let you into the arena soon."

Daire thanked him, and he led me through the door and into another room, this one with bright overhead lights on to help us see. There was already a group of people dressed in vests and helmets with lights attached. They all held obviously fake lime green automatic rifles. Daire led me to two lockers that still had vests, helmets, and a laser gun, then slipped off his suit jacket.

"Come on, boy, let's show these amateurs how it's done."

A young man no older than me turned toward us. His shaggy

blond hair stuck out from under his helmet and his grin stretched across his entire face. "Hey, Daire! Brought us some prey this time, huh?"

Daire rolled his eyes and huffed. "Fionn, this is Zed. He's a bit of a professional."

Zed barked out a laugh and stepped up to us. He held out his hand, and I took it in a firm shake. "Professional in laser tag and in real life. You're Fionn Killough. Pleasure to meet you, man."

I cocked my head. "Do I know you?"

"Nah, but I know you. Everyone in my occupation does."

Daire cleared his throat and leaned in closer to me. "He works in the same society as Ardan, sir. He's an associate of ours," he whispered.

It was funny how quickly Daire slid back into his role of second-in-command, but it made sense when we were around someone who'd done work for us.

Zed certainly wasn't someone I'd suspect as a Society associate. He had a baby face and an innocent look. Though, I supposed he used that to his advantage.

"What is someone like you doing in a place like this, Zed?" I asked.

He threw his thumb over his shoulder at a younger man who couldn't have been older than eighteen. Probably closer to fifteen. They appeared to be related, with the same floppy blond hair and big blue eyes. "My younger bro, here, loves laser tag."

I frowned. "You're brave to be admitting he's family."

Zed snorted out a laugh. "I have faith in my abilities, sir, and I know how to protect my own."

I simply nodded, and he took that as a signal to go back to his brother. Once he was gone, I whispered to Daire, "Is he trustworthy?"

Daire smiled as he pulled out the vest from my locker and yanked at the sides to undo the Velcro keeping it together. He slid the vest over my head and pressed the sides together again.

"I wouldn't put your life in danger, boy. I didn't expect Zed to be here tonight, but he's been loyal to the Company, and he's building up his portfolio."

"What if he could add our names to that list?" I trusted Daire, but I had an inherent suspicion of hit men.

"He'd make the biggest enemy in America. His affiliation has a special relationship with your uncle. They wouldn't risk it." He placed the helmet on my head and plopped a kiss on my mouth. "Now come on, Mr. Killough, let's show these guys how it's done in the real mob."

I laughed quietly. "In the words of true Irishmen, feck yeah."

He shook his head, and while I grabbed my laser gun, Daire suited up in his own vest and helmet.

An employee walked through the door and clapped his hands, gaining the attention of the crowd. He went through the basic safety rules and the dos and don'ts, before he waved at an entrance on the opposite side of where we'd entered.

"Through that door is the arena. It'll be mostly dark with some dim lights to guide you around. When the timer counts down, your vests will light up in the middle with a color to show what team you're on. You do not want to shoot your own teammates, since that will take points off you. When you get shot, your vest will go dark for five seconds before you're able to shoot again. It's a point system. There are two teams. In case of an emergency, there are glowing buttons on the walls under a hard casing. Open the cover and hit the button. The lights will automatically come on and we will find you." He waved at a large screen above his head. "You have twenty minutes to succeed. There will be TVs like this around the arena to show you how much time you have left. You have two minutes after the door is opened where no shots are allowed. We will be opening the door in five seconds."

A countdown of five came on the screen, and the employee moved to the side of the wall near the entrance.

"Good luck, you're going to need it. Start the countdown!"

I watched the clock on the TV intently, clutching my laser gun tightly in my hands as the time began to tick downward.

Five.

Four.

Three.

Two.

One.

All our vests lit up and mine turned green, while Daire's went red.

"Looks like we're enemies, boy," Daire murmured right as the door to the arena opened. "Run, because when I catch you, I won't be lenient." He slapped me on the ass as the crowd of laser taggers filed out.

I winked at Daire before I followed everyone else. As soon as they were through the door, they began to run, so I did, too. I went left and found myself in a huge room with all kinds of obstacles, from small wooden fortresses to foam ball pits, but to get to these kinds of locations, we had to go through a maze of walls.

I turned right, then left through the labyrinth, doing my best to avoid any of the other players. As I made another left, I froze when I came face-to-face with a young boy, but he showed me his green vest. We laughed before we went on our way.

I moved as swiftly as I could, ducking behind a half wall as a young woman passed on the other side. Once she had her back to me, I rose and rested my elbows on the half wall before I whistled. She spun and her red vest was all I needed to see before I shot at her chest. Her vest beeped and went dark, and she groaned.

"Damn it." She pouted.

"Better luck next time." I laughed as I crouched again and snuck forward.

I rounded a corner and shot another guy, and he cursed me, then grinned.

"Good job, man."

I winked at him, a bolt of pride firing through me. The atmosphere was intoxicating, the dimmed lights and thrumming rock music working its way into my system. For the first time in forever, I felt free. There wasn't any pressure bearing down on me and no fear of failure.

I managed to get three more people before I rounded the corner to a little girl, no older than eight, sitting on the ground with her face in her hands. She hiccupped with a small sob. The vest she wore was lit up red and it reflected around her, almost like a warning sign.

I hesitated, a primal part of my brain whispering it was a trap, before my empathy won out. I walked over to her and crouched. "Are you okay? Do you want me to find someone for you, sweetheart?"

She glanced up, and I immediately zeroed in on her smile.

"Damn it." I stood and turned but was met with Daire, who raised his gun and shot. My vest beeped and it went dark. "What the hell, Daddy?"

The little girl giggled and jumped to her feet. She clapped her hands. "That was awesome." Then, she held out her palm to Daire. "Pay up, mister."

I gaped at him. "You paid a little girl to trap me?"

Daire's grin took up his entire face as he tugged out a couple fifties from his pocket and passed them over to her. She skipped away, clearly happy with her score. What a little terror. I bet she would succeed in her future.

He booped me on the nose when I glared at him. "Always be prepared for the unexpected, boy. Just because she's a little girl doesn't mean she won't be the end of you."

"This was a lesson?" I paused as my vest lit up again, and Daire raised his gun. "Wait!"

He shot me again and the vest went dark. "And don't stick around to BS with your enemy." Cupping my cheek, he stroked a thumb across my lips before he leaned in to steal a kiss. "Run because I'm going to chase you."

My instincts kicked in before my brain did, and I spun on my heel, running as fast as I could. I passed a few of my teammates, but I ignored them as my heart hammered so fast it felt like my whole chest was rattling.

I turned a corner and froze as I came face-to-face with Zed—his gun pointed at me. I swallowed before he winked and nodded down at his vest, and relief washed through me when I realized he was a teammate. It wasn't even a real game, yet tension swarmed me like a hive of bees, and I couldn't stand still. I needed to keep going and return the favor to Daire.

I gave him a sharp nod before I was off again. Goose bumps prickled on the back of my neck, and I could tell he was watching me, yet I didn't stop.

I managed to shoot three more people before I glanced at the timer on the screen above us, the countdown finally reaching a minute left. Fuck. At this rate, I wasn't going to find Daire again.

If Sloan had been here, he would've told me that was plenty of time. With that in mind, I took a deep breath and raised the gun, focusing on the path ahead of me. I kept close to the walls, sneaking around corners and shooting anyone on the opposing team before they could get me in return. As thirty seconds flashed on the screen, I finally found Daire.

He had his back to me, pointing his laser gun at Zed, who grinned in return at him. Zed glanced over Daire's shoulder at me, and even though it was difficult to see in the dark, he raised his palm to Daire as if he was giving up, but something about the way he flicked a glance in my direction told me what he was doing. He was sacrificing himself. It was almost as if he knew I wanted to shoot Daire at least once.

I gave him a small nod in thanks before I snuck up behind Daire. "Hey, Daddy."

Daire spun around, gun raised, but I was faster, shooting him straight in the chest. His vest went dark, and I whooped as a loud buzzer echoed around the arena, signaling the end of the game.

"You're not the only one who can use a distraction." I stuck my tongue out at him, and Zed laughed, slapping Daire on the back.

"You've got a lot to teach him," Zed said.

Daire snorted. "You're telling me something I already know."

I gazed between them. "What? I did exactly what you did. I used a distraction to kill my prey."

"You were already dead. Twice." He held up two fingers to me, lips pursed, though amusement flickered in his eyes. "Can't kill me if you're already six feet under, boy."

I huffed. "That doesn't count."

He winked. "Let's argue over some greasy food."

He grasped my elbow as my belly chose that moment to growl in appreciation at the thought of burgers. Straightening, I pointed at him. "We're still going to discuss this."

We didn't. The conversation was firmly over as we enjoyed all the greasy food from the bar that Daire had promised me. I shouldn't have enjoyed it as much as I did, but it'd been a long time since I'd had something that wasn't prepared by five-star chefs.

On the car ride home, I shot Daire a grin. "We should take Sloan there."

He laughed. "Yeah, he might enjoy it."

"I'm serious. He needs to relax sometimes." I stared out the window as the streetlights rushed by, a reminder of how quickly the world passed. It was hard to believe it'd been eight years since Daire and I had begun fucking, and it had taken us this long to be something more.

"Are you going to tell your uncle that?" Daire laughed as he turned his SUV in to the driveway that led to the garage under his building.

"Fuck no. I was hoping you could." I nudged him with my elbow when his laughter grew louder.

"He's already mad at me about the Aodhan thing. I'd rather not push my luck, boy. You like my cock, and if he decides to kill me, you won't be able to enjoy it anymore," he teased with a wink.

"Good point. Maybe I should tell Conall to talk to him about it."

"He'd be the only one who'd survive that conversation." Daire pulled the vehicle into his parking spot and put it in Park.

"The only one who Sloan might actually listen to." I chuckled.

"Careful, it sounds almost like you respect him," he said, clearly amused.

I shrugged. "Conall's not too bad."

Without giving him a chance to respond, I slipped from the SUV and unbuttoned my suit jacket to make me feel more relaxed as I waited for Daire. When he reached me, I laced my fingers with his and tugged him.

"Come on, Daddy Daire. You're going to give me a real tour of your penthouse now. There are some rooms I haven't seen yet."

He yanked me back and wrapped his arm around my shoulder as he led me into the elevator. "There's only one important place you haven't seen. My office. The other door is just the bathroom for the guest room," he said while we rode upward.

The doors opened, revealing the entrance to the penthouse. Once we were inside, he hooked his hand into the lapel of my jacket and yanked me toward the stairs.

"Oooh, Daddy, you're getting rough with me. Are you trying to turn me on?"

He chuckled and guided me up the black steps to the second floor of his home. He slapped me on the ass playfully, and I gasped at the pleasant sting, even through the layer of my pants and underwear.

He led me to the door I'd seen but never entered and opened it, then stepped aside so I could move into the room. I paused as soon as I passed the threshold, gazing at the orderly office. In the center, toward the back, was a black steel desk with a black office chair. A laptop was open in the center of the desk. Other than that, there was nothing else except for three walls of black shelves stuffed full of books. The right wall had floor-to-ceiling windows, looking out toward the Manhattan skyline. Lights sprinkled across the horizon, glittering like a thousand diamonds.

I took one step after another, moving toward the shelves, and picked up a book randomly. Red in color, it was plain except for the gold font on the front. *The Truth About the Mayans*. Each title that I came across was related to history.

I replaced the original book and turned to Daire, who leaned against the front of the desk with his arms crossed. "You like reading?"

He smiled, soft and sweet—in a way I hadn't seen before. "I do. I enjoy reading about history. We as humans should always be aware of the mistakes we made in the past, but unfortunately, we don't learn from them."

"Why—" I shook away the tiny prickle of hurt and tried again. "Why didn't I know this?"

He made an amused sound in the back of his throat. "Because it wasn't important to the job. You didn't need to know."

"And now?" I asked, hesitant but hopeful.

He stared at me for a long moment before he shoved off the

desk and ate up the distance between us. He cradled my face, and I pushed up on my tiptoes to get closer. "You wanted to learn about the real me. Here I am, opening up to you, boy."

I dislodged one of his hands to nuzzle his jaw and inhaled his spicy masculine scent. My dick twitched and I ground my hips against his. "Tell me more, Daddy. *Fuck.* Please."

"This doing it for you?" The amusement in his voice tickled my insides. The serious Daddy Daire was hot, but this one? The carefree Daire—the one I made happy? Fucking stunning.

"What can I say? I get hard when there's feelings involved," I teased.

He laughed. "Okay, boy, get ready to come in your pants." He carded his fingers through my hair and tugged my head back. "My first history book was given to me when I was eight as a birthday present. From Sloan."

I cocked my head to the side in surprise. "Uncle gave it to you?"

"Yeah." He turned his head to the bookshelf with a sentimental gleam in his eye. "We'd known each other for a few weeks by then. My father had already joined the Killough Company. I was a quiet, shy boy. Sloan thought I was odd. He told me that, too. Then, he found me watching a documentary on TV when he came to visit our house with his father. He asked me why I wanted to watch something about dead people. I told him I enjoyed history. I liked to consume information about it whenever I could. My birthday was a week later, and he showed up with this."

Daire walked over to his desk and opened the first drawer. He pulled out a thick book and held it toward me. I took it and cradled it like the treasure it was. The cover was old and frail, brown in color with a drawn image of two Roman-type figures fighting on the front. The title *History of the Peloponnesian War* spread across the cover.

"It's an account written by Thucydides, an Athenian

historian. He served as a general in the war between the Peloponnesian League and the Delian League." He stared down at the book warmly, and I brushed my hand over the cover. I could feel Daire's connection to the work, despite not fully understanding his love for history.

I had absolutely no interest in ancient history, but hearing Daire speak about it was something else entirely. Need clenched at my insides. Daire wasn't just giving me information about his past, he was sharing these soft, tender parts of himself that many would never know. There wasn't anything hotter.

I placed the book on the desk carefully and took in the sharp lines of my Daddy's cheekbones and his dark eyes—soul searching for a glimpse of the man underneath the somber mask.

Daire. The good son. The reliable one.

He was the best friend and second-in-command who never questioned Sloan's orders.

He was the history lover who enjoyed reading and had walls of books.

He was the skilled strategist who built the impenetrable fortress to protect our illegal crimes behind the facade of a hospital for the rich.

But the most important part was that he was my Daddy, and I had all of him now.

I brushed my hand over his chest, my breathing growing more rapid. "Thank you."

"For what?" He leaned down, lips ghosting over mine.

"For sharing this side of you. That's all I wanted."

He chuckled. "There's a lot more about me to know, boy."

"I can't wait to find out." I surged up into his mouth and grasped his face between my hands, melting into his kiss as he hauled me closer by my hips. With our bodies pressed together like this, everything was perfect and where it needed to be.

Everything else in the world could go to hell because I had Daire kissing me. My Daddy.

He slammed me against the nearest bookshelf. Books went toppling around me, but he didn't seem to care as he picked me up under the ass. I wrapped my legs around his waist and grappled at his shoulders. His kiss was scalding, and I sank into the burn. Our passion was aflame, and I would gladly turn to ash—as long as I could have him for the rest of my life. Happy. Content. With Daire.

Nothing else mattered in this moment—the apprenticeship, the Company. I would let it all crumble as long as Daire was pressed against me.

"Daddy." He drank down my moan as his tongue brushed against mine. "Please."

"What do you need, boy?" He nibbled my bottom lip and tugged. "Tell me."

I inhaled deeply, taking in the aroma of his cologne and storing it in my memories so I'd never forget what he smelled like. "I need your dick."

He grinned, flashing me straight white teeth. "Yeah?" He nuzzled my cheek and licked a stripe over it. "Want me balls deep inside you? Fill you up with my cum until you're leaking?"

I whimpered. My hole clenched in anticipation and my stomach fluttered.

"Have you been a good boy?"

"The best. I've been the best." I tightened my legs around his waist, ignoring the twinge of pain from something sharp digging into my shoulder. "Please, give it to me."

"One day, boy, I'm going to fill you up with so much cum that it'll pool in your underwear. We'll be in a meeting with all the men, and all you'll be able to focus on is the mess in your briefs. You'll always be reminded you're mine, won't you?" He bit along my jaw, claiming his territory. "Fuck, boy."

"Use your dick on me," I begged with no shame. When it

came to Daire, I was his—body and soul. He could do whatever he wanted.

He dropped me back to my feet, and I wailed in disappointment, which quickly warped into a moan when he spun me around and slammed my chest against the shelf again. More books wobbled and tumbled from their spots, clattering against the wooden floor.

A shiver swept down my spine, and I trembled as he yanked at my pants. I wriggled my hips to show off my ass.

He gripped my hands and slammed them against the shelf. "Hands stay there. Do not move them. Understand, boy?"

I whined in answer and received a sharp slap to my underwear-covered ass for it.

"Words. Daddy needs to hear the words, boy." His tongue traced the shell of my ear, chest pressed firmly against my back. The familiar outline of his bulge rubbed the cleft of my ass, and I trembled harder. Fuck.

"I understand, Daddy. I won't move my hands."

"Good boy." He nibbled the top of my ear before he was gone. The weight of his body against my back lifted, and I held in the urge to whimper in disappointment. The sound of a drawer opening met my ears, but I was too scared to turn around in case I was punished for it.

Then, he returned. He shifted the collar of my suit jacket and dress shirt so he could kiss the back of my neck, and the feel of his lips sent a wave of desire crashing through me, landing straight in my balls. My dick twitched where it was stuck in my underwear. We hadn't even started, and I was already on edge, ready to fall over the cliff of pleasure.

He yanked down my underwear to join my pants, and I shivered as the cool air hit my heated skin. "I'm going to fuck you nice and deep, boy. You'll feel me in your ass tomorrow when we go see Sloan."

I groaned. "Yes, please, Daddy Daire."

"Will you be good for me?" He bit the back of my neck, and I crowed.

"So good, Daddy. I swear."

"Who do you belong to?" He slapped my ass, and the blow stung, but also had a spike of pleasure heading straight for my dick.

"You. Only you, Daddy Daire."

He smoothed a hand over my right asscheek, and I gasped. "Good boy. You own me, too. I'm so proud of you."

My dick bobbed and precum dripped down to the hardwood below. His words wove around to embrace my heart, healing the cuts from all the hurtful words he'd thrown at me over the years. Daire was my protector. My Daddy.

I bit my lip to stop a moan at the familiar sound of the lube bottle opening. Then, his fingers were at my hole. I kicked my pants and underwear lower until they fell around my ankles so I could spread my knees wider.

"You desperate for it, boy?" Daire nuzzled the side of my neck.

I whimpered. "Yes, Daddy."

"Will you be good for me?" His finger slipped between my cheeks and teased my entrance, petting across my hole.

"So good. Only for you, Daddy." I turned my head, and he planted a kiss on my mouth as he pushed his finger past the tight ring of muscle. "Please. I like the stretch. I don't need your fingers, I want your dick."

"Hmm." He pressed his nose to my cheek and breathed me in. "Do you deserve my cock, boy?"

"I'm good," I whined. "I'm so good for you."

"You *are* very good. A boy that any Daddy would be proud of."

I cried out and brought my fist to my mouth to bite down on my knuckles—forgetting about his rule. Embarrassment burned my cheeks at the shameful sound that left me. His praise alone almost had me coming. How fucking pathetic was that?

"No, no, boy. I told you not to move." Daire curled his fingers around my wrist, gently pulled my hand away from my face, and guided it back to the shelf. "I want to hear all the noises you make. Let Daddy hear you."

He added a second finger, and I pouted over my shoulder at him. "Please use your dick. I need you."

He grunted and removed his fingers.

I sighed in relief as the slick tip of his dick nudged my entrance. I arched my back, giving him the right angle to just slip on in.

He laughed deep in his throat. "You're desperate for it, boy."

"Yes, Daddy. For you? Always."

"To think, I nearly let another man steal you. I'm an idiot." He pressed into me.

I gasped, fingernails scratching at the shelf, and half chuckled, half moaned. "You said it, not me, Daddy Daire."

He slapped my right asscheek and surged into me so forcefully that my nails dug even deeper into the wood.

"Look at you." Daire groaned. "Sucking me in like a good boy. All the way to my balls." As if to make a point, he slammed balls deep into me. I keened, throwing my head back when he struck my prostate. Desire pummeled through me, and the sounds that ripped from my throat would've been embarrassing if I was in my right mind, but all I could think about was Daire's dick in my ass, his fingers digging into the skin of my waist, and his mouth sweeping across my cheek with a warm breath, teasing my skin into goose bumps.

My grip slipped with his next hard thrust, and before I could catch myself, I'd knocked books to the floor. My dick throbbed, and despite the urge to reach down and stroke my length, I couldn't. Daddy Daire had told me to keep my hands in front of me. I was his good boy so that was exactly what I would do.

"Fuck, you feel so good, boy. Do you know what you're doing to my cock right now? You're so tight you're strangling me. You're drawing me in, like you want me to live here . . . ."

I shivered as his fingers stroked over my cheek—his soft touch a delicious contrast to the way he ravaged my hole.

"Do you want me to sleep with my dick in your ass, boy? Will you drain my balls dry and beg me to stay inside you?"

I tightened my grip on the shelf so forcefully that the wood dug into my palm. My head dropped forward. Daire tugged on the collar of my shirt and attacked the back of my neck with his teeth. He could litter me with his marks until it hurt to move, and I'd say "Yes, please. Thank you, Daddy."

He nuzzled my neck, a soft brush of his nose where his teeth had just been. "What do you think, boy? Would you like my dick in you all the time?"

I whimpered. "Yes, Daddy. You're so wide, Daddy. I can feel you here." I shoved my hand under my shirt and jacket and laid my palm on my stomach. "You're rearranging my guts, Daddy Daire."

"Fuck, boy." He planted his hands on my hips in a brutal grip and began to hammer into me. His dick slid out, then back home with the kind of force against my prostate that had me screaming. I wanted him to stay inside me forever. Just me and him. Together. "Didn't I tell you hands in front? I should spank you for breaking the rules."

I squeezed the shelf again and held on as he slammed into me. While his thrusts were unrelenting, they were controlled. My Daddy knew exactly what he was doing.

Pleasure built at the base of my spine and my stomach tingled. My balls tightened closer to my body, desperate for release.

"Please, Daddy." I wiped my cheeks and the back of my hand returned with traces of tears. I felt so fucking needy for everything he was willing to give me. "Let me touch myself. Please. I've been so good, Daddy."

I hadn't. I'd broken the rules a few times already, but I knew my Daddy. He was forgiving.

He growled into my ear, and I cried out as he punched my prostate with another roll of his hips. "You're such a good boy. *My* good boy. Jerk yourself off, Fifi. Show Daddy how much you love his cock inside your tight little hole."

I trembled, a wave of desperation flooding me. *Finally*—the permission I needed. I spat in my palm and jerked my dick fast and hard. My need to come barreled through me as rough as Daire's dick was fucking me. "So good, Daddy Daire. I love it so much."

He seized my chin and dragged my face toward him before slamming his mouth against mine. His thrusts were relentless against my prostate and felt so fucking good. I was drowning and burning in pleasure—a desperate shivering mess. My arms wobbled, knees buckled, but before I could fall, my Daddy's strong arms curled around me to keep me steady.

"Be a good boy and listen to Daddy. Come for me." He clamped down at the back of my neck, and that was all it took for my world to crash around me in a mind-blowing orgasm. My balls nearly withdrew completely into my body as my release hit me with the force of a semitruck.

Cum splattered across the spines of books and over the shelves.

Daire wasn't far behind me. His arms squeezed me tighter while he groaned sweet praises into my ear that had my dick twitching before warmth filled my insides.

He rested his forehead on the junction between my neck and shoulder, chest heaving. "Fuck."

"Did that feel good, Daddy Daire?" I asked.

He laughed and leaned over to kiss me, and I whined into his mouth. "Perfect, boy. You are perfect."

"Only for you. You're the one who gets this side of me." I cuddled back into him, and he hummed.

"Good boy," he purred. "Now how about we clean up, hmm?"

"Sounds amazing."

He slid out of me. I quickly turned to grab him by the lapels of his jacket before he could back away. His cock curved up and was shiny from lube and cum.

"Thank you for the date and for sharing this with me." I waved at the books, then frowned at the pile scattered across the wooden floor. I bent to pick them up, but he grabbed my elbow and drew me into his strong embrace.

"We'll handle it tomorrow, boy. I only want you in my arms right now and for always."

I shivered. That's exactly what I'd wanted to hear for the last eight years.

16

FIONN

The ride to Sloan's house was filled with silence, thickened by the tension that stifled the air between us. Aodhan didn't say anything to us, and by the concerned expression on Daire's face, he thought it was strange. It was weird for Aodhan to be quiet based on our short acquaintance. He'd always been mouthy and confident. Daire didn't bother to ask if he was all right, and neither did I.

When we arrived at the house in Southampton, Aodhan finally smirked at Daire.

"Give your brother a hug for good luck?"

Daire rolled his eyes and slipped out of his Mercedes, and I followed him from where I sat in the back. Aodhan was right behind us as we stalked up the front stairs of Sloan's house. Mr. Hopper opened the door and bowed his head slightly as we entered.

"Mr. Killough has asked the Reardons to wait outside his office. Young Mr. Killough, your uncle wishes to see you in the basement," Mr. Hopper drawled. The elderly butler always looked blasé; his stoicism wasn't anything new.

I gave him a sharp nod and turned to Daire. With a smile, I reached out for his hand and squeezed it. "I'll be right back."

Daire swooped down to kiss me, and I froze. I hadn't expected him to do that so casually in front of Company men. I wasn't going to complain. I returned his kiss and held back a whine when he pulled away.

"Remember who you are, boy. You're a Killough. This company is your birthright." He brushed his thumb over my cheekbone.

I closed my eyes, reveling in the tender moment while in his strong arms, before I gave him another smile. "Yes, Daddy."

Mr. Hopper coughed, his eyebrows jumping just enough that I could hardly recognize the usually foreboding man. The moment may have been fleeting, but it was enough that I considered it a win. It was rare for anyone to catch him by surprise. Grinning wider, I winked at Daire and left him and Aodhan there as I walked down the hallway toward the stairs that led to our special torture room in the basement.

I descended the stairs and paused at the bottom. In the middle of the torture room a man hung naked by his ankles. Blood flowed from various cuts down the length of his body until it trailed over his arms and dripped off his fingers like waterfalls pooling onto the cement floor below.

A few of our men stood to the right side of the room, quiet and waiting, while Sloan sat in a chair on the left. His elbows were on his knees, hands covered in blood that dripped onto the floor with the rest of it. His white dress shirt was splattered in blood and the stains were stark against the pale material. The sight of him was sinister, a reminder of his power.

Sloan's cold stare tracked me as I stepped farther into the room. "Fionn."

A queasy sensation bombarded my stomach, twisting and knotting until I thought I was going to puke. Bile burned my throat. This wasn't the first time I'd seen a dead body—even one so mutilated. I wasn't sure I'd ever get used to it. It was rare for my uncle to be so hands-on with . . . . When he did there was usually a point to prove.

"Uncle. Mr. Hopper said you wanted to see me. Aodhan's here."

Sloan hummed and held out his hand to one of the men on the other side of the room. The man handed Sloan a damp towel. "Good," Sloan murmured as he took his time to carefully clean his hands of blood. "Do you know who this man was?"

I glanced at the body. His face wasn't familiar—though, that meant little with how torn apart he was. "No, Uncle."

Sloan smiled, a menacing quirk of his lips that sent a shiver up my spine. "His name was Markus Gill. His wife was Rina, the sister of Reed Olsson."

Oh—Reed Olsson was a man we'd recently captured. He'd stolen drugs from Sloan and hidden them. Four of our men—Cillian, Rowen, Aspen, and Fallon—had taken turns in torturing Reed for information. In the end, it was our specialized thief, Oisín Kelly, who managed to get it from Reed. Oisín discovered that Reed placed the drugs in the most obvious place—his sister's house. As payment, Oisín got to keep Reed as his own.

I nodded.

"Hm. Some of our men questioned me about leaving Reed alive. They wanted him dead." Sloan crossed a leg over his knee and held out his hand. The man who'd given him the towel opened his suit jacket to pull out a sheathed cigar. Sloan popped the end of the cigar in his mouth and our man lit it up for him. "They complained I was weak to let Reed live."

I waited. My fingers twitched as Sloan took a puff of his cigar before blowing out a stream of smoke. The sweet aroma of tobacco and cherries tickled my nose.

"The thing about being the boss, Fionn, is that we get to decide when it's beneficial to kill someone and when it's not. I could've killed Reed, yes, but he was still useful. By giving him to Oisín, I fulfilled a favor and kept one of my most important men happy—ensuring the strict loyalty of a valued asset. Reed is Oisín's toy now, but also his responsibility. Any trouble he causes, Oisín will have to pay for." Sloan took another puff and stood, rolling his shoulders, before he filled the air with more smoke. "I killed Reed's sister to prove a point. Her husband, this coward—" He waved at the hanging body. "—ran away before we could get there. Left his wife behind. It took a while to find him, but we did."

I swallowed and fought to keep my attention on my uncle—I could taste the metallic tang of blood on the air.

Sloan walked toward me and stopped right in front of me. "This waste of space wasn't useful, so he died. If someone talks to the cops, they aren't useful. They die. Do you understand?"

I tilted my chin up to meet him head-on. "Yes, Uncle."

"Aodhan. Should he die?"

I shifted with unease. Aodhan was Daire's brother. He would never want him dead, but what did that matter to Sloan? To the Company? He certainly would never run to the police. "No, Uncle. I think he could be useful."

Sloan made a sound in the back of his throat. "He directly questioned my authority and touched what belonged to me. Did you know that?"

I licked my lips nervously. "Yes, Uncle."

"What use do I have for a man like that?"

My fingers twitched at my sides. Sloan's gaze was hard on me, demanding responses. I curled my hands into fists, then uncurled them again. I wanted to give him answers —I had a duty to him and the Company—but I also needed to protect Aodhan for my Daddy. He'd always been alone in fixing Aodhan's mistakes, and now he had me to help. "He kills, right? And he's good at it. We could always send him out on dangerous assignments."

"He defied my orders." Sloan raised his dark eyebrows. "How do we trust him?"

I took a deep breath. "Send someone with him. Someone who can keep him in line."

Sloan's mouth curled into a smirk. "Hmm. Good." He patted me on the shoulder, and a shot of pride joined the terror of giving the wrong answer. "Go wait for me outside my office. I'll be there shortly." He flicked a look at the men. "Get rid of the body and clean up. Call Caden."

I held in a snort of amusement. Caden was a Kings of Men MC biker who worked under Jamie Shannon's boyfriend, Hunter. A small new chapter was set up in New York, and they had begun to work closely with us. Caden ran a *cleaning* service that dealt specifically in bodily fluids and corpses.

Sloan slapped me on the back, and I took it as a gesture to go upstairs like he'd ordered. I tilted my head in respect and made my way toward Sloan's office, where I found Daire and Aodhan waiting.

Aodhan was leaning against the wall, unimpressed by the expensive and *very real* Paul Cézanne painting that cost well over two hundred and fifty million beside him. Daire stood straight with his arms crossed. They were in a quiet conversation, and I was surprised to see a small smile on Daire's face. Maybe for once Aodhan wasn't causing trouble.

"Hey, Kitty," Aodhan greeted with a wide grin.

Daire shot me a surprised glance and his face melted into a warmth that made my chest squeeze. I didn't care who was watching as I strode directly into his waiting arms. I kissed Daire's jaw, and he gripped my hand. I tilted my head back so he could slant his mouth over mine in a drawn-out kiss that had my toes curling in my freshly polished shoes.

"Hi," I murmured against his warm mouth.

"Hey, boy. How did it go?" Daire brushed his nose against mine, and I sighed in pleasure.

"I think I did good?"

He hummed. "I didn't expect any less. Good boy."

I shuddered under his praise. "Sloan looked happy when I answered one of his questions. I can't remember the last time that happened."

Before Daire could respond, Sloan's familiar footsteps echoed through the hall. I turned to see him striding down the hallway still wearing his blood-splattered shirt. I'd expected him to get changed, but I supposed he appeared more dangerous to Aodhan if he looked like this. He had washed his hands, though, which left his skin clean.

He paused when he reached us and gestured for Aodhan to follow him with his finger.

When Daire and I went to do the same, Sloan shook his head.

"No. Only Aodhan. We need to have a discussion." He pointed at us. "You two stay here."

I hesitated, but Daire placed his hand on my shoulder and squeezed it in reassurance.

Aodhan winked at me. "It's okay, Kitten, I can handle the big bad wolf. Maybe he'll blow me—I mean blow the house down."

Sloan rolled his eyes and strode into his office with Aodhan cackling behind him.

The moment the door *clicked* shut, I groaned. "Sloan's going to kill him, isn't he?"

"No," Daire said with a certainty that surprised me. I glanced at him, and he gave me a gentle kiss. "If he was going to kill him, he would've done it already. What did he say to you downstairs?"

I took a deep breath. "That as the boss we have to choose who lives and who dies based on their usefulness."

He chuckled. "Makes sense. Sloan's a tactician. Everything he does is planned, and while he can't account for everything, he's quick on his feet when he needs to be." He waved his hand toward the office door. "Aodhan is one of the best hit men in the world, maybe even better than Ardan—don't tell him I said that."

I laughed.

"Sloan can use him. Aodhan's a loose cannon, but with the proper motivation, he can be . . . managed."

"Maybe someone to watch over him?" I offered, remembering what I'd suggested to Sloan. "There are many men we can trust to keep an eye on him."

"Not many who can keep up with him." Daire frowned thoughtfully. "Aodhan is like a cheetah on cocaine. He's always on the go, moving at a hundred miles per hour even when he's standing still. He has enough energy for a thousand men."

"We have a lot of men, I'm sure we can find someone." I sighed and wrapped my arms around his neck, and he curved his around my waist, dragging me against him. He swooped down for a kiss, and I closed my eyes, relishing the taste of his mouth against mine. Everything about *this*, about us, felt just right. He loved me and wanted the world to know. I was enjoying every second of this new feeling. I didn't want any of it to end.

"You are so beautiful, boy," he whispered against my cheek. He traced my cheekbone with his mouth, dotting kisses across my skin until his teeth were nipping at the top of my ear. "I want to eat you up."

"That can be arranged," I murmured with a wide grin. "Any time, any place. I'm yours to feast on, Daddy."

Daire chuckled hotly in my ear before he nibbled on my lobe. "You're such a good boy. I couldn't find a better boy than you."

A shudder of pleasure danced down my spine, and a keen slipped from me before I could stop it. I flushed, but Daire's chuckle deepened as he pulled back to cradle my face in his huge hands. He stroked his thumb over my cheekbone and tilted my chin up, peppering me with more kisses.

I didn't know how long we stood there, kissing gently without any real rush, before the door to Sloan's office opened again. I didn't jump away like I might've once. Instead, I slowly broke our kiss. When I turned out of Daire's arms, I was met with Aodhan's amused face.

"Don't stop on my account." He smirked as he shut the door behind himself.

Daire grunted. "How did it go?"

Aodhan shrugged. "Looks like I'm going to be sticking around for a while."

"You can get your own place," Daire responded without missing a beat.

Aodhan laughed. "Yeah, whatever. I'll be in and out of New York. I have a new partner."

"Who?" I was curious who Sloan thought could match Aodhan. There hadn't been much time between our conversation and him turning up here, which made me wonder if Sloan had already decided to pair Aodhan up with one of our men before I suggested it.

Aodhan crossed his arms and raised his eyebrows. "An Italian. Your ex, Kitten. Michele Scotti."

"He's not my ex. We never—" In the end, it didn't matter. "Why an Italian?"

Why did Uncle choose Michele, of all people? How could we trust the Italians after they'd hidden the book from us? We still hadn't heard from Elio.

"Apparently, I have a special assignment. The boss arranged something with Folliero. We have a common enemy." He winked at me. "Too bad, huh? Will you miss me?"

"No." I mirrored his posture and crossed my arms. "Stop calling me kitten."

His laughter grew louder, and he bent his fingers, making a scratching gesture at Daire. "Rawr."

Daire pinched the bridge of his nose and exhaled. "Aodhan, stop."

Aodhan held up his hands, then made a zipping motion over his mouth. "I'm done. And now I have to go meet my new boyfriend." His laughter was back, loud and boisterous—this wasn't the same quiet man who'd been in the car with us. This was the real Aodhan. "Don't do anything I wouldn't do." With a final wink, he stalked down the hallway like a man on a mission.

I watched him go with a frown as the door opened again. Sloan stuck his head out.

"Fionn, come in here for a moment. I want a word."

A sharp shot of fear fired through me. I took a deep breath to center myself. With a small smile to Daire, I followed Sloan into his office and gently closed the door.

By the time I turned around, Sloan was already in the leather chair behind his desk. His hands rested on the solid wood in front of him. There wasn't any tension on his face, and I took the relaxation as a sign that I wasn't in any trouble.

I snagged the guest chair in front of his desk. "Did you get it figured out with Aodhan?"

The soft scent of lavender filled the room and I let it soothe the fear. Now that I could admit I didn't hate Conall, I liked some of the things he'd done around this place. His essential oils were a nice touch with surprisingly therapeutic benefits.

"Yes, we did. Aodhan will be staying with the Company for a while longer. He'll be working with the Italians to fix a problem. Elio reached out and asked for help, and honestly, it benefits the Company, too." Sloan opened the top drawer of his desk and removed a shiny silver case. He opened it and pulled out another cigar, eyeing me with a conspiratorial smirk. "Don't tell Conall." He held up the cigar. "He doesn't like it when I smoke too much."

I chuckled. "That sounds like him."

Sloan raised his eyebrows. "What happened between you two? Suddenly you're more . . . *amicable*."

I shrugged. "I want to make you proud, and Conall's your pet. He's important to you, which means I need to get along with him."

That wasn't the entire truth. After Conall helped me through the Michele and Daire situation, it was difficult to hate him. If anything, I considered him more of a friend, though I would never admit that out loud. When we passed each other in the house, we'd stop to talk or share a smile. It was nice not to use so much energy disliking him. Conall was smarter than I'd first suspected.

"Good." An emotion I didn't recognize passed through Sloan's gaze as he cleared his throat and grabbed his cigar cutter.

After trimming the end, he shoved the cigar into his mouth and seized a box of matches. He made a show of lighting up. I'd never been interested in smoking, even cigars, but Sloan had been doing it for as long as I could remember. My grandfather had died when I was young, but he'd been a cigar smoker as well.

Sloan shook the match before he dropped it into the glass ashtray in front of him. He took a long puff before blowing the smoke out through his nose. "There's something we need to discuss. Something you may not like."

My throat went dry and a pit opened in my stomach. I fought to hold back a shudder. Nodding, I sat up straighter. "Of course, Uncle."

I refused to look away as his emotionless stare bore into me.

Most people thought of Sloan as ruthless and cold, and while he *was* those things, he'd also tried his best while raising me. It had to be hard for him. He'd just brutally lost his brother, and suddenly, he had his kid to take care of. Sloan had always made time for me when he could. Some nights, we'd sit at the kitchen island eating olives from the jar as we talked about our day. Other nights, he'd give me lessons about being the boss of a large organization like the Killough Company. He'd made sure I was educated and prepared. A tactician in training.

At the start of my senior year, I'd demanded to be let into the Company. To be his underling. His *apprentice*. He'd needed a month to think about it before he'd finally agreed, under the provision that I graduated with high scores. During the weekends and after I finished my homework, he started to test me with hypothetical situations, and after a few months of that, he brought me out on a couple of *excursions*. They were mostly safe trips, but I got a feel for what was expected of me if I wanted to inherit the business.

Finally, I'd graduated with a solid GPA, and that was the last time I truly remembered Sloan being proud of me.

He was still my uncle, even if he wasn't able to fully show me how much he cared for me while I was his apprentice. I trusted him.

Sloan exhaled another puff of smoke through his nose and sighed. "Lorcan O'Guinn. Lor. The one who stays here."

I frowned, acid stirring in my stomach whenever that name was mentioned. God, I fucking hated him. "Yeah, I know the one. He teaches some of our men's kids with Dr. Mifflin."

"Mm-hmm." Sloan placed his cigar on the ashtray and threaded his fingers together. "He's the son of Lorcan Lee—even if the idiot doesn't treat Lor like one."

My eyebrows furrowed. I wasn't quite sure where Sloan was going with this. "Okay."

"Let me tell you a story. My father, your grandfather, was never truly faithful to my mother. He never loved her. Their marriage was set up by *my* grandfather, who was trying to strengthen his Irish alliances. So, Dad slept around a lot and Mom never cared. She didn't love him, either, and I'm sure she had her own lovers. Out of my father's mistresses, there was only one woman I knew about. Dad never loved her, but he fucked her regularly. A maid."

Sloan rarely talked about his father. From what I remembered as a child, Grandfather had never been very affectionate, either.

He made an irritated sound. "Dad wasn't a good man, but neither was my granddad. Mom tried, but Dad had me and Eoin under his thumb, while she took care of my sister."

I frowned. Sloan talked about his younger sister even less than his father. She'd moved back to Ireland when Sloan took over the Company, not interested in being part of the mob.

"He wanted us in the family business. Anyway, that doesn't matter. The only thing that does matter was what Dad told me on his deathbed. There were rumors that Lorcan Lee was his son. The maid was Lorcan's mother. I didn't know what to believe, until Dad asked me with his dying breath to make Lorcan my chief advisor."

"Is Lorcan really Granddad's son?" I asked before I could stop myself. Panic rose in my throat, clogging it.

Sloan laughed, but it wasn't in amusement. "I wondered. After Dad died, I took a piece of his hair and Lorcan's spit from a finished can of pop." He pursed his lips. "Lorcan Lee is my half brother."

"Damn," I breathed out, catching myself before I could say *fuck*. Lorcan fucking Lee. That asshole was the epitome of a loser. I'd always wondered why Sloan chose to keep him in the Company.

Sloan shook his head and leaned back in his leather seat. He tapped the desk with his forefinger. "Lorcan doesn't know. No one but you and I do now. But Lor is Lorcan's son."

It took a moment, but the dots started to connect. "Lor's my cousin. Your nephew." I stood, nearly knocking my chair over. The panic intensified and swept south to my lungs, making it

difficult to breathe. This was the perfect time for swearing—
fuck!

Sloan raised his palm before I could say anything else. "This
doesn't change anything, Fionn. *You* are my apprentice. I needed
you to know the truth. Lor doesn't know yet, and I want to keep
it that way. He's a good kid who needs some guidance and
resources. His father has barely had anything to do with him."

What about me? I wanted to scream. Sloan treated Lor more
like a son than he did me lately. I'd worked my ass off for this
company, *for Sloan*, yet as soon as he discovered who Lor was,
he took him under his wing.

Pain sliced through my heart, and I breathed through the
agony that tore me to shreds on the inside. I nodded sharply.
"Understood, Uncle."

"Fionn—"

"Excuse me, sir." I raced out of the office before Sloan
ordered me to stay. Until he gave me direct instructions, I could
escape, and I couldn't stay in there for a minute longer.

I nearly knocked Daire down on my way through the hall. I
had to get out of here. Sloan said nothing had changed, but that
was bullshit. Everything had changed. I would lose everything.
It didn't matter if I was still his apprentice. He liked Lor better
than me.

Everyone did.

Lor laughed along with our men and cozied up to Conall
and Vail. He might look like some brooding goth, but he had
them all wrapped around his finger. They loved him. *Fuck!* And
Uncle Sloan was keeping him herc in the house. *Why?* If anyone
found out he was a Killough, too, they'd all want him to be the
boss.

Talk about keeping *useful* people close.

I took the grand staircase two steps at a time and raced
down the hallway until I crashed into my room. I slammed the
door shut before I broke down in the hall. I tried to take a deep

breath but choked on the panic rising in my throat. Terror and anger assailed me, and I didn't know if I wanted to scream or cry.

Both. I wanted to do both.

I couldn't breathe, couldn't push the air through my lungs. Why couldn't my body do what it was supposed to?

Tears burned in my eyes, and I clenched them shut, trying to hold the tsunami at bay.

Is this how my entire world crashed and burned? All because of a bastard and his son?

I tried to stumble to my bed, but my legs gave out, and I collapsed to the floor. I punched the hardwood until my fists bled and finally let myself scream.

Pushing to my feet, I forced my legs to work so I could get to the window and stare out.

I would *never* give up my hard work for that . . . asshole! Never!

17

DAIRE

I hesitated at Fionn's door, hand floating in the air ready to knock. I didn't know what Sloan had said to him, but it couldn't be good with the way Fionn had rushed out of the office. Following Fionn wasn't a choice. I had to make everything better for my boy. If that meant defying Sloan, then so be it.

Sighing, I rapped my knuckles on his door before walking in.

He was standing beside the window, his shoulders stiff and posture rigid. Everything about him right now reminded me of the boy I'd tried hard to ignore over the years. This wasn't Fifi or *my boy*, this was Fionn, the overworked and stressed nephew of Sloan Killough.

"Fionn?" I rushed to him and wrapped my arms around his waist. I pulled him back against my chest and held him as tight as I could. "What did he say?"

From this angle, I caught the tightness of his jaw and the moisture in his eyes as he stared out toward the massive lawn and the greenhouse Conall liked to visit. The remnants of tear tracks stained his cheeks. "Did you know?"

"Know what?" I grasped his shoulders gently and turned him

toward me, and he kept his hardened stance, as though he wasn't sure if he could trust me or not, and that hurt the most. His knuckles were bloody and I brushed my thumb over them gently. My heart gave a painful tug.

"Lorcan O'Guinn is my cousin. Sloan's nephew."

"What?" I gaped. "Cousin? Nephew? How?"

He searched my gaze, and while he was, the realization hit me. There'd been reports but nothing concrete.

"Lorcan Lee?"

He grunted. "Apparently, he's Grandfather's son."

"Fuck. I've heard the rumors, but I didn't think they were true." I held him tighter.

His mouth twisted in displeasure. "Yeah, well, apparently he is. Sloan's known since his father died. This entire fucking time. He's known who *Lor* was, too, and he didn't fucking tell me. This is like one big cosmic joke. This nobody can take everything away from me. The Company is *mine*."

"Fionn, listen to me. Look at me." I clasped his face between my palms and turned his head so he had no choice but to stare into my eyes. "Sloan will not do that. He trained you from the very beginning. You are his apprentice. He chose you."

"Because he had no other choice. Now he has Lor, and he likes him. Everyone does."

I frowned. "And you think Sloan doesn't love you, Fifi?"

He tried to pull away from my hold, but I didn't let him. "Let me go, Daire."

"No. In this room I am your Daddy, and you will listen to me."

"Daire." He struggled harder and went to shove my chest, but I dragged him into my arms.

We'd wasted too much time already, and I wasn't going to let this come between us. I refused to watch him wonder *what if* as though Sloan would ever consider giving the Company to anyone but Fionn. That'd never happen. Sloan loved Fionn like a son. He was hard on Fionn, sure, but only because he had to be. Sloan wanted nothing more than for Fionn to succeed, to gain the confidence and willpower needed to be *the* boss.

"This company is yours. Sloan knows that, everyone fucking knows that, boy. Even Conall."

He trembled so much that I felt the vibrations down to my bones.

"Let me go," he said, voice dark and unrecognizable. All the agony he felt dripped out through his tone, and it shattered my heart into pieces. This wasn't my boy. He was broken, trapped in a shell of fear. I had to bring him back to me.

"No." My grip tightened. "Never."

He swung, and I didn't have time to duck out of the way before his fist connected with my cheek. I stumbled backward—surprised more than hurt—and he made a move toward the door to escape. I came back to my senses before he could reach the exit and wrapped an arm around his waist as he struggled.

"Let me go, Daire. You fucking asshole, let me fucking go or I'll have your head for this."

"No." My cheek throbbed, and I made a mental note to praise him on his punch later, when he wasn't fueled by the kind of fury that could destroy a man.

He kicked, and I moved just in time to avoid my cock being a target. There was nothing I could say that would calm him down. He was panicking about losing his place not only in the Company, but in his family, and no words would get through to him while he was like this. I needed to find a way to center him quickly.

I forced him toward the bed as he continued to fight me the entire way. His yelling echoed around the room, but I didn't think anyone would come in.

I threw him onto the mattress face-first. When he went to get up again, a scream tore out of his throat. Before he could move, I dropped on top of him, pressing my arm against his upper back to hold him down.

"Fucking get off me! I'm going to have you killed for this. I'm the fucking apprentice. I'm Sloan's nephew. Fuck you, Daire."

"You are my boy." I pressed my weight down on him as he kicked up at me again. "I am your Daddy. I'm going to give you what you need. Even if you fight me the whole way through it."

"Fuck off!" The sound that left Fionn came from the deepest recesses of his chest, so painful that it was like a knife straight to my heart. I'd never expected to see my boy like this, and I never wanted to again.

My hand came down hard on his ass, the *crack* of it reverberating louder around the room than his screams had. He froze and a choked gasp fell past his pretty lips.

"You will listen to me," I ordered, my voice calm yet firm, leaving no room for argument. I struck his ass again—this time hard enough for a moan to crawl up and out of his throat. "I'm your Daddy, boy, and I have you. Do you hear me?"

He sobbed, his voice broken and raw. "It's my company."

"It is, boy, it *is* your company. Sloan's not going to give it to anyone else."

Another smack to the ass and the cries quieted down. I didn't let up, striking his cheeks over and over again—until there were only moans slipping out of his pretty mouth. His spine was still tense, but his shoulders had relaxed and he was no longer struggling.

"Are you okay?" I murmured into his hair, rubbing a soothing circle on his ass.

"Yes."

I winced at the rawness in his voice.

"I will be. Thank you, Daddy."

"We're not done yet." I grabbed his shoulders and sat him up on the bed, smoothing my thumbs over his tear-streaked cheeks and wet chin. He stared at me like I'd hung the moon even as sadness lingered in the depths of his eyes. "I'm going to take you apart now, boy. I'm going to strip you naked and lie you down on the bed. Then, I will eat you out until you writhe under my tongue—begging to come. Only when I'm done with you will I fuck you until you can't remember your name. Is that all right with you, baby boy?"

"Yes." The breathiness in his tone made me smile. "Please, Daddy? I need you so bad."

"Come here." I pulled him in close. Stroking my fingers down his neck, I took the time to trace every dip and curve of his jaw and face. I petted my thumbs under his eyes, down his nose, across his eyebrows, and around his ears. I wanted my boy to feel my devotion with every touch. I wanted him to feel loved. Worshiped.

He closed his eyes, exhaling through his nose as I leaned forward to press a kiss to his cheek, licking at the trail of tears he'd left behind. "Daddy."

"I'm right here, boy. I'm not leaving you. Ever."

I took my time undressing him, one piece of clothing at a time. His tie, then his suit jacket. Once his shirt was unbuttoned, I kissed the expanse of his chest and stomach, mapping the upper half of his body with my hands and mouth. I pressed my nose into his armpit and inhaled, and he moaned.

"You smell so good. Fuck, you make me hard, boy."

"Please take care of me, Daddy," he whimpered.

"Always." I traced my hands over his ribs and up again to his shoulders before I slid his shirt off his arms.

Next, I worked open his belt and pants before dragging them and his underwear down over his ass. He lifted his hips, and I pulled the clothing off his legs completely, along with his shoes and socks, leaving him naked for my hungry eyes.

I scraped my nails over his thighs, and he trembled. His cock was already hard and leaking at the slit. "Does that feel good, Fifi?"

He leaned forward, chin tilted toward me, silently begging me to kiss him. I placed my lips on his, our kiss slow and sensual as I continued to explore every curve, muscle, and dip. I avoided his cock, and when my fingers skimmed over his inner thighs close to his balls, he whined.

"Shh. Not yet," I murmured, mouthing kisses along his jaw. "I have you, baby boy. Trust me. Let Daddy take care of you."

"I do," he whispered, his words almost lost on a gasp. "I trust you with my life, Daddy."

"Good. I would die for you, boy. I'd give you the world." I sucked his earlobe between my lips and nipped it with my teeth. "Tell me, what do you prefer? Me eating you out or sucking your cock? Today's about you."

He let out a long breath. "Cock, please."

"Good manners, boy." I tugged his lobe before I grabbed him under the knees and pulled him to the edge of the bed. I shifted until I was on my knees on the floor in front of him. His face was flush with pleasure and his pupils were blown. "You're such a good boy. You're mine, aren't you?"

"Yes, Daddy Daire." He spread his legs and his cock bobbed in front of my face. "I belong to you."

I brushed my hands over his knees and up his thighs before I dipped forward and darted my tongue out, pressing the flat of it over his cockhead. He inhaled sharply, then whined as I swirled my tongue around the underside of his dick. He tasted salty and clean, and I was addicted.

I licked down his length, following the visible lines of his veins as if it were a game. I feasted on every reaction, from his shivers to the way his mouth opened in a silent gasp. He was beautiful like this—vulnerable, with his eyes still wet from tears.

I took the head into my mouth and sucked while he whimpered. I kneaded my fingers into his legs, massaging the muscles as I took even more of him between my lips. Swiping my tongue under his rigid length, I eyed him to savor his wrecked appearance. Right now was about him, about making him feel wanted and needed. He was *mine*, and I was going to give him everything I could offer.

I cupped his ball sack in my palm and squeezed. The carnal wail that left him went straight to my trapped cock. His breath hitched and he rocked his hips forward, driving his length deeper into my mouth. His euphoria was so fucking mesmerizing that I hungered for more, to bring him to absolute bliss.

I tightened my hold on his balls again and sucked him all the way down my throat, and he keened, arching his hips off the bed and shoving even deeper. My gag reflex kicked in and I choked.

Fionn quickly pulled back, eyes wide. "I'm sorry, Daddy. I didn't mean it."

I coughed into the back of my hand before laughing once I'd caught my breath. "Boy, it's fine. You are fucking beautiful, did you know that?" I stood and cradled his cheeks so I could kiss him gently. "Now, I'm going to fuck you. Do you want it hard or soft?"

His breath caught. "Hard, Daddy Daire. So fucking hard. Make me forget for a while."

I nuzzled his cheek, and he closed his eyes with a peaceful sigh. "Anything for you."

After giving him another kiss, I leaned over to the nightstand and opened the top drawer to grab the lube. I threw the bottle on the bed before I guided him backward until he was in the center of the mattress. I took a moment to appreciate the length of his lithe body, all flat lines and small muscles converging to make a gorgeous specimen of a man. My baby boy.

I removed my clothes, aware of his gaze eating me up as skin was revealed. He licked his lips, eyes dark and hungry, and I smirked down at him when I kicked off the final piece—my underwear. My cock bobbed free, hard and ready to feel his tightness around me.

"Do you want this, boy?"

He exhaled. "No, Daddy, I *need* this. I need you."

That's all I desired to hear. I slipped back onto the bed and settled between his spread legs. I pressed my weight down onto him and kissed him, our mouths moving like a well-rehearsed dance. He whimpered and whined, rolling his hips up so his cock rubbed against mine. I brushed my nose over his when he pouted.

"Please, Daire, fuck me."

I reached for the lube again and flipped open the lid to slick up my fingers. I opened him carefully, taking him apart with two fingers, watching as his eyes rolled back and precum beaded at his slit. He moaned, hole clenching around my fingers.

"Get your cock inside me, Daddy."

I chuckled at the pure desperation in his voice, making it deepen and shake with fervor. His cheeks were pinker than usual and his tongue swept out to wet his lips as he stared up at me.

I used the lube on my cock before I shoved his legs up to his chest. He whined, toes curling, as I aligned my length with his hole. I didn't ask if he was ready because it was very clear in the way he rocked his hips, eager to feel me pressed against his entrance. If he didn't need this so much, I might've lectured him on his behavior. Not only for the hit, but for his impatience.

My jaw still throbbed, and between Sloan's punch yesterday and Fionn's this morning, I suspected I would end up feeling the pain for days. Like uncle, like nephew. I understood Fionn's anger, but we'd need to talk about it later.

I dug my thumbs into his hip bones, keeping him still as I thrust, my cock opening him up until I was fully inside. We both groaned.

"Daddy." He shuddered against me. "Fuck, you feel so good. So fucking wide."

I slammed my mouth against his, and he grabbed my face, his kisses aggressive as his teeth nipped my lips. He rolled his hips, and we both moaned again when I slid even deeper.

"You're so tight, boy." I grasped his thighs and shoved back, staring down at where I was balls deep in his hole. Tantalizing heat spread through my stomach and farther south, settling in my sack at the erotic sight we made.

"Please, Daddy Daire." Tears pooled in Fionn's eyes and he scrunched them shut. My passion warred with the empathetic pain I felt for him. I wished he could see himself the way I did. He always acted like he wasn't good enough, and sure, Sloan pushed him, but Fionn was damned near perfect already.

"I love you, Fionn Killough," I whispered.

His eyes popped open and he stared up at me.

"I love you so fucking much, and listen to me when I tell you that you are *so good*. I am proud of you and everything you've done, and not just for the Company. You are the best and the only person who can take over after your uncle. I will be at your side the entire time. I won't ever leave you. You are mine, and I am yours."

He gasped and grappled at my shoulders. "I love you, too, Daire. Fuck me. Make love to me."

I smiled and shifted into a better position before I began to hammer into him. The echoes of skin slapping against skin reverberated around the room. The outside world ceased to exist as I lost myself in my boy. There was me and Fionn on this bed and no one else. He was my boy, and I would give him exactly what he needed.

We kissed and fucked, driven by an intense appetite for each other. I couldn't get enough of him, but simultaneously it was also too much of him—I wanted to explode. He murmured Daddy like a prayer, and despite years of not practicing Catholicism, I felt like a worshiper when it came to him.

I reached between us and grasped his cock, tugging the rigid length in time with my thrusts. He clamped around me, a vise that welcomed me inside, and pleasure seeped through my veins like poison. I could die right now, and I'd be the happiest man who ever existed.

His fingernails dug into my shoulders and he threw his head back with a whine. He was unraveling beneath me. Pride swelled in my chest at my success in making him fall apart. After this, I'd put him back together again.

"Come for me, boy," I growled. "Show Daddy how much you love his cock."

Fionn trembled as he arched his back. Sweat gleamed on his forehead and he panted. He thrust up into my fist, riding the waves of his pleasure. Euphoria hit him hard. Then, he stiffened and gasped as he came, his cock jerking under my strokes. Cum splattered across his stomach and chest, some reaching as high as his chin and nose, and if I wasn't so focused on fucking into his tight hole, I might've laughed.

"Oh fuck," he sobbed.

I continued to pump into him, and the sounds he made had my balls heavy. He shuddered and laughed. It was clear he was overstimulated from his orgasm. I was pounding on his prostate, making it feel all the more pleasurable and painful for him. A suitable punishment for the earlier punch.

"Fuck." His mouth dropped open and he winced, then moaned as I hammered into his hole at a grueling pace. I was so close it hurt. "Daddy. Shit. Oh fuck." He trembled harder, his cock jerking as if trying to rise again. "Come in me, Daddy Daire. Fill me up."

My orgasm hit me hard, a sensation I hadn't quite felt before, and my world tilted on its axis. My balls drew tight to my body and my insides melted from the heat. A wave of intense torment washed through me as I came, aching so powerfully that I thought I was going to pass out.

When I pulled out, my cum spilled onto the bed. I collapsed beside him, breathless and feeling every bit of my age.

He sighed and shuffled onto his side, throwing an arm around my waist. "I needed that."

"I know you did, boy." As the pleasure wore off, the throbbing in my jaw picked up again and I flinched.

He frowned and touched the spot where he'd punched me. "I'm so sorry, Daddy Daire. I didn't mean to hit you. I was angry. That's no excuse. Fuck."

I shook my head and laid a gentle kiss on his forehead. "You're right, it's not an excuse. It won't happen again, do you understand? I am your Daddy, boy, but I will not tolerate that, even when you're upset. There is no excuse for it, am I clear?"

"Yes, Daddy." He nestled his face against my neck and sighed. "I'm so sorry. Thank you for being here with me."

"I understand why you were upset, but trust me when I tell you that this company is yours. Not Lor's. Sloan wants *you* to lead. Lor's a good kid, but he's not a Company man." I stroked my hand up and down Fionn's spine and tugged him closer, burying my nose into his hair. He smelled like sweat and sex, and it was perfect.

"I panicked. Sloan likes him more than me."

"He fucking does not," I argued, surprising him into glancing up at me with wide eyes. I sighed in frustration at Sloan's lack of communication. He was a great boss but not the best uncle. "You remind him of Eoin. You look like him, and he might not say it, but Sloan's scared of losing you. Lor is easy to reconcile because he's not Eoin's son. You *are*. What did Sloan say to you?"

Silence filled the room, and for a moment, I wasn't sure if he'd answer. "He said that I'm his apprentice and it doesn't change anything." He groaned. "But he's told me so many times that I'm not ready to be boss."

"Of course you aren't ready, boy. He's holding back because he's afraid to lose you. The moment the Italians showed their face, he hesitated and pulled you back from what you were learning." I growled. "Then, Reyes happened, and now he's not teaching you what he needs to because he's being a fucking coward."

"Uncle's not scared of anything," Fionn argued.

I laughed. If only that were true. "Usually he's not, but now he has enemies who've grown balls, and that puts the two people he loves the most, you and Conall, in danger. So yeah, he's scared, deep down inside. He's still human."

Fionn frowned and stared at my chest.

I shook my head and patted him on the ass. "Up. I took you apart, and now I'm taking care of you. We're going to take a shower."

He groaned and flopped half on top of me. "Do I have to move? My legs feel like they weigh a hundred pounds each."

I raised my eyebrows and slid out from under him so I could stand. I turned and grabbed his knees, dragging him toward the edge of the bed. Ignoring his protests, I heaved him up into my arms bridal style. He threw his head back and laughed as I carried him to the bathroom.

"I'm your Daddy, let me take care of you." I winked at him. "I'll get you bathed and dressed, then we're going back downstairs. Understood?"

He smiled up at me, and the tenderness of it tugged at my heart. "Yes, Daddy Daire."

After I settled him in the shower, I lathered up a cloth and washed his body. The same crevices I had loved on earlier were getting attention again—from under his armpits to the crack of his ass—before I guided him under the water and watched the soap swirl around the drain. I shampooed his hair, taking the time to massage my fingers through his brown locks.

His eyes closed, and I relished the blissed-out expression. This was how it should always be.

Once we were done in the shower, I dried him and dressed him, and he sighed in contentment.

"Thank you."

I kissed him. "You're mine, boy. Remember that."

"I'll never forget."

———

Weeks flew by, and we kept busy.

Fionn called Folliero, and he'd promised Fionn that he had a lead and would get in contact with us soon. Fionn trusted him, so I had no choice but to go along with it. I didn't have to like it. Sloan had put Fionn in charge of this job for a reason, and I was at his side no matter what.

Since the whole Aodhan debacle, Sloan was colder to me, and I didn't blame him, but I also didn't push. Sloan was many things, but he was smart, and he knew I had his back no matter what.

Fionn didn't talk about the Lor situation, either, and he asked that I not mention it, so we moved forward as if it had never happened. As far as I could tell, Sloan, in all his wisdom, hadn't shared that info with Lor. Sloan had secrets—nothing new there.

In a lot of ways, life was back to normal.

Except the part where I now had Fionn in my bed. Or more specifically, between my legs with my cock in his mouth. He stared up at me, tongue rolling around my cockhead and eyes dark with lust.

"Like this, Daddy?" He smooched the underside of the tip, and I groaned, bending my knees and spreading them farther.

I stroked my fingers across his forehead and carded through his hair. "Just like that, boy."

My phone rang, and Fionn groaned.

"Don't answer it," he said.

I shook my head. "It's Conall." I'd specially chosen that ringtone for him, so I knew who it was. I reached across the mattress and grabbed my phone off the nightstand, then swiped the screen to accept the call. "Sir?"

"Daire, there's been an explosion at the new salon," Conall said.

I stiffened.

We'd learned that Thiago Reyes was starting a line of salons down in Miami, using them as points of contact for selling drugs, which had him in the Company's territory. To mess with Reyes, Sloan was going to open his own slew of salons, starting in New York City and venturing into Miami. All of this was to fuck with Reyes's head before we took him down.

Today, Sloan had plans to show four of our men—Cillian and Rowen Shaughnessy, Aspen Kavanagh, and Fallon Maher— the new shop and inform them of our future business endeavors. Sloan had also taken Conall with him.

I sat up and dragged Fionn into my arms. My hard-on flagged at the news. "Is everyone all right, sir?" I put the phone on speaker so Fionn could hear it, too.

"I was hurt. I think I have a broken arm, but I'm at the Midtown apartment now and Rory's here. I wanted to let you know what was going on. It was a shit show."

"Who do you think set the bomb?" I asked when Fionn frowned.

Conall cleared his throat. "I don't know. Sloan dropped me here and took the guys and left. I think he's going to find out. Remember Sidorov?"

Sidorov was a Russian, and while usually Sloan hated dealing with them, Sidorov had a loathing for our Russian enemies as much as we did, which made having an alliance with him beneficial. He had the women to work the salons, and we had the money and power to support them.

"I bet Sloan's headed out to see him." Conall huffed, irritation slicing through his tone.

"Fuck." I brushed a hand over my face. "We're coming to you now."

"You don't need to," Conall protested.

"We are," Fionn chimed in, already moving to slide off the bed. He grabbed his pants and shoved them on, hiding his sexy brief-covered ass. "We're already at Daire's penthouse, and it's near Midtown."

"Yeah, okay. That . . . uh, sounds good."

Fionn hesitated before rushing through getting dressed. He was worried about Conall, and so was I. There was a vulnerability in his tone that I didn't think I'd heard from him. Clearly, the shock was wearing off. We needed to get to the Midtown apartment fast.

"Hang tight, sir. We'll be there very soon." I ended the call and dressed.

We went straight down to the garage to my SUV, and I drove us to Sloan's Midtown apartment, parking in one of the designated visitor spots. Fionn was out of the vehicle before I turned off the ignition, and I had to nearly run to catch up to him on the elevator. His foot tapped impatiently, and his eyebrows furrowed. There was nothing I could say that would calm his nerves because I felt the same way.

Bomb.

We were usually the ones who set them, not the target. The fact that Conall had been hurt in the blast meant Sloan would be out for blood, and I pitied anyone on the other end of that anger.

We made it to the apartment and knocked on the door, and as soon as it opened, Fionn shoved his way past the guards inside. I followed, nodding at the guards as I slipped by.

Conall was sitting on the couch in the middle of the living room, his arm in a sling but not in a cast. His long dark hair was wet and skin shiny as if he'd showered before he was patched up.

Dr. Rory Higgins sat beside Conall, and they were talking in low voices, but when Fionn burst through the door, Conall gave us his full attention and smiled.

"Hi."

Fionn rushed over to Conall and sat on the opposite side of Rory. "Are you okay? What happened? Tell me everything."

Conall sighed and ran his uninjured hand through his hair. "I can't tell you much because Sloan dropped me off here and took off with the guys. You know what he's like." He shrugged, then winced in pain. "We stopped at the site for the salon to check it out. Sloan was telling the guys about his plans, and I walked ahead of them. I was about halfway across the street when I was thrown off my feet and landed awkwardly on my arm. There was debris and dust everywhere. My ears were ringing. I was dizzy. Next thing I knew, Cillian was at my side and helping me stand, and Sloan was calling my name. Cillian led me to Sloan, and then we were in a car on our way here. It was sudden."

Fionn ran a hand down his face. "Fuck."

Conall's mouth pulled upward at the corner. "At least they didn't get my face. A few scratches, nothing permanent. You're stuck with me for a while longer."

Fionn frowned. "Not funny." He shook his head and smiled. "I kind of like you, so you're stuck with us for more than a while."

Conall placed his hand on his chest. "Aw, Fionn, that's the nicest thing you've ever said."

He rolled his eyes. "Don't get used to it."

"Want to call me Uncle Conall?"

"No." Fionn snorted. "Absolutely not."

Conall pouted. "You're no fun. Give your Uncle Conall a hug?"

"You've spent too much time around Fallon." Fionn's phone chose that moment to ring, and he pulled it out of his pocket. He jumped to his feet. "It's Elio. I'll be back." He swept farther into the apartment, and I took his abandoned seat beside Conall.

Dr. Rory cleared his throat and stood, walking deeper into the apartment to give us privacy.

I touched Conall's elbow. "How are you really feeling? Is there something I can do for you?"

He gave me a sad smile. "Can you bring Sloan home? I know he's out there trying to figure out who did it, but I want him here. I'm scared he'll get hurt while I'm not with him."

I chuckled quietly. "Sloan's a big boy, sir. He can handle himself, and I pity the person who's responsible for this."

Conall frowned. "This is bigger than someone like Sidorov. What he has with us is once in a lifetime. I don't see him making a stupid mistake like using a bomb to try and kill us."

"You believe it's Reyes?"

He made a face. "Yeah, I do. This is a war, and Reyes pulled out the big guns."

I nudged him gently with my shoulder. "Good thing we have even bigger ones than he does. Trust me, someone will die for this."

"As long as it's not Sloan or one of ours." Conall glanced at me carefully, eyes narrowed. "Are you and Fionn good?"

"We're great," I said.

He grinned. "Glad I don't have to order Sloan to kill you for breaking Fionn's heart again."

I smirked at him. "You and Fionn have become close."

"He's a good guy, and Sloan loves him, so he matters to me,

too." Conall paused, then leaned in closer. "I like him, he's funnier than I expected, but don't tell him I said that."

I made a zipping motion across my mouth. "My lips are sealed."

We grinned at each other before Fionn came storming back, eyebrows furrowed in concern. He paused in front of us, staring at his phone for a long moment, then sighed.

"Elio found the book. One of his men took it behind his back."

"I'm assuming that man is no longer alive," Conall drawled.

Fionn gave him a *what do you think?* look. "He's getting men to bring us the book now. Apparently, he had a look at it and it's all in code. He couldn't work it out."

I stood and wrapped an arm around his shoulder, dragging him closer and laying a kiss on his cheek. "Well then, good thing we have you on our side, huh? You enjoy a good puzzle."

His eyes turned bright and determined. "You know me so well, Daddy."

18

DAIRE

It took Fionn just under nine weeks to work out the code, which was a record, according to every other one of our smartest men trying to work on it. I didn't expect it to take that long, but I didn't understand anything to do with what the detective had done. No one could figure out what Diaz was using to hide her informants' identities. When Fionn tried to explain it to me—it had something to do with numbers and math, which made me drown it out immediately—I brushed him off with a simple kiss and an "I trust you."

In those months, a lot had happened in the Company, which meant our resources were spread thin. Sloan had sent two of our best men, Cillian and Aspen, along with Jamie Shannon, to Miami to send a message to Thiago Reyes. They killed Thiago's cousin, Joaquin, in retaliation, and that meant Sloan was prepared for even more attacks from Reyes's men.

"What did you work out?" I asked from where I lay on the bed beside Fionn, who was curled over the book that Folliero had given him. The code had driven Fionn crazy, and it had taken every part of my Daddy-ness to distract him when he needed a break.

Fionn turned to me, eyes bright with pride. "A meeting time, date, and place. There was a phone number, too, but it was a burner phone and out of service now. It was all too long ago."

"So what's the next step, boy?" I stroked my fingers down his naked back, tracing the ridges of his spine until I reached his tailbone. "That's over eight years ago. Too long."

He sent me a grin. "Usually, yes, but I know something you don't, Daddy."

"What?" I shuffled to sit up and cuddled in closer to him. Laying my head on his shoulder, I stared down at a pile of numbers and words on the legal pad he was using. My gaze met the date and address that he'd finally figured out.

"This—" He tapped the address with the end of his pen. "—is a parking garage across from an independent bank. Real Time Financial. *That* bank is owned and run by Ciro Armetta, the cousin of Alonzo Armetta."

"One of the five families' bosses," I said.

In New York City, there were five Italian families. Folliero was the kingpin of them all, but they each had their own territory. They belonged to Sloan in a lot of ways. They couldn't do anything that would affect the balance of power in the city without the permission of Elio, then Sloan. There was a lot of tension between the families, which had been the cause of some gunfights and, ultimately, the Giordanos trying to invade Folliero's dominion. It was a mess that Sloan had to fix.

"Right. Well, I say cousin, but if you want to get technical, he's Alonzo's first cousin once removed. The son of Alonzo's cousin." Fionn tapped the pen harder against the legal pad. "What you may not know is that Ciro is paranoid. He believes everyone is out to get him, and I also think he's one of those preppers. Last I heard, he even has a bunker." He rolled his eyes. "Anyway, he is renowned for keeping all his security footage. *All* of it. Which means that even though this meeting happened an eternity ago, he probably still has what we want."

I stared at him in awe. "How do you know all of this, boy?"

A flush spread across his pale cheeks even though he grinned. "Because I like to know who we're dealing with, and that includes family members. I don't trust Alonzo as far as I can throw him because that man is a psycho. Have you seen how he treats his own son?" He shook his head. "So, I did a deep dive, and I have dossiers on each member of the five families . . . and the Sabbatinis in St. Loren, the Leawoods in Ft. Leawood, and the Scullys in Dallas. Actually, I have dossiers on *all* our allies and enemies. Anyone who has anything to do with the Company."

I frowned and turned him so our chests were touching. "Does Sloan know this?"

He shrugged, his blush deepening. "Yes and no. When he wants data about someone, I give it to him, but I don't think he's aware of how much I dig. I know everything, from how much money they have in their bank accounts to when they take a shit."

"How?" This was entirely new information about Fionn, and I was thrown for a loop.

He laughed. "Guys in the Company mock me, but there are those outside who respect me enough to work for me. Diaz had informants and so do I."

"Fuck, boy. You make me so proud." I dragged him in for a deep kiss, and he moaned, eyes slipping closed as he rocked his hardening length against me.

I took him apart, making him cry out as I bent him over and ate him out, and he came with the kind of force that made me miss being young. But the sight alone had me painting his ass and lower back with my cum.

Then, I wiped him down, and we dressed. We headed out of my penthouse to my car, which I used to drive us to the bank in the middle of Manhattan Valley. Fionn walked like a man on a mission, and I merely followed—his shadow and soldier. I was his in every way, both in body and loyalty. My life belonged to him, and every day I saw him in a new light. He was stronger than he let our men believe. He was also cunning, but he was quieter than Sloan about it.

A few choice words from Fionn, and the employee he talked to practically fell over her own feet to run and get the manager.

As soon as the door she disappeared through opened again, I sized up the man who stepped out. Ciro wasn't what I'd imagined. He *looked* like a young man with short dark hair, light green-blue eyes, and a five-o'clock shadow. He was taller with a sinewy build. He had to be older than Fionn. If he'd owned the bank for over ten years, he'd have to at least be in his mid-thirties. His gaze was suspicious.

Fionn greeted him with a nod. "Ciro Armetta."

He frowned at Fionn as he came to a stop in front of him. "Fionn Killough. What are you doing here?"

"Is that how you say hello?" Fionn grinned and held out his hand.

Ciro hesitated before he shook the offered palm. "Hello, and how can I help you?"

I narrowed my eyes at him and gave him a once-over. Was he seriously a prepper? He seemed too . . . calm. Reserved.

Fionn released his hand and pointed at the entrance we'd come through a moment before. "There's a parking garage across from this bank, and we need video footage from eight years ago. I know you keep all the security footage, and I want a copy."

Ciro stared at Fionn for a long moment, tongue pressed to the inside of his cheek. His gaze cut across the bank, almost as if he was searching for someone, before he tilted his head to silently ask for us to follow him.

He took us inside the building and down a wide hallway with other office-like doors attached. He stopped in front of the farthest, down at the very end, and typed a code into a keypad.

The door opened, and he gestured us inside. Once we were past the threshold, he followed us in and closed the door behind us. Numerous locks engaged, and the sound was ominous, but Fionn didn't seem surprised as he casually took a seat at a table. The area reminded me of a police interrogation room without the two-way mirror. The décor was plain and boring, all whites and creams, and there was only a table and four chairs, two on each side, as furniture. There was, however, a wall of televisions with live footage from inside the bank and outside, too, including the garage across the street.

"It's safer in here," Ciro said as he marched over to a seat on the opposite side of the table from Fionn. He collapsed and sighed in relief. "That was close. There's always ears everywhere. You can never be too careful." He gave me a look and waved his hand at the chair beside Fionn. "Sit, sit!"

Now *this* seemed more typical for a prepper with a bunker.

I did as he insisted and sat down.

"This is my safe room. Completely soundproof and there are no signals in or out of here. It's secure." He patted his hands on the surface of the table. "Now, tell me, what are we looking for?"

Fionn pulled out his phone from his pocket, opened his app with notes, and showed Ciro. "Date and time. I need all surveillance footage of the garage a few hours around that."

Ciro narrowed his eyes. "You shouldn't leave important information on your phone. Anyone can hack it." Then, he snorted. "I can get it for you, but it'll cost you."

Fionn smiled, but there wasn't anything nice about it. The expression reminded me of the cold and aloof Fionn, the one who had something to prove, and yet it also looked a lot like the expression Sloan made as a dangerous warning. "Do I look like the type of person you should be trying to bargain with? I could make Alonzo's life hell, and how would your lunatic cousin like that, hmm?" He leaned back and crossed his leg, completing the perfect boss appearance, and I couldn't help but appreciate the long lines of his sinewy body in the custom-made suit. The power exuded off him.

I hid the smirk that threatened to slide onto my mouth.

The corner of Ciro's mouth twitched, a subtle sign of his irritation. "We're allies."

"And we can make your cousin's life hard in this city." Fionn shrugged. "Your choice."

Ciro laughed tightly. "I will have the footage to you by end of day."

"Wise choice." Fionn stood, and I followed. He straightened his suit jacket. "If I don't have it by this evening, I will visit again."

"You can't make demands like this," Ciro snapped.

"You're right, but let's put our cards on the table. I now owe *you* a favor. Not your cousin, you." Fionn grinned. "And having a favor owed to you by a Killough is a rare commodity, don't you think?"

Ciro swallowed and nodded. "Deal."

Fionn and I spent the rest of the day at my penthouse. I did paperwork for Sloan's legal businesses while Fionn perused Diaz's notebook to see if he could find more information. He'd decrypted secret meetings that had nothing to do with the Company, which he said would be beneficial for us, and I believed him. If we knew about informants of other criminal enterprises, we could trade the secrets for something we wanted.

Finally, I decided he'd had enough of straining his eyes on that notebook. I rose from my desk and went down the steel steps to the living room, where he was seated on the couch, a pen clutched between his teeth as he frowned down at the book.

I leaned across the back of the couch and curled my arms

around him, earning a smile in response. "Enough of this. We're going out."

"Where?" His eyebrows furrowed. "We have a lot of work to do. Between the rat, Reyes, and the businesses—"

"Shh." I kissed his cheek and moved around to the front of the couch. I grasped the notebook and threw it on the cushion beside him before I dragged him up. "We're going to Southampton, where you're going to update your uncle, say hello to Lor—"

Fionn opened his mouth to protest. He'd barely spoken to Lor since Sloan had told him the truth about Lor's relation to them, but that wasn't anything new. Fionn's attitude toward Lor had grown saltier, and Lor had noticed, if his sad pouts that he directed at Fionn meant anything. The boy had no one his age, and it was obvious he wanted Fionn to like him.

"No. No more excuses, boy. Sloan isn't giving the Company to Lor, and Lor isn't the kind of person to join a mob. He's an academic, like Vail. I've let you have your tantrum over it, but we're done now. If you keep up with this attitude, I will put you over my knee and spank your ass red in front of everyone."

He shuddered and his pupils went wide. "Yes, Daddy."

I plopped a kiss on his mouth. "You can drive today. It'll be good practice."

He coughed, nearly choking on his own saliva. "What? I don't have my learner's permit. If they pull us over—"

"Then, I will handle it. You *need* to know how to drive, even if someone chauffeurs you around for the rest of your life." I stroked my thumb across his jaw. "I'm putting my foot down about this. You will get your learner's permit and then your license. Am I clear, boy?"

He licked his lips, eyes darkening as he stared up at me with lust that would give anyone a spiked heart rate. "Yes, Daddy Daire."

"Good boy." I brushed my nose over his. "Now let's go."

I grabbed my keys and dragged him toward the door. He huffed at the rough handling, but he didn't protest.

As soon as we arrived at the SUV, Fionn froze, as if the reality of what we were doing had hit him. He swallowed visibly and glanced toward me. "I don't think now's the right time to learn. You should drive. I can study first, and when it's quiet with the Company, I can get into the driver's seat."

"Fine."

He relaxed but hesitated when I smirked.

"I'm driving until we get to the Hamptons, and then you're taking over." I held up a finger when he opened his mouth to protest. "No arguments. The city is too busy for a learner, but as soon as we get out of here, you're in the driver's seat."

He sighed in defeat and slid into the passenger seat, while I took the spot behind the steering wheel. The traffic through the city was hell, but it started to peter out as we headed toward the Hamptons. As soon we reached an area I decided was quiet enough, I pulled the SUV off to the side of the road.

Fionn gave me a panicked look. "Daddy, I don't think—"

"Shh." I turned toward him and stroked a finger down his cheekbone. "You're okay, boy. Don't fret about this. We'll take it slow." I smiled in encouragement. "Come on, let's swap seats."

Despite his obvious dread, he did as I'd directed, sliding out of the passenger door so we could change sides. The moment he clutched the steering wheel, the anxiety in his eyes deepened and he glanced at me for reassurance.

I grabbed his hand and dragged it from the wheel so I could lay a kiss in the middle of his palm. "We'll start slow. How much do you know?"

His expression shuttered, shame filling his eyes and making his cheeks turn a bright red. "I . . . know the traffic rules and where the accelerator and brake are. This vehicle is automatic, so I don't need to change the gears."

"Right." I laid a hand on the back of his neck and caressed it soothingly. "We'll go slow. You can drive a manual another day. Right now, you just need to know *how* to drive and be confident. It's all about keeping calm and driving not only for yourself, but for others, too. There are shitty drivers on the road, boy, and you need to watch them and be prepared to react to their stupidity. Do you understand?"

He raised his chin. "Yes, Daddy."

"Good. Now I want you to take us to the house. The Mercedes is yours to control." I pointed where his feet were, each foot on a different pedal. "Only use your right foot. If you use two, you could end up hitting them together, and trust me, you don't want to do that."

Fionn removed his left foot from the brake immediately and blanched nervously.

I smiled. "You have this, boy. Guide the SUV out into traffic."

He straightened his back and stared with an intensity out on the road. He checked his mirrors without me telling him to do it, put the SUV into Drive, and hit the accelerator slowly. The Mercedes rolled forward. I stayed silent, letting him gain confidence. He drove about a quarter of a mile before he took a deep breath and guided the car onto the road.

"All right, now let's get onto the 495," I murmured with encouragement.

"Do you think I can do this?" He glanced at me from the corner of his eye.

"Yes, boy, I do. Now turn left up here and get us onto the interstate." I brushed my fingers over the back of his neck. "You're a Killough. You can do anything, and this is *your* territory. Remember that."

He took a deep breath and did as I'd ordered, taking the turn and guiding the car onto the 495. He hit the accelerator as we merged into the interstate traffic, which wasn't too bad right now, but he was going slower than the speed limit. Behind him, cars honked, and he winced every time the sharp shrill blast of a horn blared at him.

"Keep calm, boy. That's one of the most important things about driving. Don't panic." I rested my hand on his thigh and squeezed it.

He exhaled loudly, his gaze never leaving the road in front of him. A red Ferrari roared up beside us, and the guy gave us the middle finger. I rolled my eyes and tugged out the gun I kept in the glove box before pointing the muzzle at him, and even from here I could see his eyes widen before he zoomed forward.

Fionn laughed. "Daddy, put that away. We don't need a reason for the cops to pull us over. I'm already driving unlicensed."

I smirked and opened the glove box again, stashing the Glock back inside. "Patience is a virtue and that guy needed to learn a lesson."

"The only one you should be teaching anything to is me." His hands tightened around the steering wheel, but he was doing well, considering this was his first time and I'd thrown him in the deep end with Interstate 495.

"You're doing good, boy, and I'm so damned proud of you. You're staying calm, and all you need to do now is go a little faster."

He sucked in air between his teeth. "I don't know if I can."

"Yes, you *can*." I squeezed his thigh again. "Faster, boy."

"Fuck." He inhaled, then exhaled again, and the car began to pick up speed. When he reached 70 mph, his hands shook a little, but he focused on the road.

"Good boy," I praised gently. "You're doing great. When I get you to the mansion, I'll give you a reward."

"What kind?" He sent me a quick glance, and I laughed.

"You'll have to wait and see."

"You're mean, Daddy Daire." He smiled anyway.

"Now that I have you here with no way to escape, talk to me. How are you feeling about the entire Lor thing?" I studied his face, watching the way his eye twitched and his mouth pinched.

"What do you want me to say?" His knuckles turned white. The speed he was driving at went up and down, as if he was struggling to focus.

"Start with the truth on how you're feeling. You've been so wrapped up in figuring out Diaz's notebook that you're ignoring the other issue, and as your Daddy, I'm not going to let you do that anymore." I gave him a pointed look. "Talk."

"Are we doing therapy?" he teased, but I saw this for what it was—a distraction.

I narrowed my eyes at him, and he sighed.

"There's nothing to say. He's my cousin. Even if Sloan doesn't give the Company to him, who says *he* won't want to fight me for it in the future?" His eyebrows furrowed in frustration.

"Who says your brothers won't do the same?" I asked.

He frowned at me. "Because they've had nothing to do with the business."

I grinned. "And neither has Lor. If anything, he's averse to the idea of criminal life. He studies it with Vail, but has he ever done anything illegal?"

"No, but . . . ." Fionn sighed, and I laughed.

"Boy, you can't argue your way out of this. Like with Conall, your hatred for Lor comes from your own insecurities."

He huffed and rolled his eyes. "Sure thing, Dr. Phil."

"You'll get a spanking for that later. Merge into the next lane."

He glanced in his mirror and did as I instructed, so distracted by our conversation that he drove with a confidence I'd only seen in people who'd been behind the wheel for years. "What I'm saying is that I don't trust him."

"You didn't trust Conall, either, and now you two are besties."

He snorted. "We are *not*. I respect him a little now, that's all. Can we not do this, Daddy?"

"Why? Is it making you uncomfortable?" I asked.

"No, but I don't see the point. Lor is my cousin. I can't change that, but it doesn't mean I have to be nice to him." His jaw twitched, a visible sign he was gritting his teeth.

I sighed. "He doesn't know that, boy. He's as innocent as you are in this. Your problem with him isn't because he's related, but because you think Sloan pays more attention to him."

"That isn't true." The words left him too quickly, and the sharp bite to them told me everything I needed to know.

"You've said it yourself, so you can't deny it. You think Sloan cares more for Lor than you."

"Uncle doesn't know him," he snapped. "Lor could betray us. His father's not exactly trustworthy, is he? He's supposed to be Sloan's advisor, but he's never around, too busy flaunting money around the city in the local whore houses. Who says he's not the rat?"

"He might be," I agreed. Lorcan had always been on my list of potential traitors because Fionn was right. The man was slimy, and there was no love lost between him and Sloan. The only reason Lorcan was on the board was because Sloan's father asked Sloan to put him there. "But Lor isn't his father. Are you Eoin?"

"That isn't fair." He sent me a glare.

"Exactly, so why are you treating Lor like shit, boy?"

He braked a little too hard, and there weren't any cars in front of us, so I assumed I'd pissed him off, but I was happy to leave the conversation like that. Fionn was the kind of person who needed to ruminate over the information before he came to a reasonable conclusion because, despite being a young man who acted like a brat at the best of times, he was also incredibly intelligent. The problem was that his emotions always got the best of him and didn't give him a chance to reflect on himself.

Soon we were heading toward the exit to Sloan's house, and I directed Fionn, all his nervousness about driving gone as he focused on doing what I told him. When he pulled the Mercedes to a stop and put it into Park, I grinned widely at him.

"Well done, Fifi."

He stared outside the window at Sloan's house, and his eyes widened. "Fuck. I drove here."

I laughed and hooked my hand around the back of his neck, dragging him over the middle console for a hard kiss. "Nearly all the way, but it's a start. The 495 is no joke, and you did really good, boy. When you're confident, we'll navigate the city."

He chuckled as I unbuckled his seat belt.

We both slid out of the SUV, and he met me on my side, dragging me into a hot messy kiss that had my toes curling with the desire to take him to his bedroom and have my way with him, but that wasn't why we'd come here.

Instead, I dragged him inside the house, ignoring Mr. Hopper as he grunted a greeting to us in his gruff, no-nonsense tone.

"Where is Lor, Mr. Hopper?" I asked.

The older man raised his chin as he closed the door behind us. "He's in the guest apartment with Dr. Mifflin, sir."

I inclined my head in thanks, but before I could head up the stairs, Fionn grasped my elbow. I glanced at him, and he winced.

"I don't think now is the time to talk to him."

"Fionn—"

"I know what you're going to say, Daddy." He shot Mr. Hopper a look when the older man cleared his throat. "And I understand that I need to put aside my differences with Lor, but

I'm not ready yet. I swear, I'll treat him with more respect, but I can't talk to him right now."

I cradled his face between my palms, and he stared up at me in a way that made my heart sting. A vulnerability shone through, begging me to let this go, and I couldn't force him to do something when he didn't want to. I smiled and laid a gentle kiss on his perfect mouth. "Promise me to think about it, okay?"

"I promise." He hugged me, and I drew him in as close as I could get him, relishing his warmth.

Footsteps echoed around the foyer before they stopped. "Am I interrupting?"

We pulled apart and glanced toward Sloan, who stood beside the staircase. He had his arms crossed and one eyebrow raised.

"I—" Fionn's phone buzzed and he tugged it out of his pocket. "I have the footage." He grinned at me, then Sloan. "It's fuzzy, so I'll need to send it to someone to get it cleaned up, but I have it."

"What are you talking about?" Sloan walked closer to us, coming to a stop at Fionn's side.

"I decoded Diaz's notebook. The phone number of the rat was a burner phone no longer in play, but she also included a date, time, and location for the meetup." Fionn straightened, smiling proudly. "They met at a car garage in the city—right across from Real Time Financial."

"Ciro Armetta's bank," Sloan said.

Fionn laughed. "Yep, and Ciro's notoriously paranoid, so Daire and I went there today and asked for the recordings. He just sent them over." He waved his phone at Sloan. "And I know the perfect person to up the resolution. There's a couple of hours of footage in here, but if Zak can clean up the visuals, we can look to see if I recognize anyone."

Sloan's mouth curled into a smirk. "Good job, nephew."

Fionn froze and swallowed. He squared his shoulders and returned the grin. "Thank you, Uncle Sloan."

"Well, then, I'll let you get to work." He winked and turned to walk back the way he'd come, probably to head to his office.

Fionn licked his lips and moved toward me, and I opened up my arms to bring him into a hug, laying a kiss on his forehead.

"You've done amazing, boy. Now let's finish this, all right?"

"Yes, Daddy Daire."

19

FIONN

A day after sending the video footage to Zak, Daire and I received an urgent message to meet Sloan in the dining room. Luckily, we were already at the house. When we arrived, Sloan was pacing, while Conall watched him with concern, his finger tracing the deep red collar around his neck while he did.

"What's wrong?"

Conall winced. "Cillian, Aspen, and Jamie didn't get Joaquin Herrera like they thought. Instead, they killed Joaquin's cousin, Noa Garcia."

"Garcia? As in Santiago Garcia's sister?" I had a whole set of notes about him, too. Technically, the Norse Lords MC over in Pleasant Beach, California, weren't our allies. They were impartial when it came to mob wars, but I liked to know about everyone we had dealings with, regardless of their commitment to us or lack thereof. Santiago—also known as Fenrir—was also Ardan Murphy's ex-lover.

Sloan blew out air through his nose and stopped behind the chair at the head of the table. He crossed his arms over the top of it and leaned his forehead onto his wrists. "Exactly. This entire assignment has gone backward. I thought I could trust them."

Conall rose and laid a hand on the middle of his back, rubbing comforting circles. "They are the best. If this happened to them, imagine what would've happened with someone else. They made a choice, and it was the wrong one."

"They blew the bomb in the salon up without confirming they saw Herrera."

"It was raining hard," Conall argued lightly, snuggling up to Sloan. "All they could see were umbrellas, and according to their sources, it should've been Joaquin walking into that salon, not Noa. Anyone else would've made the same mistake, even you, Boss."

"So, what now?" I licked my dry lips, eyeing Sloan carefully. He appeared more ragged than usual, the dark circles under his eyes a tad more prominent. The brown roots of his hair were outgrowing the bleached blond, a sign he needed to call the hairdresser in to redo it. This was my uncle stressed in every way, and my heart ached with the urge to help him however I could.

"I called a meeting. They'll all be here soon." He waved his hand at the seat to his left. "Sit down. It's going to be a long night."

"Yes, Uncle." I took the first seat, while Daire stole the chair beside mine. Under the table, he laid his hand on my thigh and squeezed, and I gave him a small smile in response.

It didn't take long for the cavalry to show up, and the dining room was full of our men. On our side of the table sat Cillian, Corbin, and Ardan, while Aspen, Conall, Jamie, and Rowen took the other. As soon as Sloan explained the situation, the chaos began. Questions were thrown at Ardan, who had an informant tell him that it was Joaquin who was killed, and accusations of their failure were thrown at Cillian, Aspen, and Jamie. I watched without a word as Sloan ordered them to return to Miami to finish the job, and they didn't hesitate, shooting to their feet and leaving immediately.

Then, came the conversation about Fenrir and if he was going to retaliate.

"This isn't good for us or our relationship with the Lords. If Fenrir decides he wants revenge, the president of the club will no doubt support him," Sloan said with a sigh. "The only positive we have from this is that he will be angry at Thiago."

One could only hope he'd be pissed at Thiago fucking Reyes.

Ardan threaded his fingers together on the table. "Santi never wanted his sister to be part of the Cartel. He begged her not to help their cousin. He will put half the blame on Reyes as well."

That was something. We wouldn't take the full blame.

Daire hummed beside me, and I gave him my attention. "Whether he'll go after us or Thiago for revenge remains to be seen."

My stomach turned nervously. I'd never met Fenrir, but I'd heard a lot about him. He was great at his job as a hit man, and I didn't want any of my family in his crosshairs.

Ardan laughed, but there was an edge to it that I didn't like. He was usually the calm one, the reserved person who showed little emotion. "He'll come for us. When, we won't know. Santi's more calculating than Thiago. He waits for the opportune moment. He's a hit man and good at it, too."

My gaze slid to Sloan, and the expression on his face hardened, a subtle change that I noticed immediately because of how long I'd lived with him. "Right now, we need to focus on Thiago and his plans. He's more likely to react out of anger." His jaw ticked in irritation. "Which is why I propose we send the ones we love away for a while."

I winced, aware of the outburst that was going to explode from Conall, and I wasn't wrong.

"Bullshit." He jumped to his feet and smashed his fist onto

the table. He pointed a finger at Sloan. "No," he snarled. "I know what you're doing, and you can kiss my pale arse because I'm not fucking going anywhere. You hear me?"

I reached for Daire's hand under the table, and he laced his fingers through mine, the pressure a welcome comfort. His warmth seeped through me because of how close he was, and I needed all the stability he offered. He was my pillar, my wall of strength.

Conall and Sloan argued, and I vaguely listened to them because it was all the same—Conall telling Sloan that he refused to hide while Sloan was in danger and claiming his spot was at Sloan's side. The thing I'd come to respect about Conall was that he didn't back down, and he knew the truth—that Sloan needed him. After they argued came the passionate kissing, and while others thought it was hot, the fact that Sloan was my uncle made it objectively not so for me, so I kept my eyes on the other men.

It wasn't until they were done and Sloan mentioned my name that I returned my attention to him.

"A lot of things are happening, and we need to keep on top of all of them. Ardan, Fionn is close to finally catching the rat."

Ardan turned amused eyes on me, his eyebrows raised in surprise, and I made a point not to be insulted by the expression. Not many people trusted me to get the job done, and I was going to prove them all wrong.

I sat up straighter. "We have a video of Diaz and the rat meeting together. It wasn't easy to get. This was five years or more ago and not many people keep security footage for that long, but they were stupid and met across from an investment bank with a manager who's notorious for keeping up to ten years of recordings." Actually, he never deleted any, but it was information they didn't need. I didn't want to come across as a know-it-all and if I gave them a detailed overview of everything, I'd look like one. "Now we've got an IT guy cleaning up the visuals so we can see who it is. We should have a name within an hour or two."

Zak had found Diaz on the footage, but now he was clearing the photos of the men and women who came out right before or after her to see if we could recognize anyone.

"And when he does, I want you to be ready, Ardan." Sloan pointed at him.

Panic hammered away at my chest, and I lost my breath for a moment. I straightened. "Uncle, I deserve to finish the job."

"Do you?" His gaze drilled a hole in me as he leaned an elbow on the table. I stared back, not willing to concede defeat. If he wanted me to run this company, I needed to take charge and that meant finalizing this rat issue.

Daire squeezed my hand, and I'd almost forgotten he was still holding it. I must've been nearly strangling his in my alarm.

Rowen cleared his throat. "Boss, do ye need me here? Because if ye don't—"

Sloan's attention fell to him instead, and I sighed, leaning back in my chair. I let them talk some more and sent Daire a small smile in thanks. He leaned against me, and I breathed in his cologne, letting his presence be the steadiness I needed.

I vaguely listened as Sloan gave Rowen the job of promoting more recruits to soldiers, and once Rowen left, Sloan turned back to me.

"Okay, Fionn, you're in charge of this rat issue. What do we do next?"

Four sets of eyes fell on me, Daire's included, and I took a deep breath to center myself. This was my chance to make an impression on my uncle, and I wasn't going to fail.

"I'll call my IT contact and find out how far along he is with cleaning up the other people that left the garage in that time frame."

Sloan waved his hand. "Do it, then."

I jumped to my feet, nearly knocking over my chair in the

process—which made Conall chuckle—and escaped from the dining room so I could have privacy. As soon as I was in the hallway near the kitchen, I tugged out my phone and found Zak's contact information. I tapped on his name too hard on the screen. My hand was shaking as I placed the phone against my ear.

My heart galloped and I touched a hand to my chest as I tried to calm myself. A few rings later, Zak answered.

"Hey, Fionn. The person I wanted to talk to. I *just* finished cleaning up the images. I'm emailing you now."

"I could kiss you." I pumped my fist in the air. "You're the best, Zak. I'll send over the second half of the payment now." I ended the call and quickly opened my inbox, finding the email that Zak had sent me.

"Who are you going to kiss and should I be worried?" Daire's amused tone had me turning toward the door, where he leaned against the frame, and I grinned at him.

"No time for jealousy, Daddy. Your boy's about to solve one of the Company's problems." I bounced on the tips of my toes, unable to stop the excitement from surging through me until my skin was full of goose bumps and my insides buzzed. I wanted to shout at the top of my lungs and do a dance, but instead I stayed calm like Sloan had always taught me. *Emotionless in front of your men,* he'd said, *and never celebrate too early.* Maybe he should've exercised that caution when it came to the Miami situation, though Ardan's man *had* said that it was Joaquin they'd killed. It was his mistake, not Sloan's.

I stalked back into the dining room, and Daire was right behind me, his strides long and purposeful.

Sloan glanced up at me when I entered. Ardan had left, and so the only people in the room were Sloan and Conall. I took the seat to Sloan's left again.

"He sent the images." I opened the email on my phone as Daire took the chair on my other side. The very first photo attached was of Diaz in her car coming out of the garage, and I showed the screen to Sloan. "Confirmed she was there. So, Zak's also given me photos of the people who left the garage around the same time as her. We should be able to recognize someone."

Sloan smirked and stared at me for a long moment, and I waited, prepared to hear whatever he was about to throw my way. I'd seen my uncle in many different moods, but I thought this was a good one. "I'm proud of you. You've done good work."

I froze, his words echoing in my mind until they finally sank in. *Proud. Good work.* I didn't think he'd ever said those words to me together, and I wanted to bask in this moment, my chest filled with bubbles of happiness that left me breathless.

Smiling, but not so large that Sloan would think I was acting weird, I forced myself to stare down at my phone again. If I saw Conall rub Sloan's shoulder with his own sense of pride, I didn't acknowledge it. I swiped through the pictures until a familiar face hit me square in the chest—I was suddenly gasping for an entirely new reason.

"Who is it?" Conall asked.

Beside him, Sloan leaned back in his chair and crossed his arms. He seemed calm, but it wasn't him I was focused on. Instead, I couldn't tear my gaze away from the photo and the face I'd known since I'd first moved into Sloan's home.

Daire's hand rested on my lower back, the weight of it bringing me down to Earth and the reality of what I was seeing.

I exhaled, my breath stuttering. "Donal."

Conall's eyes widened. "McMahon?"

"Yes," Sloan said, earning my attention almost immediately. "Donal McMahon."

"You knew," I murmured, not quite sure if I believed it or not, but it made sense because Sloan wasn't surprised. He was too relaxed. Donal had once told me that Sloan knew more than he let on, and Daire had said Sloan always did something for a reason, and now I understood more than ever. "How?"

"Donal's been angry since Carolina's death. She bought the drugs from one of our men that day she OD'd, and he's blamed our business ever since." Sloan glanced toward Conall, whose eyes were wide, and reached over to slide his fingers into Conall's. "His anger festered until it became toxic."

"How long have you known?" Daire asked, and I stared in his direction. Sloan never left him out of this sort of information. Didn't he know? He inclined his head at me, gesturing that he was in the dark about this as well.

The corner of Sloan's mouth twitched. "After Rourke dealt with Diaz. His reaction to her death gave it away."

"What?" I gaped at him, slamming my hand down on the table. "Then, why didn't you tell us? Why send me and Daire on a wild goose chase?"

He leaned forward, back straightening until he sat in his chair like the boss he was. The power he exuded paralyzed men, but I wasn't just anyone. Sure, he scared me, but I was still his nephew. "I needed you to prove you could handle this situation. It took you a long time, too long, but you did it."

I shook my head in disbelief. "He's been in our meetings. We've discussed sensitive information with him."

"After we took Diaz out, he became less of a problem." He shrugged. "His fire was extinguished. He didn't know who worked for us in the police department and who didn't. Diaz was the only detective who was outspoken about our illegal activities. But I was careful, only giving him just enough that he didn't get suspicious without putting the Company in danger."

"So you let him get away with it?" I frowned.

"No. I was waiting for you to figure it out. Do you know how many secrets he could've shared in the time it took you to work out who the rat was? Too many."

"You should've told him, sir," Conall said quietly, his eyebrows furrowed in confusion.

Sloan hummed. "I required proof before I acted on anything, and you needed to learn how to get answers, no matter how long it takes."

"So, this was another lesson?" I stared at him, not quite sure what all of this meant. Was he actually proud of me or was this a game to him? I'd spent years doing everything I could to find answers. And he'd known. *He'd known.* I slid my gaze back to Donal's clear face through the windshield of his car. This man who I trusted—believed in—had betrayed us by telling valuable secrets to a detective gunning for us.

Daire slid his chair closer and laid a kiss on my cheek, and I fell into him.

"Are you two together now?" Conall asked quietly, and I wasn't sure if he was trying to soothe the tension or whether he was genuinely curious.

"We are." Daire pressed another chaste kiss to my temple. "And he's my boy, so forgive me when I tell you, Boss, that this was a shit lesson."

Sloan raised his eyebrow. "Are you questioning me?"

"Yes," Daire said.

I touched his arm and shook my head at him. "It's fine." I didn't understand, but Sloan was the boss. I turned back to him. "I trust you. What do we do now?"

"Now we go kill him." Sloan rose and buttoned up his suit jacket.

I stared at him again, taking in the tall imposing man who'd been nothing but strategic and sneaky my entire life, and I wondered if I'd be like him one day. Would I put my nephews through what he'd done to me? Sloan never had children, but I wanted kids, so it wouldn't be my nephews who'd take over after me.

Could I put my children through hell?

I slid my gaze to Conall, and he shrugged when he caught me looking.

"You said you wanted to finish this. Now's your chance," Sloan said.

I swallowed the lump lodged in my throat at the thought of murdering Donal. I hadn't expected the rat to be someone I would care about, and now that it was, I wasn't sure how I felt. Everything was happening so fast. The lump I swallowed caught in my chest, where it became heavier than a boulder.

Daire pressed his forehead to my temple. "You don't have to do this, boy."

Sloan narrowed his eyes at Daire and pressed his fists down onto the table, leaning on them. "No, he doesn't, but Fionn's not a child anymore, and he's my heir. As boss, we do things we don't like. We kill people we thought we could trust. Our friends. It's part of the job."

I took a deep breath and squared my shoulders. "I'm ready. Let me do it."

Sloan smiled. "Good." He stood straight again. "Then, let's go pay him a visit."

20

FIONN

I took a steadying breath, urging myself to stay calm. We were nearly at Donal's house, and I was prepared to do the worst thing I'd ever done in my life, and I still didn't know how I felt about it. My mind was a chaotic mess. I knew it was bad when Conall kept glancing at me from the front passenger seat of the car. For the first time in I didn't know when, Sloan decided to drive one of the BMWs, and Daire and I were in the back seat.

"You don't have to do this," Daire whispered to me again, his hand gripping mine tightly. "I'll do it for you."

"No." I gave him a wobbly smile. "Sloan's right. If I want to be boss, I have to be prepared to kill anyone, even friends. Donal betrayed us and that's unforgivable, no matter how angry he was about Carolina's death. He needs to die now."

"More than that," Sloan said from the driver's seat, glancing in the rearview mirror. "You will torture him, make it hurt."

"Sloan." Conall touched his elbow, eyebrows furrowed. "You're asking too much of him."

"Am I, Fionn?" Sloan stared at me pointedly. "Am I asking too much of you?"

I raised my chin. "No. I will do whatever the Company needs from me. This is my legacy and I won't let you down."

Sloan nodded, short and sharp, before he focused on the road ahead of him again.

I closed my eyes and settled farther into Daire's warmth. He was my strength, and with him at my side, I felt like I could take on the world—or torture a man I'd admired.

"How long have you really been together?" Sloan asked, keeping his eyes on the road this time.

Conall glanced at us over his shoulder, eyebrows raised in question. *Were we going to tell Sloan the truth?* The tension between Daire and Sloan was already at an all-time high and I didn't want to make it worse, but I didn't have time to come up with a suitable answer before Daire spoke.

"About eight years." Daire's jaw twitched and he cleared his throat. "We were sleeping together before we were *together together.*"

We'd talked about this before. Why was Sloan asking questions again?

"You were fucking for how long before you entered a relationship?" The curse word out of Sloan's mouth and the sharpness in his tone had me wincing. Damn it.

Conall gave us a sympathetic smile because we all knew this would put Sloan in an even worse mood. I wasn't stupid. Sloan could be cold and emotionless, but I was his family.

"We only started dating this year." Daire exhaled and drew me closer. "I'm not going to lie to you, Sloan, I led Fionn on for too long."

"Daire—" I started, but he shook his head.

"I want this out in the open, boy. Your uncle deserves to know." Daire rubbed the back of his neck and sighed. "I was an idiot. I've been sleeping with Fionn since his eighteenth birthday party. He wanted more, I didn't, and I didn't treat him the best."

M.D. GREGORY

"I knew you only wanted sex, and I accepted it," I whispered.

He chuckled sardonically. "I should've stopped the sex completely if I wasn't going to give you more. Instead, I couldn't let you go, either, and I hurt you in the process."

From the corner of my eye, I saw Sloan's grip on the steering wheel tighten, and I winced, aware of the small gestures that gave his anger away.

"So, let me get this right . . . ." Sloan's voice dripped with venom, a deep-seated fury that sent a tremble straight up my spine. "You used *my* nephew, the future of the Company, as a cum sock?"

"Cum sock?" Conall snorted. "That's imaginative."

Sloan shot him a glare, and Conall hid a laugh behind his hand, looking out the window. "Sorry, Boss."

"I wish I could tell you that it was more than that, but it wasn't." Daire cringed and gave me a sad smile. "I used Fionn, and I deeply regret it. But I've also loved him for a long time."

"How long have you loved him, then?" Sloan snapped.

The car swerved a little, and I wasn't sure if Sloan wasn't paying attention or if he was avoiding something, but my stomach swayed with the movement, churning relentlessly.

"I don't know what to tell you." Daire dragged me even closer and pressed a kiss to my forehead. We'd finally jumped over our hurdles, and we were here—*happy*. I didn't want my uncle's reaction to ruin us. "I can't pinpoint the exact moment it happened, but Fionn's always been important to me."

"You were okay with them before," Conall pointed out to Sloan with a grin. "What changed?"

"The fact that I found out my best friend used my nephew for his body and hurt his feelings." Sloan yanked the wheel, and I groaned when we pulled into Donal's driveway. "This isn't over."

"It *is*. I will let you give me lessons when it comes to business, but this is my private life. Daire is my Daddy."

Sloan hit the brakes, and I went flying forward, only saved by Daire's firm hold and the seat belt that jammed at the sudden movement. He spun around to stare at me. "Your what?"

"Daddy. Daddy Daire." I raised my chin, defending what I had with Daire. I'd do anything for Sloan and the Killough Company, but this wasn't something he could take away from me. I refused to let him. "He's my Daddy, and I'm his boy. You have Conall, the pet who you fuck in public. That's your thing, this is mine."

The iciness in his gaze didn't diminish, but his posture relaxed slightly. His jaw twitched and his nostrils flared as he slid his attention to Daire. "If you hurt him again, I'll string you up by your balls and remove body parts, one limb at a time, friend or not. Am I clear?"

Daire gave a sharp nod. "Yes, Boss."

Sloan grunted, an uncharacteristic sound from him, but it was soothing. This anger showed that he actually cared about me. The calm persona had finally snapped and it was because a man had broken my heart.

Conall cleared his throat before grinning. "Is this family moment over or should we sit in the car a little longer and talk about how much we love each other?"

"Do you love my uncle?" I pressed my lips together to stop from smiling, more than ready to watch Conall squirm.

His eyes widened and he rushed to open his door. "Look at the time. We're very busy men. Time to pay Donal a visit." The door shut firmly behind him.

The night lights of the house glimmered across the car and over Conall, making him glow.

Rolling my eyes, I cocked my head toward Sloan. "When are you going to do the *I love yous*, Uncle? It's been about eight years. Most couples are *married* by now."

"Are you telling me to propose?" Sloan drawled, traces of amusement lingering in his tone.

"What? No. I do not want *him* as my uncle." The corner of my mouth upturned before I could stop it. Okay, maybe I liked Conall a little bit. More than a little, but that was for me to know and everyone else to assume.

Sloan shot me a smile over his shoulder. "Don't you worry about us. I'll tell him I love him when I'm ready."

"So, you *do* love him, then?" I gaped.

He rolled his eyes. "What do you think?" With that, he winked and opened his door before exiting the car.

"Did you just hear what I heard?" I spun around to Daire, and he laughed.

"If anyone asks, I didn't hear a thing." He nudged me with his shoulder, a tender smile on his face. "But yeah, boy, I did. Are you surprised?"

I thought about it for a moment before I shook my head. "No. I'd be more shocked if he wasn't."

A sharp tap of knuckles on my window made me startle, and I shot Conall a glare through the glass.

He stuck out his tongue.

Rolling my eyes, I exited the car while Daire did the same on his side.

"Have you always been this impatient?" I straightened my suit jacket.

"*Always*, but you never stuck around me long enough to find out." Conall patted me on the shoulder while Sloan snorted.

"You've also never seen him in the bedroom. He's always eager for my cock." Sloan smirked when Conall's cheeks flushed a deep red.

"Shut up, Boss."

Daire chuckled, but one sharp glance from Sloan and he stopped. The tension between them thickened. Sloan's strong irritation at Daire leading me on was apparently still lingering on his mind. With a glare, Sloan spun on his heel and stalked toward Donal's house. All I could do was send Daire an apologetic smile before I followed.

Daire and Conall were right behind us as Sloan knocked on a solid brown door. Donal's house wasn't anything to sing about. It was a simple two-story home with gray bricks and a brown roof. He usually had a full green lawn out front, but the winter had killed most of it.

Donal opened the door, and the smile he wore on his face dwindled slightly when he saw us. He tightened his robe around his body and his eyes burned, shining with something I couldn't quite put my finger on as he shifted aside to let us in. "Boss, a personal visit?"

"I hope you don't mind, Donal," Sloan said as he entered the house. I followed, and behind me was Conall and Daire.

Donal led us toward the living room, straight to the left, and we followed. "Not at all. You're always welcome here, sir."

He fell into his armchair and gave us a strained smile. I'd been around Donal enough to know that he felt something wasn't right, and now that we were here in his house, my stomach churned. This man sitting in front of me wore his night clothes and slippers and was ready for bed, and now I had to end his life. I'd told Sloan I'd handle the rat, and I would, but that didn't mean I had to be happy about it being Donal. I still couldn't wrap my head around his betrayal, whether he was angry about Carolina or not.

Daire and I took a seat on a couch to the right, while Sloan and Conall sat on the three-seater to the left. Donal always had a lot of furniture because he'd always expected to have a big family, but most of his kids—minus Carolina—had moved away.

"How are you, Fionn?" Donal asked, the tautness in his shoulders disappearing. I wished he wouldn't relax around me, especially because of what I was about to do to him. "Good?" His attention narrowed on Daire's hand as he slipped it into mine, our fingers threading together.

I swallowed around the nausea that rose in my throat. This was my future, my job. Sloan trusted me with this, and I wasn't going to ruin or squander the chance. He'd told me he was proud of me tonight, and I'd ridden a high. Daire's hold was reassuring, a reminder that he was my backup no matter what, and it kept me centered.

I pressed my lips together. "Why did you do it?"

Donal's eyes dimmed and I could tell he knew what we were talking about. His chin dipped forward and he sighed. "I was stupid."

"You're a traitor," Sloan said sharply, the slice of his words nothing more than daggers. Right now, he was the cold mob boss, the one who had decided that Donal was no longer useful. He'd made a choice like we'd discussed when we were choosing what to do with Aodhan. "You told Diaz our secrets."

He fell back into his navy armchair, worn from use. "Not all of them. Some, yes. She wanted more, but I didn't give them to her. I only told her about certain drug distributions."

"Enough to affect our profits and make our lives harder." Sloan leaned forward, elbows on his knees as his dark eyebrows furrowed. "But you didn't just feed that information to Diaz, you sold us out to Toscani, too. The rogue Italians."

Donal glanced down at his hands, where he was picking at the skin of his thumb, the only sign that he was nervous. Otherwise, he didn't have the reaction of a man who knew he was about to die. "I'd hoped it would be a hit to our drug business." He sighed. "Boss, we could've lived on our brothels and other ventures. We don't need the drugs."

"No," I said, drawing everyone's attention to me. "We oversee all illegal avenues of enrichment on the East Coast. It's about dominance, Donal. The Killough Company owns this side of the US, and that includes drugs. That isn't going to change."

Donal smiled sadly. "You are a good boy, but you don't

understand the loss of a child. What it does to you. I don't regret what I did."

"We don't force anyone to buy our product. That's their choice." It was supply and demand, and while I *knew* what drugs did to people, I couldn't let myself see it that way. "Carolina chose to abuse drugs."

He laughed, the sound miserable and solemn. "Addiction is an illness, and we feed them their poison."

"What did you expect from a mob?" Sloan tilted his head. "That's what we are, and your daughter's death, as sad as it was, doesn't change what the Company is. Sex, drugs, protection, it's always been the same. *You* don't get to decide when it changes, even if you are an old friend of my father's."

Donal shook his head. "You're not a father."

Sloan's gaze slid to me. "I am."

I sucked in a breath between my teeth, my heart clattering against my ribs.

Sloan's attention turned back to Donal. He stood, tall and foreboding. "Your grief doesn't change what you did. Where's your wife?"

"Gone." Donal crossed his arms. "I thought it'd come eventually, the closer Fionn got to the truth. I sent her away a few months ago, and you'll never find her. She doesn't know anything about the Company." He paused, swallowing. Shit. He'd told us she was spending time with her sister. We thought they were having marital issues. "She won't say anything. She's already lost enough. Don't go after her. Please. Do me this one favor as your father's friend."

Sloan stared at him, and I stared at Sloan. I waited, squeezing Daire's hand.

"Very well. She'll be safe as long as she doesn't open her mouth." Sloan stepped toward me and unbuttoned his suit jacket. He pulled out a Glock and passed it to me, and I raised my gaze to him. "Get this done."

"No torture?" I whispered, hoping. There was always time to flay someone's skin in the future, but this was Donal.

"No. One bullet to the head." Sloan turned back toward Donal. "Despite your betrayal, you were once a good friend. You guided me when I needed it, and thank you for that, but this is how your life ends."

I released Daire's hand and stood. The Glock was heavy in my palm, but not as heavy as the duty Sloan had given me. I wasn't putting a random man to rest, rather a general, a man who'd worked in the Company longer than even Sloan.

Daire was at my side, saying nothing but using his presence as support as I walked toward Donal.

Donal gave me a small smile as he stood, his kind eyes forgiving. He held out his hand to me, and I glanced at Sloan, who nodded, so I shook it. "You're going to be a good boss, Fionn. Stand strong and fight. Always fight."

"It's been a pleasure, Donal." I let go of his hand and raised the Glock to his forehead.

He straightened and closed his eyes. He began to murmur a prayer, and I took a steadying breath before I pulled the trigger. Donal's head flew backward, and his body collapsed on the armchair. Blood splattered across the wall, painting the white with sprays of red.

It was done.

I swallowed, ignoring the ache in my chest as I stared at Donal's body. Buzzing filled my ears as every sense narrowed in on the old man in his chair. *Dead.* I did that.

Behind me, Sloan's voice filtered through the white noise flooding my brain. "Daire, call Caden to clean up this mess. I don't want this tied to us. Tell him to make sure no one finds the body."

Hands touched my shoulders, and I breathed through the panic that sliced through my chest. I focused on the strong hold, on the scent of Daire's cologne tickling my nose as he cupped my cheeks.

"Boy, you're fine. Look at me."

I opened my eyes again, and he was there. A guarantee. An inevitability. My Daddy.

"You did good."

I smiled. "I know."

Daire grinned.

21

DAIRE

Sloan's glare was sharp as a dagger in my back, and while I wished I could blame him, I couldn't. He knew the truth now, that I'd used Fionn for my own pleasure, and he deserved to be angry. While he had two other nephews in America—three if you counted Lor, I supposed— Fionn was his pride and joy. His *son* in a lot of ways. And here I was, his right-hand man, having broken his adoptive son's heart.

"Why did you send Conall home?" Fionn asked as we entered The Gold Coin, a bar in the middle of Manhattan. We'd come here to celebrate Fionn's victory, and he deserved all the attention. Despite Sloan already knowing who the rat was—and I was still pissed about that—Fionn had found the proof we'd needed. To take out a man like Donal, who'd spent years of his life in the Company, we'd needed top-notch evidence of his betrayal. The men who were loyal to Donal would want to see it.

"Because we're getting some weird reports of Reyes's men in the city." Sloan glared around the bar, as if Reyes would pop up, but there wasn't anyone other than patrons and a group of our men spread across the room as protection. "I don't want Conall anywhere near here unless we're sure it's safe."

Fionn raised his eyebrows, and Sloan sighed because he was easy to read.

"You matter, too, but you deserve to celebrate this win, and we have enough men. Conall can be back at the house with Vail and Lor. Fallon's been teaching Conall some self-defense techniques." By the tone in Sloan's voice, he didn't particularly like that very much. "The least I can do for the boys, after everything they've done, is protect their man. Between Conall and our bodyguards, he'll be safe. Vail's important to Cillian and Aspen."

"And to Rowen and Fallon," Fionn said.

Sloan waved his hand as we walked toward a round table and took a seat. Everything about the bar—or it was more like a pub—had an Irish feel to it. The walls were lined with pictures of Ireland, and I smiled as I stared at them from where I sat at the table. I'd never been, despite Sloan going over to the country multiple times to catch up with relatives and the allies who lived over there. I made a mental note to take Fionn one day because I know for a fact that he hadn't left the US.

The brown brick walls and low lighting would've been calming if it wasn't for the already loud volume of rambunctious drunks. It was past midnight, but the people of New York City were only just getting started. The smell of beer filled my nose, and I would've winced if I wasn't used to it already.

"Did our guys give us anything else other than Reyes's men being sighted around New York?" I asked, finally drawing my attention to Sloan as he settled into the seat.

"No." Sloan's eyebrows furrowed in irritation as he slid off his thick wool jacket and laid it over one of the spare chairs beside him. "Until we get more information, we can assume it's not entirely safe. Reyes is up to something."

"Uncle, why not take him out for good? I don't understand."

Sloan snorted. "I know you think I'm a god, but I'm not. Even with the best men on our payroll, Ardan included, Reyes isn't an idiot. His house is a fortress, and his security is excellent. He never keeps to a schedule, which makes him unpredictable."

"Like what we do," Fionn murmured.

"His men are loyal to him." I settled my elbows on the table and glanced at the menu board hanging on the wall behind the bar. "They aren't easy to turn. At least the ones close to him aren't."

Sloan hummed. "Right now, he's testing his limits, playing with fire to see if he'll get burned." His mouth quirked.

"And you enjoy it." I smirked at him when he glanced in my direction, and his gaze hardened. He'd mostly ignored me up until now. Sloan and I had grown up together, and I knew everything about him. As much as he'd hate to admit it, he usually let his enemies push a little before he destroyed them. Nothing more than a predator playing with his prey. It was a game to Sloan, even if he pretended it wasn't. "You like the challenge."

Sloan didn't answer. He rose from his seat. "The first round is on me in celebration of your success, Fionn. What do you want?"

"I usually drink whiskey, but I might try something else. A beer? A Guiness?" Fionn hesitated, and I reached out to rub circles on his back.

"Maybe a Murphy's?" He didn't drink much, and I thought he might like something different from the stereotype. "They're good."

"Do you tell him what he can and can't do, too?" Sloan's razor-sharp tone had me wincing. I hated it when he was this mad at me.

I raised my chin. "You do the same thing to Conall. I'm only suggesting something he might like, and I'm not going to stop just because you're angry at me . . . sir."

"Uncle, Daire is my partner." Fionn raised his chin toward Sloan. "And I love him. Please."

"I'll get you a Kilkenny. You'll like it better." Then, Sloan headed toward the bar.

I sighed and pinched the bridge of my nose. "He's pissed at me, and he's proving a point."

"He'll come around, give him some time. You shouldn't have told him, Daddy. It wasn't any of his business." Fionn leaned his shoulder against mine, and I wrapped an arm around his waist, laying a kiss on his jaw.

"If we hadn't told him now and it came out later, he would've been even more angry. At least we told him before he found out from someone else." I shrugged. "He's still your uncle, Fifi."

"Right, but I'm an adult. If I stuck around for eight years for sex and nothing else, that's on me. You might have broken my heart, but you never promised me anything except fucking. I could've walked away."

Behind us, someone lit up a cigar, and the sweet smell joined with the rest of the scents, the atmosphere deepening as an older man rose from his seat and began to sing a Gaelic song in the corner of the bar. I imagined this was what pubs were like over in Ireland, too. My grandfather had talked about it all the time.

"We should go to Ireland this year," I said instead of arguing with him.

He blinked like an owl, his hazel eyes big and wide. "Really? I've never been."

"I know, me neither. That's why we should go. You have great aunts over there, right?"

He made a disinterested sound. "Sure. Sloan's aunts and his cousins. His sister, too. I've never met her. Though I met a couple of our family members when they came over here last time. Remember Tiernan?"

"Unfortunately," I murmured.

Tiernan was a year younger than Sloan and had strong ambitions. I knew his mom when I was a kid, but she'd moved back to Ireland shortly after I'd met Sloan. I'd met Tiernan three times since, and I sensed an underlying impatience, like he desired more. Then, there was his clear jealousy of Sloan and his position.

"I wouldn't trust them as far as I could throw them. Tiernan's the worst." Fionn shrugged. "Sure, they help the Company over in the UK, but there's something about him. He's . . . ."

"Deceitful?" I offered.

He rocked his hand from side to side. "Maybe. Or slimy, like he's waiting for something to happen to Sloan. I can't say he wouldn't defend the Company, but if he had the chance at power, he'd take it."

I watched some of our men as they filtered through the door and took tables of their own, and I relaxed a little. The cavalry was here. We'd called them in on the way here, and now that Fionn was safe, I could enjoy and celebrate his victory, even if Sloan let him off the hook a little by not having him torture Donal. If it'd been anyone else other than Fionn doing the job, I don't think Sloan would've relented, even if the one being killed was Donal. Despite what he might say, Sloan had given Fionn an easier job because he loved him. He didn't want to see Fionn hurt over torturing an old friend.

"I agree," I said, turning my focus back to Fionn. "His brothers aren't much better."

He shrugged. "I haven't met Kyran. He's the youngest, but I have records on him. He's quiet, but I don't think I'd trust him, either. Senan, though?" He shook his head. "He thinks with his dick more than his head."

I laughed. "Okay, Fifi, time for you to get out of *your* head. No more thinking or worrying tonight. We're here to celebrate you and your victory."

"Is it one, though? Sloan already knew who the rat was." His shoulders slumped, and I tightened my hold around his waist, yanking his dress shirt out of his pants so I could slip my fingers under it and caress the warm skin of his hip.

"He had no proof and needed it. You found it for him, and you finished the job. You killed Donal. So yeah, it's your victory." I cupped his cheek and turned his face toward me.

He gave me a small smile before I dipped in to give him a quick kiss that turned into something longer. He moaned, tongue flicking against my lips, and as I opened my mouth to let him in, steins of beer were slammed down in front of us.

Fionn jumped away from me and his cheeks flushed a deep red as he gave Sloan an embarrassed grin. "Sorry."

The sound that came from the back of Sloan's throat was all irritation, but it wasn't at Fionn—not with how hard he was glaring at me. I rolled my shoulders but didn't break his stare. If he wanted submission from me right now, he wasn't going to get it. Fionn was mine and I wasn't going to apologize for it, even if I'd admitted I'd been an asshole to him. I would spend the rest of my life making up for it.

"Drink," Sloan ordered as he fell back into his seat. "You deserve it."

A few hours into celebrating—Fionn more than anyone because he'd switched back to whiskey and was mixing up his drinks—my phone buzzed. Fionn wobbled to the side, but I steadied him with a palm to his shoulder as I grabbed my phone from the table and checked the text message that'd come through.

MCGIBBS

Reyes spotted in NYC.

Attached was a grainy photo of Reyes in Central Park, talking to a man who was clearly his. They had their heads bowed, and it was daylight in the picture, which meant it'd been yesterday, at the very least, considering it was now early morning and still dark.

"Fuck." I flipped my phone to show Sloan, and he squinted before his ice blue eyes turned dark with anger.

"That bastard." He tugged out his phone and began to type furiously on it. "We're going to have to inform the men. I'll get Rowen and Fallon here and call Jamie to bring back Aspen and Cillian. It's no good to have my best men in another state when Reyes is *here*."

Fionn swayed toward me again, and I caught him before patting his hand. "That's enough to drink for a little while, Fifi."

"Why?" He pouted. "You said I could celebrate."

"You can, but you're drunk."

He was a lightweight, and as adorable as it was, now that we knew Reyes *was* in the city, we needed to be extra careful.

Sloan made a sound I ignored. In the hours we'd been here, Fionn had dominated the conversation, but I hadn't missed the glares Sloan shot at me whenever I opened my mouth. His anger was palpable.

"I'm going to step outside and make some calls. This place is too fucking loud." Sloan narrowed his eyes around the pub and shot to his feet, stalking toward one of the side doors. I watched him for a moment and rose to follow.

I placed a kiss on Fionn's cheek. "Stay here, boy. I need to speak to your uncle."

He grinned up at me. "Yes, Daddy Daire."

I smiled, my insides warming at how carefree he appeared like this. Stopping beside one of our men on the way out, I pointed at Fionn. "Watch him. He's drunk."

The Company man gave me a firm nod in agreement before I followed Sloan. He was on his phone when I got outside, and I shivered, regretting that I hadn't taken my jacket with me. It was too fucking cold, but I didn't plan on staying out here for long.

The alleyway outside was dank and the stench unbearable. It smelled like old trash, and while it was mostly dark, the flood of lights from the street lit up the area so I could see Sloan well enough.

He had his phone pressed to his ear, and he hummed in acknowledgement to whoever he was talking to. "Make it happen." He jabbed his thumb on the screen and turned, pausing when I walked toward him. "If you're here to offer excuses, Daire, I don't want them."

"You're pissed at me."

"Yes, I am." He stepped in closer. "I'm fine with you being with my nephew. I was more than okay with it when I realized it was first happening because I trusted you to take care of him. Fionn's an adult, and he can have sex with whoever he wants, even you. What I didn't expect was you using him and making him feel like a waste." He held up a hand when I went to talk. "I don't care about your excuses. I won't have anyone treating him less than what he's worth, which is a lot. He is a Killough." He shoved himself in my face in a *very* unSloan-like way that had real fear pouring through me and leaving me paralyzed. "And I would die before I let anyone hurt him because he's more than my nephew, he is *my son*. I raised him, and I'll rip you limb from limb before I let you break his heart again." His voice took on a deep growl.

"I won't, Sloan." I sighed and tipped my chin down. "I love him."

"You better take care of him or I'll make you regret ever looking in his direction." His nostrils flared. "Rowen and Fallon will be here soon." He strode past me, leaving me in the cold of the early morning to think about the threat in his words. I didn't know how to prove to him how much I loved

Fionn, but I had a long time to make up for the hurt I'd caused.

I followed him inside, and we happily stayed silent with each other. Sloan talked to Fionn and so did I, but when it came to each other, we didn't say a word. Sloan and I drank in moderation, and Fionn slowed down, too, because while we weren't going to let Reyes ruin the night completely, we couldn't be smashed. Though, Fionn was past that point.

Sloan rose to make a call to Conall, and I sighed when he left the loud bar again.

"What's wrong, Daddy?" Fionn snuggled against my side and laid a gentle kiss on my neck, right above where the collar of my dress shirt started.

I turned toward him and cupped his face, cradling him like the precious boy he was to me, and laid my mouth over his, kissing him gently. The pub around us disappeared because Fionn *was* my world right now.

"There's never anything wrong when you're here, boy." With a final press of my lips against his, I smiled. "You deserve everything, and I'm going to make sure you get it. I promise."

The corner of his mouth ticked up in response. "I'm going to remember that."

I laughed right as his phone rang. A deep mournful sound erupted from the Samsung and he scrunched up his nose as he picked it up from next to his half-empty beer. I raised my eyebrows when he glanced at me, gaze thoughtful before he grinned widely.

He answered the call. "Mom. It's too fucking early in the morning. Why are you calling me?" I didn't hear what she said, but Fionn rolled his eyes in response to whatever it was. A few moments later he made a face at me, moving his mouth in silent words that mocked whatever she was saying, and I shook my head with a chuckle. Fionn was past the point of drunk. I needed to take him home soon. "Mom, stop. I don't give a flying fuck if Deer's out drinking and can't afford a taxi home. Get one of his friends to pick him up, yeah? Fuuuuuck. You're so annoying. It's all about Deer and Bell. You fucking know you have another son, right? Me. My name's Fionn, in case you fucking forgot. I'm your oldest, the one you sent to Sloan because you *couldn't handle me*."

I widened my eyes. Sober Fionn would never have said any of this, and I liked the brazenness with Annabelle. She deserved the snarky attitude.

"Uh uh uh, don't use the tears on me. I'm done. You can stop calling me now, *Mother*. You're not getting any more money. Goodbye." He ended the call and slammed the phone on the table before flipping the bird at it. "Kiss my ass, woman." He burst into giggles and flopped against me. "Tell me you're proud of me, Daddy."

"So proud, boy." I pressed a kiss to his head and breathed in the scent of his sweat-soaked hair. He could smell like a dumpster, and I'd still want to get a good whiff. "You did good."

He hummed in pleasure. "Thanks, Daddy."

The side door opened, and Sloan walked back in with Rowen and Fallon at his side, looking as elegant as they usually did. Rowen was easy to spot in the crowd with his reddish-blond hair and clean-cut beard, while Fallon stood out as well, but mostly because he was attractive. He had long blond hair and an innocent smile, one that didn't match someone who belonged to a mob.

They were talking, and Rowen glanced at the menu board, pointing at it, and Sloan laughed. Fallon came straight over to us, and the moment Fionn spied him, he cheered loudly and jumped to his feet, dragging Fallon into a hug.

"Oh. Hi." Fallon chuckled, clearly unsure what to do about this new version of Fionn. "How much have you had to drink?"

"Lots! I like you, Fallon." Fionn tapped his chest. "And I'm sorry if I was ever an asshole to you, okay? You're a good guy."

Fallon cocked his head and fluttered his long blond lashes. "I'm hot, too."

Fionn snorted and rolled his eyes. "Yeah, but my Daddy's hotter."

"Your . . . . You know what, I'm not going to ask. Maybe later." Fallon bounced his way around to Fionn's other side and plopped down on one of the spare seats. Rowen and Sloan joined us again, with Sloan retaking the chair beside me and Rowen snatching the last one between Fallon and Sloan.

"Is this what it's like in Ireland, Rowen?" Fionn asked loudly, to the point it was almost a shout.

Behind us, someone was singing in Gaelic again, and while the person was obviously tipsy, they weren't half bad, even with the slurring that came with it.

"Aye, it is." Rowen smiled and his face softened, his eyes growing distant for a moment before Fallon touched his shoulder.

It was enough time for Fionn to start speaking about Reyes. "Okay, listen, this is what we're going to do. We're going to find all the Cartel motherfuckers in the city and take them all down right? So—" His hands flew in front of his face dramatically and he brought out the finger guns. "—this is my idea. First—"

I held back a laugh. "Enough, boy." I touched my lips to his cheek and squeezed his thigh under the table. It was time to take him home. He wouldn't be able to fight any Reyes men in this state, not to mention, he'd never been in a real gunfight. I wanted him away from the action until I had him trained better. I sent Rowen a smirk when I caught him looking at us. "Let me get you some beers. What do you want?"

Fallon's attention went straight to Rowen. "You're the expert on Irish beers. What should I have?"

Rowen snorted. "Eh, nothing here is quite as good as at home." He wrapped his arm around Fallon's shoulders, and I smiled at them, well aware of what it was like to be so fucking in love with someone. The thought made me lean over to give Fionn another kiss because I couldn't resist.

"But if ye must choose, don't be going for the stereotype. Guinness is okay, but I reckon ye'd enjoy a Murphy's."

"Murphy's it is!" Fallon leaned against Rowen, who kissed him on the temple.

"All this love. I love love. Don't you love love, Daddy?" Fionn muttered so that only I could hear, and then he heaved a dreamy sigh.

I chuckled quietly and stroked my fingers over his back.

"Since we're celebrating, I'll have a good vodka and 7UP. Been a while since I did that. Make it a double," Rowen said.

"It's on me." I sent him a wink, which earned me a pout from Fionn as he poked me in the belly.

"Only I'm allowed to be on you, Daddy Daire." The whine in his voice turned my belly warm because he was so damned adorable. If he was sober, I'd take him home right now to fuck him, but I wasn't going to do that while he was more than halfway to smashed.

I laughed and kissed him on his supple mouth again. I couldn't get enough. "You're drunk." I stroked my fingers over his chin. "But you're cute when you're jealous."

"I'm not." His pout deepened.

"Fionn." Sloan's sharp tone cut right through the moment, and Fionn turned toward him with his big innocent eyes.

Anger grabbed me, and I bit my tongue for a moment to exhale through my nose before I faced Sloan, too. "With all due respect, Sloan, he's my boy. I can handle him." Despite my irritation and all the words I wanted to say, I inclined my head forward in the respect I spoke about, but I didn't look away. I faced him as a Daddy to my boy who wouldn't back down in defense of Fionn.

"He may be your boy now, but he's still my nephew, and the future of this company. I won't have him embarrassing me."

I gritted my teeth so hard I swore I heard one of them crack. "Then, I will handle it . . . sir."

His stare hardened, and I kept my eyes on him, my chin raised. Sloan was many things, scary among them, but I'd known him for too long and his firmness came from the way he was raised. Niall Killough wasn't always a fair man, and I understood why Sloan was the way he was, but that didn't mean I was going to let this go. Fionn trusted me to take care of him when I was his Daddy and this was one of those moments.

Finally, Sloan's eyes shifted, and an understanding passed across his face. He still wasn't happy, and I wasn't sure if ever would be, but he tilted his head toward the bar, giving me permission to go. Whatever fury he held for me simmered below the surface of his tight facade, but now he was giving me a chance to prove to him that I could care for Fionn and give him everything he needed and wanted.

I left the table and headed straight to the bar, ordering Rowen and Fallon their drinks. While the bartender went to get the alcohol, I turned to watch Fionn and the boys as they talked. Fionn's face was bright and flushed from the booze, his hands moving as he spoke. His energy was electric, and now that he had an audience listening to him—Sloan included—he was putting on a show. The more I watched him, the harder I fell in love with him. How did I go so long thinking I only wanted sex with him?

When the bartender brought back the drinks, I paid and tipped her with my card before I walked back to the table with the glasses. I passed Rowen his vodka and Fallon his beer before I retook the seat beside Fionn, and we all raised our glasses.

As I raised my beer to take a drink, a loud *bang* echoed through the pub and almost instantly, everyone fell silent. Even the singing had stopped. Sloan shot to his feet, and that was enough for my senses to go on high alert.

Fionn and I turned to look at the door, where Rowen, Fallon, and Sloan were glaring. My spine stiffened when my eyes fell on Thiago Reyes walking through with confidence that a man strolling into a lion's den shouldn't have. Like in the picture sent from our men, his brown hair hung around his shoulders, and as much as I hated to admit it about an enemy, he was handsome. The suit he wore was purple striped and fit his muscular body perfectly.

Reyes was a man on a mission, his smirk assertive as his gaze glided around the room until it settled on us. The moment he found us, he walked in our direction, a dozen men at his back, his cousin Rafael included.

I sat up straighter, my arm around Fionn's chair protectively as Reyes came closer.

"Sloan Killough." He stopped beside us, his smirk widening.

"Thiago." Sloan's eyes darkened precariously. "You're in my territory."

"And you killed my cousin." The corner of Reyes's mouth jerked, a quick movement that showed his irritation.

"It was a shame that we got the wrong cousin, but all's fair in love and war." Sloan sat back in his chair and crossed his arms, his suit pulling tightly around his arms to show off his muscles.

Around us, our men waited for directions, while the other guests watched with quiet confusion. They had no idea what they were a part of, and I hoped it didn't come to anything physical while innocent bystanders were around. We tried to avoid that. It was one thing for mobsters to die, but if people who weren't part of it did as well, the cops and feds took it a lot more seriously—we didn't need that heat.

Fionn leaned against me, and I murmured "I've got you, boy" loud enough for only him to hear.

"Next time, it'll be a brother or . . . a lover." Sloan's words hit their target.

Reyes's nostrils flared despite him keeping his composure. "Do you think you're upsetting me by threatening Manny? He has balls, Killough, and he doesn't need to be hidden away, guarded by twenty-seven men."

I inwardly cursed at the threat. He had someone watching Conall. I laid my hand on my stomach, close to where my gun was holstered under my suit jacket, and Rafael's gaze flicked to me. He gave me a short shake of his head. A warning. If I went for my gun, he would go for his, and there would be bloodshed. The only thing that stopped me was Fionn's weight against my side. He was too drunk to defend himself.

Sloan stiffened and shifted forward, and the mobsters on each side watched, ready for whatever fight was coming for them. "If you go near my pet, Reyes, I will cut you up into small pieces and feed you to your beloved Manny. He'll know that every bite he takes is a part of you."

Reyes made a sound of disinterest. "I want compensation, Killough."

The laughter that ripped from Sloan's chest was abrupt and mean, and I internally winced because Sloan was done playing games. *Fuck.* This was going to get bloody. "Like I said. It's war. You started it by approving collateral damage and hurting my pet."

Fionn stood, and I was there at his side as he moved in closer to Sloan, offering support. The inebriation I'd seen before was still there in him, an underlying imbalance in the way he stood, but he seemed to have a clearer head. He was an apprentice in every way right now, and I was so damned proud of him.

Sloan squared his shoulders at Reyes. "Don't make me shoot you here in this good establishment. I don't want to cause issues for the owner."

Reyes's body went rigid and he clenched his jaw despite flashing his teeth in a smile. "You won't, but you don't care about anyone else's bottom line. There are too many witnesses. And cameras."

He nodded up at the corner of the pub, but I didn't look

because I'd already seen the security cameras when we'd arrived. I'd checked for them as I'd trained myself to do since I'd joined the Company.

"You and me. Outside. Fist fight. No weapons," Reyes said.

Fallon's laughter startled me. "Is this the fifties?"

Reyes tossed him a glare. "If it was, a washed-up entertainer like you would be sucking cock for a living, not sitting at a table with real dangerous men."

I supposed there was a compliment in there somewhere because he'd admitted that he was threatened by us.

Rowen growled behind me. "Watch yerself."

Reyes rolled his eyes, and I stepped in closer to Fionn, everything inside me urging me to protect him no matter what. "What do you say, Killough?"

Any other day, I might have thought Sloan would say no, but it was four in the morning and the months had been long. Reyes hadn't just hurt Conall in a bombing, he'd walked into Sloan's territory without fear. The bastard was testing Sloan's pride, and if I knew anything about Sloan, it was that he hated men who thought they were better than him. As far as he was concerned, no one was.

Sloan nodded. "Outside."

I cursed him under my breath. This wasn't going to end well. Even if we won, it'd come with more consequences. Reyes's men wouldn't let their boss get hurt. But Reyes knew where to hit Sloan and his words slammed right into their target.

Sloan shot around and stalked toward the side door, and Rowen and Fallon followed. Fionn was already heading there, too, and I was nowhere else but at his back, ready to protect it if needed. Men from both mobs exited the door until the alleyway was full, brimming with unmitigated testosterone and cockiness. Every hair on my body stood up, aware of the immediate danger around us, around *Fionn*, and there wasn't anything I could do.

Sloan slid off his wool coat and suit jacket, then passed them to me with his gun, and I folded the clothing over my arm. The gun stayed in my hand. By the time I looked back, Sloan's dress shirt sleeves were rolled up and he was as ready as Reyes.

Reyes's gun and jacket were on the ground in front of the circle that the men had formed, and Fionn was closer to Reyes's possessions than I was. He was also too far from me, but the spot at his side was already filled by Company men. There was no way I could get to him before the fight began.

"Ready to get your arse kicked?" Sloan asked with a lip curl.

Instead of answering, Reyes punched, and Sloan ducked and spun, his hands raised in front of him as his smirk widened. My heart jumped straight up into my throat. Sloan hadn't been in a fight like this since he was young, and we were no spring chickens anymore. I didn't like what was happening right now, but all I could do was watch.

"Is that what you call a punch, Reyes?"

Reyes's nose scrunched as he sneered, moving on the balls of his feet. "I'm only getting started, Killough."

Sloan shrugged, unfazed. "So am I. That's why your cousin, Joaquin, is the next to die."

I glanced toward Fionn, watching the way he focused on Sloan raptly. Despite still being buzzed, he was the apprentice, Sloan's nephew in every way. He was ready to protect Sloan if needed. I wished I could be over beside him, but it was better this way. Our defensive positions meant we could cover more ground if it came to that.

I blinked and returned my focus to the fight. I'd missed some of the punches that had been thrown, but I caught the moment Sloan slammed his knuckles into Reyes's gut, eliciting a cheer from our men. On one side of the circle, Fallon threw his arm up in the air with a "Good one, Boss!"

Reyes pressed a hand to his stomach and glared, but he kept his eyes on Sloan. The fight was violent, and they both moved with the kind of proficiency expected of men who'd spent their whole lives having people wanting to kill them. They were both sons of mob bosses.

Fionn's concern filtered through as I looked at him, a wince on his face when Reyes landed a punch to Sloan's jaw, blood splattering across the asphalt. Sloan returned the favor with a hit to Reyes's cheek.

The bloodshed didn't stop there. Each attack was vicious and full of hatred, and after a while their energy began to decline. Sloan had a split lip and Reyes's head had a laceration on it. The vigor from the crowd quieted, some of the steam disappearing with every minute the fight went on.

I shifted my attention from Sloan to Fionn, caught between defending my boss and keeping an eye on my boy. He was my life, and I couldn't imagine anything happening to him. I trusted the Company men to protect him, too, but there was no one better than me to do it.

Fionn glanced at me and smiled, and as corny as it was, my heart skipped a beat. I couldn't help but wink back in return, causing his grin to widen. I turned my attention away for a second, not long enough that something should've happened, but it did. From the corner of my eye, I caught a Reyes soldier going for Sloan's back, ready to attack, but it was Fionn who intercepted him by grasping his shirt and yanking him back.

Pride swelled in my chest at his quick reflexes as Fionn pointed at the soldier.

"Don't fucking cheat." He rocked slightly but kept on his feet. This was my boy, the future of the Killough Company. Even drunk, he was on top of his game.

Everyone else kept their eyes on the fight, seemingly uninterested in the Reyes soldier and what he'd done, so when the soldier jumped toward Reyes's gun beside his jacket, no one moved. I lunged forward, but it was too late. A shot rang out in the narrow alleyway, and the bullet ripped through Fionn's chest, then another. Three times the soldier fired the gun, and three times Fionn's body shuddered with the hit.

The fight stopped, but so did my world.

I was frozen, staring at Fionn as the blood drained from his cheeks. His gaze slowly slid to me. Eyes wide, he opened his mouth as he stumbled back a few paces before crumpling to the ground with a gurgling gasp that ripped through my very soul.

"Fionn!" I didn't recognize my own voice, but everything after that was pure adrenaline and anger. I raised the Glock still in my hand—Sloan's—pointed it at the soldier who'd shot Fionn, then pulled the trigger. The bullet went straight between his eyes and his head jerked back. He collapsed to the ground, body limp.

The world around me was an eerie quiet that drove an excruciating ache straight into my chest.

All at once, chaos hit.

Shots rang out. It was as though everyone had come to their senses, and whatever had slowed the world around us had hit Play again because it was speeding forward and gunshots echoed.

Rushing toward Fionn was like walking through water, my legs nothing but jelly. I couldn't move fast enough, couldn't get air into my lungs, but I made it and fell onto my knees beside him.

Then, Sloan was there, right beside me, sorrow in his eyes and twisting his mouth before the mask was back.

I used my hands to apply pressure to the wounds, desperate to stem the bleeding. Fionn couldn't die. I wouldn't let it happen.

Fionn stared up at me but didn't understand, pain plastered across his handsome face. I wanted to comfort him, but my brain was buzzing, and any coherent thoughts were impossible. All I could see was blood, spreading and pooling across his chest, wet and getting worse, and everything inside me screamed.

"You're going to be okay." Sloan pressed a kiss to Fionn's forehead.

Fionn let out a wretched sob. "Uncle Sloan, it hurts."

I ducked my head to kiss his ear and murmured, "You'll be fine, boy. We need you to be fine." This was Eoin all over again. I wasn't there when that horror happened—but now I was. I couldn't do a damned thing. I was fucking useless. What kind of Daddy was I?

Someone called out from behind us. Irish. One of ours. "We need an ambulance."

A bullet flew past my ear.

Sloan hissed and slapped a hand to his side. "Grazed," he muttered when he saw me looking.

I jumped to my feet and shot around, aiming for every Cartel member I could see. I didn't care that I had no cover— they were all going to regret what their soldier did. My left thigh burned, and I glanced down briefly to feel the wetness growing across my pants. I'd been hit. I ignored it and focused on pulling the trigger.

Our men were dragging bodies into the pub, more Company men joined us, and my brain screamed *kill, kill, kill, they hurt my boy.*

Finally, Sloan yanked my suit jacket, and I went back to my knees beside Fionn's limp body. Sloan sent me a wild look. "The hospital is nearby. It will take longer for the ambulance to get through the chaos than for us to take him there."

I nodded in agreement, panic jackhammering in my chest and crawling up my throat. Together, we slid our arms under Fionn, who whimpered, and hefted him up.

Hospital. We had to get him help.

"Move," Sloan shouted, and we rushed out of the alley and toward the hospital as fast as we could.

22

DAIRE

The hospital was cold, but I wasn't sure if it was because of the actual temperature or if it was because of the current iciness that slid its way through my blood. Everything moved at a hundred miles per hour around me, but all I could do was focus on the door they'd wheeled Fionn through. Heart in my throat, I could still see him lying on those white sheets, pale, except for the blood that pooled on his chest. The same blood covered my palms from where I'd pressed down on Fionn's torso.

Somewhere outside, I'd dumped the gun I had into a trash can at Sloan's orders. We didn't have time to find one of our men so they could dispose of it, and we certainly didn't have time to think about anything but Fionn and the pained groans that stuttered out of him.

I stared down at my shaking hands, and my thoughts became stagnant. My boy was hurt, and I couldn't do a damned thing for him. I hated this. *Hated*.

"Fuck." The exhaled curse word from Sloan startled me into focusing on him. He sat in the waiting room chair beside me, his hand pressed against his side where he'd been grazed.

The doctors had tried to look at his injury, but he'd waved

them off, demanding all eyes be on his nephew. They hadn't been so persuaded with the injury to my thigh. They'd forced me to a bed and taken the bullet out before cleaning it up, which was the most I'd let them do.

"I'm going to kill Reyes."

"Not if I get to him first," I murmured, rubbing my hands together to stave off the cold. Reyes had hurt Fionn, and nothing would save him if I ever got my hands on him. Fionn was my world, and sitting here not being able to do a thing was driving me crazy.

Sloan scrubbed a palm over the back of his neck, closing his eyes. "I did this. I let my arrogance get the better of me."

I didn't deny it. Sloan was many things, but he wasn't infallible. Reyes knew that, too, and he'd used it against us. Sloan was as human as the rest of us. He made mistakes. This was one of them, and now Fionn was fighting for his life.

"I called Conall and let him know."

I nodded, not trusting my voice as emotion clogged my throat.

"He'll live. Fionn's strong." Sloan sounded as if he was trying to convince himself.

"You should tell him that," I finally managed to get out, eyeing a woman in front of us as she begged the doctors to save her boyfriend. Her sobbing filled the already noisy ER and she was ragged. I might look a bit like that, too.

"He knows."

I shot him a frown. "He doesn't."

"What?"

I shook my head. "He doesn't know, Sloan. He's not you, and he never will be, just like you aren't your father. You send him small signals, thinking he'll pick up on them, but he doesn't." I touched a hand to my chest, pain resonating from there until I thought I was having a heart attack. But I didn't care. I could die here and now. As long as Fionn was okay, I wouldn't care. "He has a big heart when it comes to the people he loves, and he's so desperate to make you proud. You're hard on him, and I know it's because Niall was the same with you, but Fionn doesn't react well to it. He'll be a good boss one day, but you have to stop being hot and cold with him. You tell him he needs to do better, but you don't give him a chance to prove it. You're too busy trying to protect him from the more dangerous assignments."

I shouldn't be saying this to him, but with Fionn shot, all bets were off.

"Either he's all in or he's not and you make someone else your apprentice. Before Conall came along, you'd given him important tasks, and then the rogue Italians happened. You pulled him back because you panicked. You can deny it all you want, but you did. You fucking panicked that something would happen to him."

Sloan stared at me, a tic in his jaw and his eyes burning. I was on a roll.

"He thinks he's failing you, and I get it. Niall taught you to be emotionless. Cold. But Fionn's a different kind of boss. He can be a good one, but you need to stop and look at what you're doing to him. You and Eoin had each other growing up. You had support. Fionn has no one. His brothers and mother abandoned him. His dad is dead. His uncle is too busy being a mob boss to stop and be family. For a long time, he was alone. Even *I* failed him. I used him, and I can't take those years back, but I can make up for them. I can spend every minute of our future treating him like the most important person in the world because he is to me. But I know you love him, too."

I hadn't finished. There were a million things I wanted to say to Sloan—like how he set Fionn up to fail by smothering him in bubble wrap, then getting frustrated when he hadn't hardened up enough—but Sloan knew what he'd done wrong. I didn't need to throw it in his face, even if he deserved it.

Silence fell between us.

Despite all the crying and yelling happening around us, only the two of us existed right now. I didn't miss the sheen in his eyes and it was new. I didn't dare speak anymore, though, because I'd said what was necessary.

Sloan swallowed and turned his gaze toward the doors where they'd taken Fionn. "I didn't know the first thing about kids when Annabelle gave him to me. I had maids. I thought they could raise him. But when he arrived, he looked so much like Eoin. He had the same twinkle in his eyes. This . . . hopefulness. He was so innocent, and I didn't want to ruin that. Eoin would never forgive me. So, I wasn't going to let him join the Company." His mouth twitched. "I thought I could raise him the way my father raised me and Eoin, but you're right. He was softer than us. Gentle. And so smart. He made me laugh in ways no one but his father had. When I came home to him, it wasn't just a house, it was a home."

I sighed and scratched at the dried blood on my palms. *Fionn's blood.*

"And then, he asked to be my apprentice. Eoin would never have wanted him to be a mob boss. He would've hated the idea. But Fionn begged me. I couldn't say no." Sloan's mouth quirked and there was a softness on his face that I didn't feel right looking at, so I watched the sobbing lady again. "I was okay having him work under me until Conall was taken. It reminded me how easily I could lose someone I loved. Fionn. My pet. I needed them to be safe." He cleared his throat and leaned back in his chair. "You're right, though. I should tell him how I feel, and I will."

"Good." I licked my dry lips as the doors opened and a doctor walked out. He caught my eye and headed over to us, and I straightened immediately.

"Are you Fionn Killough's family?" The doctor wore blue scrubs and a white coat with a badge attached.

Dr. Julien D'Antona.

347

Sloan and I both stood. I winced at the sharp pain that shot through my thigh.

"We are," Sloan answered.

He had a young face and was probably in his early thirties. With vibrant blue eyes and dark hair swept off his forehead, he was handsome with dimples in both his cheeks. He gave us a grim smile. "Fionn was very lucky. Only one of the shots managed to hit an organ which was punctured. Two of the bullets were clean through his chest, but the third caused issues. We performed an emergency surgery, and his spleen needed to be removed. It was successful. He bled a lot and needed a transfusion, but he's in recovery right now. We have him in ICU to keep a close eye on him for the next twenty-four hours. If all goes well, he'll be transferred to a private room tomorrow."

Relief was like a punch to the stomach, and I nearly collapsed. I would've landed on my ass if Sloan hadn't grabbed my elbow to keep me upright. Dr. D'Antona frowned between us.

"Now that Fionn is in a safe spot, you need to have a doctor check on you." He gave Sloan a pointed look. "My nurses informed me you refused help multiple times despite their insistence. You're injured, and I won't let either of you see him until *you* have been examined." He raised his chin. "Now, you can follow me." I opened my mouth to argue, but he glared. "Do you want to see Fionn? I only allow healthy visitors. Come with me."

I glanced at Sloan, and he returned the stare. I went with him for an examination.

A few hours later—too long if you asked me—Sloan had his bullet graze cleaned. Dr. D'Antona led us to staff showers, much to my surprise, and he ordered us to wash up while he attained some scrubs we could use as clothes—the cops hadn't shown up yet and any missed evidence wasn't our problem. Actually, their incompetence worked out perfectly for us. Clearly they had too many witnesses to deal with.

I'd never met a doctor like D'Antona, and because of how badly I wanted to see Fionn, I wasn't in the position to argue.

Once we were clean and dressed in the scrubs, Dr. D'Antona led us to the ICU. He stopped right outside the doors and turned to us, a serious expression on his face.

"I know this shootout was the consequence of a mob war. I've seen my fair share of injured men and women because of organized crime. It's not my job to judge you, even if I wanted to." He pursed his lips. "But I will say this. This hospital belongs to me and every other doctor and nurse and personnel. It's a safe haven, a no-go zone if you will. We heal here, not hurt. I will let you into this ICU, but I expect that you understand and agree to keeping your drama away from my patients."

Sloan inclined his head. "We agree. We're only here to see my nephew."

The doctor nodded sharply and opened the doors. We washed our hands before he led us into Fionn's room with its glass walls. Fionn's breathing was even, his chest rising and falling with strong movements despite an involuntary wince every now and then. A face mask covered his nose and mouth, helping him get air.

I swallowed as a wall of emotion smacked into me and stumbled over to a chair beside his bed. I grasped his hand, not too tightly, but with the desperation I needed for myself. He was here, alive, and all was right in my world because of that fact alone. I kissed his hand again and again.

"Fifi. Fuck, boy." I laughed at how ridiculous I sounded, but if Sloan heard me, he didn't say anything as he took the other side. The doctor left us alone.

Machines beeped around Fionn, sounds that reminded me he was breathing.

Fionn's lashes fluttered and he let out a sigh. I held my breath, and Sloan leaned forward, the face of a man as desperate as me for Fionn to wake. He reached for Fionn's other hand, and I saw Fionn squeeze it.

"Fifi, are you awake?" I asked. "Boy?"

Fionn's tongue poked out and he turned his head slightly. Lashes fluttering again, he slowly opened his eyes. When I caught sight of those hazel gems behind his eyelids, I couldn't stop the wretched noise ripping from my throat.

"Hey," I whispered gently.

Fionn gave me a small smile. "Hi, Deedee." His scratchy voice through the mask made me wince. My poor boy.

"I thought I told you that we aren't using that nickname," I teased, and he laughed, then grimaced in pain. He tugged down the mask before I could lecture him about it.

"Daddy Daire, is that better?" He scrunched up his nose and turned to look at his other side, at Sloan. "Hey, Uncle Sloan. You're here."

Sloan huffed. "I wouldn't be anywhere else. You're too important."

Fionn sucked in a breath. "Oh." He frowned and his nose scrunched up more. "I am?"

Sloan sighed and pinched the bridge of his nose. "Fuck, Fionn."

"Why are you swearing? You don't swear." He glanced around back at me. "Am I dead and in an alternate reality?"

I snorted and laid another kiss on his hand. "No, boy, you are very much alive and here with us, where you belong and will stay."

"I curse when I need to," Sloan grumbled, then smirked. "And right now's the perfect time for it. The fact that you don't know what you mean to me . . . . I thought you were smarter than that. You're more than my nephew, you're my son. I'd kill anyone who dared to touch you the wrong way. Daire's lucky I didn't cut his balls off."

He gave me a pointed look, and I cringed. Yeah, I deserved that.

Sloan shifted uncomfortably. "You're my family, a Killough. I haven't told you enough how proud you make me, and how there will never be anyone else to take charge after I'm gone. You're it. My legacy." He squeezed Fionn's hand again. "I should've told you more. It's no excuse, but I forgot that you weren't me. I was used to having to guess my father's feelings, and I thought it made me tough, but your *Daddy* reminded me that I had Eoin. Your brothers are selfish."

"Not as much as his mother," I muttered.

Sloan raised an eyebrow at me.

Fionn groaned.

"What does that mean?" Sloan grumbled with a frown.

Fionn shook his head. "Nothing."

"Fionn's been giving his mother money because she's been asking for it." I sent him an apologetic wince. "He needed to know, boy."

Sloan's entire posture changed from a worried uncle to an overprotective and dangerous mob boss. His eyes darkened and his mask slid back into place. "I'll handle her."

"Don't," Fionn said weakly, taking a shaky breath. "I did it already. I told her no more. I'm not weak."

"Stop putting words into my mouth," Sloan snapped a little too harshly. He cursed himself under his breath. "That isn't what I said. Your mother knows better. I warned her that if she asked you for money, I'd stop her payments completely."

"You'll be punishing Deer and Bell then, too."

"So be it," Sloan growled. "That's on her. *You're* my responsibility, not her and your brothers. She should've thought about that before she called you for cash."

"Let's change the topic," I cut in. "Fionn's too unwell for this right now. Look where he is." No one needed reminding, but we all gazed around the ICU anyway.

"I want to officially adopt you." Sloan's words were direct and unrelenting, and both Fionn and I turned wide eyes on him.

"What?" Fionn tilted his head. "Why? I'm twenty-six. I don't need you to prove anything, Uncle. I know you care about me."

Sloan awkwardly tugged at the neckline of the blue scrubs he wore, and I held in the urge to grin at his discomfort. "I've let too many situations happen since you became my apprentice. Before you took on that responsibility, we had good times, didn't we?" He shook his head. "That changed after you officially joined the Company. I was hard on you, tried to be my father. I can't promise I'll change overnight because I *need* you to survive this, Fionn, and being the boss isn't a walk in the park. People will betray you, people you trust and care for, like Donal. I want you prepared for the future you chose, and I can't do that by being kind. The men and women who want to kill you for being a Killough? They won't be. Neither will the cops or the feds."

Fionn's lips quivered, but he pressed them together. "I know, Uncle."

"But you *are* my son and everything of mine is yours."

"Even Conall?" Fionn teased, and I laughed abruptly, smothering it with my hand. Fionn grinned mischievously through another wince of pain.

"No." Sloan stared at him, unruffled.

Fionn's eyes met mine, and we both laughed, until he groaned and touched his chest. "That hurts."

"Well, you did get shot three times. Don't do that again, boy." I squeezed his fingers. "I'll spank you if you do."

Fionn waggled his eyebrows. "Don't tease me with a good time, Daddy Daire."

"Okay, both of you. Enough." Sloan glared at us.

"Oh, he doesn't like the PDA when it's someone else," I said, and Fionn tried to laugh again, but it came out as more of a cough. He cringed in pain, and I rubbed his shoulder. "But it's fine when he fucks Conall in front of everyone."

Sloan growled, which did nothing to ease our amusement, and after a small while, he was smiling, too. "You've made your point."

"Oh, I'm just getting started, Uncle." Fionn flashed him a wide smile.

Sloan patted his thigh gently. "Before you do, you haven't answered me. Would you allow me to officially adopt you?"

"You never asked, you said you were going to," I pointed out, which had Sloan rolling his eyes.

"Fine." He dragged a chair closer to the bed and took a seat. He held on to Fionn's hand again. "Fionn, allow me to adopt you as my son. Can I do that?"

Fionn hummed and pouted in thought, and Sloan groaned, which had Fionn chuckling again. "I'd like that, Uncle. Very much."

The smile Sloan gave him was as real as it was going to get. "Me too."

An hour later, Fionn fell asleep when his pain started to get worse. The nurses gave him more pain relief, and he drifted off to somewhere nice. Sloan left to go home and check on Conall.

I stayed with Fionn until Sloan messaged me a few hours later.

BOSS

Come outside to the hallway. Now.

Frowning, I rose and placed a gentle kiss on Fionn's forehead. He grumbled but settled again quickly. Nodding at his nurse as I went past, I rubbed my eyes as fatigue hit me. It was well into late morning, and I was beyond tired, but I couldn't bring myself to go home, not until Fionn was ready to join me. I'd showered, so I wouldn't stink up the place, at least.

As soon as I got through the locked ICU doors, I paused at the sight of Sloan standing to one side with his arms crossed, looking displeased as two men in suits—detectives, I presumed —stood in front of him with notepads and pens. Every nerve inside me buzzed, alight with alarm and ready for whatever action the cops wanted to throw at us.

I stalked over to them and caught the conversation as I came to a stop.

"Thiago Reyes has been arrested for obstruction of justice, and we'll be adding charges to that. Work with us, Mr. Killough, or you'll find yourself in the same position."

Sloan smirked and squared his shoulders. "I have nothing to say to you other than it was dark, and I didn't see a thing."

One of them, a short man with thinning brown hair and a thick mustache, grunted. "Do not make us arrest you for Obstruction of Governmental Administration in the Second Degree like Mr. Reyes. We will do it."

"That's a mouthful. Try and I'll be out within the hour. My lawyer is that good," Sloan drawled.

I stepped in beside Sloan. "Why are you here? Sloan's nephew has been shot. You should be out finding the shooter, not harassing Sloan."

The second detective, a man with a clean-shaven head and a scar below his mouth, laughed. "You're funny. We know who you are. Daire Reardon, Killough's ass kisser. Mr. Killough's nephew is in here because of his mob ties. You brought this on yourself. Both of you can answer our questions. What happened this morning?"

"I went for a piss at six. Is that what you want to hear?" I cocked my head. "I haven't brushed my teeth yet, but I'm hoping to do that soon."

"There's a nice bathroom down the hallway." Sloan pointed to our left. "Very clean."

Detective Mustache made an irritated sound. "With your

witness statement, we could put Reyes away for a long time, Killough. Wouldn't that be nice?"

Sloan's smirk widened. "It was dark. Now, if you would be so kind, gentlemen, my nephew's waiting for me to return."

"Enjoy it while you can, Killough, it won't last long." Detective Scar waved his hand dismissively, and they walked away, looking over their shoulders more than once as they went. I waited until they'd turned the corner before I slid my attention to Sloan.

"They're going to be trouble."

"They already are." He frowned down the hallway. "They have what they want. They can arrest me at any time, but I don't know what they're waiting for."

"Prime annoyance value?"

He growled in frustration. "They've already put Reyes in handcuffs."

Fuck. I took a deep breath. "What do you want me to do, sir?"

Finally, Sloan turned back to me and gripped my shoulder. "Protect Fionn. Whatever happens, he's yours to defend with your life. Am I clear?"

"Yes, sir."

23

FIONN

"I'm *fine*. I wasn't even in the ICU for a long time." I rolled my eyes.

Considering my injuries, I was very lucky. It hurt sometimes to breathe too deeply, but the doctors had me on some nice painkillers, and they'd sent me to a private room about four hours after I'd woken up. They were more than happy with my progress, and I wasn't in any immediate danger.

Daire glared at me as he fluffed the pillow behind my back, which only made Sloan's mouth twitch in amusement.

"I'm making you comfortable, boy, so sit back and say *thank you, Daddy* like a good boy."

"Uncle," Fionn whined, but Sloan held up his palms toward him.

"You're the one dating him, not me, kid. You're on your own."

Daire chuckled as he shoved the pillow behind me, and only when he was satisfied did he sit back down in one of the armchairs beside the bed, right next to Sloan.

Sloan had been home at some point because he was back to wearing his suit. From what Daire had told me, Sloan had brought one for Daire, too, so they both looked like their usual selves. Sloan's suit was navy, a favorite of his, while Daire had on black, and it took everything in me not to say something like "*black again, Daddy?*"

"The nurse said it's a miracle I'm not in more pain," I reminded them as I tugged at the neckline of my horrible hospital gown. Sloan could've brought me something better to wear, too, but apparently this stupid thing was a requirement. "And that I woke up so quickly. They expected I'd be in the ICU for longer."

The sooner I got out of here, the better. Being in bed was the last place I wanted to be, but Sloan had insisted it was important for me to listen to the doctors.

"As soon as you're a little better, we'll transfer you to EK Memorial," Sloan said.

I smiled. "The Eoin Killough Memorial Hospital. I liked that you named it after Dad."

"Yes, well, he was my best friend." Sloan frowned. "I wish *he'd* raised you. He would've done a better job than me."

"You didn't do too bad," I teased as my grin widened. "It wouldn't have been easy being a boss of a billion-dollar enterprise *and* the guardian of your nephew."

Daire laughed while Sloan rolled his eyes.

"You were a good kid." Sloan shrugged as the corner of his mouth flicked up. "Eoin would've been proud of you. Maybe it's time I told you how he really died."

Daire's laughter choked off, and he groaned, falling back into the armchair.

Sloan shot a narrowed gaze at him. "You told him." He didn't sound surprised.

It was my turn to chuckle as I shook my head at him. It was easy to see that they'd been friends for a long time. Despite Sloan being the boss, there'd been an easy interaction between them since I'd woken up that I hadn't seen in a while, probably since I was a kid. They smiled at each other, and warmth spread through me as I watched them—two of the most important men in my life. This was what happiness felt like, and if it took me getting shot three times to make it happen, then I'd do it all over again. I didn't tell them that, of course.

I winced when a sharp pain volleyed through me and held up my hand as both Daire and Sloan looked at me in concern. "Don't overreact. I'm *fine*. Jesus. Uncle, don't you have a pet to go home to?"

"I do, but you're important to me, too." Sloan sighed. "I didn't show you that before, and it's going to change. You're my family, bo—" He winced, firing Daire a glare. "He was my boy before he was yours, and now I need to find something else to call him."

Daire snorted out a laugh. "Too bad. I'm his Daddy, you're only his *Dad*."

Sloan grunted, but I didn't miss the grin that took over his mouth.

"I have a name, you know," I said.

"Fifi?" The grin shrank into a smirk. "What are you, an elderly lady?"

Daire groaned and rubbed his face while I laughed. "Be glad I told him he couldn't call me Deedee like he wanted."

Sloan raised his dark eyebrows and opened his mouth, but whatever he was going to say was gone as soon as two men in suits—detectives was my guess—walked into my room. Sloan jumped to his feet, spine straight and shoulders tense as they headed straight for him.

"Sloan Killough, we are escorting you to the precinct for questioning. Think we wouldn't find your gun, Killough? Well, we did." The detective with a brown mustache grabbed Sloan's shoulder and spun him around, then yanked his arms behind his back to slide handcuffs over his wrists.

"Are those necessary?" Sloan drawled in a blasé tone.

"You're a danger to us," Detective Mustache said with a wry grin. Fucking lying bastard.

I shuffled backward to sit up straighter.

"What's going on?" I demanded, but they ignored me as they slapped the cuffs closed around Sloan's wrists.

Daire stood and stepped forward. "That gun—"

"Shut up, Daire." Sloan sent him a pointed look, and Daire's lips pressed together unhappily. I didn't know what had happened, but I was good at putting two and two together. Whatever gun they were talking about was Sloan's, but Daire had been the one who'd fired it and probably killed the man who'd shot me. Daire was about to tell them the gun was his, if only to protect Sloan, but Sloan wasn't going to let him do that.

Daire came to stand at my side, his jaw tight and eyes furious as he watched the detectives. "Don't worry, Boss, we'll call the lawyers. This is ridiculous."

"They'll try to charge me, but it won't stick." Sloan smirked at the detective in front of him, a tall man with a scar across his chin. "But it's cute that you're trying."

"We'll see," Detective Mustache grumbled, tightening the cuffs until he had Sloan hissing between his teeth. Mustache grinned, and I lunged forward, ready to fly out of bed and punch his smug face, but Daire caught me before I could.

"Not now, boy," he whispered into my ear before kissing the top of the shell. "They want us to react."

"Fucking pigs," I snapped at them, ignoring the agony that ripped through me as I fought against Daire's hold.

"Watch yourself," Detective Scar sneered, pointing a stubby finger at me. "Or you'll be in cuffs, too, boy."

"Don't call him boy." Daire bared his teeth at him.

Detective Scar rolled his eyes and grabbed Sloan by his elbow, while Mustache grasped the other. Together, they began to lead Sloan out of my room. All I could do was watch, helpless, as they dragged him off. Sloan glanced at me over his shoulder as he went, winking with a sharp nod.

"Fionn, you and Conall are in charge for now," Sloan called right before they yanked him through the door.

He was gone.

Numbness spread through me for a moment as I stared after him. When panic should've begun, something else settled inside me instead—determination. They'd come into my hospital room and ripped Sloan from my side where he was supposed to be. My uncle trusted me to take care of business now, and I was going to do more than that. I was going to destroy those cops.

I went to stand, but Daire placed his hands on my shoulders and shook his head. "No. You aren't healthy enough yet." I opened my mouth to argue, but he shushed me quietly. "Fifi, listen. You can't do anything right now. I'll call the lawyers and get them down to the police station. The best thing *you* can do is get better."

I sighed in frustration. Fucking Reyes. This was all his fault. "Fine, but I want you to call in the cavalry. Get Cillian, Aspen, and Jamie back here—"

"Sloan already did that."

"And I want the men ready. Where's Rowen and Fallon?"

"They're with Conall." Daire took out his phone and sat on the edge of the bed. I watched him typing on the screen, so I kept talking.

I exhaled in relief and rubbed my chest, wincing. "Good. Conall needs to be protected. Around the clock. When our enemies hear Sloan was arrested, they're going to get overconfident. I want every man working. If there's even a sign of any of them being unsettled, I want people to come forward. Now is not the time for hesitation. We need to be united. This company doesn't have room for men who might rat us out the first chance they get."

Daire's eyes sparkled with pride and he smiled. "Yes, sir. I'll let the men know. We also have men outside your room now, protecting you."

"What?" My mouth popped open in surprise. "Since when?"

"Since they moved you here. Sloan's orders." He shrugged. "He loves you. A lot."

I fell back against the pillow behind me and rubbed my face. "Call the lawyers. I'm going to start making plans. I'll need to talk to Conall, too."

"Yes, Boss." Daire cupped the right side of my face and kissed my left cheek before laying his mouth across mine. I moaned, returning the soft kisses that turned my insides warm and as wobbly as jelly. I touched his wrist, and he stared at me with a look that would've had me naked if I wasn't in the hospital.

"Daire, that gun they found. I know it was Sloan's, but did you touch it? Could they find your fingerprints on it?"

He sighed. "Yes. They could. We didn't have time to dispose of it the right way. You were hurt. Dying. It was chaos. We had no men around, and we were going to get one of the guys to come and retrieve it, but you were rushed into the operating room and we weren't thinking clearly."

His words were a sucker punch to the chest, and I gasped harshly. "We need to get rid of it. Find someone in the department who can make it disappear, right?"

He exhaled. "Yeah. We still have some friends there. I'll see what they can do for us, but even if they take it, they still arrested Sloan on obstruction, something that they can get all of us on if they want."

I nodded. "We stay strong. It's obvious they're gunning for Sloan. They want him, but they'll come for you, too, because you're important to the Company. They're just getting started."

"Maybe." He shook his phone at me. "That's why we call in the experts. I'll get the lawyers down there immediately."

"Okay. I trust you to do what's necessary." Despite the worry that played on my mind as I thought about my uncle being taken to the precinct, a sudden onslaught of tiredness hit me and my eyes began to burn. I yawned, and Daire sifted his fingers through my hair gently.

"Take a nap, boy. We'll sort everything out. I promise. Nothing will bring this company down. Nothing."

I smiled. "Thanks, Daddy."

EPILOGUE I
DAIRE

Drip. Drip. Drip.

The blood hitting the floor echoed around the basement. The steady beat was an applause for Fionn. I smirked, a deep-seated and revenge-fueled satisfaction sliding through me until it settled low in my stomach. I couldn't tell if I was horny or not from the sight in front of me.

Sloan was in jail after being officially arrested, which was what we'd expected to happen. He'd had his arraignment where he'd plead not guilty, and the judge had set the indictment for forty-five days, giving us time to make some *arrangements* when it came to the grand jury. Since then, Fionn and Conall had taken over as the bosses like Sloan wanted.

Fionn flicked his wrist, dancing the knife he was holding in a circle. The silver blade gleamed under the low lights as he stepped in closer to one of his victims hanging upside down by a rope attached to his ankles. The man struggled, but the more he moved, the more blood trickled from the slice in his neck onto the floor.

"What did you call me last year?" Fionn tapped the handle of the knife against his bottom lip in thought.

He'd never looked hotter than he did now, outfitted in his blood-spattered white dress shirt with a predatory glint in his eyes. He was hungry for vengeance. Since Sloan had gone to jail, he'd stepped up and taken control of the Company alongside Conall. They were unstoppable together, and I couldn't be prouder.

"Hmm, I believe it was *The Little Bitch*, right?" He turned to look at Ronan, who stood beside me with the stoicism of any good bodyguard. "I did hear them correctly, didn't I, Ronan? They called me a little bitch and said I wouldn't last a week as boss." He idly grabbed the man's hip and pushed him, letting him swing.

Ronan nodded sharply, the corner of his mouth twitching as though he was holding back a smile. "They did, sir. You heard perfectly."

The guy Fionn was standing in front of—Hopkins—whimpered. "I'm . . . I'm sorry, sir. I'm sorry. Please. *Please.*"

Fionn hummed and rocked on his feet in thought. "No, I don't think I'll forgive you. You mocked me. Men have died for less."

"I won't do it again. I won't." Hopkins sobbed, tears joining in with the blood on his face. He struggled against his restraints, wriggling and attempting to kick, but we'd tied him too tightly for all that. "Please, sir."

His friend, Miller, groaned as he slowly regained consciousness. He was taking longer than Hopkins, and he had yet to find out what waking up would entail. I suspected he'd react like Hopkins had—crying, begging, believing the entire situation was one big mistake.

"Too late." Fionn pressed the knife against Hopkins's neck again, effectively stopping his twisting, as if that would save him from another slice in his delicate meat sack. "You should've shut your mouth from the beginning."

Pride struck me firmly in the chest, making my lungs swell

with emotion. A week and a half after Sloan had been arrested, and Fionn had truly stepped up. He'd shown his true strength, and I knew Sloan would be as proud as me. Fionn didn't need me to guide him. He and Conall did an amazing job by themselves. They had both been paying attention to Sloan all this time. I was only here for support.

Instead of cutting Hopkins's throat and ending it all, like I'd expected, Fionn drove the knife into Hopkins's stomach, eliciting a pained scream from his victim. Hopkins struggled, crying harder, and Fionn's smirk was downright sexy as fuck.

He stepped back, leaving the blade lodged in Hopkins. Blood smeared his palms and fingers. Without a care in the world, he held out his hand to one of our men at his right. Duffy quickly grabbed a wet cloth and passed it to him so Fionn could wipe his hands.

Duffy hesitated, something akin to admiration flashing in his blue eyes. He was a compact man, one of the shortest guys we had in the Company, but he had wide shoulders, a blond military fade, and a background in the army. He'd probably seen all kinds of shit overseas, so the fact that Fionn had his respect spoke volumes for how much Fionn had grown.

"Thank you, Duffy." Fionn gave him back the cloth and crossed his arms. He glanced at me, and I winked.

The smile I got in return did all kinds of things to my insides, and desire joined the pride. This was my boy. *Mine.* He'd come so far in the small amount of time he'd stepped up. He'd shown the confidence that I'd seen in Sloan at Fionn's age. The things I wanted to do to him after this would make a porn star blush.

My cock throbbed and pressed against my underwear. It took a lot of effort not to reach down and give myself a squeeze. Now wasn't the time or the place, but it was tempting.

Miller had begun to wake up and realize what was happening around him. He wriggled, a gargled yell catching in his throat. Unlike Hopkins, who convinced his little minions to be assholes, Miller was a follower. He was weak—the proverbial sheep that Sloan liked to speak about. Yet Fionn wanted to make an example of what happened to men who *followed bad role models* as well as led a rebellion of words or actions.

Fionn shushed him. "I'll deal with you next."

Miller opened his mouth, but I grabbed a cloth from the workbench and stalked over to him, shoving it between his lips. He stared at me with wide eyes.

"The boss said shut your mouth." I smirked and stepped back to my original position.

"Thank you, Daire." Fionn's voice was smooth and calm.

I bowed my head toward him. "You're welcome, sir."

The men needed to know who was in charge. Out here, it was Fionn and Conall. In the bedroom was a different story, but that came later. I'd show Fionn just how hot he looked when we were behind closed doors. I'd be his Daddy.

Fionn grasped the handle of the knife lodged in Hopkins's stomach and jerked it out, blood arcing and splattering across Fionn's white dress shirt and over his exposed skin. He'd rolled his sleeves up earlier, leaving his forearms bare. His veins strained as he closed his fingers around the knife in a tight grip, and my mouth watered. What kind of pervert was I that the sight of my boy dripping with blood was hot?

"Daire." Fionn glanced toward me again, and I straightened, shoving aside my filthy, *vulgar but delicious* thoughts.

"Yes, sir?"

"Do we have other men who can do Hopkins's job?" He raised his eyebrows, eyes glinting with smugness.

I nodded. "Yes, sir. Plenty."

"Hm. And are they loyal and have they run their mouths about me?"

Hopkins's sob echoed around the basement, and he sounded like a wounded cow. Snot oozed out of his nostrils and ran up his cheeks and toward his forehead as he cried louder. "Please, sir. Please."

I eyed Hopkins, pleasure for his downfall simmering low in my gut. When Fionn had told me what they'd said about him, I was downright furious. If I'd been given permission, I would've rained hell down on him and Miller, but it was Fionn who'd wanted to dole out the punishment, and what a great job he'd been doing. He wasn't just going to kill them; he was dragging it out and torturing them.

"Any other man who can do his job is loyal to you, sir." I grinned menacingly at Hopkins.

"Good, then his death won't affect us." Fionn spun toward him, and before Hopkins could utter a word, Fionn sliced his throat. Hopkins gagged and gurgled on blood. His mouth opened and closed, and his nostrils flared like he was trying to suck in precious air.

Fionn stared—he was a man possessed by the sight in front of him. Enamoured might have been a better word. This was the first life he'd taken so cruelly, and he looked as beautiful as a vengeful angel.

Miller yelled and struggled harder. I stepped toward him and smacked him over the head with my open palm.

"Shut up."

Fionn shook his head at me and held out the knife in his bloody hand. "Finish him off for me, Daire. I made my point. Let's show Miller what a *loyal* soldier looks like."

I inclined my head and took the knife from him. "Of course, sir. Anything for my boss." I sent Fionn a smirk as I headed toward Miller. He trembled. *Good.* I wanted him to be afraid.

Fionn shifted over to the side of the room where I'd been and took a seat. He threw a leg over his knee and leaned back. He was a sight to behold—a king on his throne, and in this basement, I was his to command.

"Make it hurt." Fionn raised his chin, and in that moment, I saw all the training that Sloan had given him. This man was Sloan's son.

"With pleasure, sir."

Blood pooled on the floor beneath both bodies by the time I was done. The men were already working on cleaning the mess up when I reached out for Fionn and took him upstairs. When the blood was gone from our skin and we were in new suits, I dragged him toward me and cupped his face, kissing him deeply.

He tasted like the olives he'd eaten out of the jar earlier.

"Let's go for a ride, boy," I murmured against his lips.

He shivered and gripped my shoulders with the desperation I saw from him when he was about to come apart under my hands. "Ride? Like on your bike?"

His entire face lit up in excitement. A lot had happened over the last few months, from the bomb, to Fionn working out Diaz's notebook, to Donal, and then Fionn being injured at the bar fight. Finally, Sloan was arrested and sent to jail. We hadn't had the chance to just have fun, and because of that, I hadn't taken him on my bike yet like I'd promised.

"Yeah. What do you say you let your Daddy take care of you for a while?" I kissed the corner of his mouth, catching a taste of the olive juice there. He reminded me of a dirty martini, salty and perfect. I couldn't get enough of him. I had a lot of years to make up for, and I'd told him I'd do everything in my power to earn his forgiveness. "I'll make the missed work time worth it."

"You always do, Daddy Daire." Fionn slid his tongue across my jaw and nuzzled right under my ear. "You can have me whenever you want me. I'll just text Conall, and then we can go."

"Mm-hmm." I patted him on the ass. "You do that, boy. I'll get supplies."

He leaned back and grinned at me. "Why do I like the sound of that?"

I waggled my eyebrows at him, and he laughed. The sound worked warmth through me. Seeing a happy Fionn was worth everything. While I'd hurt him, now I could heal him and give him the world he deserved.

He pulled out his phone, and I went around to my side of the bed—at least, the side I slept on when we stayed at the mansion. I grabbed out a few packets of lube from the cabinet and shoved them into my pocket, then decided to get a few more *just in case.*

When he was done, I slid my fingers through his and led him out of his bedroom, down the grand staircase, and toward the front door. Mr. Hopper nodded at us when we passed, his grave expression nothing new, but he'd taken Sloan's arrest harder than I'd expected. He looked a lot older than usual.

We grabbed extra jackets on the way out and slid them on. It was still cool outside, and it was colder on the bike with the wind against our faces.

Once we were outside, I gestured to the Ducati. Fionn had stayed the night at the mansion, while I'd gone home to handle some business. I'd brought back the bike this morning. "Ready for the ride of your life, baby boy?"

His lips twitched and the late afternoon sun glimmered over his hair, making it shiny. "I've already had the ride of my life, and it wasn't on a bike."

I laughed loudly. "Brat."

His grin nearly split his face before he bounced toward the bike with an excitement that had my chest feeling floaty. The boss of the Killough Company was gone, leaving behind my happy boy, and I loved this side of him as much as I did when he was confident and in charge.

The sleek black Ducati shimmered in the afternoon sun, and I stopped to appreciate the fine lines of the vehicle—I couldn't help it. I loved my toys, but not as much as my boy.

"Come on, Deedee, let's go." Fionn waved his hand to usher me forward impatiently, and I shook my head.

"Didn't we talk about that nickname?" I walked toward the bike. I'd hooked two helmets on either handlebar earlier in the day, anticipating taking him for a ride. I grabbed the deep forest green helmet and turned toward him to place it over his head. I was careful, taking my time to make sure the buckle was securely fastened under his chin. He deserved to be cared for.

"Blah blah. That's all I hear. Let's go! Fifi and Deedee, taking a ride on the town. It's like Thelma and Louise but gayer." He winked through the open visor, the mischievousness beautiful to see now that he'd transformed some of his former anger and jealousy into confidence.

This was the real Fionn, the man he should've been the entire time. He'd grown and spread his wings, letting go of the grudges that had ruled his existence.

"I can't decide if I want to laugh or spank you later for being a brat."

"Both. Both is good."

I groaned and slammed on my black helmet before I slid onto the bike. I hit the ignition, and she roared to life. "Hop on behind me, boy. Keep your arms around me, and remember what I said before. Move with us, not against."

"Yes, Daddy Daire." He flipped down the visor and nearly jumped onto the passenger seat behind me. I had to keep the Ducati steady, and I held in the urge to reprimand him, reminding myself that he was excited.

He thumped his hands on my shoulders. "Let's gooooooo."

I reached back and clutched his arm before dragging it around my waist. "The other one, too," I ordered loudly so he could hear me over the vibrations.

He did as I'd instructed and cuddled me, his grip tight as he snuggled against my back.

"Good boy," I said.

He shivered so hard I felt it. I patted his arm as I began to drive. I was careful as we first got onto the street—and he moved with me in the way I wanted him to—but as we made it onto the bypass, I picked up speed. I zoomed past cars, zipping in and out between them like I always did, and Fionn followed my lead as if he'd been on the bike his entire life.

I caressed his wrist under his jacket in praise. He'd know what it meant.

Fionn hooted joyfully, and the sound was music to my ears. I'd never get enough of it. He let go of me, and I quickly checked my rearview mirror to see his visor up and him spreading his arms wide, feeling the wind on his face. The move was dangerous, and it took every ounce of my willpower not to order him to hold on to me again. Instead, I gripped his thigh near my hip, holding him tightly to make sure he didn't fall while I slowed down slightly.

He whooped and pumped his hand in the air. "This is freedom!"

He must've been shouting as that was the only way I'd be able to hear him. Despite my apprehension and fear, I chuckled and patted him on the thigh. To my relief, he finally hugged me again, plastering himself to my back.

I took us off the bypass toward one of the quieter beaches. Most of the time it was empty because not many people—except locals—knew about it.

As I slowed down at the residential streets, a chill against my chest made me shiver and I glanced down. I realized a few buttons to my dress shirt were open, which sometimes happened when I rode the bike in a suit.

"Fuck." I shook my head and grabbed my shirt, keeping it together.

"What's wrong?" Fionn shouted over my shoulder. He reached around and found the issue right away, though, and he dipped his fingers under my hand and between the open buttons to tickle my chest and stomach.

Warmth spread through me like a wildfire, and my cock

hardened under his caress. He knew all the right spots to touch me, and my body was reacting. Thank fuck I'd brought the lube. The vibrations of the Ducati weren't helping my situation.

Fionn slid his hand from my shirt and went lower to cup and squeeze my cock.

I groaned. "Fuck, boy." I didn't know if he could hear me, but I was sure he could feel what he was doing to me.

I needed to find a quiet spot and *fast*.

The perfect place came close to the beach in a parking lot with no cars and no houses around. I flew into a spot and turned off the bike. Rays of sunlight danced over the ocean, and it couldn't get any more romantic if I tried. My bike, my boy, and a beautiful location.

Fionn dismounted, and I was right behind him so I could grasp his helmet and rip it off before doing the same to mine. I dropped them on the ground as gently as I could with how excited I was, and yanked him into a hard kiss. He whimpered, shoving onto tiptoe so he could rock his hard cock against mine.

"Daddy," he moaned into my mouth, desperate and hungry. "Please."

I'd been waiting all day for this moment, and nothing was going to stop me from taking what I wanted. I'd fantasized about fucking him since he'd first had Hopkins and Miller dragged into the basement.

I flipped him around so he was facing the Ducati. "Hands on the seat, boy. Don't knock my baby over, got it?"

He whined, and a tremble worked its way through his body. "Yes, Daddy Daire. Please. I'm so fucking hard."

I growled low in my throat and worked at getting his pants and underwear around his knees, then dug into my pockets and pulled out the lube packets. I shoved my pants down, too. Hot lust burned its way through me, and the need for him had me nearly bursting. My cock throbbed even as the cool air tickled around it.

He thrust his ass back toward me. *"Daddy."*

"I'm trying, boy. I'm trying."

I was so far gone that I didn't care if anyone saw us. At this rate, I'd probably come as soon as I was inside him. I dropped a packet and grunted in frustration, but I finally managed to get one between my teeth so I could tear it open. There was no finesse in the way I smeared my fingers with lube and pushed them into Fionn's hole. I was gentle, yet rough, and by the way Fionn moaned, he loved every second.

He arched his back, raising his ass up higher for me. The bike wobbled as he gripped it tighter. "Fuck yes. Right there. Please, I want your cock, Daddy Daire."

I didn't have the mental capacity for speech. All my blood was in my cock. I stretched him as much as I could before my patience disappeared and the desperation took control. I needed to feel his tightness around me, sucking me into him until I was balls deep.

I snatched the packet of lube I'd dropped and ripped it open, which was a little harder this time now that my fingers were coated in it, but I managed. Once I had the lube spread on my cock, I dropped the trash and lined myself up to his perfect hole. The moment I began to enter, my world narrowed in on the overwhelming pleasure of *home*—that's what Fionn was to me in every way. He let me be inside him while also being a part of his life. He was everything to me, and I wanted to marry him.

The thought made me pause. Marry? I smiled. Yeah. I'd love to make him my husband.

"Move, Daddy." Fionn rocked his hips backward, and I slid in more with the movement.

I groaned. "Fuck, boy." I clasped his hips, my nails digging into his delicate skin, and thrust deep into him. We both moaned at the sensation of being connected.

He whined and whimpered, searching over his shoulder, and I knew what he needed. I plastered my chest against his back, our clothes a barrier I hated right now, and kissed him as I started to fuck him. I began gently, one small thrust after another, before our lust engulfed us and I couldn't hold back. We were needy and hungry for each other, and this wasn't one of those slow, tender moments.

I straightened and fucked into him hard. He slapped the seat of the Ducati, his sobs and pleas fueling me to thrust even faster. The area was quiet around us, and other than the birds chirping, the only sounds were our moans and my balls slapping against his ass.

"Let me touch myself, please. Please, Daddy."

I grunted. "Yes, come for me. Show Daddy how much you love his cock, boy."

He spat in his palm, and even though I couldn't see it, I knew he'd grabbed a hold of himself. Skin on skin noises echoed around us, and some birds in a tree to the right of us flew away. The crashing waves farther down the beach was a distant song in my ears, but all I really cared about was the moans coming from Fionn.

Pleasure built in my spine, and I was close. "Daddy wants to come, boy. Do you think you can come for me first?"

He whined. "Yes, Daddy Daire. Just a little more . . . ." A gasp slipped from him, then another moan before he stiffened and his cum spurted across the black leather seat of the Ducati and down the side.

I wasn't far behind him, the urge to fill him up sending me over the orgasm cliff. I braced, my back going rigid as I unloaded inside him. I hissed as a few shivers worked their way through me until my balls were empty. I was sensitive as fuck and had no choice but to pull out.

Drops of cum came with me, splattering across the asphalt. "Fuck, boy, you're beautiful."

Fionn laughed as he yanked up his pants, but he didn't do them up as he turned to me. His flushed cheeks highlighted his prettiness. "Was I a good boss, Daddy?"

"The best, boy." I didn't care to deal with my pants. My spent cock could hang out. I dragged him closer and laid a kiss on his forehead. "Such a good boy."

He shuddered and moaned. "Thank you for the ride, Daddy."

"Which one?" I nuzzled his cheek, inhaling the scent of his sweat. Perfect.

He chuckled. "Both, of course."

EPILOGUE II
FIONN

"Marry me."

The words nearly had me bouncing right off Daire's cock. I froze with him balls deep inside me and stared down at him lying on the bed, looking unfazed for a man who'd just proposed while I was trying to ride him.

"What?" I blinked, and his cock jerked. I swore the bastard grew bigger in my ass, too.

His mouth twitched and he curled his fingers around my shaft, using the precum beading at my slit to slick it up so he could stroke. I shuddered and inwardly cursed him for distracting me because I was caught between the urge to go back to using his cock to peg my prostate and demanding answers.

I rubbed my hands over his chest and tweaked his nipples, and he groaned, rocking his hips up and ripping a whimper from me.

"Fuck. Don't do that. Tell me what you said." My voice came out ragged and desperate—it almost didn't sound like me. "Please, Daddy."

Daire grinned smugly. The bastard. He knew exactly what his cock did to me and how to use it to his advantage. "You heard me, boy."

"Say it again." I rolled my hips, and he grappled at my sides, digging his thumbs into the dips of my waist. "Go on. I want to hear it. *Need* to hear it."

He made a growly sound that went straight to my balls, and I moaned as I rose, then fell straight back onto his hardness. "Marry me, boy. Be mine forever. I've fucked this up for too long, and I want to take you down to the courthouse and marry you yesterday."

I hummed and squeezed his pecs, sinking my nails into his skin.

He hissed, baring his teeth, and I grinned as I continued to bounce on him, the echoing slaps of our flesh music to my ears. He was close. I could tell by the way he was panting and the shudders that slid down his body. A flush spread up his neck, and it was the sexiest thing. I loved seeing him like this, below me and letting me take control. He was my Daddy, but he still gave me the lead when I craved it.

"Are you going to give me an answer?" He strained, the muscles in his chest bulging as he dug his heels into the bed and fucked up into me. I nearly fell right off his cock and would've if he didn't have his hands on my hips.

I huffed out a laugh, happiness bubbling deep inside my chest. "Yes. *Yes*. But I don't want to wait. I don't want a big fancy wedding. Do what you said. Take me to the courthouse and marry the fuck out of me. Make me your husband."

He slid his left hand up, stroking across the bandages that hid my healing wounds, before he dragged me down so he could kiss them, too. I wished I could feel his mouth on my skin. "What about Sloan?"

I winced.

It'd been three weeks and two days since Sloan's arrest. Daire had promised me and Conall that everything would work out with Sloan, and I trusted him.

We were working together to get him out from behind bars, but that took time and blackmail material. We also had to keep Conall away from it—as smart and driven as he was, when it came to Sloan, he lost all sense of reason. Threatening cops or lawyers wouldn't do him any favors, so our own attorney, Henderson Cashmore, instructed us to keep Conall away.

"We can have another wedding later if he wants, but I don't need anyone there, Daddy. Just you and me."

"What about Conall? He deserves to be there." He kissed down my neck and across my chest to my bandages, and I shuddered as pleasure coiled itself low in my stomach. I staved off the orgasm that tickled my balls. I wasn't ready to come yet.

"Fine, Conall and maybe one more person. That's it." I pouted down at him.

He smiled as he fell back onto the bed and placed his left hand on my hip again. He was handsome like this, all soft around his hard edges as he stared up at me with the promise to give me the world. He was a Daddy when he needed to be and had spanked me a few times when I was a little too harsh with Lor—hey, I'd been nicer recently—but he also touched me like I was made of delicate gold. Whenever I did something great as boss, he told me how proud of me he was, and that gave me a heart boner quicker than anything else.

"Aodhan?" Daire asked, thrusting up into my hole and hammering my prostate.

I cried out, using my hands on his chest to steady myself as a vicious shiver stroked down my spine. All sense of reality went straight out the door as desire assaulted me worse than the three bullets to my torso.

"Fuck, fuck, fuck! Whatever you want, Daddy. Please. I'll do whatever you want." I chewed my bottom lip, squeezing my ass around him. "Come for me. Want you inside me."

He cursed and seized the back of my neck, dragging me down for a rough kiss. His mouth was scalding against mine, and he pounded his cock into me as if our lives depended on it. In that moment, I was flying high. I had my Daddy, and I was so fucking in love that it hurt, but it was the kind of agony I could obsess over. Daire was mine now. Eight years was worth it, if it meant we always got to this point in our lives.

I dug my knees deeper into the bed and ground down harder onto him. We both groaned.

"Good boy, such a good boy for Daddy. Show me how much you want my cum. Ride my cock." Daire's voice turned guttural. The world narrowed in on this—us in a bed with his big hands swallowing my waist while I bounced on top of him right after he'd proposed to me. I would remember this day forever, and nothing could stop me from coming.

I chased my orgasm by sinking down on his dick a few more times before everything came to a sharp halt. My balls drew up closer and my hard-on jerked, spraying cum across his belly and chest, some shooting as far as above his head. I laughed as I stared down at his flushed face and how he gnashed his teeth. He growled, and then warmth filled me, spreading fire all through me.

"Daddy, Daddy. Fuck." I chanted his name as the rolling waves of pleasure continued to ripple through me.

He enfolded me into his arms and dragged me down until we were chest to chest, my cum squishing between us, but neither of us cared. His mouth covered mine, and I kissed him lazily.

"I love you, Daddy Daire."

He smiled and my heart fluttered. "I love you, too, boy. Very much. You and me are forever, okay?"

I hummed and closed my eyes, breathing in our combined natural scents. "Forever, Daddy."

———

I stared down at the grave, not quite sure what to say. I hadn't visited the graveyard since Dad's funeral, but after a nice talk with Daire's parents at brunch the other day—they loved me, and despite their favoritism for Aodhan, I liked them, too—I'd realized it was time I went to talk with my dad. Daire's parents were Catholic and assured me that Dad would hear me, but I wasn't so sure.

I stood in front of his headstone, staring down at the picture of him with his wide smile, and I hoped that he could. I held the card in my hand tightly before taking a deep breath and stepping forward to place it on top of the granite.

"This is for you, Dad." I wrung my hands together and glanced over my shoulder at Daire, who stood near the path to wait for me. He'd told me to go over to the grave first and talk with Dad, but I wasn't really sure what to say. Looking at Daire now, though, words came to me, so I turned my attention back to Dad's smiling face. "I'm with Daire now. He's my fiancé, soon to be husband. That card on your tombstone, it's an invitation to our wedding. It's only going to be at the courthouse because I can't wait very long to make him my husband, but I hope . . . . Well, I hope you'll be there in spirit."

Nothing happened.

There wasn't a breeze or some woodland animal showing up as a sign he was here with me, but somehow, I *knew* he was beside me. It was almost as if I could feel his presence. A comfort washed through me, and I smiled.

"I love him, Dad. He's a good man. Uncle Sloan was kind of pissed at him, but they're fine now. I really, *really* want to be his husband." I swallowed and turned to gesture at Daire to come over. He ate up the space between us and stood at my side. "I hope you're happy for us, Dad."

"He would be," Daire murmured, pressing his nose against my temple to breathe me in. "I knew Eoin, and he would only want you to be happy."

I grinned up at him. "I am. Very happy."

THE NEW GOTHENBURG WORLD

Ki Brightly & M.D. Gregory would like to invite you to explore further into the seedy underbelly of New Gothenburg.

http://www.gothenburgworld.com

We have an official reading order here:
https://www.gothenburgworld.com/reading-order

———

Kings of Men Motorcycle Club Series
Ki Brightly and M.D. Gregory

1. *King's Killer*
1.5. *King's Rogue*
2. *King's Eyes*
3. *King's Criminals*
4. *King's Pawn*
5. *King's Undertaker*
6. *King's Undercover Fed*
7. *King's Virtuous Son*
8. *King's Barber*
9. *King's Ex-Cons*
10. *King's Silver Knight*

———

The Killough Company
M.D. Gregory

1. *The Boss*
1.5 *Boss's Christmas*
2. *The Professional*
3. *The Assassin*

———

The Reyes Cartel
Ki Brightly and M.D. Gregory

1. *High*

———

The Love Me Series (MMF)
Ki Brightly and Kiki Jested

1. Love Me STAT
2. Love Me Slow
3. Love Me Sweet

———

City Hall Series
Ki Brightly & M.D. Gregory

1. Staking His Claim
2. Denial
3. Cuffed
4. Sold for the Night

———

The Courtesan Hotel

1. The Madam's Baby Boy by Ki Brightly & M.D. Gregory

———

The Bully Series
Ki Brightly

1. Bully Beatdown
2. Bully Rescue

———

The Norse Lords MC
M.D. Gregory

1. Thor

———

Irish Roulette
Ki Brightly & M.D. Gregory

1. How Did You Survive Without Us?
2. How Do You Survive With Us?
3. How Did You Survive Alone?
4. How Do You Survive a Kiss?
5. How Do We Survive Together?

———

The Fool Series
Ki Brightly & M.D. Gregory

1. Fool's Gold
2. Fool's Errand

———

The Sweeney Mob
Ki Brightly & M.D. Gregory

1. Legend

———

The New Gothenburg World

Vengeance and Payback Duet
Ki Brightly & M.D. Gregory

———

The NGU Polar Storms
Ki Brightly & M.D. Gregory

———

His Princess Series

———

Other Books in New Gothenburg

Santa's Bratty Elf by Ki Brightly
The Promise by Ki Brightly and Meg Bawden
Bent, Not Broken by Ki Brightly and M.D. Gregory
Curved: A Bent, Not Broken Novella by Ki Brightly and M.D. Gregory
You've Got to be Kitten Me by Ki Brightly & Meg Bawden
Yes, Sir by Ki Brightly & Meg Bawden
Dirty Secret by Ki Brightly & M.D. Gregory
Best Belly Buddies by Ki Brightly & M.D. Gregory
Bound to Him by Ki Brightly & M.D. Gregory
Speak and Obey by Ki Brightly & M.D. Gregory
Say Uncle by Ki Brightly & M.D. Gregory (Smashwords)
The Family Pet by Ki Brightly & M.D. Gregory (Smashwords)
Fan Service by Ki Brightly
Diamonds Under the Mistletoe by Ki Brightly
Fan Service by Ki Brightly
Leave Me Broken by Ki Brightly & M.D. Gregory

———

Other Books in St. Loren

Sin & Supplication by Ki Brightly & M.D. Gregory
I'm Not Your Butler by Ki Brightly (Smashwords)
Cuddle Bear by Ki Brightly
The Ownership Clause by Ki Brightly
The Family Bond by Ki Brightly & M.D. Gregory (Smashwords)

Other Books in Ft. Leawood

The Chaos We Create by Ki Brightly & M.D. Gregory (Smashwords)

THE VANHEIM WORLD

Ki Brightly & M.D. Gregory would like to invite you to explore the paranormal world of Vanheim.

No Peeking by Ki Brightly
Gutsy by Ki Brightly

Printed in Great Britain
by Amazon